Praise for *Closer Home*

"A quick read with emotional depth you won't soon forget."
—Kathryn Craft, author of *The Far End*
of Happy and *The Art of Falling*

"*Closer Home* is a story as memorable and meaningful as your favorite song, with a cast of characters so true to life you'll be sorry to let them go."
—Sonja Yoerg, author of *House Broken* and
The Middle of Somewhere

"Kerry Anne King's tale of regret, loss, and love pulled me in, from its intriguing beginning to its oh-so-satisfying conclusion."
—Jackie Bouchard, *USA Today* bestselling author of
House Trained and *Rescue Me, Maybe*

"Kerry Anne King's prose is filled with vitality."
—Ella Carey, author of *Paris Time Capsule*
and *The House by the Lake*

CLOSER HOME

a novel

KERRY ANNE KING

LAKE UNION
PUBLISHING

Text copyright © 2016 by Kerry Anne King

Published by Lake Union Publishing, Seattle

www.apub.com

Amazon, the Amazon logo, and Lake Union Publishing are trademarks of Amazon.com, Inc., or its affiliates.

ISBN-13: 9781503951259 (paperback)
ISBN-10: 1503951251 (paperback)

Cover design by Shasti O'Leary Soudant

Printed in the United States of America

First edition

To my brother, Warren, who kept my secrets, taught me the art of climbing trees, and always loaned me his books. To my mother, who allowed the climbing and encouraged the reading.
And to my father, who loved and shaped us all.

CHAPTER ONE

It's amazing what a little makeup can do to make a body look normal.

Except for the fact that she's lying in a coffin, Callie looks just like the last picture I saw of her on the cover of *Stars Now*. Same curly, artfully mussed-up hair; same porcelain-perfect skin. The pout is missing, but under the circumstances this one small oversight can be forgiven.

On closer inspection, I discover the thing that can't. "Her fingernail is chipped."

The hovering undertaker startles visibly. "Pardon?"

"Her fingernail is chipped. There. See? The right ring finger." I point at the irregularity that mars the otherwise immaculate nail. My own unmanicured finger is perilously close to hers, and I dare to touch her, lightly. Her skin feels like Silly Putty—cold and stiff—and I jerk my hand away.

The undertaker moves in closer, reeking of breath mints and hair gel. Dandruff speckles the shoulders of his black suit jacket. "I see," he says, but clearly he doesn't. His manufactured sorrow grates against my skin, and I'm tempted to elbow him in the ribs to see if he gasps for air like a real boy.

"You'll have to fix it," I tell him. "She'd never be caught dead out in public like that."

There's a moment of shock before I hear what I've just said, and then I start to laugh, a wild, uncontrolled sound on the border of hysteria that blows in out of nowhere and catches me off guard. Tears lie just behind the laughter, pricking my eyeballs, closing off my throat, and I don't know what to do with them.

The undertaker is not amused. "Considering the circumstances, I feel that we've done a highly professional job of restoring her—"

"Restoring?" I turn on him. "Like a car that's been in an accident? Or a piece of furniture, maybe? You can't restore her unless you can get her breathing again, and I'll tell you this right now: if she wakes up in that coffin and notices you've put her on display with an imperfect fingernail, she will crucify you, no matter how good the rest of your work has been."

His mouth opens and then closes again, and a dark flush rises up his neck and into his face. The veins in his temples bulge a little. It makes me feel better to see him experiencing real emotion, and my tears recede.

"It's too late to fix a fingernail," he says. "Nobody will notice."

"I'm warning you. Ever see *Poltergeist*? She'll come for you."

He swallows, the flush giving way to a sudden pallor born of fear or anger. Maybe both.

"I'll see what I can do before we bring her out. Let me take you to the relatives' room." He puts a hand on the small of my back and shepherds me toward the door. I let him steer me, turning my head over my shoulder for one last glimpse of my baby sister. She looks like she's asleep, and I take care to close the door quietly so as not to disturb her rest.

***

Dale is waiting for me in the hallway. With his hair all trimmed and a sports coat on, he looks strange and unfamiliar. My throat tightens. I feel lost and very much alone.

"All right?" he asks, and he's just Dale again, solid and familiar.

I nod, although I'm far from all right, repressing a mad impulse to fling my arms around his neck and burst into tears. We fall into step behind the undertaker, side by side, not quite touching. My right heel slips in and out of my shoe with the sort of friction that is already rubbing into a blister. I can't remember what possessed me to buy high heels. They clop unevenly on the floor, and I feel ungainly and off-kilter.

"How does she look?" Dale's voice sounds matter-of-fact, like we're talking cars or building projects, but his jaw is clenched tight.

"One of her fingernails is chipped."

"God forbid."

"I told the guy to fix it."

Dale stops. I carry on a few steps under the force of momentum before my feet figure out what to do and I turn to face him. His eyes lock on mine, level and insistent. "A horse, Lise. A fucking horse kicked her in the head."

I drop my gaze, unable to meet the naked intensity of his. "She looks like Callie. Go see her for yourself."

"I'll pass."

A silence stretches between us, broken only by the uneven clicking of my heels on the tile and Dale's even tread. A runnel of sweat caterpillars from my armpit down my side and under my breast. Where there's sweat there may be stink, but I don't dare sneak a sniff test, not here, and I wish myself miles away. *Not much longer,* I tell myself. We'll be seated in a few minutes, and everybody's attention will be on Callie's coffin and off me.

But the instant we step out of the hallway and into the foyer, all hell breaks loose. It's jammed with people, and it seems to me like they all have cameras. Small handhelds, smartphones, movie cameras, professional cameras with giant lenses. There's even one of those movie cameras on wheels.

Every one of those lenses points in my direction and I'm assaulted by flashing lights. My head spins. Beneath the onslaught, my last shreds of self-confidence flee, leaving me feeling frumpy and countrified. The little black dress that seemed so perfect when I pulled it off the Dressbarn rack is clearly inadequate. My hairstyle is outdated, my makeup all wrong. I curl my close-bitten fingernails inside my fists so nobody will see.

And then Dale's fingers close around mine, warm and strong. Grounded. He bends his head and whispers, "Smile and keep moving."

Contorting my face into something that may or may not resemble a smile, I cling to his hand and move along beside him. Unlike me, Dale has made little concession to the fact that this funeral is star-studded and infested with paparazzi. He's wearing blue jeans with his sports coat but manages not to look out of place. Most likely because he doesn't care what anybody thinks.

One of the photographers plants herself in our path. Corkscrews of brilliant red hair frame cheekbones so sharp they could slice a steak.

"Friends or relatives?" she says. "What is your connection to Callie?"

"She's my sister." The words spill out of my mouth before I remember my resolution to keep my mouth shut.

"*Ohhhh.* You're her." A hunger flares in her eyes. She takes a run of pictures, her camera click-whirring as punctuation to the run of questions she throws at me. "Annelise, right? How long has it been since you saw Callie last? Why did she say you were dead? Are we going to discover any other long-lost family members?"

"Move." Dale's palm covers the camera lens and shoves it away.

"Pardon me?"

"You're in the way."

"But we're all just dying to hear from Annelise. The fans will go crazy." Her voice modulates into a throatier register as she lays one manicured hand on Dale's sleeve. "Did you know Callie? Did you go to school together? Ooh, did you maybe date her?"

I close my eyes, clinging to Dale, braced for the coming storm. He doesn't anger easily. But when he does get pushed over the edge, I don't like to be anywhere nearby. In my head, I'm already playing out what he's going to say, how she's going to react. Maybe he'll yank that camera off its strap and smash it on the floor. She'll take offense and wreak vengeance in the tabloids. There will be a terrible headline.

REDNECK WRANGLING AT
COUNTRY STAR'S FUNERAL

Maybe she'll even press charges, and he'll end up in jail.

Dale surprises me. He lowers his voice to a conspiratorial whisper, leaning in toward the photographer. "Have a little respect for the dead. Catch me later and I'll tell you everything I know."

His arm circles my waist, warm and steadying, and he steers me around her. She lets us go. I believe, for a moment, that I'm done with the media and will be allowed to sit down.

No such luck.

We're ushered into a small room, meant to be private. Three photographers squeeze in behind us before the door clicks shut. Bright flashes nearly blind me.

When I can see again, I realize the room already has two occupants. One is a teenage boy dressed from head to toe in black. He's got a black piercing in his nose, and another in his lip that pulls it into a permanent sneer. His fingernails are painted black, and I'm pretty sure he's wearing eye shadow. Despite all of this and the sulky expression on his face, he's a pretty boy, the type that teenage girls find irresistible and parents hate.

Beside him, holding his hand, is a girl who must be Ariel.

I haven't seen Callie's daughter since she was six. Back then, she was a bouncy, talkative little thing, with a fuzz of blonde curls and a vocabulary way beyond her years. She'd peppered me with questions, hung out in my studio, begged me to teach her how to play a song on the piano and the guitar.

At sixteen, she is completely unrecognizable as that bubbly little girl. Her hair is still blonde, but straight now, and pulled back in a severe ponytail secured by a simple black band. She wears no makeup, no jewelry. Her black dress is cut on classic lines that do nothing to soften a body that's all narrow angles. My eyes search her face for a hint of family resemblance—my father's chin, my mother's eyes—but come up empty. She must look like her father, but since Callie refused to tell anybody who that is, Ariel just looks like a stranger.

And not a friendly one at that.

"Annelise," she says. An acknowledgment, nothing more. A sense of lost time rocks me. Somehow I've been expecting she would still be six. That she would call me Auntie Lise and run into the shelter of my arms. Maybe even sob while I offer comfort.

Her gaze is direct, a challenge, and my stomach does its sinking thing again. The boy releases her hand and drapes an arm around her shoulder. *Mine,* the gesture says, in a way that makes me want to snarl at him to stand up straight and wash his face. *It's Callie's funeral,* I remind myself. Ariel is an orphan who never even had a father to lose. So I summon up a polite smile and hold out my hand to her friend.

"I'm Annelise."

He looks at my hand for a little too long, as if he doesn't know what to do with it, and then he offers me his paw, fingers only. His skin is damp, his grip flabby.

"Shadow," he says.

"Seriously?" I bite my lip to hold the word in, but it slips out anyway.

"It's a statement," he says, looking bored. "Most people don't understand."

What he means is, most people are stupid. Including me.

6

All the while the flashbulbs are going off, recording the moment for Callie's public, and I'm thinking I should kiss Ariel, or give her a hug, but the glare she gives me warns me away.

Her gaze shifts to Dale, and I draw a breath of relief. He's good in social situations, much better than I am. Or at least he always has been in the past. At the moment, he and Ariel are locked eye to eye with a level of intensity that makes my skin tingle. Neither of them says a word, and I'm casting around for an icebreaker when Ariel beats me to it.

"I see you brought your boyfriend to the funeral." Her voice drips with contempt.

"I see you brought yours," I retort. Blood rushes to my face. I can feel the heat, a toxic mix of anger and embarrassment. Her lips curve in a slight smile, as if my response is exactly what she was looking for. I remember too late that the room has ears.

The instant the words leave my lips, the photographers home in on Dale, flashbulbs popping, cameras clicking and whirring. His face is tight, and I see his eyes cut toward the door. For a heartbeat, I think he's going to jump ship and make a run for it, but I know better. Dale has never run away from anything in his life.

"He's not my boyfriend," I blurt out, trying to repair the damage. "Dale was friends with your mom. The three of us grew up together." I'm not sure if she even hears me. Her gaze has gone back to Dale. The camera people certainly aren't listening.

When the undertaker glides into the room with his I'm-not-really-here steps, I want to kiss him for rescuing me from a sixteen-year-old girl. Maybe it makes me a coward, but I'm more than happy to take his arm and let him lead us back out into the foyer, and then down the chapel aisle to the very front row. My knees are wobbly, and an electric zing keeps running through the fingers of my left hand, a nervous buzz that always hits me when I'm wound up too tight.

My guide eases me into a seat, and there I am, safe as I can be for the moment with my back to the crowd and Dale's solid strength beside me. I suck in a deep breath and try to relax. There's nothing expected of me right now. Nothing I need to do but sit back and watch the show, because Callie's funeral is more of a stage play than a service to honor the dead.

The venue itself reminds me more of a theater than a chapel. Crimson carpet, plush black theater seats, a high arched ceiling painted with blue-and-gold cherubs. Callie's open coffin is on display at the center of the stage. Artful overhead lighting illuminates her face and golden hair in a soft glow so that she looks to be sleeping. Scarlet rose petals are heaped all around her body, spilling into drifts on the floor, startling and dramatic against the white of the coffin. I wonder whether the damaged fingernail is still visible.

Mourners walk up the steps singly and in pairs, pausing by the coffin to pay their respects and look up at the cameras. I recognize many of the faces from TV, album covers, movies. Some I have never seen before. One and all, I figure they could show up at the Grammys without bothering to swing by home to change their outfits or fix their hair.

Apart from me and Dale, I'm guessing the only person in this room who holds any true grief over Callie's passing is Ariel. She sits on the other side of Dale, eyes straight ahead, shoulders rigid. Shadow, seated on the far side of her, tries to put his arm over her shoulder, but she shrugs him off without so much as a glance in his direction.

When the procession finally ends, a young man mounts the steps to the podium and stands beside the coffin in a too-long silence, just enough for dramatic effect. Black suit, black hair, face so pale he could play a vampire without stage makeup. When his audience stops rustling and coughing and goes still with waiting, he begins to deliver the eulogy in a mellifluous voice. Not much resemblance to the truth of Callie's life in what he proclaims in heartfelt tones. The polished speech carefully skirts any mention of the life my sister led before she became Callie

Redfern. I wonder what would happen if I bounced up out of my seat and told them the truth.

Her real name is Callista Jean Redding, and wherever she picked up that southern drawl, it sure wasn't her hometown, which is about as far north as you can get without crossing into Canada. It's true enough that her father is deceased, but her mother is still alive, more or less, putting in the hours and days until death shows up to claim her. And, of course, there's me, the sister who pretty much raised her.

The truth is, Callie orphaned us, not the other way around.

***

After the service, there are cameras again, and an overwhelming press of bodies and voices. My undertaker friend gently grasps my arm and draws me away, and I'm more than grateful to duck into the back of a limo when he opens the door. Ariel is already in the backseat. Before I have time to ask what they've done with Dale and Shadow, the door closes and the driver shifts into gear.

Ariel glances at me and then turns her whole body away, keeping her gaze focused on the window. I know I need to reach out to her, but two intersections go by and I'm still fumbling for the right words.

"I'm sorry I wasn't here," I offer, finally. My voice comes out like I'm a chain smoker with a twenty-year habit.

"This is such a sham," she says, biting off each word between her teeth. "I can't believe you went along with it."

I want to tell her that the funeral had a life of its own from the beginning. Callie's publicist. Her agent. Her adoring public. What do I know about planning funerals for the rich and famous?

"She hated horses," Ariel says. There's accusation in her tone, and I blink, failing to see what a horse has to do with anything.

"Are you blaming me for how she died? Because that's not fair."

Ariel rolls her eyes. "Don't be stupid."

I'm at a loss, but then we pull into the cemetery and I see for myself what she's talking about.

Men are lifting Callie's coffin out of the back of a hearse. But instead of carrying her to the grave in dignified pallbearer tradition, they heave the coffin up onto what looks like a parade float. It's a flat-bed wagon, draped in black fabric, strewn with crimson petals. A horse waits between the traces. The horse is golden, a palomino quarter horse, exactly the type that killed her. Roses have been woven into its mane and tail. In the distance I can see the other cars in the funeral procession driving down a different graveyard lane, but the camera people are all right here. Waiting.

"She hated that horse." Ariel's voice sounds all at once younger, vulnerable.

"Is that . . . I mean, surely not?"

"He didn't even tell you." Her voice wobbles a little. "Fuckin' Ricken."

I think she's going to break down, finally, and I start running through responses in my head. A pat on the back. An arm around the shoulder. But Ariel is made of tougher stuff. She draws her hand across her eyes and takes a shaky breath. "Come on. Let's get this shit over with."

Just like that, she's out of the car, ignoring the cameras and the voices clamoring for comments. Her back is straight, her chin high. She carries herself as if she owns the world. I lack her confidence. I've managed somehow to snag my stocking. There's a run starting at the inside of the left ankle, stretching halfway up my calf. I've got a blister rubbed into the heel of my right foot. And I can feel my upswept hair slipping off to the side, the combs not quite holding. Should have left it down, worn flat sandals. Hell, maybe I should have just worn my jeans.

Maybe I'll just stay where I am.

But a man opens the limo door and holds out his hand. Not my undertaker from earlier, but he wears the same slicked-back hair and the same look of manufactured grief. His breath also smells like mint. Probably breath and hair are standard-issue, as much a part of the undertaker uniform as the inevitable black suits.

"Right this way," he says, and I let him lead me toward the wagon. Flower-bedecked chairs flank the coffin. A young man in work jeans and a T-shirt lugs over a set of portable steps.

My undertaker guide offers me his hand. "May I help you up?"

"You've got to be kidding."

He arches one perfect eyebrow. Does he pluck them, or do they grow that way? The rest of his face is smooth and so hairless I wonder if he waxes instead of shaving. Men in my world don't do this sort of thing, but here in Vegas, anything is possible.

"The family rides with the deceased to the grave site. Much easier than walking, yes?"

His lips jerk up at the corners as though he's just ordered himself to smile. But his eyes have scanned my legs in a purely businesslike way, and I feel like he's registered both the blister and the stocking run.

"We'll walk."

"Is there a problem?" A man nudges the undertaker aside, clearly signaling that he'll take it from here. He's short, the top of his head about level with my chin. No black suit for him; he's wearing something charcoal colored and perfectly tailored. Black shirt, skinny tie, a pair of dark glasses obscuring his eyes.

"Annelise! Oh my God, you look so much like poor Callie." He takes both of my hands, leans up, and makes a kissing gesture aimed at my cheek, missing by at least an inch. I know who he is, although we've never met: Callie's publicist, Ricken. The man responsible for this whole travesty of a funeral. His touch makes me shudder; his voice is seared into my memory like a brand, casting me back in time to the night I learned of Callie's death.

***

The coroner calls first. He's polite and matter-of-fact. Is my name Annelise Redding and is Callie Redfern my sister?

Yes, and yes.

Most of what he says next flows over me like water, except for the phrases that change everything.

There's been a tragic accident.

You're the next of kin.

The idea of Callie dead is too surreal for belief. Surely there's some mistake and she's still out there in the world, busy being Callie. But the words "I'm sorry for your loss" have been spoken and refuse to be unsaid.

Sleep is out of the question. At least five times I pick up the phone, planning to call the coroner back to ask if there is a mistake, but every time my hands start shaking and I start pacing the floor instead. It occurs to me that a drink might settle my nerves. Getting the cork out of the wine bottle isn't easy, given the way my hands are behaving, but I manage it in the end.

One glass isn't enough. I have another. By the time the phone starts ringing again, I've stopped counting.

I sit and stare at the unknown number. The area code is 702, which means somewhere in Nevada. Nobody I want to talk to there. No more news I want to hear. The phone stops ringing and I breathe a sigh of relief. But it starts up again almost immediately. Same number. What if it's Callie, calling to say there was a mistake and she's alive and well? What if it's Callie's daughter?

So I answer. There's a male voice on the other end, his voice brisk and impatient.

"I'm looking for Annelise Redding."

"Who is this? Do you have any idea what time it is?"

"I'm terribly sorry; were you sleeping?"

"What do you want?"

"Is this Annelise?"

"That depends on who's calling."

"My name is Ricken. I'm Callie Redfern's publicist—she left me this number in case of emergency. But if Annelise isn't available—"

"It's me. I mean, I'm Annelise."

"Oh, good. You had me worried there for a minute, since you're listed as next of kin. I had no idea who to call next."

Hunching my shoulder to hold the phone against my ear, I go to pour more wine. The bottle is empty. I hold it upside down over my glass and give it a little shake. One lone red drop collects on the lip of the bottle and hangs there.

"I just wanted to let you know we have everything well under control," Ricken says.

The drop falls, a splotch of color in the bottom of the glass, no more, and I set the bottle down and turn away to the dark window.

"Annelise?"

"I thought I died when I was ten. Car crash, wasn't it?"

He laughs, like I've said something funny. "Show business. You can't take it personally. I'm sure you'll agree it would be best to have the funeral here, in Vegas."

I shake my head, then realize he can't see that. My mouth feels dry, like sandpaper, and it's difficult to speak.

"Home is here."

"Not for Callie."

This isn't about Callie, I almost tell him. Just this one time, it's not about her.

"All of her friends are here," Ricken says. "And her daughter. I'm sure you can see that Ariel needs to be in her own surroundings now."

"Our mother can't travel so far."

"I understand." He doesn't. This man is very bad at even pretend sympathy. "Maybe that's for the best. Don't you think it would be kinder to spare her the funeral?"

I figure what he really means is that a drooling old woman vegetating in a wheelchair would be an embarrassment and inconvenience to Callie's friends. But he has a point. These days, our mother believes that Callie is sixteen and out on a date, when she remembers her at all. What would a funeral do to her? I've lost track of Ricken, but he's still talking.

"Look, of course you want a small-town, simple funeral. But that's not what Callie would have wanted. I doubt that you would be able to accommodate the security requirements, in any case. Have you thought of that? Fans, other industry professionals. How big is Colville again?"

"You pronounce it like 'call,'" I tell him, the only argument I can muster. "Callville. Not Coleville."

"*Call*-ville." He stretches the vowel out way too far.

Befuddled, shell-shocked, and more than a little drunk, I surrender. "Look, I appreciate you asking for my input, but really—"

"We need your permission."

"I don't understand."

"You're next of kin, and Callie's executrix. We can't proceed without your say-so, and I'm calling at this unforgivable hour so that I can get started on arrangements. We have a lot of work to do, and not much time."

I find myself agreeing to let him handle everything, and the next thing I know I'm sitting there listening to a dial tone and thinking that even in death Callie has the ability to turn my whole world upside down and inside out.

***

"Annelise?"

I blink. Ricken's head is cocked a little to the side, one eyebrow lifted. Clearly, he wants something. He speaks slowly, enunciating every syllable as though I am deaf or otherwise impaired. "The guests are waiting by the grave. Can I help you up into your seat?"

I take another look at the conveyance and the horse. Ariel stands with her back turned to all of us, chin up, arms ramrod straight at her sides. Another limo pulls up and parks behind ours. Dale climbs out and heads in my direction. The sight of him fortifies my courage.

"We'll walk."

"Annelise, we went to a great deal of trouble—"

"You're welcome to ride up there, Rick."

"But—"

"We're not going to ride on a goddamn float. What are we going to do—throw candy at the mourners?"

I start walking. The blister has rubbed raw and the stupid heels sink into the grass with every step. I'm afraid I'm going to lose a shoe altogether. But then Dale catches up and falls in beside me. I breathe a sigh of relief, knowing I can grab on to his arm if I lose my balance or trip over my own feet. We've only covered a short distance before I hear the sound of running footsteps and Ariel appears on my left.

"Don't suppose either of you know where the grave is," I mutter, trying not to move my lips in case there's some rabid lip-reader out there with a movie camera.

"Follow the crowd," Dale says.

"No worries," Ariel chimes in. "You watch—Ricken will make it look like he planned it this way. Just keep walking."

Sure enough, a black-suited undertaker appears in my peripheral vision, striding as fast as he can without actually breaking into a run. A lock of hair has escaped from its confines, straying onto his forehead, which is damp with sweat.

"This way," he gasps, steering us across the grass and onto a narrow paved road.

I hear a clip-clop of hooves and the rumbling of wheels on the road behind us. Some of the photographers latch onto us. Some stay with the wagon.

"Told you," Ariel says.

The grave site looks more like a miniature golf heaven than a place to bury a body. Not a crumb of dirt to be seen. There isn't even a visible hole, just a rectangle of Astroturf, and at the center a harness made of heavy straps. Our guide positions Dale, Ariel, and me on one side of the machinery. Shadow arrives from somewhere and sidles up to Ariel.

She glares at him. "Where were you?"

"Don't be like that." He reaches for her hand. "The all-powerful men in black said it was just you and Lise in the family limo. I hitched a ride with my parents."

"You should have stayed with them," Ariel says, but she clings to his hand all the same.

The pallbearers, all with bent heads and downcast expressions, unload the coffin and carry it to the contraption of straps and pulleys, where they carefully set it down. A cleric in a black cassock, carrying an enormous Bible, moves into position.

I feel like we're on a movie set, what with all of the cameras and the staging and the grief as artificial as the fake grass we're standing on. Callie can't really be in that box, even though I saw her there with my own eyes. She moves through my memories, alive and vibrant. Six years old, pigtailed and blue jeaned, running through tall grass in the park, airplaning her arms and squealing with glee while our father lumbers behind in exaggerated slowness. A sullen teenager, pushing the lawn mower erratically around the yard, muttering curse words and deliberately missing long strips and chunks. Sixteen and pregnant with Ariel, her face glowing with passion as she defends her right to have and keep her baby.

Callie is contrary and changeable as the weather, not a lifeless, carefully painted body about to be buried under six feet of earth. The emptiness in my stomach fills with lead. Tears well up behind my eyes and I blink them back as fast as I'm able. I won't let the curious onlookers see me cry.

The minister utters words that are meant to be healing. They flow around and over me like water—meaningless, senseless. I count the minutes until I can break away from the crowd and retreat to someplace private where I can lick my wounds.

But then the music starts. "Closer Home," the song that catapulted Callie up the charts to fame. Her voice on the recording is as clear and clean as if she's standing right beside us.

The wider I wander, the farther I roam
The more your love finds me
And leads me back home
Closer home, closer home
You always bring me closer home.

As the familiar music curls around me, heat rises through my blood. My jaw sets in a hard line. My shoulders go tight.

"Easy," Dale whispers in my ear. He reaches for my hand, but it's clenched into a fist and I can't—won't—let it go.

God knows I loved my sister. How could I not? I half-raised her; she is a part of me. But my anger matches that love, measure for measure. Standing at the place where she will be forever laid to rest, with her voice singing out the loss and betrayal that is "Closer Home," all of my heartbreak hardens slowly into hate.

CHAPTER TWO

Dale can't stay. Nor does he want to, although he doesn't say so. His small-town roots run even deeper than mine, and I can tell that the constant invasion of privacy and the pressure from the paparazzi and curious fans grate on him.

Besides, he has responsibilities back home that outweigh any reason to hang around after the funeral. Spring is a hectic time for his contracting business, and while he's got good workers who can cover for a day or two, he needs to be on-site to make sure his projects are up to the standards that have made him a success.

He could have taken a cab to the airport, but by tacit agreement I drive him instead. I've got the keys to one of Callie's cars, the subdued Lexus with dark-tinted windows. We drive in silence, partly because I hate driving in traffic and need to focus on the road, partly because we are both busy with our own thoughts. My emotions are a confusing mess of grief and anger, and it's a relief when Dale leans over and turns on the radio. His preference tends toward classic rock, but he scans through the country stations, abiding by the rule we made up when we first got licensed to drive—the driver controls the tunes. He settles on a station and I draw a deep breath, sliding into the music and letting it take me into a better space as it always does.

Until "Closer Home" starts to play.

"Sorry." Dale reaches for the knob, but I put a hand on his wrist.

"It's everywhere. Leave it."

My whole body feels sore, as though I've been systematically beaten from head to toe. The muscles of my shoulders and thighs and lower back are all clenched into knots. I make an effort to relax, but the minute I loosen up a little, the tears threaten. If I ever really get started crying, I'm afraid I'll never stop. I opt for letting the tension stay.

The airport exit comes up. I pull over to the passenger unloading area and we sit looking at each other. Dale leans over and pecks me on the cheek. "Don't worry about anything back home. I've got it."

"Call me when your plane lands."

The car door slams behind him. He turns to wave, and then he's walking away. Something breaks inside my chest and I almost fall out of the car in a sudden rush to call him back. I can't get any sound past the tears that are flowing now in earnest. So I just stand there, weeping. The door to the terminal opens, and I feel like if he walks through it, he'll be lost to me forever.

"Dale!" I barely manage to croak his name, but still he glances over his shoulder and then runs back to me. I fling myself against him, and he wraps his arms around me and squeezes me. Tight. Tight.

Strong. Solid, like always.

Only this time his breathing, too, is ragged, and his heart beats faster than its normal steady tempo. I'm reminded, again, of how small and selfish I have become. Callie was his friend, too, and unlike me he has never been on the outs with her. He must be grieving. Maybe sometimes I should be strong for him, instead of the other way around.

So I pull myself together, sniffle, and edge away from his embrace. "I'm all right, really. It's just . . ."

"It's just that she's dead," he says, softly. "You do know that grief is not only normal but also sort of expected, right?"

I snort-laugh at that, and he uses his T-shirt to blot my tears.

"TSA might consider that too much liquid for carry-on," I quaver, surveying the wet patches.

Dale grins. "Fuck 'em. You okay?"

I nod.

His thumb catches one last stray tear, and then his warm hand cups my chin. There's a softness to his face and his eyes hold mine in a way that makes my insides shiver. He bends his head and kisses me. Just a gentle kiss, but his lips linger long enough to make my heart do a double flip.

"Don't forget to come home," he whispers, and then I'm standing alone and cold, watching him walk away from me.

***

I wake to a gentle tapping at the door. My eyes open on a strange room, morning light creeping across the floor through a crack in the window blinds. For a minute, I can't remember where I am or what I'm doing here, and then my memory floods back. I'm in the guest suite at Callie's Vegas house, which means she's really dead and the funeral wasn't some horrible dream. Whoever is knocking is not going away, so I get out of bed and pad across the carpeted floor, limping a little on feet that feel bruised as well as blistered from yesterday's punishment.

My room in the house I rent back home is just big enough to hold a twin bed, a dresser, and a nightstand. This room reminds me of a suite in a luxury hotel. There's a microwave and a fridge in an alcove, and an open door reveals a small sitting room complete with a sofa and armchairs.

The tatty sweatpants and tank top I've slept in look grubby and inappropriate to the surroundings, and I know my face is a mess because

I didn't wash off the makeup last night. So I barely crack the door and peer out. A young woman clad in a crisp white blouse and black slacks stands there, holding a breakfast tray.

"Good morning. I hope you slept well."

My stomach lurches at the thought of food. My head feels stuffed full of cotton, my tongue like sandpaper.

"What time is it?"

"It's almost nine," she says, brushing past me and carrying the tray into the sitting room.

That can't be right. I'm normally awake at five. I rub at my gritty eyes and try to think, but my brain refuses to get with the program.

The young woman sets the tray on the coffee table and crosses the room to open the blinds. As she expertly adjusts the strings, warm light pours into the room. "Ricken said I was to bring you breakfast and let you know that everybody will be here by eleven to go over the will."

"Everybody who?"

"I'm sorry, I don't know. Can I set up your tray?"

She doesn't wait for approval, lifting lids and arranging pretty little glass bowls of fruit, yogurt, and oatmeal. I swallow again and shake my head. "I don't think I can eat. Coffee, maybe?"

"I'd be happy to get you some."

She closes the door just in time for me to make a mad dash to the toilet and heave repeatedly, and uselessly, into its perfect porcelain whiteness. My empty stomach tries to turn itself inside out. When the nausea eases, I cross to the sink and rinse my mouth, then splash cold water on a face that is far too pale. There are bags under my eyes that weren't there a couple of days ago. I look old and tired. My whole body feels heavy and strange, like it doesn't really belong to me.

The girl returns with a carafe, a cup, and a little silver pitcher of cream. My stomach is still iffy and the first swallow is touch and go, but by the bottom of the cup I begin to feel vaguely human, enough for my brain to start engaging with the day. I can't face some sort of meeting without getting cleaned up a bit, and I don't want Callie's people to think I'm a total backwards hick. I should shower and put on makeup and try to find something decent to wear. I opt for a long soak in the Jacuzzi instead.

I'm only five minutes late, but when I limp down the spiral staircase and find my way into the study, four sleek, shiny-looking people are already there, waiting for me. Ricken has shed the suit but manages to look even more pretentious in blue jeans and a silky black turtleneck. He makes the introductions, not bothering to get out of his chair, and I try to file their names away for future reference.

Morgan Jensen, attorney, is a suit-and-tie guy who could be type-cast for a legal thriller. He gives me the tips of his fingers to shake, and his pale eyes don't hold my gaze for more than a heartbeat before sliding away. Genesis, the accountant, is young and curvy and giggles as she air-kisses my cheeks. Her fingernails are a high-gloss pink with sparkles, and her blue eyes are a hue not known to nature. Callie's agent, Glynnis, looks like a woman to be reckoned with. I'm pretty sure her sharp gray eyes don't miss a solitary detail about me, including the run in yesterday's stockings. She looks like she might even know things that haven't happened to me yet.

Everybody has a drink in hand, and Ricken goes to the sideboard and pours one for me without asking what I want. It's amber colored and tempting, but I just sit there, holding the glass, feeling disembodied and out of place. A tray of appetizers sits on the table—tiny toast and cheese and what I think is caviar. My eyes focus on the shiny purple-black spheres. Somebody is talking, but the words fade as I drift into another memory.

***

Blue sky overhead. Bright sun on water. A breeze thick with the smell of the lake. Small waves slap against the sides of the boat and wash up against the shore. My fishing rod feels alive, the tip bent, and my skinny arms feel the strain of trying to hold it and wind the reel at the same time.

"Catch a big one," Callie squeals, bobbing up and down. The boat rocks and she sits down, fast and hard, catching hold of the side.

"Easy," Dad says. "You'll have us over the edge. Just sit still."

There's a glint of silver as the fish breaks the surface of the water, shining in the sunlight before going back under. I crank the reel faster, my arms aching with the effort. A piece of hair is stuck in the corner of my mouth, but I can't let go to fix it. Again the fish breaks clear, and then it's beside the boat, flipping its tail and splashing. It's enormous. My blood runs high with the hunt. It's the first fish I've ever caught by myself.

Dad drops the hand net under it and scoops it up.

Wrapped up in the orange netting, thrashing about in the bottom of the boat, it doesn't look so big. All at once I want to put it back, but it has a hook stuck through the side of its jaw. Dad picks up his heavy silver fishing knife and hits it on the head.

Smack.

The fish goes still. Its jaws gape. One of its eyes is smashed, and it's not pretty anymore. Dad works the hook out with a little sucking sound.

"Way to go, Lise!" he says. "Big enough to eat for dinner."

He holds up the limp body, slippery in his hands, and examines it. "This looks like a girl trout. Let's see if she'll help us catch more fish."

His blade flashes and slits my trout's belly. He digs in with his finger, stripping out a glistening sac of pale-orange eggs. Dad rinses his hand and the egg sac in the lake, blood swirling into the clear water. Then he hands the eggs to me. I show them to Callie, wanting her to see how beautiful they are with the light shining through, each one a little jewel.

She makes gagging noises. "Gross. How can you touch that?"

Dad laughs. "People eat 'em, Callie. Rich people pay a heap of money for fish eggs. Call it 'caviar' and serve it up on a silver platter."

"You're making that up." But she takes another look at my handful of eggs all the same.

"Nope. All true," Dad says.

"I'm going to be rich when I grow up," Callie announces. "But nobody's gonna make me eat fish eggs. Not ever."

***

"Annelise?" Ricken's voice startles me back into the present.

"Did Callie eat caviar?"

He blinks and stares at me blankly, his mind having stayed right here while mine went traveling. "It was brought in fresh," he says finally. "Today. If you don't like caviar, we can certainly get you something else."

"Never mind," I tell him, shifting my gaze down to the array of tabloids and newspapers splayed out on the coffee table in front of me. Most of the rags are focused on Ariel, poor little motherless heiress of Callie's fortune. There are lots of pictures of the casket and the celebrity mourners. There's even a graphic shot of Callie sprawled on the ground beneath the hooves of the horse that killed her.

Last but not least, my own face stares up at me, looking countrified and frightened beneath a headline.

REDFERN SISTER BACK FROM THE DEAD

I tighten my fingers around the glass in my hand, trying to focus on the voices swirling around me. Hard as I try, I can't look away from the picture of the horse. Callie's face is turned toward the camera, mouth open as if in surprise, eyes wide. That dark shadow under her head might be blood.

"Does Ariel know the meeting was at eleven?" Glynnis asks, consulting her watch.

"Teenagers. No sense of time. I'm sure she'll be here in a minute," Ricken answers. "Let me freshen your drink. How is the memoir coming along?"

"I've got the ghostwriter signed. Publishers are drooling." She accepts her drink back from Ricken with a nod but sets it down on the table beside her.

Ricken refills his own glass and takes a swallow. "Hold out a bit before you finalize any offers. We need to create more drama."

I close my eyes, pressing the cool glass against my hot cheek. More drama is the last thing I need.

"We really must get started," Glynnis says. "I've got another appointment this afternoon."

"I'll go fetch Ariel." Ricken gets to his feet.

"Maybe it would be best to begin without her," Morgan says. "Reading through the will could be . . . upsetting for her, don't you think?" His forehead is damp with sweat, though it's cool in the room.

"That makes sense," Glynnis agrees. "This must all be very difficult for her. We can explain things to her later."

Ricken sinks back into his chair, but he's frowning.

Morgan clears his throat and turns the process of opening his briefcase into a theatrical event. He dials the combination lock, one slow click at a time. Flicks the latches. Lifts the lid slowly and finally hands a legal-sized envelope to each of us.

"Morgan?" Ricken says. "How about if you highlight the main points for all of us, and then we can read through on our own and ask questions as they arise?"

"Certainly," the attorney says, adjusting his glasses. "I've prepared a summary, but it's really a very straightforward will. To begin, each of us inherits ten thousand dollars as thanks for services rendered."

This strikes me as extravagant generosity, but Ricken and Genesis exchange a look that clearly says they had expected more. Glynnis just nods, as if agents are gifted with sums of this sort on a daily basis.

Morgan clears his throat and continues. "Annelise is named as executrix and also as guardian for Ariel—"

"I'm sorry, what?" I can't believe what I'm hearing. Me, responsible for Ariel?

"You are Ariel's legal guardian until she comes of age," Morgan says, as if this arrangement of the words makes their meaning any more comprehensible. "There is also a trust fund of one million dollars for Ariel, of which Annelise is the trustee until Ariel's twenty-first birthday, at which time Ariel will receive the lump sum. There is a separate trust for Ariel's college expenses, of which Annelise is also the trustee."

I take a swallow of the drink in my hand, feeling the burn and hoping it will head off a full-on anxiety attack. What do I know about handling this kind of money? My mother's slender finances are enough to hurt my brain, and there's nothing complicated about them. The thought of being responsible for a million dollars makes my head swim. But the money is nothing compared to the whole guardian thing. I'm a terrible choice. Just look how I ruined Callie.

And with that thought I'm drifting again, the voices receding into a meaningless murmur.

***

Callie sits astride the frame of our open bedroom window. Her long, tanned legs are nearly bare, the too-short denim skirt rucked up to her hips. Her hair shines golden in the light from our bedside lamp. Outside it's pure dark, the sky speckled with stars.

"This is not a good idea." I'm lying on my bed, staring at her over the top of my book.

"It's a very bad idea. That's why I'm doing it. Come with me."

A breeze blows in, carrying with it the smell of adventure and maybe even magic. I run both hands through my tangled hair, glance down at my worn sweatpants, then back up at my perfect little sister.

"No."

"C'mon, Lise. Lighten up for once."

"It's midnight. You have school tomorrow."

"So?"

"What if you get caught?"

She shrugs. "That's half the fun." Her lips purse and her brows draw together in a sudden frown. "If you tell . . ."

"Who would I tell?"

Mom's barely been out of bed in a week. I've managed to get enough liquid into her to keep her hydrated, but her skin hangs off her bones and her eyes are dull and flat. She'll be fast asleep, knocked out cold by a handful of pills, and there will be no waking her before morning. Dad is sitting in his armchair, staring at the TV, nearly at the bottom of a fifth of Crown Royal. If I tell him Callie is fixing to escape out the window for a tryst with a boy, he'll bluster and shout but he won't do anything.

"Well, if you do tell, you'll be sorry," Callie says.

I know that's the truth. The last time I crossed her, she put itching powder in my deodorant. She's taller than me now, and strong. So I let her go, leaving the window open so she can get back in.

***

Morgan says something, but I'm not listening. I don't hear his words, I just see his eyebrows go up and the other heads turn toward me.

I should have stopped Callie from going out that window. Tackled her, beat her up, tied her to the bed. Maybe that was the night she got pregnant with Ariel.

My God. What if Ariel is having sex with Shadow?

The thought slams into me like a line drive. Maybe the two of them are in her room right this minute making a baby Shadow that I'm going to end up responsible for. In my mind, the baby has black fingernails and piercings and makes Damien look angelic by comparison.

Panic sets in. I can feel my insides quivering as if they've been turned to jelly. There's enough voltage going through my hand to power a small electronic device.

"Has anybody seen Ariel this morning?" My throat is parched and tight and I take another swallow out of my glass, a long one this time, as though it's water. Alcohol burns all the way down to my stomach and up into my nose. A coughing fit follows, and when I'm done, all eyes are fixed on me like I'm the new display at a freak show.

The intensity of their expressions is beyond any reasonable reaction to somebody accidentally inhaling a drink. Genesis is no longer smiling. Her eyes are narrowed, lips thinned. Ricken is actually pale. He gets up, pours himself another drink, and swallows the whole thing before pouring another. Glynnis is the only one who doesn't seem perturbed. She smiles at me, her sharp eyes softening a little.

My hands are shaking so hard a little wave of amber liquid sloshes over the edge of my glass. Carefully, I set it down and lock my fingers together in my lap, on top of the untouched will.

"I'm sorry, I don't think I heard what you said," I tell Morgan.

He clears his throat. "In simplest terms, you inherit the bulk of the estate."

It's my turn to stare. It's a damn good thing I've already set down my glass.

"I what?"

"Apart from the bequests already mentioned, and the two trusts for Ariel, you inherit everything. All of the money, the property, and the business."

The circle of faces wavers and distorts. My skin feels cold, my limbs heavy. None of this makes any sense.

"Why?" I ask, hoping somebody can tell me. "She told everybody I was dead. Why would she leave me everything?"

Nobody answers. Nobody says anything, in fact, until Morgan clears his throat again. "Genesis, could you please tell Annelise what this bequest is worth?"

"There will be estate taxes, of course," the accountant says, "but at last quarter's accounting, Callie's net worth was just over one hundred million."

I know that number can't be right. My ears are buzzing. I can't understand why Morgan is sweating; the air in the room is frigid. I wrap my arms around myself to stop my shivering.

"I'll prepare hard-copy statements for Annelise," Genesis goes on. "Callie's investments were extensive, and there are a number of business interests. Plus the real estate, of course."

Ricken returns to his seat and gives me an oily smile. "This must feel overwhelming. But we are all here to support you. Callie relied heavily on her team to manage the finances and the business so that she could focus her energy on her music. You won't need to worry about a thing. I, for one, came prepared with a contract for you to sign today, so there will be no lapse at all in my services. It just needs a minor alteration, since I had expected you to be signing on behalf of Ariel, but that's easily done."

He's already got a pen in his hand. He pulls out a document from beneath one of the tabloids on the coffee table and crosses out a line. Genesis leans over to retrieve a briefcase leaning against her chair.

"I won't rush you," Glynnis says. "We've got plenty of time to sign papers. You've got enough on your plate for today, I think."

I try to smile at her in thanks, but my lips feel frozen. The scratching of pens as Ricken and Genesis make their little alterations makes my skin twitch. Morgan, who knew what was coming and was already prepared, pulls a document out of his briefcase and holds it out to me.

"I've also brought an agreement for you, since I assume you'll want the same law firm to deal with your interests and the estate. It will simplify things for you. Do you need a pen?"

Black ink on white paper. Little squiggly, meaningless marks. The high ceiling feels like it's going to fall on my head. The walls are closing in. My heart is racing like a pack of horses on the home stretch and I can't breathe.

And then it hits me, like a bolt of lightning out of the blue.

Ariel doesn't know.

As if things aren't rocky enough between us, now there's this. I have to tell her. Now, before any one of these piranhas gets a chance. I'll tell her I don't want the money. I'll make up some sort of excuse for Callie; I'm good at that. But any way I spin it, it's bound to feel like a betrayal.

I set the unsigned agreement down on the end table beside me and get to my feet. The room spins once, then steadies. And then I walk out the door, not bothering to excuse myself or wait for a break in the conversation.

"Annelise?" Ricken calls after me. "We'll be ready with the contracts in a minute."

I keep walking. Once I'm out of their sight, I stop and lean against a wall for support, focused on breathing until my heart slows down and my vision is clear. It's tempting to bolt up to my room and lock myself in, but I want Ariel to hear the news from me. Might as well get it over with.

When I knock on the door I saw her vanish behind last night, there's no answer. I knock again, louder.

The door isn't locked. I turn the knob and push it open.

I step into a spacious bedroom that looks nothing like the cramped quarters Callie and I shared. No posters on the walls or clothes crumpled on the floor. A granite counter runs along one wall, complete with a microwave, minifridge, and sink. French doors lead out onto a small patio, surrounded by a high fence. A door to a walk-in closet stands open; two other doors are closed.

The room is empty.

"Ariel?"

No answer. The first door opens into a bathroom. The mirrors are steamy. A damp towel lies discarded in the middle of the tile floor beside a Jacuzzi tub. I hang up the towel and move on, holding my breath.

The other room has to be the bedroom. If I find her in bed with Shadow, I don't know what I'll do. Sneak away, maybe. Come back later. But the image of the Shadow baby is a powerful motivator and I knock once, then enter.

There is a bed, but it's neatly made and there's no sign of Shadow. I breathe a little easier.

Ariel sits crossed-legged in the middle of the floor, the contents of an open cedar chest spread out around her. Her hair is wet and tangled. She's wearing flannel pajama bottoms and a baggy T-shirt, and her face, when she looks up at the sound of the opening door, reminds me of the child she once was.

I cross the room and sink down onto the floor beside her. My fingers trace the smooth wood grain of the chest while my eyes sort through the visible contents. On the floor are some of Ariel's baby clothes. A picture of Callie at the KISS concert she snuck off to when they played Spokane in '96. A stack of *Rolling Stone* magazines.

"I have a chest just like this. Our grandfather made them for your mother and me."

These days, mine is being used to store music books and CDs. Callie's, on the other hand, is full of mementos and odds and ends of clothing and jewelry, not all of them hers. She was always and forever engaging in what she called "borrowing," usually without permission and often for keeps. I reach in and fish out a sweater, soft angora in a delicate rose color. "I wondered where this went."

"It's yours?"

"It was, until Callie decided she wanted it."

Shut up, Lise. Don't speak ill of the dead.

Callie's favorite childhood blanket is folded up in a corner of the chest and I pull it out, poking my fingers through a hole in the center. "I could have sworn I saw her stuff this in the trash can."

Ariel takes the blanket from me, poking her own fingers through the hole. Her fingernails are bitten down to the quick. "Why would she throw it away?"

"I'm not sure. I remember we were almost late for school because she wanted to take it to the first day of kindergarten. Mom said no. Callie never would listen. She stuffed it in her backpack."

"What happened?"

I shrug. "I don't know. When she got in the car after school that day, she wouldn't talk. You could see she'd been crying; she was still sniffling. And when we got home, she went into our bedroom and stuffed it into the trash can. Never saw her with it again."

A little warm spot burns through the cold of my long-held anger, remembering. I lean into the trunk, caught up in memories. Callie's favorite teddy bear. A Barbie doll, clothed in '80s rock 'n' roll regalia. And then, poking out from beneath yet another of my missing sweaters, I see the tattered green corner of a notebook.

"Oh God." I choke on something that is half laughter, half-undefined. Shoving aside the other objects, I grab the old journal and pull it out. Written on the front cover in curly letters with a little heart dotting every *i* is the familiar inscription: *None of your business. Do NOT read this and that means you, Annelise.*

"Let me see."

I hesitate, holding on even as Ariel's fingers clutch the book from the other side.

"She wouldn't want us to read it."

"It's not like she's gonna know."

"I'm not so sure about that. She's probably floating around in ghost form, watching us. Read this diary and she'll go all crazy. Throw caviar at us while we're sleeping."

Ariel giggles. "Come on. What can it hurt? I want to know who she was back then."

Don't we all, I'm thinking. Me, I'd like to know who she was, ever.

My niece looks up at me, still holding her end of the book, and there's a sheen of tears in her eyes. I think how I feel about my own mother slipping ever further away, and about everything that is lost with each evaporated memory.

I let Ariel take the book. She hugs it to her chest. "I don't think she'll mind. Not really."

I'm still worried about what Ariel will find in those pages, but I shrug and let it go. At least the diary has served to break the ice a little between the two of us. "If you read anything that . . . well, if you have any questions, just ask." I get up, stretching out a cramp in my left thigh from sitting cross-legged.

"Okay," she says, her voice distant. The book is open in her lap already and her head's bent, hair screening her face. I've been dismissed. I know I need to tell her—about the will, about the money—but I can't. Not right now. Since I'm not going to sign any contracts until after we talk, I can't go back to the meeting. So I climb the stairs to my bedroom, making sure to lock the door behind me. I feel unutterably weary and lie down across the bed. When sleep comes for me, I surrender to the sweetness of oblivion without a fight.

CHAPTER THREE

It's too early to be awake, but my eyes are wide open, staring at the ceiling, and my brain is already racing. I feel like I've been turned inside out and upside down, and when I get out of bed and look in the mirror, my face doesn't look like it belongs to me.

The rest of yesterday is a blur. I didn't leave my room and barely even got out of bed. Ricken knocked twice, and I told him both times I'd come down later. The same girl who brought me breakfast showed up with a dinner tray and a manila folder. I managed to choke down a few bites and then went right back to sleep.

The folder, untouched, sits on the dresser, right beside my hairbrush and jewelry. I haven't opened it, but I know what's inside. All of those contracts. It makes sense to sign them, but I still haven't talked to Ariel.

I need time.

I also need coffee. At home, I have a pot that wakes up at the same time I do. I haven't yet investigated Callie's kitchen, but the idea of fixing my own coffee, maybe even my own breakfast, appeals to me. I need something normal in the middle of a situation that is anything but.

The kitchen is dark and I stumble around and clatter into things for what seems an eternity before I find the light switch. Callie must have a coffeepot somewhere, but I can't find it. All I can locate is a Keurig and a bunch of tiny, flavored K-Cups. I want plain coffee—no chocolate or vanilla or hazelnut—but the kitchen is huge and it would take forever to search for something else. By the time I've figured out how to program the machine, I'm wishing I'd taken one of the cars out in search of a coffee shop. I miss my own little kitchen and the ritual of grinding beans, measuring them into the filter, listening to the pot gurgle.

But the first scalding sip makes me feel better. Brain cells start waking up, and suddenly I'm ravenous. The fridge is well stocked, but not with anything of interest to me. I see fruit and cottage cheese and yogurt, but all of those serve only to make my stomach swirl. What I'm craving is grease and salt. Fried eggs and hash browns. Bacon. Sausage. In this fridge, there's not an egg to be seen, only a container of egg substitute.

A soft click. Footsteps. I spin around, heart hammering, to face a short, stout woman in sturdy black shoes and a white apron. Her hair is covered under a hairnet. Her brown eyes are not friendly, even though her words are carefully polite.

"I can get you something, señora? Breakfast, perhaps?"

"I can get my own. I don't suppose there are potatoes somewhere, or real eggs?"

"It is nothing for me to fix it. I can send to the store for eggs. How do you want them cooked?" She is already in action, wiping down the counter where I've apparently spilled an invisible drop of coffee.

It's not her kitchen, I tell myself. *It's mine.* "How about we send to the store and I cook them myself?"

She gives me a pained, long-suffering look. "We have guests for dinner. I must begin preparations now, and two in the kitchen . . ." She shrugs and spreads her hands wide, indicating that this would be a mistake.

I know nothing about guests. If I had more guts, I'd find Ricken and tell him, "I don't want guests for dinner. Cancel it."

But this is Callie's life, not mine, and I don't feel like I have the right to exert any control over events in her house. Especially since I bailed on the meeting yesterday and wasn't exactly around to be consulted about plans.

I'm not hungry anymore.

"You know what? Never mind the eggs," I tell the cook.

Clinging to my coffee mug, I wander into the hallway, exploring the quiet house. Main living area, where I've already been. Entertainment room. Game room.

Music studio.

For a long time I stand in the doorway, just looking, and then I enter.

It's an airy, spacious room with a hardwood floor and acoustic tiles on the walls and ceiling. Callie has all the latest technology. An electric piano. Microphones. Recording equipment. A sheet of music rests on the piano stand, titled "Love Me." It's a manuscript, an original song, but it's not Callie's writing. She never did write music. Hopefully, she came by this song honestly. I trail my fingers over the tops of the keys, lightly, feeling the music stir beneath them. Positioning my hands, I depress one key. It makes a small clicking sound.

If I turn around, I'm convinced Callie will be standing behind me with a knowing smile on her face. "How come you never play anymore, Lise?"

"I play."

"Only what you need to teach lessons. That's not music."

I swear I've actually heard her voice, but when I spin around, the room is empty. Enough already. I flee outside to the pool. The desert air is cool and dry. Sinking down into a lounger, I lay back and close my eyes, just breathing.

My cell phone vibrates in my pocket and I fumble for it, sending a wave of coffee flooding over my lap. By the time I get my hands on the phone, there's no time to look at caller ID and I just answer.

"Oh my God. Is it true?"

"Is what true?"

"It is, isn't it? You can stop being coy, Lise, cat's out of the bag. I always knew you and Dale had a thing, although how you've managed to keep it a secret this long is beyond me. In this town? And from me? You two should go be spies or—"

"Nancy. Breathe."

The voice on the other end of the phone pauses and obediently takes a deep breath. Nancy is Dale's sister. I love her, almost like family, but she's a hopeless gossip, and whatever her news, wherever it came from, she has got to be stopped.

"Now, back to the beginning and make it slow and simple. What in hell are you talking about?"

"Oh, come on, Lise. If you're going to be snarly, I'll go ask Dale."

"No! For God's sake, don't do that. I really need to know what you heard."

"I didn't hear it. I saw it. At Safeway. Ran down to get things early before getting the kids off to camp. There was no milk in the house. Not a drop. I can't believe the way they drink that stuff, and we were down to a crust of bread and—"

"Nance. Focus."

"Right. So I'm standing in line at Safeway. Went early partly to avoid lines, but you know how that is. They only had one open, and I wasn't the only one with the idea. Sandra McGregor was in front of me with a heaping cart, and she was discussing politics with the checker—"

"And you saw . . ."

"So I'm totally bored and looking at the tabloids. And right on the cover of *Need to Know*, there's a picture of you and Dale. He's got his arm around you, and the headline is something like 'Mystery Lover for

Redfern Heiress.' And the article is really touching, all about you and Dale, and inside there's a picture of him kissing you. So don't try to tell me they made it all up, because photographs don't lie."

My whole body goes hot, then cold. Dale did kiss me. At the airport. I haven't let myself think about that kiss. Whatever it means or doesn't mean, it's private, between me and Dale.

"Ever heard of Photoshop?" I ask her, scrambling.

"It doesn't look photoshopped."

I can tell that she's scrutinizing the image. "You're looking at a copy right now."

"Of course! I bought one for you, too, for when you get home. And one for Dale. And Mom. You're in the big-time news, Lise! This is awesome."

I take the phone from my ear and clunk myself on the forehead with it, twice. My entire body feels like it's wrapped in cotton wool. Even my ears feel fuzzy. I can still hear Nancy's voice.

"Lise? Lise!"

"Look. I don't care how it looks or what it says, it's all lies. You hear me? Dale and I are not a thing. Friends, like always. You can't spread this around. You have to make sure people know the truth."

Silence. Uneasy breathing.

"Nancy."

"Yeah?"

"What have you done?"

"Are you positive it's not true? It sure looks real."

"Nancy!"

She sighs. "Well, shucks. The local paper called and asked questions. I gave an interview."

"What did you tell them?"

"How you and Dale and Callie were always together as kids, and how you and Dale are best friends and that you went camping last summer . . ." Her voice trails off. "It's really not true, then?"

I hang up. There are no words for this. It's not her fault, not really, and anything I say is going to be horrible and wrong. I'll have to apologize later. Right now, I don't know what to do.

I can't go home.

That's the first clear thought that comes to me. The whole town will be buzzing with the juicy details of Callie's death and my supposed romance with Dale. Maybe later I'll be able to face them, but right now I can't go home and I can't stay here, and what am I going to do? I don't want to think about what Dale's going to say.

A rustling sound pulls my attention to the far side of the pool, where a tree branch hangs over the fence. The branch is thrashing in a way that has nothing to do with the early morning breeze. There's a woman in the tree. She's got a camera pointed in my direction. I cover my face reflexively, before I realize it's too late to hide. She's already got me, out here in a T-shirt and jeans with my mug of coffee. No bra. Uncombed morning hair.

I am not going to become one of those tabloid pics of some poor woman without her makeup, taken in the worst possible light, looking like a zombie. My fingers close around my coffee mug, and I consider the trajectory. If I aim right, maybe I could drop her right out of the tree, camera and all, with one good thunk to the skull.

But then there would be pictures of me in handcuffs to add to the frenzy.

She's dressed all in black with a stocking cap over her head. She clings to her perch for dear life with one hand while she holds the camera with the other. Probably the first tree she's ever climbed, or she'd have recognized the branch was not quite sufficient to bear her weight. Her face looks very young and rather frightened.

I start walking toward her. "Leave now, and maybe I won't call the cops."

Her body overbalances to the right and she lets go of the camera, grabbing onto the branch with both hands.

"I—don't think I can."

In a minute she's going to fall onto the concrete and break her skull without any help from me. Suppressing the temptation to walk away and leave her to her fate, I drag a deck chair underneath her perch.

"Let your feet drop."

"What?" Her eyes flick down to the chair, then back at me.

"Hold on with both hands, let your feet hang. The chair will be just a couple feet below you, and then you can drop."

She shakes her head vigorously. "Can't."

"If you're scared of heights, you shouldn't climb trees. Now come down before you fall down."

"Maybe we could just talk." Her voice is shaky but determined. "Why did Callie say your whole family was dead? Was your childhood abusive? Oh, and who is the guy you were kissing at the airport?"

In her excitement, she almost forgets her predicament, loosening her grip enough that she starts to slide again.

"You are going to have to let go."

"I will if you tell me—"

"Or I could just go inside and let you fall. Think you can hang on until the cops get here?"

Her feet are slipping. Stepping up on the chair, I reach up and grab her calf, giving a little tug. The other leg slides free and she's dangling by her hands now, exactly as I want her, while I support her with my arms around her waist.

"I've got you. Let go."

With a little squeal she releases her hold, and I manage to get her down onto solid ground. As soon as she has her balance, she grabs the camera and snaps a close-up. She steps back for a better shot, the pool right behind her. The little click of the shutter triggers my suppressed rage.

Another shot. Click.

My hands press against her shoulders. Frail little bird bones, no weight or substance to her at all. One good shove, and she's off-balance, both arms flailing. The camera arcs out, swinging at the end of its strap. Her scream cuts off as she hits the water and goes under, sending a lovely rainbow spray into the air.

She comes up sputtering, treading water, hair plastered to her head and in her eyes. Her stocking cap drifts up to the surface like a strange black jellyfish and then sinks again. As soon as she can speak, she starts shouting. "You ruined my camera."

"Where I come from, people get shot for trespassing. Be glad it's just a camera." Spitting mad as I am, I can't bring myself to push her back under. Instead, I reach out a hand and tow her over to the edge.

Once out, she sits there with the camera in her hands, shoulders hunched, shivering in the cool morning. A pool of water grows around her. I can see her shoulder blades through the clinging fabric of her shirt, and count the knobs of her spine. Her face is pure misery. Pathetic as she looks, I harden my heart and hold on to my anger.

"Paper or TV?" I ask her.

She swipes her eyes with the back of her hand and sniffles. "What?"

"Which paper, which station? Who sent you here?"

"I don't . . . nobody sent me." Tears start pouring down her cheeks now in good earnest. She glances up at me, and I get a good long look at her face. The hair plastered to her head is dark red.

"Wait. I remember you. You were at the funeral."

She scrubs at her face with her hands, smearing mascara into long black streaks down both cheeks. "Ricken said . . ." A sob escapes her. She's shivering, her teeth chattering.

A dreadful suspicion washes over me. "Ricken put you up to this?"

"He saw me here, yesterday, outside the gates. And he told me about the tree . . ."

"Right. Ricken told you to climb a tree and hang out over the pool." My voice drips with sarcasm, but I know full well there's nothing he wouldn't do for a little extra media buzz.

"I'm not lying!" She sets the camera down tenderly and stands up so she can dig in her sodden pocket. It takes a minute, but the business card she extracts, though sopping wet, is pretty much intact. And sure enough, there's Ricken's name and a familiar phone number.

I take it from her.

"Hey, give it back. It's mine."

I just look at her.

She has the decency to shuffle her feet and flush, but still persists. "My new camera is ruined. That's like a thousand-dollar investment. Maybe he'll give me another lead."

"My sister is dead. Are you going to find me another one?"

"I didn't think of—"

"You need to start thinking. Like Dale said at the funeral, have a little respect. Now, I'm going to walk you out through the house. And you're going to stop spying on people who want to be left alone."

"His name is Dale?"

It's hopeless. Lips tightly sealed, I lead her, shivering and dripping, across marble tile and Persian carpets, hoping that Ariel doesn't make an appearance.

Just before I slam the front door on her woebegone self, I have an idea.

"Give me your business card. I'm sure you have one."

"Are you going to—I mean—will you report me to the cops?"

"Just give it to me."

Another dig through sodden pockets and she holds out another soggy piece of cardboard. Melody Smith, photographer.

"Melody, huh? Good luck with that camera."

I slam the door. It's a satisfying sensation to hear that sound reverberate through the marble-tiled entry area. It would be even more satisfying to smash something. Instead, I call Ricken. I'm pretty sure he's not accustomed to being up this early, but hey. Maybe he hasn't even gone to bed. I'd love to catch him out in a casino, the music of the pull slots jangling in the background. Tie loose, suit rumpled, despair in his eyes.

The phone goes directly to voice mail. I don't leave a message.

I make my way back to the kitchen to find the cook already hard at work. From the looks of things, we'll be hosting a small army with very expensive tastes. I set my mug down in the sink and talk to her back.

"Do you think you could still get me some eggs?"

She glances over her shoulder. "I can send someone to the store."

"While they're at it, could we get a copy of *Need to Know*?"

At that, she stops dicing onions and turns to look at me. "What do you want with a piece of trash like that? We get the newspaper delivered every morning."

"I need to see something."

She shakes her head and makes a clucking noise with her tongue. "You need to hold to the memories of your sister that are real. That rag is all made up. You hear?"

I want to hug her for that, but instead I shrug. "There's a story I need to see."

"Suit yourself," she says. "Eggs and one junk paper, coming up."

***

As it turns out, I needn't have gone to the trouble. Ricken turns up a couple of hours later with an armful of tabloids. The only way he could look more like the cat who ate the canary would be if he actually had yellow feathers stuck to his chin.

Before I glance at the magazines, I make my first demand. "I want your house key."

"What?"

"You wander in and out of here like you own the place. Do you live here? Were you sleeping with her?"

"I don't understand. Did something happen?"

He rests a hand on my shoulder, lets it slide down my arm. I'm not sure if it's meant to be a seductive gesture or a soothing one. Either way, his touch makes my skin crawl.

I jerk my arm away. "There was a reporter in the pool this morning."

He blinks at that. "What was she doing in the pool?"

"I put her there." I shove his business card at him. "Care to explain?"

He accepts the damp rectangle gingerly, holding it with his fingertips. "Now, Lise. Is that what's bothering you? Of course I can explain."

I grab one of the tabloids out of his hands. Sure enough, there's a picture of me and Dale, his arm around me, head bent protectively over mine. I'm gazing into his face, and even I think we look like lovers.

"You're encouraging this shit!"

"Of course I am. This will totally raise the price on the memoir. And sales of her last album are already way up. You, my dear girl, are money in the bank. Everybody wants to know about the mysterious sister who has inherited the fortune. And about your lover, of course. It couldn't get any better."

"I don't understand how lies about me and my friend have anything to do with anything."

He shakes his head and wags a finger at me. "You don't understand show business."

Well, he's got that right. The pictures make my stomach turn. I should call Dale, but my hands start to sweat at the very thought. How do I even bring this up? Everybody in Colville will be talking about it. His friends, his clients.

"The cameras follow the money," Ricken says. "Callie's dead. You're not. Do your job right, and there will be even more money. Now, we have a lot of work to do. Strike while the iron's hot! The team will be over again this afternoon. You can return the contracts, and then tell us everything about Callie's childhood. We can use that to play on emotions for a while, keep things moving. Of course, everyone's very interested in you now, too, so we'll need to work on your image."

I flip through the tabloids.

Redfern Family Back from the Grave!

The Truth about Why Callie Lied!

Imposter Inherits Redfern Fortune!

Redfern Heiress Caught with Secret Lover! This headline is accompanied by a picture of me with Dale, and followed up by our yearbook photos.

I shove the magazines aside in disgust. "Here's another idea. How about we let Callie rest in peace? There's already plenty of money."

This trips him up. The concept is so foreign, it sets his jaw and brain at cross-purposes. His mouth opens and closes soundlessly before he pulls himself together. "Have you looked over the contracts yet?" he asks.

Apparently my face expresses guilt, because Ricken shakes his head and makes a clucking noise of disapproval. "You must pay attention, Lise. None of us can act without your permission. Inheriting this kind of money is not a game; it is serious business. You have a responsibility."

That word breaks something inside me. My whole life, I've been responsible for everybody. For Callie, up until she got pregnant and ran away. For my mother when she was depressed and my father when he was drunk. For making sure groceries got bought and lunches made and laundry done. For arranging my father's funeral and getting my mother into a nursing home. And now Callie's gone and got herself killed and left me saddled with a bunch of problems I don't know how to solve.

"I don't give a damn about the money," I tell Ricken. "Go ahead and have your little media party, if you must, but leave me and Dale out of it. You hear me?"

My words slide off him like water off a duck's back. "It's too late for that, I'm afraid. Once the media get their teeth into a story . . . well, you'll just have to ride it out."

I want to kick him out of the house, but the ugly truth is, I'd be lost without him. I compromise by taking the conversation full circle.

"Give me your house key."

"Annelise—"

"Give it!"

With a sigh, and an expression that clearly conveys his belief that I'm behaving like a capricious child, he pulls out his key ring and removes a key. I know damn well it's not the only one in his possession. Hell, he's probably given them out to reporters and photographers so they can sneak in and take pictures while I'm sleeping. Mentally I add *get locks changed* to a growing list of things to do.

"The team will be here at one. And the party's at six," he calls after me as I stalk away.

I give him a middle-finger salute and keep walking. He can have both the meeting and the party without me. Maybe I can go somewhere for a week or two. Use my credit card, book a flight, run away. If I step out of the limelight for a bit, maybe the press will forget about me and life can go back to normal.

A wonderful idea all around, except for one small detail.

Ariel.

The world settles back onto my shoulders. I need to grow up. Tell Ariel the truth about the will, sign the documents, and accept the facts.

I find her in her bedroom, folding clothes into a suitcase.

"What are you doing?"

She barely glances at me before turning to an open dresser drawer and pulling out a stack of underwear. "Obvious, isn't it?"

"Let me rephrase. Where are you going?"

"On a trip."

"You're only sixteen. You can't just take off without—"

She whirls to face me. "Where were you before, with all of the rules? Mom didn't care. I took off last summer—it took her two days to notice I was gone. And then she had Ricken come get me."

Her hands are clenched into fists. She looks nothing like her mother, and yet I recognize perfectly the way she stands, the defiant angle of her chin. Callie used to look at me like that when I got in the way of something she wanted. There was no point fighting with her once she got that expression on her face.

I collapse onto Ariel's bed. "God. Ricken is reason enough to run away in the first place."

She laughs and her body relaxes a little.

I start breathing again. I gather up all my courage and open my mouth to tell her about the will. But just then she looks up at me and asks, "What happened between you and my mom, anyway?"

My throat locks. The moment stretches as I search for words that will evade the truth without telling an outright lie. At last, I clear my throat and look away. "It wasn't one thing, really. It was a long grocery list."

"Don't give me that shit about how you just drifted apart. Everybody lies to me. I thought maybe you'd be different and tell me the truth."

"Ariel . . ."

"I remember. We used to visit you. You visited us. And then we didn't. I want to know what really happened."

My hands twist together, fingers laced so tight it hurts. My voice comes out small and childlike, so quiet I almost don't hear it myself.

"She stole my song."

"She what?"

"'Closer Home.' I wrote it. That last time you visited, I sang it to her."

"Oh." Ariel's hands go still.

My eyes drop to my own hands, the fingernails blanching yellow white with the pressure. My chest feels so tight I wonder if I'm having a heart attack. Breathing is a problem, but I manage to keep the air going in and out. "She came home for our father's funeral, your grandpa. I don't know if you remember."

"Sorta. There was the church, and the graveyard. I didn't really know him, but I remember all the people crying. And food."

"Lots of food."

"I remember falling asleep while you and Mom played guitars and sang. And then we didn't come home anymore. Even to see Grandma."

"I called Callie once, after the song hit gold. I told her to never come back." My voice is still small and quiet. It has to be to squeeze past the knot in my throat. "Mom missed her."

The truth is, I missed her, too. I kept waiting for her to call, to tell me she was sorry. Maybe to offer to share something of her fame.

"Sometimes I hate her," Ariel says.

"Ariel . . ."

Her face is set, jaw clamped. "I know. She's dead. So now it's supposed to be all sweetness and light and we never say anything bad about her."

I do know. It's easier to hate her than to let myself feel anything else. But Ariel needs to hear the good things, much as it hurts me to dredge them up.

"When you were little, before she got into the music, everything revolved around you. Everything. When you were born, the first couple of days after she brought you home from the hospital, she wouldn't let anybody hold you. She was so tired, getting up with you nights, she was falling asleep in the chair with you in her arms. I told her to go to bed and let me take care of you, just for a couple of hours, but she wouldn't do it."

"Well, that certainly didn't last. I guess I wasn't what she wanted after all."

"You were perfect. She was terribly young. No older than you are now when she got pregnant. I know she loved you. The fame pulled her away, but she always loved you."

Ariel changes the subject. "So how did you find out, about the song? Did she tell you?"

I shake my head. "I got into my car one day and turned the radio on just in time to hear the DJ say, 'And here's a new one from Callie Redfern, burning up the charts.' And then 'Closer Home' started to play . . .'"

Callie could sing. No doubt about that. And she had a kick-ass band to back her. "Closer Home" never sounded so good when I sang it. But she was thoughtless and careless, and now I can't put off telling Ariel the news.

"You didn't come to the meeting."

She shrugs. "Why bother? Morgan was just going to ramble on in legal speak about who inherited what. And Ricken would be moping around and trying to look all grief-stricken while lusting after Mom's money. If I'd been there, I might have hit somebody."

"Ricken. If you're going to hit somebody, ever, pick Ricken."

She grins, then turns back to her packing. "So, what do I get?"

"A cool million. When you turn twenty-one. And money for college."

Her hands stop moving, and she gives me a level stare. "I know damn well she was worth a whole lot more than that. Who gets the rest of it? That slimeball Ricken?"

I swallow hard. My mouth is full of sawdust. "Not Ricken. Me."

Our eyes stay locked for a long moment. I wait for a rush of hatred or tears of grief, but after what seems to me an eternity, she shrugs slightly and goes back to her packing.

"Cool," she says.

"Ariel, I'm not sure you understand. That's all she left you—one million and money for college. I don't know what she was thinking. I'll deed it all over to you as soon as it's clear—"

"Are you kidding? I don't want to have to worry about all that money. You have no idea what you've just stepped into."

I feel like I'm free-falling without a safety net. This is not at all what I'd expected from Ariel. For a few seconds I'm relieved that she doesn't seem hurt, but that gives way to the old, heavy weight of responsibility. Ariel's room is light and airy, but all at once it feels way too small. I close my eyes and imagine I'm back home in my little rented house, with the maple out the window and the fresh air flowing in. Last week I was complaining about being broke. Now I want nothing more than to ditch all of this money and the strings attached to it and go back to my old life.

"I'm going to go find my dad," Ariel says in a low voice.

My eyes fly open.

"Why?" I know it's a stupid question before it leaves my lips, but I seem to have no control over my own tongue.

"Are you serious?" She adds socks and a pair of jeans to her suitcase.

"Okay. I totally get why. But how, then? Where are you even going to start? Far as I know, she never told anybody who he was."

Ariel picks up the diary, dropping it into my lap. "Everybody she had sex with the year before I was born, all detailed there. Nobody could ever accuse her of being a prude."

The diary seems to burn into my skin. I shiver, the rest of me cold in comparison. "So she mentions a few names . . ."

"Six. Six names over the course of a month. And she had no love for any of them, either. Not so much as a good strong crush."

"She was sixteen. She was your mother. You shouldn't talk about her like that."

Ariel whirls on me, hands on hips. "She set herself a challenge to see how many guys she could bag over the summer. That's where I came from. How do you think that feels?"

"Sucks." I'm wishing I had a drink. A very stiff one. "I'm not sure knowing which guy it was will make you feel any better."

Ariel shrugs. "I want to find out about the other side of me."

"Callie didn't want anybody to know."

"But why?"

"She didn't want to share you with anybody. We tried to get her to tell us so she could get child support. But she wouldn't do it. Said she figured you were better off without a dad."

"Why would she even think that?"

"Your grandpa was an alcoholic. He said some things . . ."

He wasn't the only one who said things. I said plenty. And the thing about words is that once they're spoken, you can't ever really call them back.

***

It's been two months since Callie had her baby, and the added expense has swamped our precarious finances. I'm sitting at the kitchen table with a calculator and a stack of bills, trying to make two and two add up to five. Callie's fixing a bottle for Ariel. You'd think the baby was starving to death from the sounds of her, instead of chubby and pink and obviously thriving.

"Here, let me hold her." I need a break anyway. My head aches and my right eye has developed a twitch.

She hands me the baby and I snuggle her against my heart, pressing my cheek against her downy head and making the soothing little noises I didn't know I was capable of before Callie brought Ariel home.

"Almost out," Callie says, shaking the formula can. "We'll need more tomorrow."

All of my softness fades away. "I thought WIC paid for formula."

"Not enough to make it through the whole month. I called and asked for more. They said I should remember it's a supplemental program, not a free ride." Her voice takes on a sarcastic edge over the last words.

She tests a little formula on her wrist for temperature and reaches out her arms for Ariel.

My body has gone cold. "There's no money, Callie. What about food stamps?"

"All gone. You'll have to let one of the other bills ride this month." She takes Ariel from me and sticks the nipple into her mouth. The wailing stops at once, replaced by contented little gulping noises. Callie's face goes all dreamy. She looks almost like a different person when she's holding the baby. More like those pictures of Madonna and child, less like a willful teenager.

I watch them, feeling cold and helpless and lost. I've already moved money around as much as I dare. The mortgage is covered. I've paid half the electric bill and skipped the phone. There are enough groceries in the cupboard to eke out basic meals until my next payday. We've got a stash of diapers that Callie got free with a coupon.

But that's it. I've started working days at McDonald's and teaching all my music lessons in the evenings. Mom's in the hospital with the worst bout of depression she's ever had, which is saying something. There are going to be medical bills. Dad hit a point a few months ago where his drinking carried over from something he did after work to needing a couple of shots in the morning, and the whole functional alcoholic thing went out the window. Showed up to work one morning so drunk his boss couldn't help but notice, and that was the end of his job. He hasn't been fully sober since, far as I can tell. Callie applied for welfare, but I make too much money for her to qualify for more than a few dollars in food stamps, at least as long as she lives with us. Dale and I don't really talk these days, and I can't ask him for help, not with this.

"There isn't anything else," I say. "Money only stretches so far."

"We have to have formula."

"Obviously. So maybe you should get a job."

She sighs. "We've been through this. With the sort of job I'd get, we'd pay more for day care than I'd bring in."

This is true. I'm the one who crunched the numbers to figure it out. But something's gotta give, and I've got nothing left.

"Time to tell me who the father is." I hold up a hand to shush her before she even gets started. "Yeah, I know. You want to raise her yourself and all that. But we need some help here, Callie. He could at least be buying formula."

"Not happening."

I know to shut up. Anything I say at this point might as well be preached at a statue, but I can't help myself.

"She needs a father. Not just for the money, either."

"Lot of good that's done us."

"Dad wasn't always like this, Callie. It's Mom being sick and—"

"Just shut up, will you? I'm sick of you defending him. He can get off of his ass and help out. The money he spends on booze and smokes would more than pay for anything Ariel needs."

She's got her back to the door and doesn't see Dad shuffle into the doorway and stop to listen. He looks like hell. Since he lost his job, he's been shrinking. His clothes hang loose on his bony frame, as if they were made for a different man. His hair needs a wash and he hasn't shaved in a week. Tomorrow I'll have to bully him into the shower.

He sways a little, blinking, but he's sober enough to register what Callie's saying.

"I put a roof over your head," he says. "Food on the table. You could have a little respect."

My soul shrinks down small in my body, wanting to get away. I hate conflict, and there's no way this isn't going to turn into a big scene.

Callie rolls her eyes, snatching the bottle out of Ariel's mouth and slamming it down onto the table. "Oh, please. Give me a break."

Ariel starts wailing, wanting the rest of her bottle and scared by the shouting.

"Watch your tone. I don't have to put up with this from you."

"What are you going to do about it? Have another beer?" Shoving back her chair, Callie flounces across the kitchen and flings open the fridge, revealing a twelve-pack of Bud and a whole lot of nothing. She pulls out a can, pops it open, and holds it out. "Fridge is full of this shit, and there's no formula for the baby. But here. Have a beer. You know it's what you came in here for."

"Callie—"

"Shut up, Lise. He's a big man, he can speak for himself."

Moisture glistens in my father's eyes, and I find myself hoping, desperately, that he'll say no, just this once. I want this to be a storybook world where he takes the can and dumps it down the sink. At least, I want him to be shamed enough to turn around and walk away, coming back for his beer when Callie is elsewhere.

But the beer draws him in, one step at a time. As he takes it from her hand, he says, "Nobody asked you to get pregnant. If you're grown up enough to talk to me like that, you can go be someplace else."

Callie's face flushes. "Maybe you're the one who should move out," she shouts after his retreating back. He doesn't answer. Tears streak down her face as she sinks back into her chair and picks up Ariel's bottle. The baby settles almost at once, but the air in the kitchen feels supercharged and toxic.

"He didn't mean it," I say, watching the shell of my father shuffle away down the hallway, watching my sister's tears fall. "He won't even remember in the morning."

"Which doesn't change a thing," she says.

I don't know what to say and so I retreat to the facts. "Right. Nothing changes, him or the budget. Which means you need to collect child support. And for that, we need to know who Ariel's father is."

"I don't know," Callie whispers.

"What do you mean you don't know? How can you not know who you had sex with?" A little tendril of fear curls through me. I think about date rape; maybe she was drugged or blacked out and somebody took advantage. But she squares her shoulders and gives me a defiant look.

"There was more than one guy, okay? And even if I knew, I wouldn't tell. No kid needs this kind of shit."

"Oh, for God's sake, Callie. Grow up, already!" All at once my emotions are too big to hold in another minute, and all of the anger and heartbreak and anxiety spill out in a flood. "Dad's right. If you're old enough to get down and dirty with that many guys, then you're old enough to take care of yourself. I'm not the one who got herself pregnant, so don't expect me to carry the weight of you and a baby."

I feel something between us crack and shatter, but I don't apologize.

Callie goes very still. When she looks up, her tears have dried and her jaw is set at full-on stubborn. "Fine. Don't give us another thought."

"I didn't mean—"

"Yes, you did." She stands, Ariel sound asleep in her arms and oblivious to the storm.

"Where are you going?" Already my anger is evaporating into fear and loss.

"What does it matter to you?" Unlike my father, she seems to have grown taller as she walks away from me.

***

It's only now, after Callie's dead and it's too late to talk about it, that I see this was the real break between us. She moved out before the week was over and lived on welfare until she landed a gig singing for a bar band in Seattle. After that we still talked now and then, about work and Ariel and the weather. There were visits. But we were always careful and polite, more like strangers than sisters. For the first time I let myself wonder if she would have stolen my song if I hadn't said those things to her.

"I didn't mean it," I want to tell her now. "I only wanted to make you do the right thing, to find the father. Make him pay. I would have helped you for as long as you needed . . ."

But the time to set things right between us is gone, and now it's Ariel who wants answers.

"Do you think . . . ," I stop myself. Of course she thinks looking for her father is a good idea. She's sixteen and the only family she's got is me. "How are you going to find him? I mean, a name in the journal is one thing, but he could be anywhere by now."

She drops another book in my lap. The Colville High yearbook, 1997–1998. "They're all in there. Names, birth dates. I'll google them."

"Surely it can't be so easy."

"I found this." She sets her laptop down in front of me.

"Oh my God, you have got to be kidding."

I lean in to see the picture more clearly. Kelvin Marcus hasn't aged well. The washboard abs are gone, replaced by an obvious paunch that isn't disguised by a dark button-up shirt and suit jacket. Threads of gray run through thinning hair, and there are dark pouches under his dreamboat eyes.

"He's a preacher." Ariel's voice drips acid.

"Kel?" I can't tear my eyes away from the screen.

"You know him?"

"Everybody knew him. Captain of the football team. He was smoking-hot and he drove this GTO that could peel rubber in third gear. All the girls drooled over him."

She looks at the picture again, and then at me. She deflates a little. "You don't think much of him."

That is putting it mildly. Back then, I was blinded by his good looks and popularity, but unless he's done a full about-face, he is definitely not father material.

"People change," I say, as much to myself as to her. "He could have legitimately found Jesus and have a calling. But I can't imagine he's going to be ecstatic to have an illegitimate daughter come crashing into his world."

Her eyes light up and she grins. "I know, right? Like a bomb in the middle of his pretentious, hypocritical life."

"You don't know that he's a hypocrite. Like I said, people change."

"He looks like a hypocrite."

She has a point. Kelvin looks more like a seedy used-car salesman than a man of God.

"He lives in Portland. How are you going to get there?"

"There are these flying things called planes."

Only a teenager can produce this level of sarcasm. I take a breath and keep my voice level. "Where do you plan on staying? How are you going to afford all this?"

She shrugs. "I have money."

"So, what's the plan? You're just going to talk to him? A meet-the-candidate sort of thing?"

"No, I want to actually know. I can get a paternity testing kit at Walmart."

"Oh, come on. Walmart offers pretty near everything, I know, but—"

She clicks a bookmark on the laptop and brings up a product description screen.

Identi-Match. Paternity DNA testing from the comfort of your home. 100 percent reliable.

"You've been a busy girl." Apparently, all it takes is a DNA swab and the United States Postal Service to determine the father of your baby. I read through the fine print, partly because I can't believe it's that easy. Partly just to buy time.

"It won't stand up in court."

"I'm not doing this so I can get child support."

"Suppose you tell me why you are doing it, then. Really. Because if you're searching for another parent to love and look out for you, you're probably better off hanging out with me."

Her lips thin into a hard line, and she slams the laptop closed. "You're not a parent. You're barely even an aunt."

Touché. Whoever her father is, I didn't do any better than he did. I locked Callie out of my world, and shut Ariel out right along with her.

"Just forget it," she says. "Forget I said anything, okay? It's not like I need your help." Tears underlie the words, even though her eyes are dry.

God, I suck at this. But I'm not running away again, not letting her shove me out the door. I inherited the same stubborn gene as Callie has apparently passed on to her daughter.

"I don't want to forget it. But you need to think this through. What do you think is going to happen when you show up—at a preacher's house, no less—and announce that maybe he's your father? He's not likely to welcome you with open arms."

"I don't care. It's not like I want to live with him or anything. I just want to know if it's him. Okay?"

It's not that I have any empathy for Kelvin. He deserves to have his world torn apart. In fact, if that's what Ariel's little visit is going to do, then I'd love to be a part of it. I try to summon up the strength to do what I'm sure is the right thing. I'm the responsible one. It's my job to stop her.

Studying her profile as she adds a T-shirt to her suitcase, the idea of managing her strikes me as ludicrous. I'd have to lock her in a room. Probably with handcuffs on. That face is not built for acquiescence. I catch myself trying to puzzle out the ancestry of her bone structure, the jaw that would be square in a man but is rounded just enough to be feminine, the sculpted planes of her cheekbones and forehead. She didn't get those features from Callie or either of my parents. Wherever they came from, there is nothing fragile about this girl. She'll be a very strong woman, if the bitterness doesn't destroy her.

"The paparazzi will eat you alive. There was a reporter here today."

"In the house?"

"In the pool."

Ariel gives me another look, as if reconsidering something, and then laughs and holds her hand up for a high five.

"Ricken put her up to it," I tell her. "So don't you believe for a minute he wouldn't give them an inside scoop on you if he thinks it will fuel the fire."

She shrugs, and I think of another problem.

"What about Shadow? Is he going with you?"

"Yes, he's going with me. And before you even ask, Mom put me on the pill when I was fourteen. Just in case, she said."

Responsibility again. How am I supposed to have a sex talk with a teenager who has more world experience than I do? Feeling my face heat, unable to look her in the eye, I dredge up some words that are probably from high school sex ed.

"A pill won't protect you from . . . from . . . look, if he's been with any other girls, then . . ."

Ariel digs under the pile of clothes in her suitcase and holds up a box of condoms. Opened. "And I made him get tested. Okay?"

It's not okay.

"Do you love him?"

She shrugs. "Maybe. I don't think he's after the money, and he thinks fame is stupid. So." She shrugs again.

I want her to have some illusions and some dreams and a little magic. I want to tell her she shouldn't settle, that love is the most important thing and she should wait for the right guy and then . . . that's where I run into trouble. Then, what? Give him her heart and watch him stomp on it? At least she's honest with herself and knows what she's doing. So I focus on more practical matters.

"Can you trust him?"

"Depends what you mean by that. He's not a stalker or anything creepy."

"How do you know?"

"I just do, okay?"

"What about his parents?"

"What about them?"

"Do they know the two of you are running off on a wild goose chase?"

"What do they care? He's eighteen. Besides, they left on a business trip this morning, and they won't even know he's gone."

She's too young to be so jaded. My anger at my sister for the song she took from me suddenly seems a small thing compared to what she's taken from Ariel.

Innocence. Stability. A childhood.

There were years of touring with different bands before Callie made the big time. She lived in Seattle, LA, New York, moving in and out of relationships with one man after another. This residency at Caesars in Vegas has kept her in one place for three years, long enough for Ariel to put down roots and make some friends. Now that Callie's dead, she'll lose that, too.

It doesn't matter what she says, I know she's hoping to find a father who will love her, accept her, or at least give her a clearer sense of where she fits into the scheme of things. Trouble is, I know enough of Kelvin to believe that, minister or not, this will be one more dream shattered.

"Let me help you." The words are out of my mouth before I even know I'm going to say them.

Ariel zips up her suitcase and turns to look at me. "How can you help?"

"I know Kelvin. I can set up a meeting."

"You'd do that?"

My head nods. Surely I'm possessed. "Give me a little time. You could leave tomorrow."

She turns away from me and sets the suitcase on its wheels. "You're just trying to put me off. Thinking I'll change my mind."

"What does it hurt to wait a day?"

"Do you know what they're planning for tonight? You don't. Of course not. They haven't told you yet. A full-scale soirée, right here at the house. Media people, so-called friends of my mother. Celebs. A charity fund-raiser for Ebola orphans in Africa or some shit. Like Mom ever cared about orphans."

I stare at her with dawning horror. Of course it's good to feed the orphans, but even I can see that a gathering like this has nothing to do with charity.

"Ricken just said we had people coming for dinner."

"Right. He's afraid you'll say no. Just watch. Hairdresser will show up any minute now. And a makeup artist. They'll have a whole wardrobe planned for you." She tilts her head to one side. "Something elegant but with hints of country. Anything that will make you look like Mom only increases the human-interest angle. Seen stuff like this a thousand times. House will be full of paparazzi."

She's got her window open, the suitcase balanced on the ledge.

Again my mouth opens and words come out. "Let me go with you."

She freezes, then turns to look at me.

"What?"

"I want to go with you. I can help."

"You're running away. Admit it."

"Like you're not? All right. Yes. I'm running away."

She hesitates. "Shadow's still coming."

61

I sigh. "All right. You and me and Shadow. All good?"

"After you." She gestures toward the window.

My throat feels dry, my pulse thunders in my ears. I was five the first time Mom left me in charge of my two-year-old sister. I never had a chance to do something crazy and irresponsible. I'm terrified and excited in equal measure.

"Don't I get to pack a bag?"

"Now or never. If you leave the room, maybe you'll send the cops after me."

"Then come with me. We'll walk out the door together like civilized people."

"And when Ricken sees us? Or the maid, or anybody? Now you're forgetting the camera people. Either you're in or you're out."

This isn't sane, I tell myself. I've got a credit card wallet in the pocket of my jeans. I've left my purse in my room. My phone is on the nightstand.

Dale will be calling.

At first that thought pulls at me, and then, my heart plummeting into my belly, I remember the tabloids. I don't want to talk to Dale. Not now, not yet. And I sure as hell don't want to attend Ricken's little soirée. Or make a decision about the contracts.

Before reason has time to catch up with me, I'm sitting on the window ledge, poised between fates. A deep breath, and I swing my legs through the window and take the leap, old enough to know that for every such act of rebellion, there must always be consequences.

For once, I've decided I don't care.

CHAPTER FOUR

One thing is sure and certain. Never before in all my born days have I traipsed directly up to the ticket counter in an airport and asked for tickets for the first flight out.

I stand beside Ariel, my stomach doing queasy flip-flops, my left hand fisted to try to stop the electricity that persists in zapping through it. Traveling light is one thing. What in hell was I thinking, running off without so much as a suitcase or even my phone? Something could happen with my mom. Dale could be trying to reach me.

Breathe, Lise. Focus on something else.

Shadow lounges against the counter beside me, watching not the proceedings but the constant stream of people dragging their luggage in through the doors. Some of them form into a line behind us or go to other counters. Some head straight for the TSA.

"I've got a flight to Portland at two o'clock," the woman behind the counter tells us, her fingers tapping the keyboard as she speaks. "How many?"

It's noon now. I figure two is about perfect.

Ariel has other ideas. "Anything sooner?"

A furrow appears between the perfectly penciled brows. Tap, tap, tap. "Well, there is a one o'clock, but it's booked. You could try standby."

"What about first class?"

The woman glances up from the monitor for the first time, really looking at Ariel, then me, and finally Shadow. "I can check." Her voice sounds doubtful.

"Do that," Ariel says.

"I can get you on flight 879 at 1:00 p.m.," the woman says. "If you can get through TSA in time."

"We'll take it."

"Hang on just a second," I hear myself saying. "Don't you think first class is a little extravagant?"

Ariel slaps a bank card on the counter along with her ID. "I said we'll take it." The woman picks up the card. Debit, not credit, I note, and yet it covers three first-class tickets without a glitch. A moment later and the three of us are heading down the terminal and into the maelstrom of the TSA.

***

Ariel calls for a limo as soon as our plane jolts to a landing. Once again, I have the sensation that I'm just a passenger in the journey of my life, and I let the courteous driver help me into the car without asking questions. But when we pull up in front of a high-rise in downtown Portland, I realize we have a problem. The hotel, a place called the Nines, occupies the top floors and is obviously a luxury stop. There's a stretch limo parked up ahead of us. I watch the driver open the passenger door while a bellboy hovers at a respectful distance. As the passenger gets out of the car and tips the driver, my eyes widen. I've seen that face in a dozen big-screen movies.

"Isn't that . . ."

Ariel shrugs. "Who cares?"

A car pulls up behind ours, a nondescript black sedan. The man who steps out of it has a camera.

Our driver comes around to my door and opens it, but I shake my head at him. "This is not our hotel."

His eyebrows go up, the brim of his cap rising visibly.

"Ma'am?"

"There's been an error. This is not our hotel."

The man is well schooled in dealing with whims. He closes the door without further expression and gets back into the car.

"What are you doing?" Ariel demands. "I've always wanted to stay here."

"You and every other rich person traveling to Portland."

"So?"

I count to ten, giving myself a chance to get both my heart rate and my irritation under control. "Rich and famous people attract attention. Use your head. Do you want the press to know we're here and what we're doing?" I gesture out the window, where the man with the camera is snapping pictures of the celebrity.

"Oh," she says, deflating.

"So what if the media find us?" Shadow says. "Public opinion is irrelevant."

I ignore him and address the driver. "Straight ahead, please."

"I need a destination," he says, looking back at us in the rearview. His eyes are keen and close set, and his stare is a little too curious for my comfort.

"Would a Hilton be okay?" Ariel asks.

"Maybe." I watch the street go by for a few blocks. The driver is still too intent on his rearview.

"Ma'am?" he asks, his eyes flicking from me to Ariel and back again.

"Tell you what. Pull over and let us out right here."

"Aunt Lise, what the hell—"

"Just do it."

"Don't you dare!" Ariel yells.

The driver eyes us both again and pulls over. Age has its benefits. A moment later, all three of us are standing on the sidewalk watching the car drive away. Color burns in Ariel's cheeks, and if looks could kill, I'd be drawn and quartered. "I had a plan! You're ruining everything!"

"You want to see ruined," I retort, "you let those people sink their teeth into the story of you searching for your father."

"I don't know if I'm up for sleeping on the street," Shadow drawls.

We both ignore him. I soften my voice and try to be reasonable. "You saw the photographer back there. You know how they've been about your mom."

"They don't even know who we are."

"Seriously," Shadow says, "I didn't sign up for this."

"Shut up!" Ariel and I snap in unison.

"Honey, trust me. They know who we are. And that driver was memorizing our faces."

"He was a little shifty," she concedes. She gives me a long, considering look. "All right, fine then. You have a better plan?"

I do, in fact, have a plan. I can only hope it's better.

***

Shadow is not impressed with the Best Western accommodations.

He lounges on the sofa, one black-jeaned leg flung up over the back, the other bent and resting on the cream-colored fabric despite the fact that his shoes are on. His eyes are half-closed, the expression on his face bored.

Ariel and I are eating Chinese food out of paper cartons with chopsticks, not talking, but not fighting, either. We seem to have arrived at an uneasy truce. She only picks at her food, while I sit and stare out the window, wondering what in hell I was thinking.

The laptop dings with the universal sound of mail hitting the in-box, and Ariel gasps. I glance up to see her staring at the screen, white-faced and rigid.

"Honey, what is it?"

"The Reverend Kelvin has answered my e-mail." Her jaw is so tight she can barely get the words out.

Shadow rolls off the couch and slouches across the room to look over her shoulder. He whistles between his teeth. "Dude. He's got some balls."

I'm miles behind and scrambling to catch up. "But how? When did you e-mail him?"

"Last night. He isn't very encouraging."

"And you're surprised by this?" The instant the words leave my mouth, I regret them. She's miserable already; no point rubbing salt in her wounds.

"I thought since he claimed to be all holy and shit, he might at least be honest."

I sigh, setting down my chow mein and stabbing the chopsticks into it. I'm not hungry anymore.

"What exactly did you tell him? That you think he's your father and you want to test his DNA?"

"I'm not entirely stupid. Just that I'm Callie's daughter and I want to meet with him."

I get up and cross the room to look over her other shoulder.

Dear Ariel,

I was deeply saddened to hear of your mother's death. She was very young and it must be difficult for you to have lost her. God's ways are mysterious and often beyond our understanding, but you must trust that He has your best interests in his plans, always. If you let Him, He will comfort your grief and help you to find your way to a life that is useful in the service of others. We can see very little with our human eyes, and perhaps, even though your mother was not on a righteous path, she was able to make peace with Him and you will still see her in the next life. We can always hope.

As for coming out to see me, as you've suggested, I do believe you would be better served to seek counseling with a local pastor. I can recommend somebody if you wish.

May you find comfort in Christ,

Reverend Kelvin Marcus

"Bastard."

"Right?" Ariel says.

I'm not sure if I'm more bothered by the empty platitudes or the fact that he dared to tell a sixteen-year-old girl that her mother probably isn't headed for the pearly gates. Not that I haven't had these thoughts on my own, but I'm not going to say them out loud.

Ariel shoves the computer away from her and leans her face in her hands, the picture of disappointment. I pace the room until an idea hits me, like light from above.

"I feel a sudden need to go to church," I declare.

Ariel looks up, bewildered. Her eyes are red and her cheeks are wet. Understanding crosses her face like a sunrise. Her eyes brighten. A little smile turns up the corners of her lips.

"Church is for the plebes," Shadow says, unwrapping a fortune cookie.

"Call me a plebe, then," Ariel says. "I think church sounds brilliant."

***

It has not been a good night.

Ariel and I shared a bed, with Shadow relegated to the couch. As bitterly as he complained about the arrangements, I suspect he's the only one who had a decent sleep. Ariel is very quiet as we get ready for church.

She's wearing a knee-length skirt and button-up blouse. Her hair is braided in one long rope. As usual, she wears little makeup. She looks like the poster child for how a preacher's kid is supposed to look, and I dare to hope that Kelvin will be softened enough to be kind to her.

I confront my own haggard face in the harsh light of the bathroom mirror. The hotel shampoo has left my curly hair tangled and unruly, no matter how many times I run a comb through it. The makeup essentials I picked up at the nearest Rite Aid are not up to repairing the damage done to my face by grief and a sleepless night. The JCPenney dress now seems to show way too much cleavage and be all wrong for church.

All in all, I would be much happier staying right here, barricaded in this hotel room.

"You sure you want to do this?"

She nods. Her face is pale under the fluorescent lights, with dark circles under her eyes. Her cheekbones look sharper, and I realize she hasn't eaten this morning and did little more than poke at her food last night. Still, she appears anything but fragile.

Shadow has made no special preparations, other than taking a thirty-minute shower. "It's not that I don't believe in God," he says now, lounging on the couch again. "It's churches and the hypocrites who run them that bother me."

"Nobody's making you come." Ariel opens the Identi-Match box and selects a swab and a small envelope, dropping both into a quart-size sealable bag, and then tucks the whole thing into her purse.

I'd argued for something a little higher quality than what you can get at Walmart, but for reasons of her own, she'd been adamant. So we took a taxi to the nearest car rental company, and then went shopping. Walmart for Ariel's father-catching supplies, then off to JCPenney and Rite Aid for me. Ariel pointed out that we could afford a different level of shopping experience, to which I countered that I hadn't come into any money yet and was running up my credit card at a pretty good clip already.

Shadow stretches and yawns. "You know it's all a power trip, running a church. Saving souls. Like humans can actually do that. Christians act like they're all self-effacing and humble and shit, but they're really self-centered narcissists."

"You're pathetic." Ariel opens her handbag to double-check her supplies.

He blinks. "Me? How am I pathetic?"

"Like you're not a self-centered narcissist. Stop pointing at other people."

A tinge of color rises to his cheeks. "I'm just saying—"

"Christians are humans like everybody else. Some are good people and some are assholes."

"And this Kelvin guy?"

"Very probably an asshole. Also maybe my father. Your point would be?"

The verbal sparring threatens to destroy the last shreds of my manufactured calm. Picking up my own purse, I dig in it for the car keys.

"You might want to remove the tag," Ariel says, giving it a sharp yank. The cardboard comes off, but the little plastic tab refuses to break.

I shrug. "It's not like anybody will notice. We'll be late. Let's go."

Without waiting to see if anybody follows, I head for the door. Ariel is right behind me. Shadow slouches behind her.

I'm the designated driver. Not that the others aren't willing, but I'm the only one old enough to sign on the line for the rental car. Plus, I don't trust Shadow as far as I can see him, and Ariel doesn't have a license yet.

It's a cool morning, but it only takes about three blocks before there's sweat trickling down between my shoulder blades and my hands are locked on the steering wheel. It's not that I'm a bad driver. I can navigate snow, ice, and rain, dig a vehicle out of a snowbank, and drive poorly maintained dirt roads without an issue. But I'm a small town girl. In Colville, if there are three cars ahead of you at the stoplight, that's traffic. Driving in cities is not a thing I do for fun.

Shadow has taken it upon himself to act as navigator. His bored-superior voice grates on my nerves like fingernails on a blackboard. He's in the backseat, leaning forward and breathing into my right ear when he's not telling me where to turn.

Ariel is quiet, face turned toward her window. Her hands rest in her lap, open, but she is far from relaxed. I can feel tension rolling off her in waves.

"We need some tunes." Shadow's long arm reaches between the seats for the radio knob. He sets the radio to scan, stopping it on dark, discordant metal. In my opinion, this is not music. It's all noise and sharp angles that drive into my head like musical shrapnel. Shadow ups the volume. Ariel turns it down.

I hit the "Scan" button again, stopping it when we hit familiar territory.

"What is that drivel?" Shadow asks, his hand reaching for the controls.

"It's not drivel. It's the Eagles." I slap his hand. Pure reflex, but the sharp contact of skin against skin feels amazing.

"I hate country," Ariel mutters.

"It's not country. How can you kids not know the Eagles?" I edge the volume up a little, and the car fills with the familiar, comforting harmonies I love. Despite their protests, Ariel relaxes a little. And Shadow retreats to the backseat in a sulk.

Total win, as far as I can see.

CHAPTER FIVE

Kelvin is clearly doing well for himself.

The church is big enough to get lost in. People mix and mingle in the foyer. There is a coffee bar with two baristas working at top speed. Another booth sells cookies and juice. No alcohol, as far as I can tell, but it's still morning. Who knows what happens when the sun goes down?

Worship music wafts through high-quality speakers at just the right decibel level to soothe the senses and ease social anxiety without being overwhelming. Flat-screen monitors hang overhead, flashing messages:

Children's ministry and licensed
day care available downstairs.

Join a small group today, sign up at the
computer bank, east end of the foyer.

Help stop Ebola in Africa. Have you donated?

A young woman approaches, hand outstretched, a smile as big as Texas lighting up her face. "Hi, I'm Tina. Is this your first time at Worship Central? I have coupons for a free coffee if you'd like."

"I think we're going to go sit down, now. Thank you, though."

Her palm is moist and clammy. When I try to extricate myself, her fingers tighten and her other hand comes up for a double shake. I feel like I've encountered a needy octopus and pull away with a sharp yank that lacks any semblance of manners or finesse.

Her smile fades into a *God bless you, you poor sinner* expression, and she turns her attention to Ariel and Shadow. "How about these two lovely young people? Coffee? Would you like me to show you where the youth church is? So dynamic and awesome."

It strikes me that Tina is in the business of sales. Not cars, but God. She wants to close the deal, which means we are about to be prayed for, out loud, in the middle of the lobby.

Ariel saves us. "We just love Pastor Kelvin," she gushes. "We came early to get the best seats and to be sure we don't miss a single word of the service. Thank you so much for the welcome, but we're hardly first timers." She grabs my elbow. "Come on, Aunt Lise. I so don't want to end up stuck in the balcony."

We are free and on the move, even if we have no idea where we're going. The crowd is thicker now, but it's moving in the same general direction we are. I catch a glimpse of tight red curls off to the right. Ariel's still got my elbow and I keep my feet moving while I glance over my shoulder. A curly red head topping a slim, compact body vanishes into the crowd. I wrench my arm away from Ariel to turn back, but there is a press of people behind me now and I'd be fighting upstream all the way. I tell myself my swimming pool journalist could never have tracked us here, but I slide into my seat with a whole new knot of anxiety woven into my belly. My left hand thrums with electrical pulses and my heartbeat is way too fast.

The seats are a far cry from the torturous hardwood pews of my childhood. These are cushy, fold-down theater seats in blue velvet. We're not relegated to balcony seating, but we're still a long way from the platform. No danger of missing any part of the service, though. Flat-screen TVs hang at regular intervals offering a close-up view of the empty podium. I can see two men operating movie cameras on tripods.

We've only just gotten settled when the worship team takes the stage. There's a trio of vocalists. A bass player and two guitars. A full drum kit. And a sleek, shiny concert grand played by a guy with bouffant hair and a plum-colored suit jacket.

When I was a kid I loved to sing in church, my voice blending with those around me, but that was a long time ago and a whole different kind of church. Now, Ariel stands rigid and silent on my right. The woman on my left has her hands in the air before the end of the warm-up song. When the guy behind me starts chanting a stream of nonsense syllables, my first thought is that he's insane, but then I remember about tongues.

Where I come from, speaking in tongues and waving your hands in the air would be considered indecorous behavior. Only one person ever prays aloud at a time, and it's generally an authoritative male from behind the pulpit. Certainly nobody speaks out of turn. We all know that the Bible talks about tongues, but then it talks about a whole lot of other weird stuff that we're surely not expected to abide by. Stoning adulterers, for instance. Or women being consigned to a special tent at certain times of the month.

Song by song, the worship team pulls the crowd in deeper. It doesn't take long until everybody's on their feet—including us, trying to fit in—although my hands stay rigid at my sides. Voices all around me take up the meaningless verbalizations. One of the singers on the platform closes his eyes and raises his hands, an ecstatic look on his face. Somebody not too far away from me sobs loudly Voices all through the congregation call out, "Praise Jesus. Hallelujah."

One more song, slow and soulful, brings everybody down enough to take their seats and listen without emoting all over everything.

And then Kelvin takes the stage, Bible in hand.

He's wearing a three-piece suit and a perfect tie, his hair combed back in a smooth wave from his forehead. He takes his place behind a lectern and opens the Bible. On the giant screen behind him, the image of a weathered, bloodstained cross comes up. He opens his mouth as if to begin speaking, then holds up a hand as a signal for us to wait, and silently bows his head for a moment.

A soft chorus of hallelujahs and praise Jesuses echoes through the building.

Kelvin clears his throat and sweeps the congregation with his gaze, ending up directly focused on the camera. "Beloved, the Lord has commissioned me with a difficult message for you all today. Turn with me, if you would, to Romans 6:23."

He makes a show of flipping to the passage, although I'm pretty damn sure he's got a bookmark in there. Other pages riffle throughout the congregation, and then he intones, "For the wages of sin is death, but the gift of God is eternal life in Jesus Christ our Lord."

Dramatic pause.

"Beloved, most men preaching from this text today would emphasize the gift of salvation. And truly, salvation is a great and wonderful gift, the most precious gift we can imagine or comprehend. But I am going to dare to talk to you today about sin."

He comes out from behind his podium to stand at the front of the stage. "Sin is not a popular topic today. We speak instead of choice. We no longer teach right and wrong. We fool ourselves into believing that all people are good but sometimes misguided.

"Yet do not doubt for a moment that there is both good and evil in this world. Just look around you. There is evil everywhere, and yes, there is sin.

"Anybody who says otherwise is lying to you."

My hands ache, clamped together so tightly the fingertips are turning white. I breathe a prayer again, this time to Kelvin. *Please don't go where I think you're going with this. Not with Ariel sitting here.* Her face is a mask, and she sits motionless, holding Shadow's hand.

Kelvin licks his lips. "Recently, a high school friend died, suddenly and tragically. She was far too young, and her untimely death made me stop and ask myself some difficult questions. In her case, it was clear that she had made what popular culture might call 'unwise choices.' She had a great gift and chose to use it for her own selfish pleasure rather than in serving the Lord."

I flick another glance at Ariel, still rigid and unmoving beside me.

Her chin is tilted up, gaze directed straight ahead. But her eyes are flooded with tears and her cheeks are wet. I want to put an arm around her, to lean over and whisper words of comfort. But I know she won't welcome the gesture, and what words do I have to offer?

Kelvin launches into a spiel about how we are all sinners, but I lose track of where he's headed as I'm pulled into another memory.

***

It's Sunday, and Callie and I have just walked home from church. It's well past lunchtime and my stomach is growling. My butt feels bruised from sitting on the hard wooden pew while Pastor Jantzen rambled on and on. I'm also shivering. It's freezing outside and I chose not to wear my jacket. My choice, and maybe a stupid one, but I hate that jacket. It's purple and bulky and the sleeves are too short. I'd rather be cold than seen wearing it in public.

The kitchen is dark. All the lights off, shades drawn, no savory post-sermon meal to make up for the pain and suffering we've just endured. Mom is still in her bathrobe, hair uncombed, eyes dark-circled. She's managed coffee, of a sort. The kitchen smells burned, like she couldn't wait for the pot to quit perking before she grabbed a cup, and now the coil is evaporating the spill. Her hands, both of them cradling the mug, shake so hard a wave of coffee slops over the rim onto the table. She doesn't bother to wipe it up.

We know better than to comment or complain. Callie pours herself a Coke out of the bottle in the fridge while I start slicing cheese and buttering bread. *We'll fry them,* I'm thinking. *Grilled cheese smells awesome and is warm. Add a can of tomato soup and we're golden.*

Mom makes a point of asking us about church when we get home. Even at thirteen, I'm old enough to recognize the guilt she's feeling. She should have gone with us. She should have dragged Dad out of bed, hangover or not, and made him go. We should be a happy, smiling family unit. We're not.

And so she grills us while I grill the sandwiches. How was Sunday school? What was the lesson? And the sermon?

"Boring," Callie says, drawing out the *o*. "I thought he was never going to stop."

Mom doesn't respond to this, so I dare to throw in my two cents. "Most interesting thing was his tie. Three shades of purple with green splotches. Like amoebas."

Callie giggles.

Mom ignores her, but turns on me.

"He is a man of God, young lady, and you do not have an opinion about his tie." A long and blistering lecture follows, lasting until all that is left of the sandwiches and soup is the warm smell lingering in the air and the dishes in the sink. Only then am I able to escape, up to my room and away.

***

Unlike Pastor Jantzen, there is no going overtime for Kelvin. He arrives at a perfectly escalated conclusion, voice trembling with emotion as he invites sinners to come forward for prayer. The worship team silently walks up behind him and plays the opening chords of "Just as I Am," then starts quietly singing.

I grab Ariel's hand, icy cold and trembling.

"It's time. Let's go."

Her eyes are wide. She looks from me to the procession of people walking up the aisle, heads bent, tears rolling down many of their faces. As they reach the front, Kelvin touches every single one—a handshake here, a clap on the shoulder there, occasionally a hand laid on a bent head in blessing. Prayer warriors draw individuals off to the side where they kneel in groups of twos and threes.

"Maybe this isn't such a great idea," Ariel says.

"Oh no you don't. Too late to back out now."

Kelvin's sermon has pissed me off. I have a few things to say to him. And I want him to see Ariel. Here. In his kingdom, in front of God and everybody, and to realize exactly what she represents. I want to watch his face when it all sinks in.

"We're going straight to hell," Ariel murmurs, but follows along when I start walking. Shadow skulks along behind her, looking like the perfect target for an exorcism.

Keeping my head bowed and my face composed in what I hope looks more like penitence than vengeance, I shuffle behind an elderly man. Maybe Ariel is right and I'm headed straight for hell, but I have set my hand to the plow and will not turn back. It's too late, anyway. The press of people hems us in, and it would create a huge disruption to break away.

Kelvin touches the old man in the middle of the forehead with his right hand, the diamond on his finger flashing blue fire. I'm close enough now to see the foundation smoothing his skin, the touch of blush on his cheekbones. His eyes are tired. He doesn't bother to look at my face as he reaches out to put a holy hand on my shoulder.

"Kelvin. It's been a long time."

He blinks. His eyes come into focus. The hand hovers just above my shoulder, arrested in its descent.

I smile sweetly, drawing Ariel up beside me. "This is Callie's daughter, Ariel. We were in the neighborhood, so we thought we'd drop in for a little spiritual counseling."

Kelvin has forgotten to breathe. His face turns a dark reddish purple, and I think for a minute that the prayer warriors are going to have a real emergency on their hands.

"I can't talk right now," he says, finding his voice. His eyes skitter away from Ariel to the crowd building behind us and then back again. "We're in the middle of service."

"This will only take a minute," Ariel says. "Could you just swab the inside of your cheek for me?" She's got the Identi-Match swab in her hands, which are no longer shaking.

"I don't understand." He looks from Ariel to the swab, eyebrows raised in a question.

"DNA," Ariel says. "To see whether you're my father or not."

His shoulders stiffen, and his voice drops into that mellifluous preacher range. "I can't imagine where you got your information, child, but you're far from the right track if you think that I—"

"Callie kept a diary. Rather detailed notes, as it turns out." My voice cuts across his. Several people nearby turn to look. "Not hard to believe, given your way with the girls."

He swallows, hard, his eyes darting to the camera and back again. "Please. Not here. Not now."

"Where then? When?" Ariel demands.

Kelvin reaches into a pocket for a handkerchief and blots his forehead. "I'm asking you politely to leave."

"And if I don't?"

He leans down closer, keeping his voice low enough that nobody else will hear it over the music.

"I won't let you do this. I've worked too hard—"

"I could come by your house." Ariel smiles at him. "Maybe I can meet your wife. And your kids. Do I have brothers or sisters?"

"Do you really want to destroy the faith of thousands of people?"

"Oh, please. Like it's built on anything real."

Kelvin turns to me, blind panic and fury contorting his features. "Lise, make her stop."

I laugh at him. "Give me one good reason why I would want to do anything for you."

Shadow grabs Ariel's hand and tugs. "Come on, Ari. You're holding up the line."

Two big guys are working their way through the crowd in our direction, both wearing dark suits. Holy bouncers, I figure. Our time is limited.

I put my hand on his arm. "You're a goddamn hypocrite, Kelvin. All you had to do was talk to her for a few minutes, show a little kindness. But that's not your way, is it? You haven't changed a bit."

He's a good actor, I'll give him that. Keeping a righteous expression on his face, he bends his head to speak directly into my ear.

"Get out of my church."

"I thought it was God's church."

A camera flashes. I go cold, remembering that glimpse of red curls in the foyer. But before I can get a good look at the crowd, a meaty hand grasps my elbow. I look way up into a face that doesn't even pretend to be spiritual. Ariel is still beside me, her arm firmly in the other goon's possession. Shadow is nowhere.

"You'll need to leave now," my bouncer says.

Kelvin smiles, the mask of untarnished holiness firmly back in place. "Go in peace," he says. "I will pray for you."

That does it. I forget that Kelvin is supposedly a holy man of God. I forget about the cameras and Ariel and all sense of decorum. He's just plain old Kelvin from school, taking advantage of me and mine.

"Asshole!" My fists are clenched and my free arm is moving, but it connects with empty air as my bouncer drags me out of range. Overbalancing, I trip over my own feet and begin a slow-motion tumble that is stopped by the inexorable force holding my arm. One of my shoes comes off, but he doesn't miss a step and I have no choice but to scramble after him, bobbing up and down in an uneven one-shoed gait.

The crowd parts before us like magic, people staring and whispering to each other. I keep my head bent, partly to keep an eye on my precarious footsteps, but mostly to keep from being recognized. There's no need to look where I'm going, anyway. All I have to do is keep my feet moving and my personal bouncer takes care of the rest.

A door opens in front of me, framing gray sky and rain. The rush of fresh air is more heavenly than anything about the service, and I step out of the church under my own steam. The bouncer blocks the doorway.

"Don't come back."

"No forgiveness at the Church of Kelvin?" I ask. He slams the door in my face. There is no outside handle.

An airless, choking sound from Ariel spins me around in alarm. She's doubled over, both arms clasped around her belly.

"Oh my God, are you all right? Can you breathe? Are you choking?"

Ariel raises her head to look at me. Tears are pouring down both cheeks. She makes that whooping sound again, then manages to suck in a good breath.

"You—" she says, and then goes off into another fit.

"What?"

"Standing up to him like that. I thought you were going to kick him in the shins in front of God and everybody."

"Balls, actually. Shins are too good for him."

Ariel giggles. "He's like two feet taller than you . . ." She breaks up again.

The rain has switched from drizzle to downpour, and both of us are already soaking wet. My shoeless foot is in a puddle. I don't know where the car is from here. And yet her laughter sparks something deep inside me.

"This isn't funny," I start to say, but my voice cracks, and before I can help it, I'm overtaken by laughter that I can't control.

This sends Ariel off again, and the two of us stand there, whooping insanely, soaked to the skin and staggering like drunks. Shadow shows up from somewhere. Unable to get any sense out of either of us, he takes us each by an arm and tows us around the edge of the church and out to the street, where we parked the car.

"We need to go before the service lets out," he says, digging in my purse for the keys and unlocking the doors. That thought sobers me enough to let me drive, although the occasional giggle from Ariel sets me off again.

My sense of direction has been turned completely upside down, and I'm actually grateful to Shadow when he starts spouting directions. He's got some sort of app on his phone, which seems to take us on a far more roundabout journey than is necessary. On the off chance that somebody is following us, this is no bad thing, though his continual fiddling with the phone rubs my fur the wrong way.

I've just made a right turn onto a major thoroughfare when he says, "Uh-oh. That's not good."

"What?"

"You're on Twitter." His thumbs move ninety miles an hour. "And Facebook."

"This is news?"

"Let me see." Ariel grabs the phone from him. "Oh my God. Somebody snapped you in the church."

"Show me that."

I reach for the phone, but Ariel holds it out of reach.

"You're driving."

A car behind me honks, and I realize the light is green. I put my foot on the gas, paying attention to the traffic but all the while trying fruitlessly to get a peek at Shadow's phone.

More clicking. "Oh dear," Ariel says. "This is definitely not good."

"Just me?" I ask, trying to allay my panic. "Nothing about you trying to swab his DNA in the middle of a church service?"

"Nope. Just you."

"Let me see."

I stop at a red light and snatch for the phone. Ariel relents, and I find myself staring at a shot of me with my hand on Kelvin's arm, his head bent over mine. We look intimate and wholly absorbed in each other, as though he's telling me secrets.

Fabulous. My whole body is shaking by the time the light changes.

"They're spinning it as an old romance rekindled," Shadow says, snatching back his phone. "Including some speculation about a love triangle with that other guy. Dale. Some of Callie's fans are tweeting that all three of you are part of a scheme to extort Ariel's money. Oh, yeah. Here's an interesting twist: 'What if this Annelise person isn't really Callie's sister? She looks fakey to me.' Oh, and better yet: 'Maybe she's an alien or something. Just saying.'" He laughs uproariously, as if this is the funniest thing ever.

I am not amused. Exhaustion seeps through every cell in my body. I just want to wrap myself in a blanket, lie down, close my eyes, and wish the world away.

"Are we done?" I ask Ariel. "Can we go home now?" The words leave an aftertaste of bitterness in my mouth. I'm not sure that home is possible anymore.

"Are you kidding me? We're just getting started. Kelvin makes top of the dick list. Besides, I really doubt he's the one. He doesn't look like me at all. So, we do process of elimination. If all of the other possibles get ruled out, then we come back and harass him."

"You're not the one they're turning into an alien," I mutter.

She counters with heavy artillery. "I have five text messages from Ricken. Three of them are messages for you, reminding you that all business is at a halt until you sign contracts."

I'd almost forgotten about Ricken. Maybe being a scheming alien impostor isn't so bad after all. I'll settle for the relative serenity of a hotel room, pizza delivery, and two moody teenage kids watching mindless TV.

CHAPTER SIX

Dale washes his plate and fork, rinses them, and sets both in the drainer to dry. The leftover meatloaf is reaching its end date, and he scrapes it into a bowl for his old bulldog Spike, who shuffles over, drooling, to eat with a whole lot more enthusiasm than Dale was able to muster.

He finds himself pacing, sink to table to couch to window. Over and over again. Can't seem to settle to anything, although there's plenty to be done. That new deck for Bob Sanders, for one thing. He needs to draw up the plans, make a list of the building materials he'll pick up in the morning. There's also that bid to put together for the Cooper house, although he's not sure he wants to take that project on. Cooper has a reputation for being difficult: changing his mind about plans already under construction, micromanaging builds. He pays well, though, and Dale isn't sure he can afford to pass up the opportunity. Time to crunch some numbers and make some decisions.

But all he can think about is Lise.

He can't shake the way it tore up his insides to hear her cry like she did at the airport. Or the feel of her body in his arms, the scent of her hair. That kiss.

He shouldn't have kissed her. That was a line best not crossed in any case, and now there are the tabloids. Five of them stare at him from the middle of his kitchen table, all with photos that make it look like Lise adores him. The airport photo makes it look like she is kissing him back.

For Dale, there are far worse things in life than the public declaration that he and Lise have feelings for each other. On his side, it's true. The damnable part is that the story will likely drive her farther away from him. Even dead, Callie has a way of complicating things.

He shouldn't feel anger at Callie, he knows. Or think of her as selfish and manipulative, though he knows full well that she was both. Now he's supposed to somehow conjure up an image of a sweet and saintly human being. That mark is beyond him, and he gives it up and starts pacing again, pausing at the sliding glass doors that lead to his backyard. It's full dark. The first star is out, hanging bright in the sky above the silhouette of the fir trees.

Belly tight with dread, he pulls out his phone and dials. Lise always answers by the third ring, if she's going to answer at all. This time she doesn't. Still, he waits, needing to hear her voice even if it's just the message on her voice mail. But at the end of the sixth ring, another voice answers. Male. Clipped vowels, New York accent.

"Ricken." Dale's brain fumbles through all of the reasons the publicity guy is answering Lise's phone and doesn't like any of them.

"Who is this?"

"This is Dale, not that it's any of your business. Put Lise on."

"Oh, Dale! Of course. Awesome. I was going to call you. We'd like to get you back out here ASAP. How soon can you catch a flight?"

"What's happened?"

"What? Oh, you mean why do we want you out here? It's just so we can get you some interviews, a little more press time—"

"I'm not going anywhere. Where's Annelise?"

"She's not available—"

"How come you have her phone?"

Ricken's brief hesitation chills him. For a talker like this douche bag, even an instant means something.

"Now, Dale—"

"Where the hell is she? Give her the fucking phone."

"I can't do that. She's—not here—"

"Where is she? She doesn't go anywhere without her phone."

"Easy," Ricken's voice says. "We'll find her. I don't think she's in any danger."

"How can you possibly know that? Have you called the police? When was she seen last?" Dale knows Lise. She would never walk away, not from Ariel. And she takes that phone everywhere in case somebody calls from her mother's nursing home.

"Well, Ariel's gone, too. And before you start shouting, it looks like both of them went out Ariel's bedroom window."

"They could have been abducted."

"Unlikely. Ariel took a suitcase. And used her debit card to purchase airline tickets to Portland. Three of them."

Dale sinks into a chair as the world spins. "Portland?"

"I'm sure they're fine. As soon as she uses the card again, I'll let you know. Police won't even look at this until she's been missing for twenty-four hours. You sure you don't want to come out?"

He's not sure of anything anymore. If Lise is in Portland, what possible good would it do either of them for him to go to Vegas? But what if she's not? Just because Ariel ran off, there's no guarantee that Lise is with her.

"Three tickets?"

"Airline won't release names at this point, but we're guessing both Annelise and Ariel's boyfriend are along for the ride."

The goth kid's involvement is not comforting. None of this makes any sense. Callie was the one to go running off on harebrained schemes without a thought for anybody other than herself. And all Dale has to go on that Lise isn't tied up in the house somewhere is the word of a man who has worse morals than a rattlesnake. A snake will at least warn you before it bites.

"So, are you coming out?" Ricken asks.

"I'll let you know." Dale hangs up. He picks up the tabloid and reads the story again, trying to get into Lise's head. And Ariel's. Maybe they did cut and run. He's not sure what he should do. Stay put, in case she calls? Go search Callie's mansion and make sure there's not a body?

She didn't call.

Dale knows she doesn't love him, not like that, but he'd thought there was more there, at least enough consideration that she would let him know before she took off somewhere. That rankles.

Spike waddles over and presses against his knee. Dale scratches behind the dog's ears. "You think you know somebody," he mutters. The dog snuffles and drools and Dale continues to sit, his hand smoothing the brindled fur while he waits for the phone that doesn't ring.

CHAPTER SEVEN

The price of room service for three people is outrageous. On principle, I object. I point out that we could eat for a week on what this one meal will cost us, but I'm too bone weary to think of another option. I don't want to risk a restaurant, and I'm not willing to eat Chinese food or pizza for breakfast.

Along with the meal comes the morning paper, neatly folded and innocent looking. I pour myself a cup of coffee from the carafe and begin thumbing through, glancing at the headlines until one freezes me into immobility.

Heiress of Callie Redfern Empire
Visits Portland Church

At least it's not on the front page, but it's bold and black and impossible to miss even with a casual flick through the paper. I can't tear my eyes away from the photo, a close-up shot of Kelvin and me. Ariel is a blur in the background, face turned away from the camera, her paternity swab totally out of sight. Not a single pixel of Shadow, who ought to stick out like a sore thumb.

All of this strikes me as manifestly unjust. It's not like it was my idea to track down Kelvin. If they want to take pictures and put them in the paper, surely it should be Ariel they're stalking. Guilt follows hard on the heels of this thought. It's my job to protect her, a job I'm really not performing very well or we wouldn't be here in the first place.

"Let me see." Ariel grabs the paper from me and proceeds to read aloud.

"'Annelise Redding, heiress to the one-hundred-million-dollar empire of deceased superstar Callie Redfern, was seen visiting with Reverend Kelvin Marcus on Sunday. Local sources in the women's hometown confirm that Kelvin and Annelise were high school sweethearts . . .'"

I don't hear anymore, and my appetite for breakfast vanishes with the words. Trying to figure out who the unnamed sources are would be hopeless. Hell, there's probably a picture of Kelvin and me together in the yearbook, dressed up for prom. Every girl in my high school class will remember that I'm the one Kelvin asked. And they are probably still spiteful about it. If only they knew.

"Were you in love with him?" Ariel looks up. "Did Mom steal him, too, besides the song?"

"No."

I haven't thought about prom in years. Too much guilt lies in that direction, the reminder that Callie is not the only one capable of betrayal.

"Tell me," Ariel says. "Come on, I deserve to know."

"No comment." I keep my voice light but escape to the shower, the only place where I can find refuge behind a locked door. I set the temperature hot enough to nearly burn my skin, focusing on the pain to keep the memories in check. But it's too late. The wall I so carefully built has crumbled, and all the hot water in the world can't sluice away my guilt.

***

My social standing in high school isn't even on the charts. It's not that I'm actively unpopular, just marginal. I'm into music but don't have time for either band or choir, though Callie is in both. I rarely make it to dances or parties, and by the time senior year rolls around, I've never even been to a homecoming. My piano lessons are the one thing I push for, and Dad goes along with that, making sure my teacher gets paid and even footing the bill for the piano tuner once a year.

Practicing and homework eat up all my spare time. Mom is depressed more often than not, and it falls to me to see that Callie and Dad get fed and that Mom eats enough to not blow away with the wind. I've had a raft of odd jobs, all minimum wage and all lost when I didn't show up because of some crisis that needed tending. By my junior year, I'd figured out I could make more with a combination of babysitting and teaching music lessons to beginners than by working at McDonald's, anyway. So now I have a regular roster of students and precious little spare time left for social activities.

So prom isn't even on my radar until Dale brings it up.

"You should go," he says, elbow-deep in soapy water.

Dad says we don't need a dishwasher; he's got two. He means me and Callie, which is a joke that isn't funny. Really he just has me. At sixteen, Callie no longer listens to anything I tell her. Even if she agrees to help in the kitchen, a rare occurrence, she's worse than useless.

Dale, on the other hand, is quick and efficient. His mom says his wife will thank her someday, and he and his sister split all the house-keeping chores. Tonight, he's helping me out so we can get to work on a social studies project we've teamed up on.

His suggestion makes me snort. "Right. Who am I going to go with?" I've turned down so many dates by this point that nobody bothers to ask anymore.

Dale is quiet for a minute, his sunbrowned hands turning a plate under running water to rinse away the soap before handing it to me to dry.

"We could go," he says.

My stomach does a quick flip-flop as my pulse speeds up a little. Dale is my best friend, and he's making a suggestion that threatens the safe balance of our lives.

He keeps his eyes on the pot he's taken to scrubbing, not even glancing at me. It's hot in the kitchen, and the humidity is through the roof with a thunderstorm brewing outside. His cheeks are flushed, his dark hair damp and curling at the ends. A beard shadow darkens his jaw, and I'm suddenly surprised by how much muscle he's got in his arms and shoulders. Somehow, I hadn't noticed.

I'm still looking at him when he glances up at me in turn, and I flick my eyes back to the dish that I'm supposed to be drying.

"You know, as friends," he says. "Nothing weird. Not like a date."

I put the dry dish in the cupboard and take the dripping pot from his hands. "Probably have more fun than all the love struck," I say, cautiously.

"Right? Remember Kate and Evan at Homecoming? So uptight they couldn't say two words to each other."

"Until Kate spilled that Coke down his crotch . . ."

We're laughing now, back to our usual easy banter. We'd been at Tony's Eatery with a couple of other non-homecoming-going kids when the luckless duo came in. And we'd all poked fun at them mercilessly for days.

I shrug. "I guess we probably ought to go to prom, right? Like it's some rite of passage or whatever."

"It's totally lame. But we can go laugh at everybody."

"Okay."

"Really?" His eyes hold a new intensity that brings the heat to my face and makes me turn away to hide it, my heart hammering beyond reason.

When I mention prom to Dad, he totally surprises me by digging out his wallet and handing me a wad of cash.

"Go buy something pretty," he says.

I unfold the bills and lay them flat. I've never had this much money to spend on myself in my entire lifetime, and I look up at him, uncertain. He's not drunk. The level on the bottle has only just started to drop.

"Callie needs shoes," I say, half choking on the words.

Dad waves away my objection. "You work hard. Wear something nice for Dale."

I stare at him.

He pulls me in close and plants a kiss on the middle of my forehead. "I haven't always done right by you. That boy's going to make a good man. Steady."

"Oh my God, Dad. We're just friends."

I feel like the earth has tilted and I can't find my balance. When Dale and I get together to study, there's an unease between us that has never been there before. I catch him sneaking glances at me when I'm trying to sneak glances at him. I keep telling myself that he's just the same old Dale who used to put bugs in my hair. But how I feel about him is shifting like the glass in a kaleidoscope, and I find myself making excuses to avoid him.

And then Kelvin happens, like a bolt of lightning out of a clear blue sky.

On Tuesday afternoon, I leave the campus for lunch with a couple of friends and we linger too long. I'm halfway to class when I realize I've forgotten the binder with my homework in my locker and have to go back to get it. I'm going to be late for English, and Mrs. Carlson is going to flay me. I'm digging through a pile of books when I sense somebody standing beside me.

Kelvin Marcus, star of the football team and the hottest boy in school, is leaning up against the lockers so close I could touch him. He smells of aftershave and engine grease, and his dreamboat eyes are fixed on me. The bustle in the hallway slows down as my senses sharpen and focus. My heart is thudding like a whole herd of wild horses, so loud I'm afraid he'll hear it.

"Hey, Annelise," he says. "What's up?"

I can't imagine what he's doing here, unless he's going to ask me for class notes. I'm one of the smart kids; he's a notorious class skipper. He gets away with it, not because the teachers are willing to let it slide, but because all the girls bail him out and help him study.

Clutching my binder to my chest like it's a life preserver, I click the lock shut and turn away. "I'm late for English."

He puts out an arm, all solid muscle, and blocks me.

"Just a sec. Mrs. Carlson will wait."

"Are you kidding? She lives to mark people absent."

His eyes travel away from mine, down to my lips, my breasts, and then up again. It feels like he's actually touched me with his hands. My heart has skipped from galloping to pure flutter, and there's a hive of bees where my stomach is supposed to be.

"I've been watching you, Annelise."

"You have? Why?" I stare up at him, startled, my brain running through all of my recent actions and trying to think of what I've done.

Kelvin leans his head down, so close that I can feel the warmth of his breath on my cheek when he says, for my ears alone, "Have you looked in the mirror lately?"

There has to be some sort of mistake. Kelvin doesn't pay attention to girls like me. Not that I'm hideous or anything, but the girls he dates are definitely not wearing clothes they bought at the Goodwill. I glance over my shoulder for his friends, thinking maybe somebody put him up to this on a dare, but all I see is a couple of girls staring in our direction.

"Come to prom with me," Kelvin says.

All the fluttering and the buzzing inside me goes quiet, like it's been sucked out by a giant vacuum cleaner. At the same time, the sounds around me become crystal clear. Voices. The clock ticking. Kelvin's breathing.

It takes two swallows before I can find my voice.

"I'm already going."

"Fix it."

"What?"

"Change it. Go with me."

"I can't do that." Dale has always been there for me. He would never, ever break a promise. There's no way I can leave him in the lurch.

"Sure you can." Kelvin winds one of my curls around his fingers.

My breath is out of control and my head feels light. Dale was just being nice, I tell myself. Doing a friendly thing. He won't mind, really, if I go with somebody else. Probably, he'll even understand.

The bell rings for class. I'm late. It doesn't seem to matter.

"I won't let you go until you say yes," Kelvin says, his hand still playing with my hair.

Every ounce of my morality and responsibility vanishes when he smiles, lazy and confident. "Yes?"

I nod, unable to find words.

"You're late for class." He takes my hand and walks me down the hall. It's a good thing I'm holding on to him, because my knees feel a little wobbly, and tripping over my own feet now, with everybody watching, would be the ultimate embarrassment.

He releases me just outside the classroom door, slowly, letting his fingers run the length of mine. Little shivers run up and down my arm, and I feel like I can't breathe. I watch him walk the length of the hall before I open the door and go in.

Mrs. Carlson is reading something from a book. She stops and looks at me over the top of her glasses. "You are late, Annelise."

For once, I don't care. I open my books and bend my head, but there's a little smile tugging at my lips as I daydream about what Callie is going to say. And then I remember Dale, and the warm happy feeling dissolves. I'm going to have to tell him. Today, for sure, before the gossip gets there first. He'll understand, I tell myself. Surely, he'll understand. But my body feels cold and heavy, all the excitement congealed into dread.

Dale is waiting for me after school with the offer of a ride home and the chance to check out his new wheels. New to him, anyway. He's worked long hours to buy this car. A job he hates at the Golden Arches during the winter. Odd jobs for local farmers in the summer. It's just an aging Subaru, but he's polished it until it shines anywhere there's still paint. Normally, I'd be excited for him and for me. Dale having wheels is almost as good as having some of my own.

"Start her up," I say, sliding into the passenger seat. "Let's hear that engine roar."

Obligingly, he starts the engine. It doesn't roar, exactly, but it runs along like an engine should. Or at least I think so. I don't know anything about cars. Dale does. He's probably spent hours under the hood already, adjusting and tinkering.

"I like the seat covers."

"Goodwill special." He grins. "Figured with prom coming up and all, I'd splurge. Don't want to get your dress dirty."

He shifts into first and starts navigating the after-school parking lot chaos. I glance over at him while his eyes are safely on his driving and then look away, twisting one of my backpack straps in my fingers. His hand on the shifter knob, nearly brushing my thigh, is square and strong. The cuticles, stained black with engine grease, support my belief that he's been working on the car. His right thumbnail is a different story, black and blue and a little bit purple.

"What on earth did you do?" I start to reach for his hand to get a better look, but I stop myself. Two weeks ago, before this prom thing came up, I would have grabbed it without thinking.

"Stupid," he says. "Dropped a wrench on it."

"Doesn't it hurt?"

He shrugs. "Stupid's gotta learn, right? I stuck a hot needle through the nail to let off the blood. It's okay."

I catch myself wondering if his hands would feel the same as Kelvin's or different if he played with my hair or touched my waist. My face heats up at the very idea, and I lean forward to turn on the stereo.

"How are the tunes?"

Dale laughs. "If you were buying a car, you'd choose the one with the best sound system. Wouldn't even care about how it runs." It's not said in a mean way, though. More like he approves of my weirdness.

We drive in silence for a bit, the music turned up good and loud. One of his speakers has a buzz, and it grates on my nerves. I feel like I do in summer when there's a big storm rolling in, all pins-and-needles irritability. My skin seems hot and itchy and three sizes too tight.

"About prom," he begins, as if he's read my mind, then pauses and turns down the music.

"Yeah, about prom." Seems like there's a whole school of goldfish in my stomach, and my hands have gone all clammy and cold. I grab on to a flicker of anger for courage. This whole situation is Dale's fault. If he hadn't brought up prom, he and I would be the same as always, easy and comfortable together. He'd tease me about going with Kelvin, and I'd push him to take some girl.

He glances over at me, and I watch his eyes go dark.

"Spit it out." Each word sounds like it's been carved out by a hammer and chisel.

"I'm going with Kelvin." My words hang in the air between us. I wait for him to say something so I can bring out my excuses. *We were going as friends. I didn't think you'd care. It's not like we're dating or something.* If I just blurt them out on my own, they will sound too much like guilt. So I wait. But Dale doesn't say anything. He turns the music back up, and we drive the rest of the way in loud silence. When he pulls up in front of my house, he still doesn't say anything. Doesn't look at me. Just stares straight ahead, hands on the steering wheel.

"I'm sorry . . . ," I start.

"Don't be."

"Dale—"

"I've gotta go, Lise. I'll be late for work."

When Dale's mad, he generally yells. I don't know what to make of this mood, but my heart is in my shoes when I open the door and climb out of the car. My backpack feels like it's made out of lead, and I just hang there for a minute, holding the door open, looking in at my best friend, who still won't look at me.

"You coming over to study after?"

"Nah, I've got some stuff to do."

There's nothing I can do then but close the door. The maple tree over my head is bright green with baby leaves, and there's new grass under my feet. But the world feels as bleak and cold as January as I watch him drive away.

***

A thud on the bathroom door brings me back to my current predicament.

"You gonna be in there all day? Shadow needs to pee, and I want a shower."

"Be out in a minute." I can't turn off the water, because all at once I'm crying, and they'll hear me. Not just a few tears, either. Something is trying to tear me apart from the inside out. Grief doubles me over, jagged sobs ripping me open from belly to throat. I don't even know what I'm crying about. Not Dale surely, not after so many years. As for Callie . . .

Callie is dead.

I've heard this said more often in the last few days than I've heard comments about the weather. I've said it myself. God, I saw her lying in a coffin. But it's not until this minute, in a hotel shower with a teenage girl impatiently banging on the door, that I finally believe it's true.

I sit down in the bathtub and let the water pour over my head and face while this new reality shifts everything in my world. Present, future, and even the past. All of my memories have a new and darker filter. If it hadn't been for that stupid prom. If Kelvin hadn't asked me, if I'd gone with Dale, if I hadn't written a song for her to steal, then maybe Callie would still be alive.

And in a long and roundabout way, this means maybe it's not the horse that killed her. Maybe it was me.

CHAPTER EIGHT

I wake up Tuesday morning feeling like I've been run over by a logging truck. Every muscle in my body is bruised and sore. My eyelids are puffy and swollen, my brain foggy. The room is dark. Ariel snores softly. Shadow, an indistinct shape on the couch, mutters something in his sleep and rolls over onto his side. For a minute, I think it's still night, but the clock on the bedside table says 5:00 a.m.

Tired as I am, my eyes are wide open and don't want to close. I need coffee. Good coffee. The in-room swill is not going to cut it this morning. Besides, when Ariel and Shadow wake up, I'll have to talk to them, and I need caffeine on board for the conversation that's coming.

It's time to be a grown-up and make Ariel go home, wherever that is.

Using stealth that Callie would have appreciated, I slip into the bathroom to pull on jeans and a T-shirt. I splash water over my face. Drag a comb through my hopeless hair. And then I ease out of the room in search of a hotel coffee kiosk, hoping against hope it will be open at this hour.

I'm in luck.

The barista is getting ready for the day and there's only one person in line in front of me, an elderly gentleman with a cell phone pressed to his ear and a briefcase in hand. He doesn't even glance at me. I skip the fancy stuff and order a cup of good strong coffee.

"You look familiar," the girl says as she puts a sleeve on my cup and hands it over.

"Probably." I fake a smile. "I was here yesterday morning."

She shakes her head. "Janelle worked yesterday. I wasn't here." Her eyes narrow.

I shrug. "I get that a lot. Sort of face that looks familiar, I guess. Have a good day."

As I walk back to the elevators, I can feel her eyes burning into my back. The gift shop is closed and dark inside. But there's enough ambient light to see by, and on the magazine racks, I catch a glimpse of my own face staring back at me. It's all I can do to keep from running for the elevator as if the bats of hell are on my tail, but I keep my steps slow and steady.

When I open the door to our hotel room, Ariel is sitting up in bed, looking rumpled and half-awake. Her laptop is open in front of her. Shadow is nowhere to be seen, but the bathroom door is closed and I hear water running.

"Get packed. We're finding a flight back to Vegas this morning."

Ariel shakes her head. "We're flying to Pasco. Look." She turns the laptop in my direction and scoots over to make room for me on the bed beside her.

E-mail again. The open message reads:

Hi, Ariel!

There is nothing in the world that would make me happier than a chance to meet Callie's daughter. I can't imagine how you must be feeling. She was a beautiful and talented woman, and her loss is inconceivable to me. Why don't you text me when you're in town, and we'll set up a place to meet?

Timothy

With her hair tumbling around her face and that wheedling expression, Ariel reminds me of Callie. And like her mother, she's not one to waste an opportunity to exploit my weakness. She grabs my hand. Her eyes are red rimmed and bloodshot, and I suspect I'm not the only one who has been hiding tears in my pillow.

"Come on, Auntie Lise. Timothy sounds ever so much nicer than the preacher guy. We have to go now—he'll be totally disappointed if we don't."

I'm still struggling with the name on the page. "Timothy McCallahan? You're kidding, right?"

Ariel's face falls. "He's not a nice guy, then. Figures. Mom only went for jerks."

I shake my head. "Not true. Timothy was too nice, if anything. But I can't see him hooking up with your mom."

"He was in the book. Right after Kelvin. You want to see?"

No. I don't want to see. I'm disillusioned and a little sick, and the last thing I want is to read all about it. The only thing I do want to do is crawl into my very own bed at home, pull the covers up over my head, and shut out the world. Instead, I take a long pull at my coffee and promptly burn my tongue. The pain is bracing and a distraction from that god-awful emptiness at the center of me.

All at once, I realize that I want to talk to Timothy, that I need to know how this all went down. Because if he is Ariel's father and never claimed her, I'm a terrible judge of character. At the same time, the right thing to do is call off this wild goose chase and drag Ariel back home. It's not like money is an issue. We could hire an attorney to check paternity on all of these men.

"Ariel, I really think . . ."

Her lower lip quivers. Her eyes fill with tears, and she blinks them back.

That does me in. I sigh and surrender. "Oh, hell. All right, we'll go. At least Pasco isn't big on paparazzi."

She sniffles, drawing the back of her arm across her eyes. And then her arms go around my neck in a hug that's both swift and fierce, and she's out of bed and pounding on the bathroom door.

***

Pasco is not my favorite city. Too flat, too dry, too windy, but I have to admit it's pretty in May. In a few weeks the land will be brown and naked, but now the trees are in flower and the grass is lush and green. We've checked into another Best Western, this one within easy walking distance of the airport. It's clean and offers a continental breakfast. I figure if—and it's a big if—any celebrity types are hanging out in Pasco, they'll go for the Red Lion. Nobody will look for us here.

We take a taxi to our lunch meeting with Timothy. It's a silent trip. The driver doesn't talk after asking where we're going. Ariel stares out the window, pale and intense. Shadow, as usual, is obsessed with his phone.

I haven't been here for a long time, and I'm surprised by how much the downtown has changed. Most of the businesses are Mexican now, even a couple of the restaurants I remember as plain Jane cafés. The restaurant Timothy has selected doesn't look like much from the outside, but as soon as we open the door, my doubts fall away. The food smells amazing. Even better, the place is pretty much empty.

Timothy waits at a table in the corner with his back to the wall, talking quietly with the man sitting across from him. When he sees us, his face lights up and he blazes his signature smile in our direction, making me feel like the prodigal child come home. Two long-legged strides bring him across the room, and he wraps me in a warm hug.

"I'm so sorry about Callie." His voice breaks and he squeezes me tighter. I respond in kind, tears spilling onto my cheeks. I hug him back as if graduation was only yesterday and he's still my pal and not some relative stranger. When I pull away he smiles again, completely unselfconscious of the tears on his cheeks, and turns to Ariel.

"Beautiful, just like your mother." He takes both of her hands and kisses them. "I was afraid you wouldn't really come."

I find myself glancing around the restaurant, embarrassed, aware that we are making a public scene. The woman behind the cash register catches my eye and looks away, busying herself and putting on a disinterested expression. A man in the far corner is staring, but drops his gaze to his menu when he sees me looking at him. There aren't any other customers except for the man Timothy was talking to.

"I want you to meet Dennis," Timothy says, leading Ariel by the hand. The man gets to his feet, removing a pair of wire-rimmed glasses as he does so.

"Dennis, this is my old friend Annelise. And this is Ariel."

Dennis smiles and shakes hands with Ariel first, then me. He's a soft-looking man, with a chubby, red-cheeked face and a monk-like bald spot. His blue eyes are kind, and his handshake is good and strong.

"So happy to meet you both." He turns to Shadow, who is positively glowering by now, and smiles as if the boy is a sight for sore eyes. "I'm sorry, I didn't catch your name."

"Because nobody introduced me," Shadow mutters.

"Oh, grow up." Ariel slides into a chair. "None of this is about you."

A genuine hurt flashes in his eyes, and for the very first time I consider the probability that he's a human being with real feelings and that I should try to make him feel included, but then I'm distracted by wondering why on earth Timothy would invite a stranger to what promises to be an intensely personal meeting.

This is the point where the conversation promises to get awkward, so we chat about the weather and summarize what everybody's been up to since high school. We're saved by the prompt arrival of a thin Hispanic boy in a white apron who deposits chips and salsa on the table before asking, "Anything to drink?"

"Corona," Timothy says. "You want one, Denn?"

The other man shakes his head, and Timothy turns his smile on the rest of us. "Anybody else?"

"Sure," Shadow says, and I squelch him with a look.

"They're not old enough to drink. But I could use a beer."

Or three, I add silently, dreading the conversation that's coming. Timothy is the only one who seems perfectly at ease. That's one thing that has changed about him since high school. I watch him dip a chip into salsa, every movement pure grace and confidence. He was an awkward teenager—always dressed in floodwater pants, bony wrists sticking out of too-short sleeves, as if his clothes could never quite keep up with his growth spurts. Now he's perfectly put together, from the top of his smoothly combed head to his spotless shoes. I only notice the thin white scar on his left cheek because I'm looking for it.

Ariel nibbles contemplatively on the chips, forgoing the salsa, her eyes darting from one face to another as Timothy and I discuss what we know of our classmates. As soon as the drinks arrive and we've placed our food orders, she gets straight to the point.

"I'm looking for my father."

Timothy takes a long swallow of his beer and exchanges the kind of look with Dennis that implies they're so in tune with each other they can say things without passing a word between them. It's the kind of look people exchange when they've been married for twenty years. He sets down the beer and pushes it forward an inch, as if its placement on the table is the most important thing in the world right now.

"I thought that might be it. How did you know?" His eyes meet hers, dark blue and steady. No defenses, no denials. Everything about him is honest and open and *nice*. I take a breath and squeeze my hands together under the table. A nice guy would have stepped up and claimed his own kid, not waited for her to come looking with a Walmart Identi-Match kit.

"She kept a diary," Ariel says. Her cheeks are flushed. "You're not the only one in it."

He nods. "The chances are—" He breaks off and clears his throat. Dennis reaches across the table and takes his hand, and again their eyes meet and hold. "I—we—always wanted kids," he says, finally. "We've been talking about adopting—"

Shadow snorts and chokes on a mouthful of Coke. As soon as he recovers from the coughing spell, he breaks into laughter. "This is awesome. Wait until Ricken gets his teeth into this one."

Ariel's face has gone beet red. She slugs him in the shoulder with her fist, nothing gentle or affectionate about it. "Nobody's telling Ricken. Don't be a dick."

"Ah, come on, Ariel. You're missing out on the irony of the situation. A preacher, a gay man, and a country singer walk into a bar—"

"Shut up!" Her voice breaks, and she shoves back her chair and heads for the bathroom, blundering into the corner of another table hard enough to clatter the silverware.

Silence stretches out between the rest of us like a rubber band. I can't bear the waiting, so I launch into Shadow.

"You're supposed to be here to support her." I don't realize how angry I am until I hear my own voice. "She trusts you, God only knows why. This isn't about you and your stupid jealousy."

He leans forward across the table, dark eyes burning with a rage of his own. "You think you can just waltz in here after ignoring her for her whole life and shoulder me out. News bulletin: I'm not jealous. I was here before you." His gaze sweeps across all of us. "Any of you. And I'll still be here when you've all evaporated."

Another silence, dark and ugly, as we avoid each other's eyes, not knowing what to say.

Shadow shoves back his chair. "Fuck this shit. I'm going back to the hotel room."

I let him go. He's got money and a phone. He can get a cab or wander around downtown for all I care. A flicker of guilt follows this thought the minute it passes through my mind. Maybe I don't like him much, but Shadow has been there for Ariel. I haven't, and neither has her father. I let my gaze flicker over the two men, and then I escape into my Corona. The waiter comes back with food, and all three of us stare at the steaming plates sitting at the two empty places at the table.

Dennis shakes his head. "Poor kid."

Timothy sighs. "Teenagers," he says, finally, as if this is a tiff over curfew. "I teach at the high school." He smiles, ruefully. "Social graces run thin with them. They're adept at spitting out the truth the rest of us try to bury in politeness. Messy." He pushes his food around with his fork but doesn't eat.

Ariel comes back, eyes hidden behind sunglasses, hair damp. I know the moves—cold water on the face to stop the crying, hide the evidence of red eyes even though everybody and his dog already saw the breakdown. Salvage the remnants of your pride at all costs. Dennis gets up and pulls out her chair for her.

Timothy waits until she's seated and then turns to me. "Now that the ice is broken, we might as well clear the air. You're appalled by the idea of gay men playing parents to Callie's teenage daughter."

I shake my head. "No. I mean . . . I didn't expect . . . I never knew . . ." I take a long swig of my Corona to settle my nerves and give my brain time to catch up with my emotions. "Okay. The gay thing is weird. But only because you apparently were on Callie's list of beddable men and—"

He opens his mouth to say something, and I hold up a hand for him to wait.

"I always thought you were a nice guy. If you knew you might be Ariel's father, then you should have stepped up to the plate. Offered to help out."

It's Timothy's turn to laugh. "Oh, come on. You knew Callie better than anybody. You think if she'd wanted my help, just maybe she'd have come asking?" He leans forward, his gaze turning to Ariel, who is hanging on every word. "When I heard she was pregnant, I did go and talk to her. You know what she said? 'This is my baby, Tim. MINE. And I'm not sharing her with you or anybody else, you hear me?' You know how she was. There was no arguing with that."

I sit back in my chair, all the anger wrung out of me for the moment, leaving me limp as a week-old dishrag. "That's pretty much what she said to me when I told her she needed to name the daddy."

A tear rolls out from under Ariel's glasses, onto her right cheek. Another follows on the left. She wipes them away with the back of her hand, keeping her head bent. Looking at her, I feel utterly and completely helpless, my heart twisting six ways to Sunday.

"I might have pushed harder," Timothy says, picking up his empty bottle of Corona and setting it back down. "But the truth is that me being the father was highly improbable. It wasn't precisely—a successful mission." His cheeks flush with embarrassment, and he glances at Ariel but doesn't hold her gaze. "I suppose you've both read all about it."

"Not me." I shake my head and shiver a little. "Don't need to know the glorious details."

"Hang on a sec." Ariel digs around in her purse and comes up with the diary. My heart sinks as she flips through the pages to a spot she's marked with a yellow sticky note. Truth and honesty is all well and good up to a point, but I know how cruel Callie could be. Timothy doesn't deserve that.

Ariel clears her throat and then reads in a clear, steady voice, "'Timothy is the sweetest boy in the world, in and out of the sack, but I doubt he'd be interested in a second go-round. Besides, I'd ruin a nice boy like him in a week.'"

She closes the book and looks around the table. Timothy's cheeks are wet. Dennis takes off his glasses and wipes them on his shirttail, clearing his throat. As for me, I'm floating on an updraft of disbelief. My Callie scoffed at all the boys. She tormented them, teased them, seduced them, and then dumped them. The respectful words in the diary, her restraint in describing what I can only imagine from Timothy's few words was a fiasco, doesn't sound like my sister. Maybe I didn't know her much better than she knew me.

"It's not impossible, right?" Ariel fumbles in her purse and pulls out one of the paternity swabs. "I mean you—and she—" She breaks off, cheeks red and hot, and passes him the swab.

"Not impossible," he agrees. "What do I do with this?"

"Rub it on the inside of your cheek, and then put it in this little envelope."

Timothy complies, and Ariel rewards him with a smile that is full-on high-beam intensity. It changes everything about her face, turning sharp angles into curves. There's even a dimple in her left cheek. I stare at her, feeling lost and bewildered. I didn't even know that dimple was there, but then, the poor kid hasn't had much cause for big smiles in the last few days.

Ariel's mission is accomplished and she relaxes a little, taking a sip of her drink and diving into the carne asada like she's half-starved. The aroma wafting up from my arroz con pollo might be mouthwatering on another day, but now I push my plate away and lean back to escape it, stomach still dancing with butterflies. Timothy plays with the salt and pepper shakers, circling them around each other into different configurations.

"I saw the papers," he says after a long silence, eyes glued to the table. Ariel glances at me, fork suspended halfway to her lips.

"Hard to miss them." My body goes cold. An electrical charge zings through the fingers of my left hand. I tuck it between my thighs under cover of the table. "Kelvin's on the list."

I expect this to hurt him, but he nods, as though he's not surprised. "And Dale?"

That knocks the breath out of me. A dark, twisted thing slithers out of the hole I've kept it in for over sixteen years. Anger. Jealousy. Heartbreak. I want to say, "No. Of course not." But I haven't seen the list, haven't read the incriminating book. Both hands are locked between my knees now, cold and clammy. My body thrums like a plucked string, vibrating from the inside out.

Exactly the sensation I'd felt when the doors to the gym opened in the middle of the prom dance and Dale and Callie blew in.

***

Laughing like maniacs, soaked to the skin. Neither of them dressed for prom. Callie's T-shirt is black, thank God, but it's soaking wet and clings to her breasts and belly. Her hair springs into wild corkscrew curls all over her head. On her, of course, this all looks sexy as hell. Dale, one hand on her lower back, leans down close to her ear to say something that makes her laugh harder. In this room full of tuxedoed, slicked-up boys, he shines like a beacon in the middle of a foggy sea. The collar of his button-up shirt is open over his sunbrowned neck, the sleeves rolled up over muscular forearms. His hair is its usual untamed mess. Callie puts her hands on his chest, and he pulls her in for a slow dance.

I can't breathe. My whole body goes cold, and I have a strange sensation that I'm trapped in a glass bubble.

Kelvin whistles. "Isn't that your kid sister?"

"Guess she decided to crash the party." My lips feel numb.

"Day-um. Look at her all grown up. Think she'd dance with me?"

I want to think he's kidding, but his gaze follows her with a whole lot of interest.

"Hey, I thought you were dancing with me."

He laughs, rubbing his hand up and down my back and letting it come to rest on my butt. "Aw, don't get your panties in a bunch. A guy can look, can't he?"

I move his hand back up onto my waist. "She's sixteen, Kelvin."

This only serves to fuel the fire. His breath smells of alcohol and his words are starting to slur. He's made four or five trips out to the parking lot and he's obviously got booze stashed out there somewhere.

"Old enough to know better." He makes smacking noises with his lips.

She's not just my sister, she's my baby sister. Infuriating sometimes, but mine. Nobody's going to talk about her like that to me.

"You're a pig." I brace my hands on his chest and give him a shove.

His feet tangle and he staggers sideways, bumping into the couple beside us, which saves him from falling. He stands there, legs spread a little too wide, his tuxedo shirt half-untucked.

"What the hell was that for?" His voice is loud enough to be heard over the music. Several couples near us stop to get in on the drama. Somebody giggles.

My face flushes hot. I want to run for the bathroom and burst into tears, but I won't give them all that satisfaction.

"You're drunk." I infuse all the disgust I can concentrate into the words. "And you're also boring." I tear off the corsage that seemed so beautiful a few hours ago when he pinned it on my dress, and throw it on the floor. It lies there, taunting me, and I stomp on it, grinding the flowers up with my heel.

All eyes are on us now. I'm too mad to care. Head high, I stalk toward the doors with as much dignity as I can muster, given my unfamiliarity with high-heeled shoes. People move out of the way to let me by. There's laughter and whispering but one voice says, clearly, "Good job, Lise. I knew you were too smart to fall for it."

It's Timothy. As usual, he's gotten the clothing all wrong. His tux is powder blue, the sleeves too short. I can see about a mile of white shirtsleeve. But he nods at me, as if I've done something brave rather than humiliating myself and the captain of the football team in front of God and everybody.

I have no idea what he's talking about, but his approval sustains me in my long journey to the door, forestalling tears and keeping me moving.

Once outside, it's all a different story. It's pouring rain. How could I forget that? I have no coat, of course, because I didn't want to cover up the dress. No wheels. It's a couple of miles home, and I'll never make it in these shoes. Dad will be thoroughly sloshed by this time. Mom will have all of her meds on board and be in bed and dead to the world.

Dale would give me a ride if I asked him. All I have to do is walk back into the gym. Tell him I'm sorry and that I was stupid to go with Kelvin. But my pride won't let me. Ever since I told Dale I was going with Kelvin, he's been distant. Polite. Too busy to come by to study.

Probably hanging out with Callie.

I don't understand the emotions swirling through me. Dale's just a friend. He can dance with Callie all he wants to. So why do I want to scream at the very thought of the two of them together?

Drenched in rain and self-pity, I slip off the shoes and head for the street, not bothering to lift the hem of my dress or avoid the puddles. At the far side of the parking lot I run into trouble.

They've been smart enough to choose a spot well away from the streetlights, and I hear them before I see them. The car is a nondescript sedan, all four doors open with the dome lights killed. A burst of raucous laughter erupts, and then a familiar voice, "Hey, Lise. Come join us. We got booze."

In the mood I'm in, the idea tempts me. The car would be warm and dry. I don't drink—seen enough of that from my dad to know better—but my growing anger makes me feel reckless. I splash my way over to the car and bend down to look through the open door. There are four of them smooshed in there, all members of the football team.

"Come on, Lise. Get out of the rain." Frank slides over in the backseat to make room for me. In the front, behind the steering wheel, Bryce whistles and makes a point of staring down my cleavage. His eyes are glassy and strange, and I'm pretty sure he's on something besides the booze.

"Where's Debbie?" I ask him.

"Deb is a thing of the past," he proclaims. "I've got other fish to fry. Wanna take a shot? I'm free for the rest of the night. Got something for you that will warm you right up." He puts his hand on his thigh, right next to his crotch, and leers at me.

Rumor has it Debbie is home with a black eye Bryce gave her when he was buzzed up on crack. Reckless mood or not, I'm smart enough not to get into anything with him. But I'm also soaked to the skin and shivering, and it's a hell of a long walk home. Frank gives me a lopsided smile and holds up a bottle of his own. "C'mon. I'll warm you up."

He's not a bad sort. He plays football, but he also sits in front of me in algebra and is one of the smartest kids in school.

I scoot in beside him. He drapes an arm around my shoulders, more comradely than groping, and I lean into his body heat and accept the offered bottle. Just one good swig, I promise myself. What can that hurt me? It burns all the way down and makes my eyes water, but I manage not to cough or splutter. Already I feel better, and take one more drink for good measure.

Bryce laughs and drains the bottle he's holding. "Lightweights, all of you. Who's up for some good stuff?"

"I'll take a hit," another voice says, and Kelvin's face appears in the open door.

If I had a brain in my body, I would have known he'd be out here. This is probably where he's been getting his supply all night. I lean in toward Frank, resting my head on his shoulder and letting my hair fall over my face. Guys don't notice dresses; maybe from the back Kelvin won't know it's me.

Nice try.

"Lise? What the hell?" I recognize the ugly in his voice. Dad gets like that sometimes when he's at the bottom of a bottle. Frank makes things worse by kissing me.

"Get out here." A hand clamps around my arm, tight enough to bruise, dragging me toward the door.

"No." I hold on to Frank and pull back. "Let go of me."

"You're my fucking date."

I fight, but he's strong and the stupid dress tangles up my legs. Frank does nothing to help, pulling away from my desperate grasp, both hands in the air in a gesture of disengagement.

Kelvin yanks me out the door and onto my feet and slams me backwards against the trunk. I try to twist free, but he's got me pinned, his hands on my shoulders, his hips grinding mine against the car. "Bitch," he says. And then he's kissing me, all slobber and tongue. He tastes like whatever was in the bottle, only rancid.

I make myself go limp and let him kiss me. When I figure he's good and distracted, I knee him in the groin. But the damn dress gets in the way, and it's not nearly hard enough. He stops kissing me, though, doubling over with his hands between his legs. I take the opportunity to run, barefoot, carrying my shoes. Kelvin comes after me, really mad now, and grabs me from behind.

"You're not going anywhere."

Frank and the rest of the cowards are still in the car, doing nothing. Bryce grins, watching like this is a spectator sport and he's got the best seat in the house. Nobody else to be seen in the parking lot. I know I ought to scream, but my pride won't let me. I'm telling myself I can handle him, that he's not going to go further than kissing, but I'm not sure. I want Dale to come rescue me, but he's inside with Callie.

And then there is somebody else in the parking lot. Tall, gangly, awkward. Absolutely no match for Kelvin, and I'm totally surprised by the authority in his voice when Timothy says, "Don't be an asshole, Kelvin. The game's up. Let her go."

"Mind your own business," Kelvin says. He's got me by the hair now, twisting it tight so he controls my head. He kisses me again, and this time I bite his lip. He jerks away, dropping me as his hands go to his mouth. He's bleeding.

I back away, keeping my face to him this time so he can't come up on me from behind, shoes clutched in my fists as weapons. Timothy brushes past me. "I've got wheels. Let's go."

My heart hammering like crazy, I follow him, splashing through puddles. I step on something sharp and a burn flares in my right heel. The stupid dress clings to my thighs and knees, slowing me down. My head feels wobbly from the booze. But Timothy's car is right there. He opens the passenger side door for me and heads for the driver's seat.

Before he can get the door open, Kelvin is on him with a flying tackle. Both of them disappear from my sight on the other side of the car. I hear a grunt, and a wet, heavy sound as they hit the pavement. A series of thuds. I glance over at the booze car, opening my mouth to scream out for help, but all four of them are lined up in a row, just watching. Frank shakes his head a little, and the scream dies in my throat.

Clutching a shoe in my right hand, the heel facing out like a knife blade, I round the car. Timothy's pinned flat on his back, Kelvin pounding him with both fists. Coming up behind him, I hammer at the side of his face with the heel of the shoe. He yelps, twisting around to see what hit him, and I strike again. He's drunk, his reflexes slow, and the hand coming up in self-defense isn't fast enough to prevent another blow. This one catches on his ear and tears the skin, leaving a trail of blood.

He grabs for the shoe but misses, and I get in one more good smack on top of his head. The moment of distraction is enough to let Timothy use both hands to shove Kelvin backwards, writhe out from underneath him, and give him the knee in the balls he so richly deserves. I don't need to be told to get in the car, and we're off and driving. Last I see of Kelvin, he's writhing on the wet pavement, his hands clutching his privates.

Timothy's lip is split, his left eye swelling shut. His cheek is cut and bleeding. As soon as we're out of the parking lot and it's clear nobody's coming after us, he finds a place to pull over. Both of us are shivering. He turns the heat full up, but I feel like I'll never be warm again.

"You okay?" he asks.

I nod. I've never felt less okay, but I'm not hurt and I figure that's what he means. He's a different story. "Maybe we should go to the ER. You might need stitches."

He shakes his head. "My mom would have a fit. Costs a fortune."

"You're bleeding."

He checks himself in the mirror. "Face cuts always bleed. It'll be okay. Thanks for getting him off me. What on earth did you do? I couldn't see anything."

"Shoe." I grin. I can't help it, and all at once we're both laughing.

"Ow," he says, stopping at once and putting one hand over his lip.

"You need some ice on that."

"Yeah." He pulls back out onto the road and drives me home, both of us keeping the rest of our thoughts to ourselves.

"Thanks," I say, when he drops me outside my house. It seems a very small and inefficient word, but I'm about to burst into tears and need to get into the house before that happens.

"Hey, I've always wanted to kick that asshole in the balls. Thank you for providing the opportunity."

***

"Lise? Are you okay?"

Everybody's looking at me. My cheeks are wet, and I scrub them with the backs of my hands and take refuge in a long swallow of ice water.

"Sorry." I try to smile.

"Whatever are you sorry for?" Timothy says. "You've got carte blanche to cry anytime. What's it been, a week since she died?"

A wave of exhaustion rolls over me, and I want out of here and away. Oblivion would be lovely, but responsibility waits.

"We should go check on Shadow," I say.

Ariel snorts, but she looks pale and tired herself, and she's still hiding behind her sunglasses.

"I never did thank you properly," I say to Timothy as we all push back chairs and get to our feet.

"For what?"

"You took a hit for me, back then. I'm pretty sure I never showed proper appreciation."

"Prom, you mean?" His face darkens and he glances at Ariel. "Has he changed?"

"Not as much as you'd hope."

"I have to admit I was shocked when you agreed to go out with him."

"Not so much as I was that he asked me." I manage a smile and a shrug.

Timothy studies me and shakes his head. "You didn't know."

"Apparently not. What are we talking about?"

His face flushes and he shakes his head. "Wish I hadn't brought it up."

My stomach does an elevator trip down into my toes. Whatever it is, I also wish he'd kept it to himself, but it's too late for that now.

Timothy telegraphs something to Dennis and he nods, steering Ariel out onto the sidewalk with a hand on her shoulder.

"Spit it out," I say. "I already know Kelvin is a class-A asswipe. Probably not much you can tell me that would come as a shock."

He runs a hand through his perfect hair, standing it on end. If he were on TV, the expression on his face would be "man delivering bad news."

"Some of the guys used to call you the Ice Queen."

This surprises me into a giddy little laugh. "Me? You've got to be kidding."

Timothy doesn't smile. "Because you were so pretty but never went out. There were the inevitable frigidity jokes. Kelvin . . ." He stops and clears his throat.

"God." Even after all these years, shame heats my skin and turns my stomach. I definitely wish I hadn't eaten so much lunch.

"Kelvin had a bet going that he could get you to go out with him and . . . well, get you to have sex . . ."

My face burns with humiliation. I should have known. If I hadn't been so flattered by his attention, I would have seen it. In the days between Kelvin's invite and prom, girls whispered to each other when I walked by. A couple of the guys asked me out. One of them grabbed my ass while I was getting something out of my locker.

"Well," I say. "You're right. I could have happily lived my whole life without knowing that little tidbit."

Timothy won't meet my eyes. "I'm sorry I said anything."

"No, I needed to know. For Ariel." I put my arms around him and squeeze him tight, wanting to erase what he's feeling. "You're a good man, Timothy. Be happy."

He pats my back like I'm a child who needs soothing. "Take good care of her, okay? Let me know if we can help."

Outside, when Ariel puts out her hand to say good-bye, Timothy ignores it and pulls her into a hug. "Whatever happens with the testing, I hope you'll stay in touch."

She hugs him back. "You can count on it."

Dennis, who is driving, won't hear of us waiting for a cab, and they drop us back at the hotel. All the way I'm watching the streets for red curls and a camera, but I see only ordinary people doing ordinary things. Ariel leans her head against the seat, eyes still hidden by dark glasses, but her face looks softer, more at peace, and she clasps the purse on her lap as if it contains treasure.

CHAPTER NINE

Shadow is not in the hotel room. His suitcase is still there, open on the couch where he left it. His shaving kit is on the bathroom counter. Ariel registers this quietly.

"He'll be back," she says, but there's a catch in her voice. She dives straight into the shower, leaving me to the mercy of my memories.

I peel out of my jeans and into a pair of sweatpants. Shame heats my face all over again just thinking about the Ice Queen wager. I wonder if Dale knew about that, and what he must have thought of me.

Which reminds me that I owe him the decency of a call. He doesn't know where I am. He'll be worried. And nobody knows where to reach me if Mom gets sick or has a fall. A couple of days ago, Dale's voice would have been the most comforting sound in the world, but now my hand feels weighted with lead as I dial the familiar number. Each ring travels from my ear down to my toes and back again, as if I'm an empty sound tunnel. When Dale's answering machine clicks on, I freeze, mouth open, throat tight, choking on words I don't know how to say.

I'm fine, don't worry, I'll be in touch later.

But nothing is easy, not anymore. I hang up without saying a word and collapse on the edge of the bed, shaking like I've narrowly escaped mortal danger. In the bathroom, the water stops running. Ariel will be out in a minute, and I need to pull myself together. I want to escape, hit the bar downstairs, maybe get thoroughly plastered. But I need to be here for Ariel.

So instead I climb into bed, hiding my shivering beneath the covers, and turn on the TV. Clicking through the channels is mindless and soothing, and little by little my hands stop their wild shaking. I settle on an old episode of *I Love Lucy*, silly and familiar.

Ariel emerges from the bathroom in a cloud of steam. She looks about ten years old in her fuzzy sleep pants and T-shirt, with wet hair loose around her face. I expect her to climb into her bed and put her earbuds in, but instead she climbs in next to me. Not touching, but closer than she needs to be. She's got her laptop, though, and it only takes a minute for her to be thoroughly absorbed in the screen.

Watching her, I'm struck by how alone she is. Her mother is dead. She doesn't have a father. And the only person she feels she can count on is throwing a hissy fit and has gone off God knows where.

I keep running lines in my head.

I love you so much. You're all the family I have left.

It's you and me, kid.

Let me take you home.

But I've never been good at saying what I feel. And I don't want to go home, not until the media circus dies down. So where are we to go, what are we to do?

Ariel looks up from the screen and catches me staring at her. "What?"

Not a tone that encourages conversation. She's got a personal space bubble up around her so big I can feel it burning my skin. But I have to say something, and I want to kick myself when I open my mouth and spill, "So where are we headed next?"

"Yakima." Her eyes look weary and don't light up at all.

"That's not far, at least. We could rent a car."

She nods, her eyes on the laptop screen. Her forehead is puckered, lips pressed so tightly together I can see white around the edges.

"You don't have to do this, Ariel."

"I do." There's a flatness in her voice that's close to despair, night and day from the enthusiasm she had about meeting Kelvin and Timothy. Maybe she's missing Shadow, I don't know, but something's not right.

"Who is it? Does he know we're coming?"

She closes the laptop and turns up the volume on the TV, not answering my question.

The studio audience laughs loudly. I go to the TV and hit the "Power" button manually, standing directly in her line of vision.

"Ariel? Talk to me."

Something bumps against the door, and both of us shift our attention in that direction. There's the sound of somebody swiping a key and the door opens. Ariel stiffens and looks away, so Shadow's dramatic entrance falls flat. He waits in the doorway for a long moment, a bouquet of red roses in one hand, a box of chocolate in the other. Ariel keeps her eyes fixed on the blank TV, even when he kicks the door closed.

He brushes past me without any acknowledgment whatsoever. Chocolate and flowers, God help me. He looks tragic and romantic and just a little bit dangerous, right out of one of those teenage vampire movies. "You were right," he says, kneeling beside the bed and laying the flowers in her lap. "I'm sorry. I don't want you to need anybody but me."

Ariel flings herself into Shadow's arms, burying her face against his chest. He glances over her head at me and smiles, slowly, deliberately, before he bends his head to kiss her. The two of them are lip-locked in a heartbeat, leaving me in the front-row bleachers with the scent of roses heavy in my nostrils.

"I'll just put these in water, then," I say, but neither of them comes up for air. What I want to do is beat the boy over the head with his bouquet, but instead I put water in the ice bucket and leave the roses in the bathroom, then slip out the door and go downstairs. The bank of pay phones slows my steps, but I keep going, across the lobby and outside.

A walk would be nice. I could use a chance to stretch my legs and clear my head. But the weather has shifted. Wind scours against me, so full of dirt it's hard to breathe. The sky is gray with it. A tumbleweed rolls across the parking lot, pursued by a plastic bag and a rattle of dry leaves. A man strides toward the hotel, head bent, face scrunched up against the dust. I open the door for him, and we both blow back into the lobby.

"Pasco dust storm," he says, smoothing a hand over windblown hair. "Hate this place, but business is business. You staying long?" The smile, the suit, the briefcase in one hand and cell phone in the other—all shriek sales.

"Not long." I need a polite exit strategy—now—but can't think of anything.

"You look familiar. Have we met?" A worn-out pickup line if ever there was one, only I think he means it. His eyes sharpen, measuring the angles of my face, the fall of my hair.

"I get that a lot. One of those faces, I guess." My smile feels wooden, my lips numb. "Good luck with the dust!" As I turn and walk away, his eyes boring a hole into my back, I long for the good old days when I would have assumed he was checking out my ass, not fixing to identify me as Callie's sister. I take the stairs, insurance against any more curious eyes, and arrive at the door of our room out of breath and out of sorts.

I make sure to knock loudly before I let myself in. The two of them are cuddled up on Ariel's bed, but at least they're fully clothed.

I sit on the edge of my bed and pull off my shoes. The blister from Callie's funeral still isn't healed. It stings. My feet ache. I just want to be done with this day, but before I can turn off my brain, I need to discuss the plans for tomorrow.

"Okay, kids. Who's the next victim?"

"His name is Bryce and he looks like another one of Mom's real winners." Ariel's voice sounds small and tired. She leans her head on Shadow's shoulder, her face hidden by her hair.

I suck in a breath between my teeth and hold it, counting to ten.

"Bryce Halvorson?"

Ariel nods, her face still hidden.

"Ariel. Honey. No. I love you, but no."

"You promised."

No need to wonder where Ariel got her stubborn streak. I've heard both these words, and the tone they're uttered in, come from Callie's lips a thousand times. It never mattered if I'd really promised anything or not.

"But you didn't tell me his name. Kelvin is an angel of light compared to Bryce."

"And this is a surprise? Mom liked dicks. We know that."

Shadow snickers and she smacks him. "You know what I mean. So this guy's a creep. So what?"

"*This guy*," I say, exaggerating her emphasis, "is dangerous. Skip him. Move on. If he's your father, honey, you don't want to know."

"People change."

"Not that much."

"What did he do? Murder somebody?"

I sigh. "No, he kept it down to beating his girlfriend and dealing crack. He liked hurting people."

Ariel shakes her head, her lips set in a thin line. "I don't care if he's a psychopath. I need to know."

"You think that because you're sixteen—"

She flings her hands up in the air and glares at me. "Sixteen doesn't mean stupid. If I've got psychopath genes, maybe I should know before I kill somebody in my sleep or something."

"Bryce isn't your father, all right? You're nothing like him. Give this one up."

"But Yakima is, like, an hour away."

"Your mother made me responsible for you, and I'm not going to let you do this. I'm just not. So I'm going to call a cab and we'll head to the airport and find the soonest flight out, you hear me?"

Ariel plants herself between me and the phone. "You said you'd come with me. You agreed."

"I changed my mind. Move."

"Call a cab if you want, but I'm not getting in it."

"Ariel—"

"Me and Shadow can go without you."

"How are you going to get there?"

"Greyhound."

"We could hitchhike," Shadow drawls. "I've always wanted to try that."

"Sure," Ariel agrees. "The bus is too slow. Hitchhiking is an awesome idea."

"Until you get in the car with a rapist or a murderer. Think, Ariel. You're not using your head."

"Shadow will be with me." She says this as if the boy offers protection. More a liability, as I figure it. She's more likely to rescue him if it comes to trouble than the other way around.

"You can't hitchhike. That's the end of it."

Ariel leaps off the bed like she's got a rocket launcher and gets right in my face. She's as tall as I am, probably outweighs me by a few pounds. Her fists are clenched at her sides, her cheeks flushed red with outrage. "How are you going to stop me? I'm too big to lock in my room."

"I'll call the cops. Report you as a runaway."

"You wouldn't."

"Try me."

"You're bluffing."

She's right. I'm not going to call the cops. If the media got their teeth in that story, it would be like throwing fresh chum into shark-infested waters. If pictures of Ariel in the back of a cop car start circulating in the tabloids and on Twitter and God knows where else, she'll never forgive me. But if I let her take off and she gets hurt hitchhiking, then I'll never forgive myself.

It seems like an eternity that we stand there, locked eye to eye—the still center at the eye of a storm. She speaks first.

"He's not going to hurt me."

"Ariel, listen to me. I know him. You don't. He—"

"He's dead, okay? He's fucking dead and we're going to the fucking funeral and I'll never know . . ."

Her face contorts, eyes scrunched, mouth stretching into the shape of another word, but all that comes out is a sob. Arms wrapped around her belly, she sinks onto the floor with her back against the bed, wrenched apart by weeping.

I don't know what to do, how to comfort her. I stand there feeling gutshot and like I'm intruding on a private moment. It's Shadow who sits down on the floor beside her and puts his arms around her, murmuring soothing words, rocking her as though she's a small child. Her grief is so raw, so naked, it makes me want to run. If I keep listening to her, I'm going to break into pieces and join her on the floor.

I can't comfort her and I can't leave her, so I go to the phone instead and focus on practicalities. A rental car. A hotel. I'm pretty sure that the last thing Ariel needs is another funeral, but if she's hell-bent on going, then I'll be going with her.

CHAPTER TEN

When Dale walks into his house at the end of the day, there's a light blinking on the answering machine. One new message. The display shows an unfamiliar number. Probably a telemarketer, he tells himself, but can't quite silence the burst of hope that Lise has finally called. Fear follows fast on that first thought. What if she's in trouble? What if it's a call to tell him she's hurt or dead?

Spike whines and presses against his leg, asking for his usual pats.

"Just a minute, boy." Dale pushes "Play." After the beep, he hears the sound of breathing. And then, nothing.

He stares at the little red light and doesn't press "Delete." Maybe it's a wrong number. Maybe it's Lise. He can't remember ever feeling so helpless and off-balance. There's nothing he can do, not until she chooses to come to him, and her history of asking for help is pretty damn thin.

His skin itches with unrest even though it's been a long day of hard physical labor. Nothing in the fridge looks interesting, and he's not really hungry, but he knows he needs to eat. In the end, he makes himself a sandwich and manages to swallow half of it, but it tastes like sawdust and he gives the rest to Spike. He thinks about bed, but there's no way he's going to sleep. Not yet.

It's not often that he gets all wound up, but when he does, it helps to lose himself in a project, and there's that box for Ariel he's been wanting to make. Once out in his shop, surrounded by the smells of wood and sawdust, he immediately feels calmer and more grounded. A moment of puttering, pulling out his tools, and then he takes a long look at the plans he's drawn up. He's a builder, not a furniture maker, and he wants this project to be as close to perfect as he can make it. Most of the principles are the same as framing a house, just on a finer scale. "Measure twice, cut once," as his dad always says. But on this keepsake box even a fraction of an inch off true will show, and Ariel deserves nothing but the best.

He's drawn the plan from memory of the cedar chests Callie and Lise were given by their grandfather, but he's switching things up a little. He went looking for cedar, but a friend had ordered in a supply of curly maple. Beautiful red gold wood, with smooth, dark swirls and spirals that will glow once it's polished and stained.

In a moment of self-doubt, he hesitates to make the first cut. Memory shakes him as he pictures the shape of the chest in his mind.

***

Prom night. He's sitting on the windowsill in Lise and Callie's room, watching Callie stow her T-shirt into what her grandfather had meant as a hope chest. Callie's is more of a rat's nest, a mishmash of her life and the lives of others. She's like a magpie, shamelessly purloining shiny things that catch her fancy, then forgetting about them. Dale catches a glimpse of a friendship bracelet he made for Lise when they were in sixth grade and feels a sharp pang of hurt. Did Lise even miss it? Probably not, he tells himself.

"That shirt's still wet, Call. It will go moldy."

She turns to look at him and grins, her hair drying in spiral curls around her face. "Cool. I have no objection to mold." Then she frowns. "On the shirt, anyway. I don't want it all over everything else. Too bad you didn't wear a tux. One of those plastic bag things the suits come in would be perfect."

"If I'd worn a tux, you would have worn a dress, and we wouldn't be having this conversation."

He can't help his eyes moving over her body with appreciation. It feels wrong, since he remembers when she was just a little kid. But she's not that now. She's spent the entire evening making sure his hands have touched nearly every inch of her.

She catches his eyes on her and turns toward him, hands deliberately pulling down the hem of the oversize shirt she's wearing so that the fabric goes tight on her breasts. Her bare legs are brown and slim, and he's not at all sure she's wearing anything under that shirt. His heart picks up its tempo, sending heat through his body and firing the hard-on he's been fighting all evening into full throttle.

Callie, looking anything but sixteen, slides the shirt up onto her thighs. Dale swallows. He should go home. She's Lise's sister. But Lise doesn't want him, will never want him. The thought of her snuggled up with Kelvin in the back of that GTO makes him sick. He's heard all the gossip, knows what Kelvin's got planned. He wants to believe that Lise will never go for it, but then, he never thought she'd go out with a jerk like that in the first place. He thought he knew her; he was wrong.

The coals of anger that have been heating his belly for weeks flame up. Forget Lise. Callie wants him. She raises her eyebrows in a question. He makes some sort of movement of assent, and she is halfway across the room to him when they hear footsteps on the stairs. Callie freezes, her head swiveling toward the door. Dale knows those footsteps. His heart skips a beat.

The door flings open, thudding against the wall and bouncing back. Lise stands there, barefoot and rain wet, the skirt of her dress ripped halfway up her thigh. Her gaze travels from Callie to Dale and back again.

Nobody moves. Nobody speaks. It's like they've been transformed into statues. His own breathing is loud in his ears, and his face is hot with a mix of emotions he can't begin to sort and identify. He manages to break the spell and takes a step toward her, but Lise warns him off without a word, barricading her body with her arms crossed over her breasts.

"For God's sake, Dale. She's *sixteen*." Her voice drips acid. The look she gives him is equal parts hurt and outrage, and he wants to start babbling excuses. *We haven't done anything. We were just talking.* But he knows damn well what he was about to do and that stops his tongue.

"Looks like the Ice Queen melted in the rain," Callie says. "Never thought you had it in you. Was it good?"

"Best night of my life," Lise answers. The strap of the dress has slipped off one shoulder. She hitches it up with one hand. Shivers. "Get out. I need to change."

Callie, damn her, crosses the room and takes possession of his hand. "Come on, Dale. Let's go hang out in your car."

"Put some clothes on," Lise says, in the big-sister voice that always irritates Callie.

"Don't need any."

Dale can't tear his eyes from Lise's face as Callie tows him from the room. Did she, or didn't she? Her eyes are shuttered, chin high. She's shut him out. His mouth tastes like ashes as he stumbles down the stairs behind Callie.

***

In all the years that have passed, they've never talked about that night. Now it's been too long. The wall is too thick. So he does what he always does and pushes the memories away.

The wood is smooth and solid beneath his hands. Predictable. He knows how it will behave, what it will do, and there is comfort in that. One more measurement just to be sure, and all of his worry and heartache fall away as he loses himself in the process of creation.

CHAPTER ELEVEN

I'd hoped to be inconspicuous, but there's no more than a handful of mourners in the tiny chapel and we camouflage about as well as white rabbits in black dirt. There are no ushers, and I choose a row about halfway back, avoiding the statement made by choosing either front or back. We're neither close friends nor shirttail relatives.

This funeral is night-and-day different from Callie's. No open casket for one thing. Bryce is locked up tight in a shiny black coffin glittering with brass. A single wreath of white roses rests on the lid. In front of it, on an easel, sits a poster with a full-color headshot of the deceased. He's recognizable as his high school self, good-looking still, but his features have coarsened; the lines engraved in his forehead and cheeks don't bear the stamp of kindness. His iron-gray hair is shiny with gel. His eyes, even in the photo, look unfocused, as though he's three sheets to the wind with a drink in one hand.

Two women sit side by side, front and center. Their shoulders touch, but they might as well be sitting with a mile of empty space between them. One is small and plump, clad all in black with an old-fashioned mourning hat that obscures her face with netting. The other is taller and younger. Her bleached hair is short and spiky, the better to show off her heavily studded ears. She's thin to the point of skeletal, with a long-sleeved black shirt hanging off her bony shoulders. Her jaws work rapidly on a wad of gum and her fingers twitch restlessly.

Three men sit together in a row, all in button-up shirts and ties, their hair slicked back. They have the same sort of resigned boredom as people waiting on a delayed flight at an airport. One of them frowns over his smartphone, reading a message and texting a response. Two elderly women in conservative dress, both carrying prominent Bibles, sit well away from the men on the other side of the chapel.

The minister glances at his watch, clearly wanting to get on with things.

"Let not your hearts be troubled, you believe in God, believe also in me. In my house are many mansions. If it were not so, I would have told you."

He stumbles over the words as though he suspects, as I do, that if Bryce is in a place with many mansions, he's probably figuring out a way to break and enter. The sermon is mercifully short, as is the eulogy. There's not much to be said. Bryce was born, he lived, he died. Any of his more daring exploits can't be talked about in public, I suspect, due to legalities.

The spiky-haired woman sobs aloud, but her face is dry. The old woman sits quietly with her head bowed, a handkerchief held to her lips. I can't see her face, but she must be Bryce's mother. Her husband died when I was just a little kid. I'd forgotten that, but all at once I remember, clear as clear, my dad telling my mom that old man Halvorson blew his brains out in the middle of his kitchen.

I was ten. Bryce would have been the same age. A twinge of compassion twists through me. Maybe Bryce would have been different if his father had been different. I don't remember how he was in school before that day, only the bully he became later.

Ariel sits pale and quiet, her hands folded in her lap, eyes downcast. When the service is over, all the mourners file out, except for Mrs.

Halvorson. She doesn't move, as if she hasn't even noticed that everyone is gone. When I walk over and take her hand, there is a delayed reaction time before she registers the touch. She looks dried up and small, as if all of the juice has been sucked out of her and there's nothing left but skin and bones.

Her fingers are cold, the skin rough and dry, her eyes empty. She smells of old polyester and mothballs. Her blank expression reminds me of my mother's, and I look around to see if anybody is there to take care of her. Too late, too slow. Her fingers tighten around mine.

"Callie, isn't it?" she says. "One of them Redding girls."

"I'm Lise."

"None of mine could be here," she goes on, as if my name is irrelevant. "Joseph is in California. Got no car, he says, no money for a plane. Janet is busy with the babies. Three of them, and I haven't seen a one of them."

She's got me trapped, partly by the hand but mostly by her emptiness. Out of my peripheral vision I see Ariel and Shadow waiting at the back of the chapel. Ariel is watching and listening, and that makes me shudder. This is not what she needs for a grandmother. Shadow leans against a pew, playing with his phone.

"I'm not long for this world, myself. Something wrong with my heart, doctor says. It could drop me any minute. Just once before I die, I'd like to see the little ones."

All of this is delivered in a lifeless monotone. A bubble of panic rises up inside me, the thought that I'll never break away, will spend the rest of my life listening to her litany of troubles. I want more than anything in the world to detach her clinging hand, but can't bring myself to do it.

"Just like his daddy, Bryce was. Thoughtless. Thoughtless." She shakes her head, and I stare at her in dawning understanding. The minister's lack of conviction. The closed coffin. Maybe I'm wrong, though. I want to be wrong. I glance at Ariel, who has moved to the back of the chapel and is talking to Shadow.

Lowering my voice, I ask, "Mrs. Halvorson, how did he die?"

I hear soft footsteps behind me and look up to see the undertaker hovering. He's got dandruff on the shoulders of a threadbare black suit and an insincere smile pasted on his face. I catch a whiff of the inevitable breath spray. But to me he looks like an angel of mercy, come to rescue me from the answer I don't want to hear. He holds out a hand.

"Come now, Mrs. Halvorson. It's time to go to the graveside. Let me walk you to the car." She stares at his hand as if she doesn't know what it's for, then finally reaches out and lets him help her to her feet. As soon as she's in motion she forgets all about me, transferring her attention and her complaints to her escort.

"Didn't think about his mother at all, did he?" She shakes her head, leaning heavily on the supporting arm of a stranger.

Ariel's eyes follow her out the door. "Should we go to the graveside?" Her voice sounds childlike and small.

"No. You've seen enough."

Shadow puts an arm around her and pulls her close. "How about we go eat? I'm hungry."

She doesn't agree, but lets him lead her out the door. I'm okay with that. If I can get her in the car, I have her at my mercy. Back to Pasco and the airport.

But the instant I step outside the door, the spiky-haired woman runs interception. I hear my mother's voice in my head, echoes of rare childhood trips into the city wilds of Spokane. *Keep walking. Don't make eye contact.*

But this woman's right in front of me, and this is a funeral and it's already too late. Her eyes are dark brown, the pupils constricted and tiny. Her mascara is smeared, emphasizing dark circles. Her foundation fails to completely cover a bruise on her left cheekbone. "You got a light?"

"Pardon?"

She waves an unlit cigarette in my direction. Her fingers, heavy with silver rings, tremble visibly. "Lost my lighter. Really need a smoke before the grave. His, not mine." Her lips jerk up into a smile, revealing stained and broken teeth.

"I'm sorry. I don't have a lighter." I start to skirt around her, my only thought to get Ariel out of here and away. Shadow has other ideas.

"I've got a light if you can spare me a smoke." He pulls a book of matches out of the pocket of his pants and stands waiting. It takes her a minute, considering, but she nods and taps another cigarette out of an almost-empty package. Shadow leans in close to light her cigarette before applying the match to his own. She sucks in smoke all the way to her toes, holds it, then blows a long, thin stream into my face. I wave it away and step back, forgetting to play polite.

"I'm sorry," she says, as she does it again, her eyes staring directly into mine, bold as brass. "Does smoke bother you, then?"

I turn away and take a step toward the car, looking back to see if Ariel is following. "We really need to go."

Ariel glances from me to Shadow, who's leaning against the side of the building as if he plans to stay awhile. She steps up beside him, reaches for his cigarette, and inhales. Her eyes are on me as she does so, and I choose not to give her the reaction she's looking for. Not here, not now.

Spiky works on her smoke with true dedication, but once it's burned almost down to the butt, she looks at me and says, "Bryce never mentioned you."

"I wouldn't think he had. Haven't seen him in sixteen years."

"Are you his wife? Or were you, I mean?" Ariel asks.

The woman laughs, short and sharp. "Nothing so official." Her fingers and the glowing end of the cigarette are now almost touching, and she drops the butt and grinds it into the sidewalk with a sharp twist of her high heel.

Ariel persists. "So he wasn't married? No kids?"

"Him? Likely got kids planted all over the countryside. If there's a wife, he never said nothing. Didn't have a ring, for as much as that matters." She starts down the stairs and then turns back. "You guys coming to the graveside?"

I can't read Ariel's face and wait for her to answer. There's color back in her cheeks, a faint flush that could be anger or shame or determination. "I think we'll pass," she says.

Good. She's had enough. We walk to the car in silence. Ariel and Shadow pile into the back, side by side. They reek of smoke and I crack my window to let the fresh air roll in, eyeing them both in my rearview mirror.

"Girlfriend or hooker, what do you think?" Shadow asks Ariel.

"No reason she couldn't be both." Ariel's words are short little jabs. Angry, then. Good. Anger is healthy.

"Fine stepmother she'd make," Shadow says. "A whole new life of adventure, just waiting."

"Why do you have to be such an asshole?" But she's laughing, and I breathe a sigh of relief as I shift the car into reverse. As long as she doesn't get sucked into believing she's a monkey in this circus, she'll be okay. Now it's back to the hotel, and tomorrow I'll find a way to get her onto a plane and home, Ricken or no Ricken. Sooner the better. Bryce's woman might just have been measuring up the competition for his will, but if she's recognized Ariel or me, she'll definitely call in the media. I shudder at the very idea of a news story connecting me to Bryce.

I'm driving across the parking lot when Ariel leans forward and says, "I want to go to where he worked."

"What?" My foot hits the brake all by itself, and we all lurch as I slam to a stop.

"I want to see where he worked."

I crane my neck and swivel around to look at her directly. "Honey, don't you think you've seen enough? He wasn't a nice man. He didn't hang out with nice people. And there's no way to know whether he was your father or not."

I'm wasting my breath. She's going, with or without me. All things considered, I might offer a modicum of protection, or at least be there to pick up the pieces after the fact.

"Oh, hell. All right. Somebody tell me where to go."

***

Yakima strikes me as cramped, dark, and dirty, even though it's not really any of those things. The wide sky overhead is blue and cloudless, spring sunshine lighting up sidewalks and streets. Thanks to Google, locating the car dealership where Bryce worked is easy. It's not much more than a dirt parking lot full of dusty used cars. A square building, once lime green, now faded and peeling, bears the sign "Jim's Cars: Make an Offer, We'll Make You a Deal."

I wedge the rental into a space between an aging Suburban and a Ford pickup with a dented fender. Before we get our doors open, a sales guy exits the office and heads in our direction. His pants are belted low to accommodate the swell of his belly, and he hitches them up as he walks. Pinstriped shirt, blue tie, buzz-cut hair, and the inevitable toothy smile pushing back heavy jowls. He reminds me of a bulldog after a bone.

His hand is out for the shake when he's still four feet away. "Good afternoon. My name is Jim. How can I help you lovely ladies?"

He goes for the two-handed shake, engulfing my hand in one of his and then laying the other on top, politician-style. His hands are big and soft, no calluses. "We've got some almost-new cars that would be perfect for you. I've even got a hybrid. Only four years old. Single owner, well maintained. Best deal in town."

"We'd like to work with Bryce," Ariel says, beside me. "My friend bought a car from him a while back."

Jim, still clasping my hand, gives her a long, deep look. "Well, now. He's not here, missy."

She tilts up her chin and smiles at him, making sure to display her dimple. "Maybe we could come back?"

"Ah, see, that's the thing. Bryce won't be coming back. He died last week. Right here in this very lot, as it turns out. So I reckon you're stuck with me."

There's something about his voice that doesn't ring true. It's more than the whole sales-guy thing. His face is open and harmless, despite the veins in his nose and cheeks that hint of plenty of hard drinking. His eyes, a muddy shade of greenish brown, are intent, moving from me, to Shadow, to Ariel, and back again.

All at once, his touch feels intrusive and I pull my hand away.

Still smiling, Jim shakes his head at Ariel. "Now, were you here about a car, or were you here about old Bryce?"

She bites her bottom lip and drops her gaze, fiddling with the straps of her backpack. I'm willing her to be smart, but she's so damn stubborn. Words come out of my mouth before I know I'm going to talk.

"I don't appreciate your tone. My daughter needs a good used vehicle. But since Bryce is gone, maybe we'll go to a different lot."

"A car I can help you with. But I'm not in Bryce's line of work, per se, if you catch my meaning."

I'm not sure I do, but I'm beginning to.

Jim leads us across the weed-infested lot, straight to a 2010 Toyota Camry. It's probably both the newest and the most expensive car he has on offer. The exterior looks okay at first glance, but Dale has taken me car shopping a time or two, and I notice straight up that the mileage and price tag are both too high. Ariel peers in the driver's window, faking interest in the interior.

I'm beginning to fear we're really going to have to buy a car before she finally gets around to asking more questions, but Jim saves us the trouble.

"Glad to see it's really cars you're interested in. Can't tell you how many kids come around here—some clean and sharp looking like you, even—asking for Bryce. I can't exactly shoo the kids away, now. It's a free world, ain't it? Can't stop 'em from shopping for cars. What Bryce does with his customers, that's his own business. Was, I mean. Poor bastard. Don't mean to speak ill of the dead."

He crosses himself. "So what do you think of this car, then, missy?"

"Way too much money for what it's worth," I say. "How about something like this? Older but same mileage." I'm looking at an old silver Subaru. The body doesn't look like much. It's rusting in places, and the front end registers an encounter with a deer, but it's all-wheel drive and Subarus run forever.

Shadow rolls his eyes and starts playing with his phone. Ariel shoots me a look of disbelief, as if I'm seriously considering buying this car for her. Jim, on the other hand, is all enthusiasm. "This one is a fine car. Lots of folks buy a Subaru for their kid—nice, safe, long-running vehicles. I had the perfect car for you, if that's the sort of thing you're looking at. Well maintained, low miles. Thanks to Bryce, though, it's off the market."

"Why, what's wrong with it?" Ariel is all big eyes.

"Killed himself in it, that's what. Not to speak ill of the dead, but if he felt the need to take hisself out—and I get that, what with the feds closing in on his little operation and all, can't blame him going for the escape hatch—it's beyond me why he couldn't have picked something old and rusted."

"Going out with style," Shadow says. "I can respect that."

Ariel shivers and clings to Shadow's hand, but there's a flush to her cheeks and her eyes glow with excitement. "What happened to the car?"

"Blood all over the seats, that's what. Bullet through the driver's side window."

I'm skeptical. "How do you know it was a suicide? Wasn't there an investigation?" I haven't seen Bryce in years, but I can still think of plenty of reasons somebody would want to shoot him. Especially if he was dealing drugs to kids. Hell, the woman at the funeral looked more than capable of putting a bullet in his brain.

"Watched him do it," Jim says. "Me and Mike. Nobody else was on the lot. Bryce walked over there and got in. Lit up a cigar, turned up the tunes. Mike was walking over to tell him to knock off the cigar in the car; brings down the value, you know? Even smokers don't want a car that smells like some other guy's old smokes. And bam. Blood on the window and he's dead as dead. Cops investigated, sure, but didn't ever tow the car away. Still on my lot, and now I've gotta call in a special cleaning crew."

"I want to see it," Ariel says.

"No. Ariel, no. I absolutely won't—"

"You can't stop me." Her eyes are scanning the car lot.

"Over there, I bet." Shadow points toward the far side of the lot where it borders on a narrow alley. A strand of yellow crime-scene tape drifts in the breeze.

Ariel is already in motion. I've got to stop her. Maybe I'm not parent material, but viewing a bloody suicide scene can't be good for a kid, especially when the deceased might be her father. I can't imagine what the hell she is thinking. As for Shadow, who is facilitating this macabre viewing, my hand aches with the desire to smack him upside the head. So I trot after them, picking my way between cars. I hear Jim puffing behind me.

"Ariel, wait!"

She doesn't. I'm too far away to stop her when she reaches the car and looks in the window. It feels like I'm caught in a horror movie. My feet move too slow; my voice falls on deaf ears.

Her face contorts in a grimace, and she cups both hands over her nose and mouth. Shadow turns away, gagging loudly, and bends over to vomit into a little patch of weeds. Two more steps and I can smell the decay, even through the closed door. An irrational fear strikes me that Bryce is still in the car with brains dripping out of his shattered skull.

"Don't take much blood to make a stink," Jim says. He sounds nasal, and his breathing is louder. "Come away from there now, kids. This ain't no joke."

Ariel turns on him, fierce and urgent, all of her pretenses stripped away in the face of the reality this car represents. "Nobody said it was funny, okay?" She's digging in her backpack, and I realize, too late and a dollar short, what she's planning to do.

When the swab and envelope emerge from a pocket in her backpack, Jim lumbers forward, faster than you'd expect from a man of his size, and plants himself between her and the car. His face has lost all of its softness, the bone structure beneath the fat establishing itself under duress.

"Just what are you intending to do?"

She stares at him, deer in the headlights, not a word to say. I'm sure as hell not going to help her talk her way into that car. I'm hoping Jim is going to do something sensible. Ban us from the property, maybe. Call the cops.

Ariel chokes back a sob, then looks up at him from under wet lashes. "All right, I lied. He is—was—my dad, okay? I never got to meet him. My mom just told me, and I came all the way here to find him but now he's d-dead . . ."

Even my eyes fill with tears in response to the waterworks she's put into play. Shadow smirks, or at least I think that's what he's doing. Hard to tell with that thing in his lip.

Jim's gaze turns on me. "You're not her mom, then."

I just shrug. Let him draw his own conclusions, so long as he keeps Ariel out of that car.

His eyes narrow, the pupils constrict, and all at once he's really seeing me, and not just as a potential sale. His stare makes me drop my eyes and shuffle my feet like I'm twelve.

"Let me get this straight." His voice is very soft, but there's an edge to it. "You just found out Bryce was your daddy, and you came to meet him without so much as telling him you were coming. And you just now figured out he was dead."

"What's wrong with that?"

Jim folds his arms across his chest and smiles at her. "I've got a couple kids round about your age. You know what they do? They get on their computers. Or their phones. And they google stuff."

"So?" But she's backed down a little. Her face looks uncertain.

"To put a bald face on it, you're lying."

"I don't know what you—"

"If you don't own a computer of your own, and I'm pretty sure you do, your friend there, he would have googled old Bryce fifty million times before you ever got here to this lot. So I don't believe you never knew he was dead. You want something. And I want to know what it is that you want." He softens his voice and smiles at her. "You can tell old Jim. I'm not about to hurt you."

Wordlessly, Ariel holds up an Identi-Match swab.

He leans down to peer at it, brow furrowed in confusion. "What is that supposed to be? A Q-tip?"

"He wasn't really my father. Or at least, I don't know if he was."

Understanding dawns, and his salesman smile comes with it. "So that's some DNA test, and you think you can swab the blood and find out if he's your daddy or not. I see, I see."

He rubs his chin, his eyes rolling over all three of us again. "I thought you all looked familiar, but I couldn't place it. Not from here, are you? Seems like I read about you in the news."

If we go now, we get a few minutes' head start on anybody he chooses to call. Because he is going to call; I can see it in his face. This is a chance to make a few bucks, easy, and get some attention for his cars while he's at it. But if he's carrying a cell phone, I haven't seen it yet.

Ariel drops the theatrics. It's almost startling to see her put herself back into her own skin. She stands taller and has more bulk to her. Her chin comes up, her eyes level with his. "It's not hurting you any to let me do what I came to do."

"Not helping any, either." He stands there, stroking his chin, considering. "You've got some money, if I remember that story correct. You'd be the daughter of the star what got killed by that horse."

"And?"

"And you can afford to pay. I'll let you get your swab, but it'll cost you."

"That's blackmail."

"Nah, just good business sense. I have something you want. You have money to pay me. Nobody's getting hurt. Now, if you want to talk blackmail, we could make an extra deal that says I don't call the local newspaper right now and tell them you're here."

I feel myself wilting inside, picturing the headlines on this one. Even if she pays him, there's nothing that says he's going to keep his mouth shut. And this time it will be Ariel in the stories, front and center.

"You're despicable." A white-hot rage heats my body from the inside out. My hands curl into fists. But I've got enough common sense left to think. Much as I'd like to clobber him with a shoe, sneakers aren't in the same class as high heels. Besides, he's big, and this is his lot and his town. It won't help Ariel for me to wind up in jail.

As a protector, Shadow is useless. The look on his face when he stares at Jim is closer to admiration than outrage. Jim shrugs, hands out and open.

"I'm a businessman. This is a business proposition."

"I thought you said you had kids," Ariel says. "What if your daughter was in this situation?"

"Since she's my daughter, that's not likely to be a problem. You telling me you don't have the money to pay? Way I see it, this is fair and square. Not even your money. Rich kid out on a joyride." His voice has been affable all along, but now it switches to mean. "Know what? I never knew who my daddy was neither. Did I go traipsing across the country? No, I got myself a shitty job. Why? Because I wasn't born in a great big house with money to burn. Now, do we have us a deal or not?"

I turn to Ariel. "We can walk away from this. Your swab is probably not even going to work on old dried blood. It's a Walmart thing, for God's sake."

"How much?" she says to Jim, ignoring me.

"I'm a fair man. Let's make it ten K for the swab and another ten not to call the media."

"That's twenty K! I don't have that kind of money."

"I'm pretty sure you know where to get it." He smiles at me, leaning back comfortably against the car. Apparently, the stink isn't bothering him anymore.

"You don't understand! My mom had the money. I'm only sixteen . . ." Her voice rises in frustration, breaking at the end of the last syllable. A red flush creeps from her neck to her chin and up over her forehead. Tears flood her eyes. She lifts her chin and blinks furiously, trying to hold them back, but they spill over and onto her cheeks.

"The funeral was only a week ago," I tell him. "There's legal stuff. Neither one of us can access that kind of money."

He shrugs. "No skin off my nose. Now, I suggest you get off of my lot before I call you in as trespassers."

"Wait a sec. Maybe we can work something out." My mind is scurrying between my bank accounts, figuring out how much I can scrape together. "I can get you ten," I tell him. Saying the words out loud makes me feel clammy and weak. I'm talking all of my savings, and Callie's money is still no more than a promise.

Ariel spins toward me, dashing away tears with both hands. "You'd do that?"

I'd much rather she come to her senses and walk away, but yes. I will do this. I dig out my debit card and hold it out to him.

He mulls over my offer. "I might be willing to lower my cost if we include a transfer of property." That smile flashes again, and it's with a sense of dread that I see where we are headed. It's too late now, though. I'm a fly and I've stepped onto his web. Struggling is only going to get me stuck tighter.

"I'll take ten," Jim drawls, confident in his position of power. "And I'll keep my mouth shut about this juicy little news story, on the condition that you take this car off my hands. It would cost me plenty to get it cleaned enough to sell. We'll write up the documents, fair and square, to show that you paid me for a car."

"Nobody in their right mind will believe we've paid ten grand for this."

He shrugs. "Car salesmen, you know? Always taking advantage of the ladies. Especially dainty little rich ladies who don't know a thing about cars."

Ariel holds out her hand. "Deal. Now give me the keys."

"Not so fast, little lady. Not so fast. We're going to do this paperwork up right and proper."

"Wait up a second. Have you all lost your minds?" I'm staring at the car in disbelief. "We can't possibly drive that. How are we supposed to get it off the lot? What do we do with it?"

"Should have thought of that before you bought it." Jim starts walking toward the office, jingling a set of keys in one hand.

Ariel stands by the car, not touching it, not moving away. Her eyes are red rimmed, her nose pink. She's not looking at the car or me or Shadow, or seemingly anything in particular. She's just standing there, staring at nothing.

Shadow seems to be in a trance of his own, and I grab his shoulder and give him a shake. "Call a tow truck."

He's got this dazed expression on his face, and I'm not sure he's even heard me. I shake him again. "Google a number, you hear me? Get a tow truck here before I'm done signing papers. And keep an eye on her."

Without waiting for an answer, I swing around and stomp after Jim. No high-end salesroom here. No shiny cars on display. Pictures and advertisements are tacked onto a bulletin board just inside the front door. The office stinks of tobacco and sweat, permeated with burnt coffee from a pot that looks like it might have been washed about ten years ago. The desk is cluttered with papers. An ashtray overflows with stale butts. I worry about what is going on outside with the kids, but I tell myself they've got each other, they'll be okay.

Buying cars is not on my top-ten list of fun things to do, even when I want a car and am shelling out the money for something I'm going to actually drive. This particular transaction is an ordeal from hell, simplified at least by the fact that I don't need to mess around with financing and credit scores. It's over relatively quickly. I sign my name on the check and on the papers that declare Bryce's suicide car as mine.

Blood money.

What if Ariel really is Bryce's kid? I don't know what that would do to her, but I can't imagine it would be anything good. On the other hand, not knowing might be worse, especially if none of the other candidates pan out. I'm torn by indecision. Would it be better to do everything in my power to prevent her getting this batch of DNA, or get it over with and see what fate has to say about her parentage?

By the time I walk back out into the sunlit afternoon, the keys to my new purchase clenched in my hand, I'm numb and cold with fear that Ariel will be where I left her, standing and staring out into space. I needn't have worried. She and Shadow have moved a sensible distance from the Death Car, sitting side by side on the hood of an old Chevy. From across the lot, they look cool as cucumbers and carefree as summertime. Funny thing how looks can be deceiving.

"Tow truck should be here any minute," Shadow calls out, as I head in their direction.

"Let's get out of here," I say to Ariel, as soon as I'm close enough to make eye contact. "You don't need to do this."

"Where's the tow truck supposed to take the car? I didn't know what to tell them," Shadow says.

"Does it matter? It's not like we're keeping it. Pick a spot. Any spot will do. Hell, send it up to the cemetery as a last gift to Bryce. Send it to his widow. Ask the tow truck guys to take it to a junkyard. Use your own brain."

Ariel has got all the backbone this boy is missing. "Give me the keys."

I put my hands behind my back and shake my head. "Please let this go."

"I have to. You don't understand." She's not going to back down, but whatever's waiting for her in that car, it's something she doesn't need to see.

"Fine. I'll do it, then." I start walking, but she steps in front of me, blocking the way.

"I have to do this myself. If I don't, I'll just . . . it won't . . ." She's so incredibly brave and annoyingly stubborn, all in one fabulous package, and she's breaking what's left of my heart. She reaches for my hand, and I let her take the keys.

When she reaches the Death Car, she hesitates just long enough to draw a deep breath. Her cheeks puff out and her face starts to mottle red as she turns the key in the lock and opens the door.

Even from where I'm standing, the stink intensifies. Holding her hair back with one hand, she scrubs at the dried blood on the seat with her swab. Then she turns back toward us, letting all of her breath out with a whoosh and sucking in another gulp through her mouth. I figure she's done and at least it was quick.

"Give me your water bottle," she demands of Shadow.

"What for?" He takes another look at her face and hands it over.

Ariel stalks back to the car, pours water onto the dried blood, and then makes another attempt at swabbing. This time she slams the car door shut behind her, then fumbles with sliding her swab into the little envelope. Her hands are shaking too hard, and she drops it into the dirt at her feet.

I run to help. The cotton is stained a dark, rusty brown. Dust and a piece of dry grass adhere to it, and I brush them off as best I can, then take the envelope and seal the damn thing up. Ariel is a shivering mess. I want to scrub my whole body and maybe my brain with antiseptic.

Putting an arm around Ariel's shoulders, not even looking toward the sales office for Jim, who I'm sure is watching us, I head for the rental, fumbling in my pocket for the keys as we walk. I'm not wasting a second getting off this accursed lot and back to safety. Wherever that is.

Ariel moves like a sleepwalker, responding to the pressure of my arm as I guide her between the cars, stumbling over uneven patches of ground. Her eyes are glazed. Her hands are icy cold, but a thin film of sweat covers her skin. Shock, I figure. I wonder, all at once, if she's seen the pictures of Callie lying dead under the hooves of that goddamn horse.

Of course she has. As Jim said, she's a teenager. She's on that laptop constantly, and I know damn well she's googled the accident and seen every ugly rumor ever printed about Callie. There have been plenty over the years. And now this.

Helplessness floods through me. I don't know how to help Ariel. She needs a nice, maternal woman to take her on. And grandparents. The kind who feed you cake and display your picture to all their friends and even the checker in the grocery store. Not somebody like me, and definitely not Shadow.

He trails along behind us, useless. I try to form a charitable thought about him. He's young, too. This whole brush with the ugly side of death has got to be an eye-opener for him as well as Ariel. I don't know anything about his family, but what sort of parents does he have that they're allowing him to visit suicide scenes?

And then I remember. They didn't. They have no idea what he's doing. I'm the one who let him come here. Hell, I drove.

I tighten my arm around Ariel's shoulder. "I'm so sorry, honey. I never should have brought you here."

She shivers. "There was a chunk of something. On the seat . . ." She stumbles and leans against me, and I get my arm around her waist to support more of her weight. Tremors travel through her body, head to toe.

"Shh, don't think about that. Let's go get you a nice warm shower, okay? And then we'll talk."

The car is only a few feet away now, a beacon of mercy. I click the locks open with the remote.

"Go open the passenger door, Shadow. Help me get her in."

For once, he does what I ask without quibbling. The car is warm from the sun's rays. It smells of car freshener and old tobacco, but that is like roses compared to where we've been. I ease Ariel into the seat, and she leans forward over her knees, face buried in her arms. My hand hovers over her head and then lowers, slowly, to rest there a moment. Her hair feels silken and soft to my touch, and I dare to stroke it.

Shadow's voice breaks the moment. "Tire's flat. Now what are we gonna do?"

CHAPTER TWELVE

I can handle a flat tire, but the timing is abysmal. Every moment we delay is another moment for Jim to change his mind and make a call. I want to dissolve into tears, to allow myself the luxury of falling apart and letting somebody else solve the problems for once. But there isn't anybody else.

"You'd better get busy," I tell Shadow.

He looks at me blankly. "What?"

"Change the tire. There will be a spare and a jack somewhere. Find them."

"I don't know how."

All at once, I see him with different eyes. The piercings, the deliberately uncombed hair, and made-up eyes are a thin disguise for a scared little boy. He folds his arms across his chest and scowls, though it's really more of a pout. "We can ask the tow truck driver."

"Oh for the love of God and money! We are not paying the tow truck driver to change a tire. I'll do it myself. Make yourself useful and find Ariel something to drink, if you can. There's a dispenser outside the office."

"I'll do it," Ariel says. Her head is still buried in her knees, her voice muffled, and I'm not sure what she's referring to.

Watching her sit up reminds me of watching a wilting plant after it gets water, only in fast-forward. Her spine straightens. Her eyes clear. She's still deathly pale, but her face no longer carries that lost, confused expression.

"I'll change the tire."

I know I'm being sexist and I shouldn't be surprised, but I am. Back in Colville, most of the girls know at least basic car maintenance. It's survival. There are a lot of isolated roads, and if you get a flat, you're pretty much on your own. But Ariel's world is a far cry from that. For some reason, I expected even a trust fund baby like Shadow to know his way around a car, but not Ariel.

"I like cars. I take shop classes." Her face has regained a little color, but she suddenly goes pale again, eyes wide. "Oh God. Like him. Like Bryce. He must have liked cars. Maybe—"

"No way. I knew him in high school, remember? Didn't give a rat's ass about cars. What he liked was screwing people over. He sold cars. He didn't work on them. Okay?"

She takes a deep breath and nods. Her eyes look up at me, blue and pleading.

"He's not going to be the one, right?"

"Damn straight."

"What if—"

"You go on like that, and I'll burn that thrice-damned swab before you can send it off."

Her lips quiver, and I prepare to backpedal, thinking I've chosen the wrong method to try to snap her out of it. But then she nods and gets out of the car. Her hands are still shaking, but she's steady on her feet. "Come on, Shadow. You can help."

I want to coddle her. Coax her back into the car, drape a blanket over her, pat her back and stroke her head. But I can see that having her do something, take action, is far more effective. She's capable and competent. After a couple of fruitless attempts at telling Shadow what to do, she takes over and does it all. He doesn't seem to care, just leans up against the car and plays with the omnipresent phone.

On Ariel's command, he removes the damaged tire and sets the spare in place. Her hands are steady now, her face absorbed. She pushes back a strand of hair and leaves a streak of black along her cheek. Shadow makes a show of brushing the dirt off his hands and his jeans. He points at her cheek. "You're all smudgy."

She rubs at it absently with the back of her hand but doesn't seem to care. "Do we have water? I'm thirsty."

"I'll get you something." Shadow sets off toward the drink machine, not moving with any particular speed. I wonder if he'd walk any faster with the seat of his pants on fire. I keep staring at the street, willing the tow truck to appear. It should have been here by now. I should have commandeered the phone and called myself, made sure it was done right.

Jim is standing outside the office door, smoking and watching us. I don't for a minute trust that he's going to honor the agreement not to call the local newspaper. When Shadow saunters over and slouches in front of the machine, Jim leaves his sunny spot by the front door and goes over to talk to him. They are too far for me to hear what they are saying, and I don't like that, either.

My skin feels too tight for my body, my chest constricted, and it's hard to draw a full breath. Shadow nods at Jim and heads back our way, carrying a soda in each hand. One for himself and one for Ariel. My mouth feels suddenly dry and my resentment builds. One of these days, I'm afraid the pressure is going to make me explode, which will be messy.

For now, I get into the car and start the engine. It makes me feel better to have wheels. At least we're not sitting ducks. We have options. Ariel gets into the front beside me, leaving Shadow to his own devices.

After a moment's hesitation, he climbs into the back, handing a cola to Ariel. She snaps it open and drinks without a word.

In the rearview, Shadow looks sullen and bored. He's not playing with his phone, he's staring out the window at the car lot. We can't leave yet, though, because of the Death Car.

"You did call a tow truck, right? They're coming?"

"Yeah."

Jim could direct the driver to the car. Hell, he could even give them my contact information so they can bill me. But I don't want anybody else to have my contact information. And I don't want to use my credit card, not now that I've wiped out my savings.

Ariel's thoughts must be tracking mine. "Let's use my card to pay for the towing. Ricken will have kittens when that charge pops up." She giggles, and some of the tension eases out of me. She's recovering better than I would have expected. It seems like forever, but it's only about five minutes before the truck rolls in. The driver is all business and doesn't glance twice at me or Ariel, although his gaze lingers on Shadow. I peg the look as more of a you've-got-to-be-kidding disgust than any sort of recognition, though. He doesn't even ask questions about the junkyard bit, just nods and says he'll take care of it.

Relief floods through me as I pull away. Maybe Jim will keep his side of the bargain after all. Maybe everything will be okay.

***

We check out of our Yakima hotel and head back to Pasco. If Jim doesn't know where we are, he can't send any media hounds after us.

It's a quiet trip. Ariel falls asleep almost immediately. Shadow is busy with his phone, the sound of his texting a low-level annoyance that I drown out with the radio. We stop to pick up a take-out pizza and secure a room in a motel at the truck stop, just outside Pasco. It's not up to my Best Western standards, but for a lot of reasons, I prefer to be outside town. There's a room available on the ground floor where I can park the car right outside the door, which is perfect for a quick getaway if we need one.

Shadow digs into the pizza as soon as we're settled in, but he's the only one with any appetite. Ariel takes a hot bath and then sits, staring blankly at a TV show I'm pretty sure she's not watching. I fall into oblivion minutes after my head hits the pillow, despite the kids and the TV and the engine noise from the big trucks.

I wake to Ariel calling my name and shaking my shoulder. My eyes won't open, and I hear her through what seems like miles of sleep.

"He's gone." Her voice sounds panicked.

Nightmare, I'm thinking, as I fight against the weight of sleep. But when I manage to get my eyelids unstuck, sunlight floods in through opened hotel blinds. It's clearly not the middle of the night, like I'd expected.

Blinking, I sit up, pulling the blankets against my chest and glancing around reflexively for Shadow.

He's nowhere to be seen. Only Ariel, standing beside my bed with her hair all mussed.

"Where's Shadow?" My tongue feels like sandpaper and sawdust. There's dried drool on my cheek. Scrubbing at my face with my hands, I yawn and stretch, willing my sluggish brain to catch up with the program.

"That's what I'm trying to tell you. He's not here. I don't know where he is."

"Honey, take a breath. Maybe he went to get coffee. Or for a walk or something."

She shakes her head vigorously. "No, he would have told me. He doesn't go off like this."

"He did before."

"That was different. That was a huff."

"Well, maybe he's having another huff. He'll be back."

"His stuff is gone."

Now I'm wide-awake. "What?"

"His suitcase. Gone. His phone. His shaving kit." Ariel climbs into the bed beside me, too far away for me to hug her, drawing her knees up to her chest, shivering. "I don't understand."

"Did you guys fight last night? What happened after I fell asleep?"

"Nothing. He was quiet, but he's like that sometimes. I was really tired and he lay beside me while I fell asleep. And when I woke up—" Her voice breaks on a sob as she lays her face on her knees.

"Oh, honey. I'm sorry." I wish there was something else to be said. "Did you text him?"

That makes her stop crying. She lifts her head and fixes me with a watery glare. "If he wants to leave, he can leave. I'm not chasing after him."

"Good girl."

Despite her declaration of independence, she sounds forlorn and desolate when she says, "I guess you still want to go back."

Oh, I do. I do. But I don't want her to just quit, either. She needs to succeed in this wild quest, or at least know she tried. "Maybe we could take a little break," I say carefully. "Go home for a bit. Rest up. And then give it another go."

"Maybe." She sighs and lies back on a pillow, staring up at the ceiling. "Want to know who's next? Maybe you could at least tell me if he's another Bryce."

"Sure. I can't think of anybody worse, so maybe it will be another Timothy."

Ariel climbs out of bed and pads over to her suitcase, digging into the front pocket. Her hands come up empty, and she tries the main compartment. Still no book.

"Shit."

Clothes fly out of the suitcase in a mad scramble as she checks and double-checks. When she turns back toward me, her eyes are wild.

"He wouldn't," she says.

The fact that she's said it tells us both that she knows he would. With a sinking feeling, I remember the look in his eyes during yesterday's bargaining. Not shock or dismay, but a sharp interest. I'm out of bed in a heartbeat.

"Get dressed. We need to go."

"What? Why?"

"If he ran off with your book, it wasn't for any good reason. Media could be here any minute. We need to get moving."

Ariel just blinks at me. "He wouldn't," she says again, but her voice lacks any sort of conviction.

I scramble out of bed and into my jeans, pulling on yesterday's socks and hunting for my shoes, which have chosen this moment to go missing. Damn, damn, and double damn. We should have stayed in a big hotel. It would have been easier to sneak away. Here there's nowhere to go but out into the parking lot. We're sitting ducks.

My elusive shoes are in the bathroom. I have no recollection of leaving them there, or of taking them off at all. I run a comb through my hair, grimacing at my reflection in the mirror. I'm all makeup smears and wild eyes, but there's no time to worry about that. I scoop up Ariel's toiletries and bolt back into the bedroom, ready to throw it all into a suitcase and get moving.

Ariel is standing in front of the window, one hand on the pull cord. A block of light from the parted drapes turns her hair to white gold and casts an elongated shadow on the grimy carpet. She's still wearing her fuzzy sleep pants and a T-shirt with bunnies on it.

"Get away from the window and come get dressed! Somebody will see you."

She doesn't move. Doesn't turn. "Too late," she says.

My heart drops like a roller coaster, taking my stomach with it. Keeping to the edge of the room, I join her at the window, only making damn sure to keep myself out of sight. What I see is worse than any-thing my imagination was able to conjure on its own.

It's like a party out there.

When we rolled in last night, the parking lot was half-empty. Now it's full of cars and panel vans. I recognize call letters for affiliates all over the state. Tri-Cities. Spokane. Seattle. Reporters, all loaded with cameras, mix and mingle, drinking coffee and chatting. There's an argu-ment going on between two camera-bearing men in the prime front-and-center real estate, punctuated with gesticulating arms.

For a second, I hope they'll come to blows and the sharks will turn on their own.

And then I remember that Ariel is standing there in her jammies, for all the world to see. The fact that they haven't noticed her yet is a miracle. Maybe if I'm quick, I can get her out of sight. But even as my hand snakes out to grab her sleeve, the tableau outside shifts.

Heads swivel toward the window in unison, as if they're all part of one big organism instead of individual bodies. Coffee cups vanish. Cameras come up. I yank Ariel sideways. She stumbles, and before she can recover her balance, I drag her away from the window.

"What in hell were you thinking, standing there like that?"

She's gone flatline. Her hands are cold, eyes blank, face slack and unresponsive.

"Ariel! Talk to me."

My mother used to go away like that. It terrified me then; it terri-fies me now.

***

Callie sits in her booster seat at the kitchen table, whining and wretched. Her face is still crusted with the milk and cereal we both ate for break-fast and lunch. It's time for dinner, and we're both hungry and sick to death of cereal. Mother sits in her chair at the end of the table, cigarette burned to a long stick of ash, the live embers almost to her fingertips. She stares across the kitchen at the scuffed cabinets, unblinking. It's like she's sleeping, only her eyes are open. I'm frightened, but I know better than to call Dad at work.

"I want to eat!" Callie pounds a small fist on the table, and the cigarette ash trembles and falls apart, a soft cloud of gray dust. Mother doesn't even blink. What's left of her cigarette is going to burn her fingers. I move my hand to take it away and then stop, watching the red coal grow upward, waiting for pain to jolt her awake. Maybe then she'll see me again, will get up and make us something for dinner.

But when flame meets fingertips, she doesn't even flinch. Her eyes move down, slowly, and she stares at her hand as if it belongs to someone else, as if it's a mild curiosity like a caterpillar. I grab the butt away and drop it into the ashtray. It burns my fingers, and I shake them and pop them in my mouth. Blisters bubble up on Mom's index and middle fingers, but she shows no sign of pain.

I'm scared, and I don't know what to do. There's nobody to call who will help me. And so I do the only things I know how to do. I feed Callie and get her off to bed. And I leave my mother sitting there at the table until at last my father comes home to take care of her.

***

Now I'm all grown up, and I'm supposed to know what to do. But that same lost feeling nearly swamps me. Ariel stands inside the circle of my arms, neither pulling away nor seeking comfort. Tears pour soundlessly down her face. I can't reach her, and helplessness creeps into me from my toes on up. Maybe she needs a hospital. Grief does weird things to people, I know, but this seems beyond normal. I'm horrible at emotions, and I don't know what to do, other than protect her from what is outside that window.

I've already failed at that, but wallowing in failure won't help her, either. So I coax her back to bed and wrap her in blankets. She lets me, but I'm not convinced she even knows what her body is doing. I fetch a glass of water from the sink, so full of chlorine it stings the lining of my nose.

Her hands recognize the glass, shaping themselves to hold it, but she does nothing with it until I say, "Drink," and guide it to her lips. She swallows the whole thing, then lies down on the bed curled up into a comma, eyes closed but with those silent tears still sliding out from under her lashes.

In the distance, I hear a deep whomp, whomp, whomp in the sky. The sound tightens my belly, makes me want to take shelter under the bed. It's not until it stations itself overhead that I realize it's a helicopter. Ariel and I are worthy of a news chopper, as if there's going to be a big car chase or a shoot-out or something. I mean, the best thing they could hope for would be a glimpse of us running for the car from the hotel room.

THE CAR.

I had completely forgotten about the car. A car is good. If we can get to it, we can get out of here. My first glimpse out the window was too full of shock and alarm to register details, and I wonder if escape might be a real possibility.

I go back to the window and peer through a crack in the blinds, trying not to move them. The light is bright after the dimness of our unlit room, and I blink. There are more cars in the parking lot now, and a raft of pickup trucks. Many of the newly arrived vehicles look like they could have driven right off Jim's used-car lot.

The truck now wedging into an empty space is more rust than metal. The right fender is bent. A woman squeezes out through a door that slams against the neighboring car. She's wearing too-tight jeans and a T-shirt, a Seahawks cap jammed down onto her head. Her arms are full of flowers. She works her way out from between the vehicles to a space left clear by apparent common consent. There are already several bouquets of flowers there. A teddy bear. Hand-lettered signs that say, "Rest in Peace" and "God Loves You, Callie." All heaped around a poster-size picture of my sister.

With all of this going on, it takes me a minute to register the fact that our rental car is nowhere to be seen.

CHAPTER THIRTEEN

"I can't believe he told them where we are," Ariel says. "Maybe they followed him or something."

"Nobody followed him. He took the car!" I shout at her. "Now how the hell are we supposed to get out of here?"

My anger at Shadow transfers nicely to her. This was all her hare-brained scheme. If it wasn't for her, I'd be safe and warm back at Callie's house, reading through financial statements and dealing with the terms of the will. And Ricken. Her tears increase my helplessness, and that makes the flames burn even higher.

"Maybe somebody else stole it." She hugs a pillow, burying her face.

"Grow up, Ariel. Shadow sold us out, stole the car, and left us stranded high and dry. Sooner you face up to reality, the better."

"Reality sucks."

"Yep. But that doesn't change anything. He's gone, he's not coming back, and he's the reason we're now screwed."

She's shivering, despite the blankets. A sob escapes her, and she stuffs the back of her hand into her mouth to silence the rest of them. As fast as it came, my anger fades.

"I'm sorry." The words ring empty. Which is the way my chest feels, as though my heart isn't even there anymore. With a sigh, I sink down onto the bed beside her. "We should call the cops and report the car stolen."

"Please don't," she pleads. "He'll be back. You'll see."

"Honey, you have to let him go. He's not worth it."

She shakes her head. "You don't understand."

"Try me."

The tears spill over and flood her cheeks. "He's all I have left."

Her voice breaks. She buries her face in the pillow, both fingers knotted into the case, weeping as though her heart will break.

Jesus God have mercy.

When I reach out to stroke her hair, she doesn't pull away, and I dare to lie down and spoon behind her to give her my warmth. Her body tenses. I hold my breath, waiting for her to pull away, but instead she snuggles back against me, and I drape an arm around her and hold her until the sobs slow to an occasional shudder.

Her breathing settles, and I begin to think she's fallen asleep when she says, "He was my best friend. We rode the limo to school together. We hung out. He knows me better than anybody."

"A limo took you to school?" As soon as the words are out of my mouth, I know it's a stupid thing to say. All I need to do is look out the window to understand why she wouldn't be taking a school bus.

"Always. I thought it might be fun to ride the school bus sometime."

There's a spark of interest in her voice, and I figure talking is good. Any subject, anything, to move her away from tears.

"Callie and I walked. A lot. Mostly because I never could get her out of bed in the morning, and we always missed the bus."

She rolls over to look at me. Her eyes are swollen, her face all splotchy. "Where was Grandma? Why didn't she drive you? Or make Mom get out of bed?"

"Grandma was . . . sick. She wasn't usually awake before we went to school."

"Mom never did like to get up in the morning. But then she was usually out partying until late. I like morning. Everything feels new. Fresh. Like maybe good things will happen." I sense her thinking about Shadow again.

"Niles was okay before he was Shadow," she says, after a long pause that fails to be silence because of the helicopter noise. "He's really a super nerd. Which is cool. I like his nerdiness. But the kids picked on him, and then he met these goth kids and took Intro to Philosophy, and bam. Shadow. Like he got lost somehow."

"I'm sorry." The more I say these words, the more they feel threadbare and inadequate, but what else can I say? I've got no life advice to offer her on boys.

"Mom got lost, too, I think. She was around more when I was little. We did stuff, like finger paints and Barbies. And she used to sing to me."

"Did she?" I prop my head up on an elbow so I can see her better. "Like what?"

"I don't know the names. Weird old songs. There was this one about a little kid who wanted scarlet ribbons or something. And her mom couldn't get them for her. I forget. Only I remember lying in bed, sick, I think. And her hand on my forehead, and her singing to me."

My turn to roll flat on my back and stare at the ceiling, digesting this bit of information. My imagination is not up to the task of framing my sexy, popular, fashionista sister embracing this song. Dad used to play scratchy old vinyl albums over and over until I wanted to scream. The Browns. Jim Reeves. Tammy Wynette. If he was feeling modern, we got Dolly Parton and Kenny Rogers.

But when Callie was sick, or sad, or scared, it would always be the same request. "Sing something." And the old songs, so engrained in my memory, would come into my head first and foremost. I didn't think

Callie remembered. I certainly never dreamed that she would have sung the same old songs to Ariel.

"You could maybe sing something," Ariel says now. "Do you know the ribbons song?" Her voice is tentative, and she's staring up at the ceiling. I can feel her not looking at me.

"Yeah, I know it." The song is not a problem; it's me. How long has it been since I sang anything? In the car, in the shower, anywhere? I can't remember. This scares me. Once upon a time, singing was more natural than talking. Now the very idea sets my heart to pounding, the nerves in my hand to zinging.

"Now?" My throat feels like it's full of rust.

She doesn't answer. After a moment, she rolls away, leaving a space between us. I feel the cold creep into my skin where her body had been touching mine, and I reach for the memory of the girl I used to be. If I close my eyes, I can imagine being a child again. That this is my bed, and that it's Callie snuggled in beside me. This makes it a little easier to get started. I draw in a breath and manage to squeeze out the first line.

My voice doesn't ring true. I've picked the wrong key. I stop, my whole body thrumming with nerves.

"You do know it!" Ariel exclaims, with the most enthusiasm I've heard from her all morning.

"Of course I do. I used to sing it to your mom."

"Well, keep going, then!"

I clear my throat, shutting off my brain and letting my memory find the melody. "Send me, God, some scarlet ribbons . . ."

My throat closes and breaks. It's too much, this song. It carries too much of then and now, of everything lost. I'm the only one who remembers. The old record, and the whispering and giggling under the covers in the dark. The childhood I shared with Callie is no longer shared. There's only me.

And then a cold hand slides into mine.

Ariel. Maybe it's not all lost after all. We're connected by one old song, generation to generation.

"My dad had that song on vinyl. I bet the album's still around somewhere. You want me to find it for you?"

"That would be cool. Auntie Lise, I want—"

She's interrupted by a male voice trumpeted through a bullhorn.

"People—I know we are all grieving Callie's death. Thanks for coming out, and for bringing flowers for her. I know she's looking down and happy right now. Let's remember the gift she left behind."

Oh, no. I know what's coming before it happens. A squeal of a microphone, static, and then the opening bars of "Closer Home."

"Sing it," Ariel says. This time, there's a spark of mischief in her bloodshot eyes, and that dimple pops up in her cheek.

"No."

"Come on, Auntie Lise. Sing the fucking song."

"Watch your language, young lady."

She's out of bed now, dancing around the room as though she hadn't been half-comatose thirty minutes ago. She picks up a shoe as a microphone and starts to sing, mimicking Callie's stage schtick. Laughter shakes me out of tears. The music moves through me like quicksilver, head to toe and back again, and my lips start to move pretty much on their own. In a minute I'm singing, too, my voice free under cover of the noise outside and Ariel's antics.

A knock at the door stops us both in our tracks. Ariel's hand with its shoe microphone sinks to her side. Both of us stare at the door as if it's a living thing that might come after us at any minute.

I wish I had Dad's Colt .38, but it's back home, tucked into the top drawer of my nightstand. Or Dale's bulldog. Hell, I wish I had Dale.

"Pretend we're not here," I say.

Ariel rolls her eyes. "They saw me, remember? They're not that stupid."

We both creep up to the door, Ariel still clutching the shoe. Not a bad idea, and I grab the other one. If an intruder breaks in, we can bludgeon him with footwear.

"Don't open it," I whisper, loud enough to be heard over the still-blaring music.

The knock comes again.

Ariel stands on her tiptoes and looks out through the peephole.

"Who is it?"

"Like I would know? Some guy."

"Move. Let me see."

"Ariel? I'm your father," a voice says from the far side of the door. "Let me in so we can talk."

Ariel shoots me a look that is half hope, half panic.

I shove her out of the way. "Let me see." The man on the other side of the door looks like an advertisement for Joe Average. Medium height, medium weight, medium-brown nondescript hair receding from a high forehead. He's clean-shaven and smiling, white teeth glinting in the morning sunlight. I don't like him.

"Well?" Ariel says. "Who is it?"

"I have no idea."

"I thought you knew all of Mom's boyfriends."

"I did. It was a small school. I don't remember this guy."

"Maybe we should—"

"Don't you dare let him in! You'd better tell me who the others are. Then I can make a better guess at his identity."

She shakes her head.

"Ariel . . ."

"You'll ruin it."

"I think that's already been done."

Ariel puts her eye up to the peephole again, then calls out through the door. "What's your name?"

"Just let me in, baby girl, and we'll talk."

Ariel reaches toward the chain and I block her with my shoulder. She stumbles away from the door and I put my back against it, bracing myself. "You're not thinking! We cannot open this door. I'm willing to bet you a thousand bucks that man hasn't ever set foot in Colville and never met your mother."

"Then why . . ." Her voice falters as reality finally sinks in. "But Kelvin knew about the money."

"Kelvin's fan base is more important to him."

"Do you think Timothy . . ."

The look in her eyes reminds me that I still have a heart. How many hits is she going to have to take? "No. I don't think that at all. There are some good and decent people in the world, and Timothy is one of them. But right now we are up against the assholes. Understand? And that guy outside the door is part of the asshole clan, sure and certain."

"What if you're wrong? What if he was, like, visiting Colville or something?"

"Did her journal say anything about boys visiting? C'mon—you really need to tell me. It's time."

The music from the parking lot is becoming annoying. It's moved on from "Closer Home" to the new album, the one with a picture of that blasted horse on the cover. I want to scream at the top of my lungs.

But at least the knocking stops, and Ariel finally decides to cooperate.

"All right," she says. "I guess I might as well tell. There are only three others. Some guy named Hunter Brasswell or Braithewait. Arlyn Thompson. And, um, Grant somebody or other. That's it."

A shiver of relief runs through me. "Did you read the whole thing?" I ask, carefully.

"Yeah."

"Is there anything . . . about Dale?"

Her eyes narrow. "That guy from the funeral? Should there be?"

"No." I can feel the heat creeping up my neck and into my face. The more I try to stop it, the hotter I get, and I turn away to hide my face.

"Then how come you asked?"

"Because he took Callie to prom. The sharks are already onto him; if Callie mentioned him, there will be a bloodbath."

Her forehead creases and her eyebrows go up. "How would they know if she mentions him or not?"

"The diary," I say, as gently as I can.

"But Shadow has it."

I don't respond to this. I wait. She's a smart girl; she won't live in denial forever.

"Oh," she says, finally. And again, "Oh."

I wait to see how she's going to take this, dreading hysterics or, worse, a return to shocked immobility.

"I thought he only told them where we were and everything. You think he sold the diary?" She grabs her phone off the dresser, thumbs moving at lightning speed.

"What are you doing?"

"I'm asking him what he did with it."

"You think he's going to tell you the truth?" I find the remote and click on the TV. If he's sold the diary, there will be speculation all over the news.

"Jerk's ignoring me. Maybe we should call the cops after all." She slams down the phone, grabs her laptop, and flops onto the bed.

On second thought, I don't think that's a good idea. The last thing we need is to have the media taking pictures of a cop at our motel door. Hell, if I have to, I can buy the car from the rental people.

"Let's wait a little," I tell her, flicking through TV channels. Commercials on all the local channels. Dramas and comedies on the cable affiliates. I flick past a talk show featuring a man in a suit and half glasses expounding on something psychological, then flick back. A ticker tape runs across the bottom of the screen: "Ariel Redfern in Pasco Searching for Her Father."

"These children of stars," the man is saying, "are inevitably damaged by their parents. Generally, they are dragged into the spotlight at an early age and made to feel that they are the center of the universe. It becomes a rush, a fix. All children seek attention. Too much of it turns into an addiction to the spotlight, to the camera."

"That's bullshit," Ariel says. "Who is that idiot?"

"Apparently, he is Dr. Ralph Newcomb, Ph.D."

"Take this case of Ariel Redfern," he goes on. "It would appear that her mother kept her out of the spotlight quite effectively. As a child, we don't see her traipsing to the awards or put on display. And yet, here we see her engaged in this publicity stunt only days after her mother's death. In grief, the need for outside recognition and acknowledgment from the fan base overpowers the healthy desire for connection with family and friends. Also, one must ask whether her guardian is manipulating her at this point."

I hit "Mute," but it's too late. Ariel stares at the screen in horror.

"They think—they really think that's what I'm doing? That I want this?" She gestures toward the window, sweeping both arms wide to encompass the parking lot and everybody out there.

"Well, this guy does. But he's not everybody."

"I can't even . . ." Her cheeks are flushed. "Like I'm Britney Spears with that head shave thing? Ick. Ick, ick, ick. I feel slimy."

"He doesn't matter, honey. He's some pretentious asshat taking advantage of your situation to look important. Which makes him pathological. Not you."

"And you. Are you manipulating the situation, Aunt Lise?" Her voice falls into a mockery of the psychologist's weighty tones. She draws a shaky breath and her lip trembles. "I just wanted to know who my father is. I always wanted to know. And she wouldn't tell me. I never thought it would get all twisted . . ."

"Of course you want to know. Especially with her . . . gone."

"I wanted it to be an adventure. They've made it ugly."

"Only if we let them."

"But there's no way out of here without making it worse. Either we hide our faces like we're criminals, or we come out waving at the camera. Like we wanted this."

"Maybe they'll go away."

Ariel has her mother's withering expression down perfectly. "Yeah. And the Pope is Jewish."

The next channel shows the motel's parking lot. Vans, fans, helicopter, and all. They are dancing out there now. Cop cars have established a presence on the perimeter.

"Sooner or later, some other celebrity will do something that attracts their attention. Then they'll all go away and we can go back to normal."

"There's never been a normal. I don't know what that is. Besides, I'm hungry. We're going to starve to death in this scumbag motel."

"Do I detect a note of criticism there, young lady? Maybe I should remind you that this whole thing was your idea."

"You were supposed to stop me! No offense, but you suck as a parental unit. OMG, what an asshole!"

"Who, me?"

"No, Shadow. He's tweeting about me and Mom. I don't believe it." She taps away again, then squeals with outrage. "And he's posted on Instagram. A whole pictorial. Oh my God! I can never show my face again. Anywhere."

"Never is a long, long time."

But I feel the same way. My head hurts. I lie back on the bed and close my eyes, focused on breathing. Surely if we can just get through this day, the media circus will pack it in for the night. The fans must have homes to go to, kids and pets to tend. Then we can call a cab and get out of here without running the gauntlet.

My eyelids are heavy. Maybe if I lie perfectly still, I can fall back asleep and make this day go away. The bed dips down as a weight depresses the mattress right next to me.

"Seriously. You have to look."

I sigh and lever myself to a sitting position. "What am I looking at?"

"You don't know Instagram?"

Any response I might have given is washed away by the pictures. Ariel, pale and lost-looking at Callie's funeral. Me and Ariel at the airport. Ariel and Kelvin. Timothy and Dennis. The kicker is a picture of me leading Ariel away from the Death Car. We look like a modern-day version of women visiting the tomb on Easter morning, heads bent, clinging to each other as though we'll fall over without mutual support. In every one of them, Ariel looks fragile and ethereal. How the boy has managed photographs that capture real incidents and yet so widely miss the mark—her incredible strength, her resilience—is amazing to me.

Through his eyes and into the lens, I guess. This must be how he sees her. All the photos look familiar. Because I was there, I tell myself. Because I was living this while he was standing around snapping his pictures. Him and that blasted phone. But something about one of them nags at me.

"Wait, go back."

"Which one?"

"Me and Kelvin."

She scrolls up and pauses, her finger hovering over the mouse pad. "What about it?"

"Can you pull up the pic from the paper in Portland?"

Her eyes flash up at me, questioning, but her fingers are already moving. "You don't think?"

"Yeah, I do."

She brings up the newspaper photo, which is black and white, and lays it side by side with the one on Instagram. They are not just similar. They are identical.

"But that means . . ."Ariel doesn't look fragile or ethereal now. Every line of her body is energized. She picks up the phone, and I figure she's texting Shadow again, but this time she places a call.

"How dare you!"

Unintelligible words from the other end.

"How much did you pay him? Don't you lie to me . . ."

Not Shadow, then. I lean in closer to listen, and Ariel thumbs the "Speaker" button. Ricken's voice comes through, tinny but clear.

"Now, sweetheart, you can't begin to understand. It was done for your best interests—"

"Really? Turning my friend against me was for my own good?"

"We need to play this up, make the most—"

"You're a total creepazoid. And you're fired!"

He laughs, his condescension so thick I want to reach through the phone and strangle his skinny neck. "You don't run things, Ariel. Your aunt does, and she doesn't know enough about the finances to risk—"

I lean in, being sure to speak slowly and clearly. "Ricken? This is Annelise. Guess what? You're fired. I will not be signing your contract."

"You can't—"

"Can't I? I'll call Morgan and Genesis and tell them both. You're out."

Ariel hangs up before he catches his breath.

"Yes!" She gives me an enthusiastic high five. Both of us are laughing. But the elation seeps out of her like air out of a balloon. She pulls her knees to her chest to support the weight of her head. "All along," she says. "He didn't just grab the diary on impulse and then run off. He's been spying on us. The flowers, the chocolate, everything . . ."

There is, of course, a picture of that, too. Ariel with her arms full of red roses, the chocolate box open on the table in front of her. She's smiling up at the camera with adoration.

"I thought he loved me."

All of the charitable things I've been trying to tell myself about the boy and what could make him behave this way go out the window at the sight of what he's done. Anger seethes in my belly, stiffens my spine, wakes something in me that seems familiar and foreign at the same time.

The phone vibrates. Both of us lean in to peer at the screen. Ricken.

"Like I'm going to pick up, asswipe," Ariel mutters. A voice mail notification pops up. Then a text message.

```
Ariel. Let me talk to Annelise.
```

She flings the phone away from her and belly flops facedown on the mattress, burying her face in the pillow. I stroke her hair.

"We can't ever find my father now. We can't even leave the motel room."

"We'll find him. No way we're going to let that little schmuck and Ricken ruin this for you. Three left on the list, yes?"

She nods, head still buried in the pillow.

"And how many have popped out of the woodwork since the diary came out, claiming to be your father?"

She consults Google. "Five, looks like."

"Any of them actually on the list?"

She flips over onto her back and looks at me. "Not a one. Why are they doing this? I don't get it."

"Money. Notoriety. I know you've seen plenty of people grabbing after their little bit of fame."

"Yeah, I guess."

"Bring me your yearbook, or did he take that, too?"

"Nah, he only took the diary." She slides off the bed and fetches me the old book. It feels strange in my hands. I've never looked at mine; don't even know where it is. My old classmates stare up at me, frozen in time. Some of them are connected to memories; some I can't remember at all.

"Okay—give me the names of all the potentials who aren't on your mom's list and we'll see if they could have known her."

A quick search of the yearbook tells us that only one of the men claiming paternity went to school in Colville during the right time frame.

"Add him to the list. We'll hire somebody to go swab the four of them, okay?"

Ariel doesn't answer at first, busy clicking links. She stops. Stares at the screen. "Oh, shit."

"What now?"

"There are twenty new ones."

We've both had enough. Ariel slams the lid shut on the laptop. I click off the TV. It's only eleven o'clock, and there are hours of daylight left to endure. Somebody else starts knocking at the door, but neither of us bothers to look this time.

Ariel's stomach rumbles loudly. She giggles, then goes serious. "I'm really hungry."

"Maybe we could order in."

She bounces a little on the bed. "You think? I want pizza."

"Again?" I should be feeding her healthy meals, but my own stomach rumbles at the idea of greasy crust and melty cheese.

We look at each other, both silently weighing our hunger against the risks of opening the door for the delivery.

"I say yes," Ariel says, "only first I get a shower. Just in case. I'm not going on camera looking like I've spent the night in jail."

"Some jail if they let you wear fuzzy pajamas."

She sticks her tongue out at me and vanishes into the bathroom. I pick up the phone to dial the number on a pizza flyer shoved into the motel information binder. The kid who answers puts me on hold, and I sit there, staring at the locked door that connects to the next room over. And just like that, I have an idea. Maybe there is a way out of here after all.

I hang up on the pizza place and make three separate calls. One to the manager in the motel office. One to Melody Smith. Last, and hardest of all, I call Dale. It being middle of the day and all, I call his cell, holding my breath and hoping he's planning and not in the middle of cutting or framing. He carries a cell phone under duress, and most of the time he doesn't answer, especially if he's working.

But it only rings twice before his voice comes on.

"Who is this?"

"It's me."

"Lise. What the hell do you think you're doing?"

Typical Dale. No expression of worry or hint that I'm in over my head and a victim of my fate. He's clear that whatever mess I'm in is my responsibility.

"Where are you?" I ask.

"Why?"

"I'm in a spot of trouble."

"I noticed. I'm already on my way. Just passed the Connell exit and should be there in about half an hour."

My fault or not, he's always ready to bail me out, before I even get a chance to ask. Damn the man, he's too good to be real. My breath catches in my throat, and my body goes weak with relief.

"Lise? You there?"

I take a deep breath and try to steady my voice. "You obviously know what's going on."

"Kinda hard to miss it. Soon as I saw the news, I headed out." His voice is matter-of-fact and calm, but I can tell he's pissed. He's got every right to be.

"They've probably scoped your truck."

"I'm driving a rental. I can get to you okay. The dicey part will be getting you out of there."

"About that—I have a plan."

He snorts. "Considering what you've been up to, I'm not sure I want anything to do with your plans."

"Just listen." I tell him what I'm thinking, and he's quiet for a minute. I know good and well the exact expression on his face as he goes through every step, looking for flaws.

"Sounds as good as anything else. All right. So the manager is primed for this?"

"Yep. I promised her a thousand bucks. I think it will hold her. There's one more thing."

"Yeah?"

"I sort of promised Ariel a pizza."

He sighs, heavily. "Fine. I'm on it."

My fingers are clutching the phone so tightly my hand aches, and I try to ease them off. "I can't tell you how much I appreciate this."

There are so many things I want to say to him, but I can't. The words are frozen and won't pass my lips. *This means everything to me.* No. *You mean everything to me.*

He's so quiet I think maybe he's already hung up.

"Lise?"

"Yeah?"

"You could have called. At the very least, you could have called." And then the line is really and truly dead. I keep holding the receiver to my ear, like maybe he's still there, maybe he'll give me a chance to explain.

Ariel emerges from the bathroom in a cloud of steam. She freezes when she sees me, her face going pale beneath the heat flush.

"What happened?"

"Rescue."

"Then why are you crying?"

I put my hand up to my face, surprised to feel the wetness of tears. The receiver suddenly feels like it's full of lead and I hang up, in slow motion.

"Who was that?" Ariel insists.

"Dale."

"What did he do, cuss you out?"

"No, he's coming to get us."

"Then what's the matter?"

What do I say to that? I can't answer her; I don't have an answer myself. So I shrug, as if I'm the teenager and she's the nosy parent. Ariel narrows her eyes and gives me a long look. Then she nods wisely, and says, "He's your Shadow, isn't he?"

Honesty compels me to some level of truth. I shake my head. "No, it's more like I'm his."

CHAPTER FOURTEEN

There's no room in the motel parking lot. Dale finally parks next door at the truck stop. Nothing for it, they're all going to have to traipse from the room to the car. He can't imagine what the hell Lise was thinking that she didn't see this coming. Well, one step at a time. He takes a peripheral course to the office, avoiding the crowd as much as possible, balancing a pizza box in his arms.

Callie's newest album broadcasts loudly from speakers set up in the bed of a pickup truck. Her voice fills the empty space in his chest with a pain he doesn't have time for. Shaking it off, he opens the door to the motel office. A wave of overheated air wafts out, heavy with old tobacco smoke and musty carpet. He nearly collides with a young man exiting, coffee cup in each hand, cap embroidered with the letters KXLT pulled down over his eyes. He grins at Dale.

"Bet you never expected you'd be sharing a motel like this with a celebrity."

Dale plants himself in the doorway, exchanging a stare for the smile and counting to himself. About fifteen seconds, he figures, until the coffee heats through the cardboard and starts to burn. "Bet there's some sort of news in town more exciting than two women staying in a motel," he says.

"Aw, c'mon. With Callie's daughter looking for her dad and everything? Where's your heart, dude?"

Dale has one, and at the moment it's connected to his fists. He reminds himself that the satisfaction wouldn't be worth the cost. He lets the kid go. It's a relief to pull the door closed behind him. The music fades into the background. A coffee urn sits on a small table with a hand-lettered sign that reads, "Guests only. Help yourself." There's nobody in the small lobby, nobody behind the desk.

He rings the little bell and a voice that could be male or female calls out, "I'll be right with you." A long fit of coughing follows. Finally, a heavyset woman emerges from the back room, rolling a walker and dragging a portable oxygen canister like a dog on a leash. A sharp tang of fresh tobacco smoke accompanies her.

Dale tries to keep his eyes on hers, but his gaze keeps being distracted by her hair, which is a bright shade of magenta. Only one prong of her oxygen tubing is in the nostril where it belongs; the other has wandered onto her cheek.

"You sure you want a room?" she wheezes. "It's not going to be a quiet night."

"I'm sure."

"Hell of a thing," she says, settling down onto a rolling chair and scooting it over to the computer.

"Hurting business, is it?"

"Oh, I dunno about that. If it lasts long enough, most likely will. For now, publicity might bring me some curiosity seekers." Her words are punctuated by wheezes and clicks from the oxygen delivery system.

"I want a specific room," Dale says, as her fingers hit the keyboard. "Number twenty."

The woman pauses in her typing; her eyes, half-buried in fat, peer into his. She nods, and her chins wobble. "Your name?"

"Dale Elliot."

"Okay, Mr. Elliot. Ms. Redding set it all up, said you'd be coming. I've got the room key ready." Her gaze holds something other than curiosity as she hands him two keys. "They are in nineteen. This key is for twenty. And this one will open the door between the rooms. Can I do anything else for you?"

"Say a prayer, maybe." He's being flippant, but she nods, seriously.

"That poor lamb. Won't be the first prayer I've said for her. May the Almighty send down a curse upon those vultures out there."

"I thought they were good for business."

"Maybe so, maybe so. But business isn't everything now, is it? You take good care of that poor motherless child. And let the lady know I won't be charging her card for that second room, you understand?"

Dale turns back and smiles at her. "You are a good person. But there's plenty of money—"

She waves her hands at him. "Hush. That's between me and my Maker. It's not like you'll be using the room. But I would enjoy a piece of that pizza, if you're in a giving mood." She inhales deeply, which sets her to coughing.

Dale opens the lid and lifts out a slice, dripping with cheese. She holds out both hands for it and grins at him. "Debt paid. Now get on with you."

Keys in one hand, pizza in the other, Dale steps out of the office and back into the blazing sunlight, scoping out the most direct path to room 20. Reporters wait by their vans or lean against the trunks of cars, eyes trained on the window and door of room 19. People are dancing now, in a space cleared in front of the shrine.

He takes his time crossing the parking lot, blending in. It's surprisingly easy to do. He's got a baseball cap pulled down low and shades on. Nobody expects to see him here, so he's free to look around. A few friendly voices rib him about the pizza, asking for a slice. He smiles and keeps walking. With the music playing and people dancing, it's a little like the outdoor concerts he's been to at the Gorge, except that in this case, the performer is dead and there's way too much media here. A fair bit of weed is circulating. He can smell it, can see it in the laid-back facial expressions and loose-jointed moves of some of the dancers.

As he passes the shrine, he pauses. Callie smiles out of a life-sized poster, her eyes seeming to hold his, that half smile on her lips, one of amusement at his predicament.

Are we having fun yet?

He wants to reach out and touch her bottom lip, trace the line of the smile and trap it in his memory. Already she is fading. It's been a long time since he saw her, and he gets lost trying to remember exactly how long it's been. At her father's funeral, as near as he could remember. Ariel was just a little kid, all big eyes and curls. He'd had a short, inane conversation with Callie, mostly weather and small talk with a smattering of questions about her career and his business. Both of them avoided the topic of the little girl who had attached herself to Lise.

If he'd known it would be the last time, how would it have been different?

He startles at a touch on his arm, half-surprised when he turns to see a strange woman. Her hair is dark, her skin copper, her eyes big and brown. About as different from Callie as a woman can be, and yet her smile is familiar, a mixture of mischief and invitation.

"I know, love," she says, patting him. "You want something to numb you up a little." She holds up a bottle and he very nearly accepts it. There would be a surreal comfort in giving in to Callie's voice, drinking and dancing with this crowd of strangers.

"Not today, thank you." He starts to walk away, then is moved to turn back and kiss her on the cheek. She tastes of sweat and dust and something sweet. Her eyes follow him as he turns his back on Callie and works his way through the crush of bodies to the door of room 20. At the door he hesitates, just for a second, then turns the key and enters.

***

"You should take a shower before this Dale guy shows up," Ariel tells me, combing tangles out of her hair.

"I'll have one later." I'm tired; I'm hungry. Getting up off the bed feels equivalent to climbing Everest right now. At the same time, I'm pretty sure I'm a mess.

"Trust me. You don't want to be seen like this."

"It's only Dale."

He's seen me at my worst over the years. Early morning. Late at night. In the middle of a bout of the flu, surrounded by tissues and empty mugs of tea. But despite all of this, I feel a fluttering in my belly at the mention of his name, and lift my hand to my lips, remembering his kiss.

"Dale and anybody who ever watches the news. Or looks at a magazine. Or the Internet." She grins at me. "They'll make up a story to match how you look. Depression. Or alcoholism." Ariel plants her feet firmly on the carpet and tugs at both my hands.

Motivated by thoughts of headlines varying on the theme of "Alcoholic Breakdown for Mystery Guardian," I let Ariel drag me to my feet. Once I'm in the shower, hot water sluicing away not only dirt but also the ugliness of the last couple of days, weariness gives way to a difficult mix of anticipation and dread.

Seeing Dale is at once the thing I most want in the world and the thing I most want to avoid. It took years for the two of us to find our way back to a comfortable friendship after the prom fiasco. We never talked about my betrayal or how I felt walking into the room and finding him with Callie. We buried all of that emotional mess without benefit of a funeral or public grieving, and now here it is again, resurrected by Callie's death and the media.

The whole situation makes me want to lock myself in the bathroom forever. But when I think about Dale and Ariel having a private chat,

I slam off the water and grab a towel. I'm grateful for the steamed-up mirror. I don't want to see how I look after the days of grief and worry and ineffective sleep. Last time I caught a glimpse of myself, I didn't like what I saw.

But the look in Dale's eyes before he kissed me drives a set of emotional reactions I haven't experienced in years. Cursing both Dale and my own traitorous heart under my breath, I grab another towel and dry a clear spot on the mirror. I look old, I think. Old and tired. My eyes are puffy and red. The bathroom lighting gives my skin a greenish cast and emphasizes the fine lines and dark circles under my eyes. Callie looked better dead in her coffin than I do right now. A wave of injustice threatens to swamp me, the old jealousy busting out of the closet where I've stuffed it. Knowing this is stupid and wrong does nothing to make me feel better. I couldn't compete with her when she was alive, and now she'll be forever perfect in memory.

Makeup might help. But I've just opened the tube of foundation when Ariel knocks. "I think he's here."

"Already?"

"Well, there's somebody in the room next door."

Shit, shit, shit.

Dropping the towel, I grab my clothes, but my skin is still damp and it takes forever to work my way into my jeans. My T-shirt looks like I slept in it, which I did, but at least it passes the sniff test. I hear Dale's voice and Ariel's answering, but the bathroom fan drowns out the words. I attempt to drag a comb through my curls, but it catches and snarls. Unless I want to break half the hair on my head, detangling is going to be a long task. Remembering Ariel's reaction to Dale at the funeral, leaving the two of them alone is not going to be a good idea. Abandoning the beauty program, I check to make sure I'm fully dressed and open the door.

They stand with a pizza box between them, open on the table. Ariel's face is a study in wonder.

"How did you know?" she asks.

He smiles. "Callie's favorite. I took a gamble."

She grabs a piece out of the box with her hands, dripping sauce and cheese, and tilts her head back to cram the first bite into her mouth. "Maybe Lise is right about you," she says with her mouth full.

I step into the room before he can respond to that. "Hawaiian with white sauce, I'm guessing."

Dale turns at the sound of my voice. "You all right?"

I can't move, can't even breathe all at once. The room is too small, and there's not enough air for the three of us.

He looks tired. There's an expression on his face I can't decipher, something in the way he looks at me that is unfamiliar. Up until this moment, I would have said I know him better than anyone else in the world. Every line on his face, every scar on his body. The way he thinks, his favorite foods, and his opinions on people and politics. The two of us share a history more entwined than most lovers.

Now he feels like a stranger. Only a week lies between us, but my internal landscape has shifted enough to account for years. I don't know what to say or how to be. My knees feel weak and my legs start to shake. My skin heats from the inside out. Every detail of my appearance— from my uncombed hair to my bare feet—makes me feel naked, my shell cracked, my heart out in the open for all the world to see.

"We'll be ready in a minute," I manage, finally, as if he's a taxi driver come to pick us up.

"No rush. We've still got to figure out a way to get through that crowd." His voice sounds tight. There's a line of tension in his jaw that makes me think he's pissed. I can't blame him.

"I'm eating pizza before I go anywhere," Ariel says with her mouth full. "I'm starving."

"Where's the car?"

"All the way over by the office. Couldn't get through."

"I've got a plan. I think." I have to do something other than stand here looking at him, so I turn and start digging through my bag for a pair of clean socks. Of course, there is no such item. I choose the cleanest-looking pair and sit down to put them on, sneaking glances in Dale's direction.

He sits down across the table from Ariel.

"Have some pizza." She holds a piece out and he takes it, rewarding her with a smile.

I want him to smile at me like that. I want him to smile at me at all.

"You want some, Lise?" Ariel asks.

My stomach rebels at the very idea. "Thanks, not hungry."

It takes no more than a minute to pack, considering that the only belongings I've got are the few items I bought for the trip. Almost immediately, I regret refusing pizza because now I have nothing to do with my hands or my eyes and I can't keep staring at Dale like a lovesick teenager. There are things I need to tell him, an apology being top of the list, but I don't want to have that conversation in front of Ariel.

"You don't like the pizza?" Ariel asks me.

"It's fine."

Dale is still holding the piece she gave him. Bits of sauce and cheese have run down over his hand and onto the table. He startles and grabs a napkin.

"Sorry. Not hungry, either, I guess."

Ariel cuts her eyes from him to me and back again. "Oh for God's sake. Just kiss her already and get it over with."

"Ariel!"

She rolls her eyes at me. "What? The two of you are making me crazy."

"It's not like that . . ."

"Oh, come on. That picture of you two at the airport is worth a thousand words. Make that two thousand."

My cheeks are flaming. I'm going to kill her. Right now, I just need to shut her up. "You of all people know how the tabloids—"

"Oh, please. Spare me. That was not a photoshopped kiss, and don't try to tell me it was." She points at me. "You're all guilty because you think you dragged him into this mess somehow, only you didn't, that was Mom. And me. As for him . . ." She pauses to scrutinize Dale, whose face gives nothing away. "I'm not sure what his problem is, but he can't keep his eyes off you. Whatever it is, the two of you are ruining a perfectly good pizza." She closes the lid on the box and picks it up. "I'm eating in the other room. Use the bed, do whatever."

The door closes behind her, and the two of us are left alone. Now that Ariel has ripped the scab off, there's no way to skate along on social niceties or pretend that everything is okay. I swallow and clear my throat, searching for a safe thing to say.

Dale starts, and it's not kissing he has on his mind. "You want to tell me what this is all about?"

"Ariel was dead set on running off to find her father."

"And you thought this was a good way to track him down? Running a dog-and-pony show all across the countryside?"

"No. I thought . . ." My voice fades away into nothing. Beneath the weight of his anger, I can't clearly remember what I'd thought.

"You weren't thinking!" He's on his feet now, close enough for me to see a vein pulsing in his forehead. He seems bigger than I remember, all muscle and sinew and rage. I want to run into the bathroom and slam the door, but I hold my ground. I have to explain, make him understand what isn't even clear to me.

"I couldn't stop her, and I didn't want her to go off with Shadow. I figured it was better—"

"And you couldn't have called?"

"She wouldn't give me time to get my phone." This sounds lame, even to me.

"Of course. And there were no phones along the way. At the airport, or the hotel. You couldn't have borrowed Ariel's phone, or Shadow's, to let me know where you were and that you were okay. Come on, Lise. Tell the truth. You didn't want to talk to me."

I have nothing to say to that. He's right.

He raises both hands in frustration. "Do you have any idea how worried I was? Do you care? Or am I even on your radar at all?"

"Look, I'm sorry!" Traitorous tears fill my eyes and start flowing down my cheeks. I refuse to brush them away and force myself to hold his gaze. "I did call once. I couldn't . . . I didn't . . ."

His hands drop to his sides. "That goddamn kiss."

Too many emotions, too many thoughts. Before I can pick one, he draws a deep breath and turns away so I can't see his face. "I'm sorry, Lise. I took advantage."

This is worse than anger. I cross to him and put my hand on his arm. "Dale. Please don't. I . . . kissed you back."

"But it's why you didn't call."

"Okay, yes. It's why I didn't call. But only because I didn't know what to say, and then there was that stupid newspaper thing. I ran. I didn't know what to do, so I ran away."

He doesn't answer. Doesn't turn. His arm feels unyielding beneath my hand.

"Please," I say again, not knowing what I'm asking for. Desperation forces words out of me that I never meant to say. "It's not the first time. I ran before, at prom. I was confused and scared, but I wanted . . . I didn't . . . and then Kelvin asked and it was just . . . easier."

I hear him take a breath that sounds like a sob, but I know it can't be. Dale doesn't cry. I tug on his arm, and he lets me turn him around to face me. His eyes are wet, his breathing ragged, and the intensity of his gaze is too much. I look away, down at my sock-clad toes so close to his familiar sneakers.

He cups my chin in both of his hands, so warm, so strong, and turns my face up to his. One moment, one long look, and then he's kissing me again. Not gently this time, not with hesitation, and all of the things neither of us has said are in that kiss. It consumes me. It's love and anger and passion all unleashed. His hands shift and my whole body is pressed against his, my softness molded to his strength.

Through the tumult of emotion and sensation, a question rises in my mind. I try to shove it back; it's going to ruin everything, but it won't be silenced.

Dale breaks the kiss and pulls away. Both of us are breathing like we've run a marathon, and his fingers hold my shoulders so tightly it hurts when he asks, "What is it?"

"Callie," I tell him, watching his face. "We have to talk about Callie."

He flinches, as if I've slapped him. "Now?"

Before I can answer, the door to the adjoining room slams open and Ariel runs to the window. "Something's up. They're all leaving."

I detach myself from Dale and sink onto the bed in an attempt to hide the way my whole body is shaking. "Pack up. Looks like Melody bought us a window."

"Melody who?" Ariel asks.

"Paparazzi chick. The one who took a little swim in Callie's pool the other morning."

Ariel spins around. "And you talked to her? What were you thinking?"

"I didn't tell her much. But you are going to."

"I am not talking to any reporter!"

"You will, because that was the deal. She'll get us out of this motel, and you'll get a chance to tell your side of the story, just once, to somebody who will give you a fair shake."

Ariel's chin juts stubbornly.

"We'll discuss it later. For now, let's just get out of here, okay?"

After a long moment, she stomps over to her suitcase and scrambles everything back into it. "So, how'd she do it?"

"Check your Twitter."

She plonks down on the bed beside me and pulls out her phone. "She's posted a picture of us having lunch in downtown Pasco and says we've been spotted there—where did she get the picture?"

I grin. "Maybe I told her there was one on Shadow's Tumblr."

"Genius," she says. "But they're not all falling for it."

"And it won't be long before the rest figure out it's a trick," Dale adds. "Better make the break while we can. Either one of you have a hat or dark glasses?"

We both look at him blankly, and he shakes his head. "What kind of celebrities are you, anyway? I'll get the car. Be ready." Before he hits the door, he turns back and jams his baseball cap onto Ariel's head.

"In case," he says, and he's gone.

The room feels empty and I can't stop shaking. Ariel stands at the window, watching.

"What will happen to all that stuff they left for Mom?"

I cross the room to stand behind her. Without the crowd, the little shrine looks sad and neglected. A teddy bear wearing an "I ♥ Callie Redfern" shirt has tipped over and lies on its back, blank eyes turned up to the sun. Some of the flowers are wilting. Callie stares directly at me from her picture, smiling slightly.

"Come on, Ariel. Grab your bag."

She lingers long enough to raise my blood pressure, but at last she comes away, and we're both waiting in the other room when Dale drives the rental over and pulls up right in front of the door.

"Ready?"

Ariel nods, pulling down the brim of the cap to cover her eyes.

"All right, then. Here we go."

Pictures I've seen in supermarket tabloids flash into my memory. Stars at the beach with their cellulite exposed for the world to see.

Drunk stars. Crying stars. Botched plastic surgeries. I'm not a star, and this is crazy. I keep my chin tucked and my head down so anybody with a telescopic lens won't get more than the top of my head.

My window reconnaissance told me everything I need to know. There are still three panel vans, parked back behind the shrine, along with a smattering of other cars that could belong to guests but might be fans or paparazzi. Impossible to tell. None closer than fifty feet. I make a beeline for the car, a warm wave of relief rushing over me when my hand makes contact with the front passenger door.

I glance up for Ariel, but she's not there.

A frantic sweep of the parking lot shows her heading the wrong way, toward the shrine and not the car.

My vision goes into fast frames.

Ariel, head down, backpack slung over her shoulders.

A glint of light beside one of the panel vans. A camera. Click, click, click.

Two reporters pop out of each of the vans. More cameras. Car doors open. Reporters swarm toward us. I'm too frozen to move or even shout at her to *get back here now!*

Dale's door opens, and he's out of the car and running toward Ariel. The two of them converge at the shrine, the camera people only a few steps behind. He says something to her that I can't hear and she nods, running the back of a hand over her eyes. Dale grabs the poster of Callie. Ariel bends down and scoops up the teddy bear, cradling it against her breast like it's alive and wounded.

One of the reporters holds a microphone toward Ariel. "Such an outpouring of love for you and your mom. Does it give you any comfort?"

"How do you feel about your boyfriend sharing private information?"

"Is Annelise really your aunt? Was this her idea?"

Another zeroes in on Dale. "Sir, are you her father?"

Ariel tucks her chin down and says nothing. Dale keeps himself between her and the cameras, carrying the poster in one hand, his free hand on Ariel's shoulder steering her toward the car, making himself a shield. I hold the back door open for her and she climbs in, hiding her face in her lap. Dale shoves the poster in beside her and slams her door shut. Once he's safely back in the driver's seat, he hits the door locks and I breathe a little easier.

One of the idiots stands right in front of the car, camera to his eye, snapping away. Dale starts the car. The photographer doesn't move. Another one comes up and leans against the window, tapping on the glass with one hand while taking pictures with the other. Ariel covers the window with the bear, blocking him out.

Dale rolls forward until the bumper of the car must be touching the camera guy's knees, but he's still standing there with a superior smile, as if he's pulled a fast one on us. Dale's white-knuckled hold on the steering wheel and the murderous expression on his face say otherwise.

"Dale, no!" I grab at his arm, hard and unyielding as an iron bar.

The car rolls forward another inch, then stops.

The cameraman doesn't move.

Another inch.

The smile is gone now, but still he doesn't get out of the way.

Two more agonizing inches. In slow motion, the camera swings away in a wide arc as he folds forward at the hips. The car keeps moving and now we have a cameraman for a hood ornament. He's shouting, scrabbling with his whole body for traction. Dale keeps driving, turtle slow.

"Dale!" I shout at him. "What if he falls?"

"Won't hurt him at this speed."

"And if a tire rolls over him?"

"Then he gets what he deserves." He jerks the wheel to the right and steps on the gas. Fingernails screech on paint as the photographer careens across the hood and takes to the air. Peering back, I see him rolling on the tarmac, then climbing to his feet and brushing dirt off his pants.

Ariel squeals with glee.

I turn on her. "What the hell were you thinking?"

"I was just—"

"You don't want people to think you're playing along with the media, but a stunt like that makes everything that psychologist said look true. Do you hear me? Sometimes I actually know what I'm talking about!"

"Lise," Dale says, in a warning tone.

"Don't Lise me! You're as bad as she is." Anger heats my blood, and it feels damn good. I'm strong and capable and right, for once. The shaking is gone. "We had a plan. Get in the car. Drive away. How hard is that? My God! Have either one of you thought about how that little stunt is going to play out on the news?"

"She wanted the bear," Dale says. He pulls the car onto the street and turns left, heading for the freeway. His eyes are watching the rearview more than the road ahead, and that means trouble. I turn around to see a car following right on our tail with a camera-wielding woman in the front seat. Behind it is one of the panel vans.

Ariel clings to the bear, silent tears coursing down her cheeks. Callie stares at me from the poster propped up sideways on the backseat, as if she's lying down for a rest.

I clutch at my anger as desperately as Ariel holds on to the bear, but it's already giving way to remorse. I'm not sorry. I won't be sorry. Why oh why am I always the one in the wrong? No one says a word as Dale exits for the freeway and merges onto the bridge. Our entourage follows.

"Now what?" I say, finally. "I'm out of ideas."

"We'll keep driving." Dale is every bit as mad as I am. I'm not sure if any of it is directed at me, but one way or the other, if somebody lit a match, the whole car would explode in one fiery ball of emotion.

"We can't drive forever," I argue.

"You have a better idea?"

"We could fly . . ."

"You want to try the airport with that lot on your tail?"

I picture the Pasco airport. Outdoor parking lot, long walk to a single terminal. No, I don't. It's not that I have a better idea, I just don't like this one.

"I couldn't leave it there," Ariel whispers in the backseat. "It looked so . . ." Her voice fades to silence.

Dale shoots me a look. Yep. He's pissed at me. I'm not happy with myself, either. I turn to look at Ariel. "What do you want to do?"

"Can we go to Mars?"

"Be serious."

"I am serious. Where else am I going to go?"

"We could drive to Vegas, if that's what you want." Dale is watching her in the rearview mirror.

She shakes her head. "There's nothing there. I can't ever go back to school. Not after this. What's left? Ricken?"

"We fired him, remember?"

She chokes on a half laugh at that, and the corners of my lips twitch, despite myself, despite everything. But then her shoulders lift in a gesture that falls short of a shrug, and a perfectly matched set of tears well up in her eyes and spill over. "You see? There's not even Ricken."

Dale and I exchange a look. I know what he's thinking, and I'm not sure how I feel about it. But where else is there to go?

"How much gas have we got?" I ask him, as he exits onto the tight, curving on-ramp marked "Spokane."

"How strong is your bladder?"

"Depends how fast you drive."

Ariel leans forward to look out the front window. "Where are we going?"

I look out the window at the endless expanse of flat spreading to the horizon, already turning brown, and my heart surges at the thought of mountains and green, green trees. "Home, Ariel. It's time to take you home."

CHAPTER FIFTEEN

By the time we hit the roundabout that marks the south side of Colville, every muscle in my body is clenched tight. Even my toes are curled. Besides that, I really need to pee, and I look with longing at the Shell station as we roll on by, but there's no stopping now, not with the paparazzi still on our tail.

We lost the panel van at the gas station just past Spokane, and the Chevy at Spoko Fuel in Chewelah. But there are two cars still hanging in there, a little white compact and a dark-green sedan. Both have Nevada license plates.

Dale pulls out his cell and hands it to me.

"Best let my folks know we're headed their way."

"I'm not so sure about leading this parade up to their place." I glance at the cars trailing us. Mr. Elliot has a zero-tolerance policy for bullshit, particularly the type we've brought to town.

"Nowhere else to go. Best to give him a little advance notice, I'd say."

I dial the familiar number. It rings and rings, but nobody answers. There's no voice mail.

"Maybe they're not home."

"They're home. Where else would they be? They're just not bothering to answer."

Ariel leans her elbows on the back of the seat. "How come we don't go to Aunt Lise's house? Or yours?"

"Because we won't be able to get rid of these asshats at my place or Lise's."

"So you're taking them to see some old guy? What's he gonna do?"

"Trust me. He's not that old." In my mind I start thinking about all the things Mr. Elliot *could* do if he so chooses, and it does nothing to relax me.

Ariel makes the sort of noise that can only be made by a teenager. "You're old. And he's got to be a lot older than you."

This I don't bother to grace with an answer.

"Where's town?" Ariel asks.

"This is it." Dale rolls down Main Street, our entourage right behind him.

"Mom grew up *here*?" There's a serious note of disbelief in her voice. "There's like . . . nothing. Where's the mall?"

"There isn't one, kid. You can go hang out at the Walmart if you want." Dale swings left off Main. No light, no traffic, so the wagon and the sedan both stay right on our tail. Past the steak house and the feed store. Across the truck route and the railway tracks, and now we're moving away from town and across the flats of what was once a lake.

Despite everything, I breathe a little easier. I know this town. It's in my bones. Already I feel a little stronger, a little more hopeful that we'll figure things out.

"Gonna wish I had my pickup," Dale mutters a little later, when he turns off the paved road and onto dirt. A road sign informs us that "This Road Is Not Maintained," in case we weren't able to figure that out for ourselves.

I grit my teeth and brace myself. Mud season is not quite over, and the road is mostly ruts and puddles. Dale grew up driving this mess and expertly navigates the car, taking us around the worst of it. Ariel has gone very quiet in the back, and I imagine how strange this place must seem to a city kid. Evergreen trees form an unbroken wall on either side of the road. Mostly cedar here. There will be pine and fir farther up the mountain. I love the trees, but even I feel a little bit small and alone whenever I drive out this way.

"That's the worst one," Dale says, slowing to a crawl to navigate around a mudhole that takes up the whole road. He goes to the left where there's a little more solid ground. Ariel squeals as the right side of the car sinks. The tires catch and spin, sending up a wide spray of muddy water, but then we're through and back onto reasonably solid ground.

The white compact follows Dale's path closely and makes it through. The sedan is heavier and not so lucky. It sinks all the way to the right axle. The driver guns the engine, spraying mud and water everywhere. The car slides gently sideways until the whole thing is sitting in the mud.

Dale grins at his rearview mirror and keeps driving. "No cell service out here," he says. "Hope he enjoys the walk."

Only a few hundred feet farther on, we turn right into a lane so narrow branches scrape against the car. A sign on the right reads "No Trespassing." On the left, another one proclaims "Beware of Dog." We bump and jolt uphill and around a corner before the driveway widens into a well-maintained gravel yard. Seconds after we pull in, Mr. Elliot steps out onto the porch, a big black dog at his heels. With his long hair and graying beard, blue jeans and flannel shirt, Dale's dad pretty much looks the part of a mountain man. Especially with the shotgun in his hands.

Ariel gasps. "He's got a gun."

"At least it's the shotgun and not the AK," I mutter, looking around for the compact. It pulls in, so mud crusted it's now brown instead of white.

"Stay in the car," Dale says. "Hit the locks, Lise." He steps out and slams the door shut behind him, and this once I follow orders. Ariel slithers over the back of the seat and into the front beside me. Her face is pale, her eyes wide.

Dale stalks over to stand beside his dad on the porch. They nod at each other, but neither one of them says a word. The dog butts up against Dale but gets only a quick pat on the head and a command to sit.

Nothing else happens for a minute. Then the front door of the compact opens, and a man gets out. Wrinkled T-shirt. Faded jeans. He's wearing a baseball cap turned backwards and he's got a camera slung around his neck on a strap. His focus is entirely on me and Ariel. I turn my back and block her with my body. "Get down."

She slides down low in the seat, but not so low that she can't peer up through the window. I follow suit.

"Get back in your car," Mr. Elliot barks.

"Hey, man," the camera guy says, smart enough to stay put but not smart enough to follow orders. "She's got to talk to somebody, sooner or later. Might as well be me. Come on, one good picture and I'm out of your hair."

"You're trespassing." Mr. Elliot pumps a round into the shotgun. He now has Camera Guy's attention, but the guy's an idiot and still doesn't get it.

"Come on, old man. You're not really going to shoot—"

Mr. Elliot lifts the shotgun to his shoulder and sights along the barrel. Dale stands beside his dad, his face like stone. The dog whines. Ariel gasps and puts both hands over her mouth. "Seriously? He's just a shutterbug. They're scumbags, but nobody shoots them."

"Nobody's shooting anybody." At least I hope not. I've never seen quite that look on Mr. Elliot's face.

"I'd suggest you get back in the car and head on back to Vegas," Dale says. "Can't be responsible for what the old man's going to do."

"You're bluffing." But Camera Guy doesn't sound too certain. He glances over at me and Ariel, gripping his camera with both hands. "You shoot me, you're in big trouble. I'll press charges."

"Hard to press charges if you're dead."

I don't like the sound of Mr. Elliot's voice, but Camera Guy chooses to risk it. Keeping his car between himself and the porch, he circles around, bent low, camera ready, toward our rental. I push Ariel's head down and lean over her, screening her both from the camera and flying bullets.

It's just the shotgun, I keep reminding myself. *He's not going to kill anybody.*

And then, in a flurry of mad barking, the dog leaps off the porch and runs at the photographer. Ariel shrieks again and puts her hands over her eyes.

"I can't watch."

A laugh bursts out of me, and I pry her hands away. "It's okay, look."

Camera Guy shouts and runs for his car, pursued by a hundred pounds of barking dog. He stumbles and goes down on one knee. The dog is on him, licking his face with great slobbery swipes of a pink tongue. His enthusiasm and weight knock the guy off-balance, and he topples onto his side where he lies screaming, trying to cover his face with his arms.

Dale strides over and grabs the camera. "Now, I'm going to call off the dog and you're going to get in your car and drive away."

"Be dark soon. Heard the wolf pack out hunting last night," Mr. Elliot says, conversationally. "Do those magazines buy animal photos?"

"Give me back my camera. I'll call the cops!"

"And tell them you're up here trespassing? Besides, there's no cell service for a couple of miles, at least."

"Better get going. Your buddy in the mudhole is going to slow you down some," Dale adds.

Ariel looks like she's walked through the looking glass, her expression equal parts anxiety and wonder. "Are there really wolves?"

"No. They're messing with him."

"But there's no cell service?"

"The towers are blocked by the mountain and the trees."

She looks at her phone, pushes the screen with her fingers, then shakes it, as if that will fix it. "I can't even *text*?" Her voice rises on the last word, close to panic.

"They have this incredible invention here called a landline. Come on. I don't know about you, but I really need to pee."

Camera Guy is back in his car, vanishing down the driveway.

Ariel is still trying to work her phone as she climbs out of the car and I steer her toward the porch. "No wonder Mom ran away."

"Annelise," Mr. Elliot leans the shotgun up against the house and gives me a hug. He smells of wood smoke and trees, and my muscles begin to relax. "We were so sorry to hear about Callie." I let my head lean into the safety and strength of his shoulder for a minute, and then I remember Ariel and pull away.

She stands at the edge of the porch, wearing the same look on her face as at the funeral, an unmistakable cloud of *leave me alone*.

Mr. Elliot respects that. He smiles at her, but doesn't try to touch her. "You must be Callie's girl. Not much more than a baby last time I saw you. You've been having quite the adventure, I understand. Come on in: Pat will be delighted to have somebody to fuss over."

He opens the door for us and bellows: "Patty! Company!"

No matter how many times I've been in this house, I always have a moment of disorientation when I come through the front door. Outside, it's a tin-sided pole building like hundreds of others around here. Inside, master craftsmen have been busy at work. The wood floors are aged barnwood, lovingly sanded and stained. The rafters are made of logs, polished and varnished to a warm glow. Each piece of furniture is handcrafted and unique. From the sitting chairs to the cedar siding, all of it is the work of the Elliot men.

Mrs. Elliot emerges, wiping her hands on an apron. Her round face lights up like Christmas morning, and she rushes over to envelop me in a hug. Where her husband is hard lines and reserve, she is all softness and warmth. She smells of cinnamon and sugar. One whiff, and a rush of longing wells up into tears that I can't hold back. I try to picture my mother baking cookies and doling out hugs, wonder about how things might have been for me and Callie if she had been different.

The warm arms squeeze me a little tighter, and a soft hand smoothes my back. Then Mrs. Elliot releases me and turns to Ariel and wraps her in an embrace. Ariel stands stiff and unyielding, her eyes wide with alarm. But then, slowly, her arms come up and she hugs back.

Mrs. Elliot releases her but lays her hands on both sides of her face, turning it one way and then the other. "You don't look like your mother, God rest her poor soul. Nor like your grandparents, either. Must take after your dad's side of the family."

Dale intervenes. "Mom, give the poor child a break. It's been a hell of a day. No rest stops between here and Pasco."

"Oh my goodness. You two head straight on back to the restroom, then. Annelise, there's one in the master bedroom, so neither one of you has to wait. I'm sure you're starving; I'll get the food on the table. You'll stay for dinner?"

"I think maybe they ought to stay longer than dinner, what with those reporters snooping around," Mr. Elliot answers.

Dale starts to say something, but I don't linger for more conversation. After directing Ariel to the main bathroom, I head toward the back of the house. Through the living room, with its high ceiling and skylights, every window looking out onto blue sky and green trees. Into the bedroom with its massive four-poster bed, handcrafted out of polished logs. And finally, the bathroom. I take my time, splashing cold water over my face, trying to smooth my crazy hair with my fingers.

On my way back, a picture in the hallway between living room and kitchen stops me in my tracks. Right in the middle of the family photo gallery hangs the tabloid picture of me and Dale kissing. It's been neatly cut out and framed and hangs between Dale's high school and college graduation photos. My heart takes up residence in my toes while my face heats from the inside out. I want to lock myself in the bathroom and never come out.

How am I going to explain the truth to Mrs. Elliot when I don't know what it is myself?

My feet drag me back to the front room. Dale is introducing the dog to Ariel. She sits ramrod stiff on the edge of the sofa, the big dog sitting in front of her, not more than a foot away.

"Ariel, this is George," Dale says.

She lifts her hand and moves it toward the dog, then draws it back. "Won't he bite?"

"Are you kidding? Did you see how he was attempting to lick the reporter guy to death?"

He's rewarded with a giggle. "I've only ever seen little dogs. They barked. One of them bit me."

Dale makes a dismissive noise. "Those aren't dogs. They don't count. Go ahead, say hello. He's going to get his feelings hurt in a minute."

George whines and stretches his head out toward her, sniffing. Ariel tentatively reaches out to touch the top of his head, then slides her hand down to his ears. Taking this as an invitation, the dog surges forward and takes a long pink swipe at her cheek.

Ariel flings her arms around his neck to keep herself from falling over. George starts snuffling at her face and arms, taking her in, and she clings to him, laughing now. Dale is laughing, too. He looks up and sees me watching and the laughter fades, replaced by a guarded quiet that's like a knife to my heart. We need to talk. This wall he's put up between us is damn near unbearable.

"Your mom has some new artwork in the hallway." The words come out before I'm sure I want to say them.

"You noticed."

"What did you tell her?"

"Nothing."

I don't know what to say to that. We're in some sort of weird space betwixt and between. Not lovers, not friends. Those kisses demand answers, and neither one of us seems to have any. Callie looms, larger than life. I don't need to say her name; I know she's there for him, too. And it's her ghost that keeps me from crossing the space between us and stepping back into his arms.

Mr. Elliot rescues us. "Grub's on. You all coming?" He smiles at Ariel and the dog. I'm pretty sure that his sharp gaze hasn't missed the tension between me and Dale, but he ignores it. "You want to give George his dinner?" he asks.

At the magic word, the dog abandons Ariel and trots over to sit at his master's feet, his tail thumping loudly on the floor.

"Sure." Ariel follows the two of them out of the room.

Dale looks like he's going to say something, but then he turns and heads for the dining room. Dinner is meatloaf and mashed potatoes, apple pie for dessert. All this, and she never knew we were coming.

Ariel eats like she's never seen food before. I alternate between ravenous hunger and a lump in my throat that makes it hard to swallow even one bite.

"I hope that camera guy won't give you any more trouble," Mr. Elliot says, swallowing the last bite of his second piece of pie and shoving his chair back from the table. "Can't believe he followed you all the way up here."

"We're just lucky there aren't more of them," Dale answers. "Wasn't easy getting away from the motel."

"Why don't you and Ariel both stay here?" Mrs. Elliot asks, smiling at me. "So much safer than your place in town. And now that you and Dale are finally together . . ." She actually clasps her hands, looking from one to the other of us and beaming. "I've always thought of you as family, Annelise. Callie, too, of course. Even when you were wee little things, I always thought one of you would marry Dale."

Ariel pauses with her fork halfway to her mouth, eyes flickering from Mrs. Elliot to me to Dale. I barely manage to keep my gaze focused on my plate, dissecting a bite of meatloaf as if it's the most important action in the world.

I can't say it's all a lie. I don't know what it is. My feelings are all over the map and not to be trusted.

"Mom," Dale says. There's a warning note in his voice, something close to a growl. She just smiles at him indulgently, like he's six.

"Oh, of course. Likely you're not talking about marriage. But that's okay. Annelise is still welcome to stay. There's the couch. Or, modern times being what they are—"

"I really need to check on my place," I break in. "I've been gone for over a week. Just want to make sure everything's okay."

"I'll drive you home," Dale says.

This was not precisely what I had in mind. My stomach twists and flutters, and there goes the rest of my appetite.

"You've hardly touched your food," Mrs. Elliot clucks, shaking her head. "Poor child, you must be exhausted. And Ariel almost falling asleep over her plate. We need to get you both squared away, get some rest. Ariel can sleep in the loft. Are you absolutely sure you won't just stay here, Annelise?"

"I need to go home," I say, quickly before she can suggest again that I share a bed with Dale.

"Oh, but honey, you must be so exhausted. And those picture people . . ."

I want to point out that those picture people took the photo she's got hanging in the hallway, but I keep my mouth shut for once. "I've been living out of a suitcase for a week. I really just want to go home."

"I'm going with you." Ariel's eyes are at half-mast. She looks a little dazed, but I recognize the stubborn set of her jaw, the way her lips are compressed. Uncanny how Callie's moods can show up on such a different set of features. It's probably safer for her here than in town, but I'm too tired to argue.

Dale sees it, too. He pushes back his chair. "I'll take you both. Thanks, Ma." He drops a kiss on his mother's forehead. "Guess Dad will have to help you with the dishes."

"Take my truck," Mr. Elliot says. "You can do something with that car in the morning."

"Hopefully, the idiots aren't blocking the road and we can get through." Dale looks at me. "You wanna take George? He'll make intruders think twice."

"Yes," Ariel answers for me.

At the mention of his name, the dog gets up, stretches, and pads over to the table, snuffling around beneath the chairs for crumbs before settling down beside Ariel's chair for her to pet his head and scratch his ears.

"Dog's not allowed at the table," Mr. Elliot says, but not like he means it. His face softens every time he looks at Ariel.

Half an hour later, my plan to get away alone for the night has been thoroughly shot to hell. George rides in his accustomed spot in the back of the pickup. Ariel has the window seat, and I'm crammed into the middle, feet straddling the hump and the stick shift. The truck smells of wood and engine grease, familiar and comforting, but I'm anything but relaxed. I'm only inches away from Dale. His strong hand rests on the knob of the gearshift, so close, yet so out of my reach. Every time he shifts gears, his arm brushes against mine.

My hands keep knotting into fists. I consciously relax them, but a minute later they're all curled up again. Dale's window is cracked open, even though the night air in May is cold. It makes me shiver, but I don't mind. I feel like I'm suffocating, and the sweet green smell of spring helps, a little.

"So what are you going to tell her?" Ariel asks.

"Who? About what?"

She doesn't accept my deflection. "Mrs. Elliot. About the two of you."

Dale doesn't answer. I risk a glance in his direction and don't know what to make of the hard line of his jaw or the way his eyes are fixed on the road.

"Nothing," I say finally.

The truck rocks through a mess of deep ruts, throwing me hard against Dale's shoulder. It takes a minute to right myself. I can't stop thinking about that last kiss or worrying about the distance between us now.

Dale slows the truck to a crawl as the giant mudhole appears in the sweep of the headlights.

"Looks like your friends weren't wolf food after all."

No more stuck car, but a mess of tire tracks remains as evidence that the tow truck came and went. My relief surprises me. Both that the camera guys are gone from here, and that they're probably both okay. Death doesn't need any more victims.

"Are there really wolves?" Ariel asks again.

"Rumors of them," Dale answers. "Haven't heard them howling or seen any myself."

"What else is there?" She sounds like a kid who has heard too many ghost stories around a campfire, and I suddenly see this road through her eyes. Deep darkness like she's probably never seen before in her city world. Nothing illuminated but a sweep of rough dirt road and thick trees.

"Deer," Dale says, missing the tremor in her voice. "Bears, mountain lions, coyotes."

"Mostly deer," I tell her. "Especially in town. Be more worried about the paparazzi than the wolves."

She relaxes, little by little. By the time we turn onto the smoothness of pavement she's asleep, her head leaning against the window. Dale drives my street twice, end to end, looking for suspicious vehicles. Sure enough, a very muddy white car with Nevada plates is parked across the street and down a ways, as far as possible from the nearest streetlamps.

"You can't stay here," he says. "They'll never leave you alone."

"Hard to take a picture in the dark." My voice sounds calm, but my insides are quaking. I can't make the shivering stop, even with my arms wrapped tight around my chest to hold myself together. The nerve thrills in my left hand are close to pain. *They're not going to hurt me*, I tell myself. *It's just pictures.* But they have already turned my world upside down. I squeeze my eyes shut to make the car go away, but behind my lids I see all of the cars and panel vans from the motel blocking my street, cameras flashing.

"You have keys to the old house?" Dale asks.

I nod, not trusting my voice. "Fingers crossed they're not onto that one yet."

Dale drives to the end of the street, takes a left, and heads across town. No headlights follow us. Everything is quiet and peaceful, but then so was the motel in Pasco before we fell asleep. My head aches deep behind my eyes. Resentment toward Callie rises up until it feels like it's going to choke me.

She got me into this. And it's looking like there's no way out.

The street in front of the old house is empty. There's a car in the driveway at the Stillwells', but it's an old, familiar Subaru with Washington plates. Lights glow behind drapes up and down the street. Most of my neighbors have been here for as long as I can remember. Some of them watched me and Callie grow up through their living-room windows. Good people, but they hold a new level of threat for me. Every one of them will want to hug me, talk about Callie, ask about the funeral.

As for the house, it's in a sad state of limbo. There's a "For Sale" sign up on the lawn. Mom's been in the nursing home for a year now, and the sign has been up nearly that long. My realtor tells me it would sell if I'd just lower my price. I know he's right. I know a house shouldn't be empty, but the thought of facing up to the memories and emotions packing up will trigger is too much for me. Even Callie's belongings haven't been touched since she moved out sixteen years ago. One of my students cleans the place once a week. I've hired another to mow the lawn in summer and shovel snow in winter. I swing by on Tuesdays and Thursdays to check on things, flush the toilets, run the water, but it's still looking neglected and empty. An abandoned house gets to feeling sorry for itself, Mr. Elliot always says.

Dale gets out of the truck and opens the tailgate for George, who bounds out and starts investigating the yard with his nose. Ariel wakes up, her cheek reddened, a line indented into it. Her eyes are still dazed and she moves like a sleepwalker. The front door sticks, like it always does. Dad planned on fixing it but never got around to it.

Ariel sways on her feet, and I put an arm around her shoulders to steady her. "We need to get you to bed."

I walk her upstairs and tuck her into Callie's old bed. George flops down on the floor, chin on his paws. When I invite him to come back down with me, he thumps his tail politely but declines to move.

Dale is waiting by the front door.

"You know that dog is going to end up in the bed," he says. "Not sure about his status with fleas."

I shrug. "Seems maybe she needs something more than a teddy bear. Thanks for bringing us."

Dale puts a hand on the doorknob. "I think you'll be safe here. If you have any problems, call one of the neighbors. Wait, you don't have your cell."

"Landline is still hooked up."

He gives me a long look. "It's been a year. You're still paying that?"

I shrug but don't meet his eyes.

"Gonna be even harder now to let it go."

"I keep thinking maybe I'll move back in. It would make financial sense."

He shakes his head. "Sometimes holding on to things isn't the best idea. Make sure you lock up tight. And don't worry about Mom, I'll talk to her."

A couple of hours ago, this is what I thought I wanted. Now the only thing I'm sure of is that I don't want him to go, but I can't ask him to stay. So I do something I never thought I'd do. I cross the space between us and kiss him.

His lips answer mine, but his body remains rigid and unbending. His arms don't come up to hold me. When I pull back to look up at him, his eyes are misery. He swallows hard, then shakes his head.

"I'm sorry."

"Dale . . ."

"I shouldn't have kissed you that first time. Opened up a whole big can of worms."

The world spins around me, but I dredge up a shaky laugh from somewhere. "It's not like I objected."

"I can't do this, Lise. All these years . . ."

I don't know what to say to that, so I say nothing. The silence stretches until breaking it feels like it's going to take an act of Congress.

Dale's the one who finally breaks the silence. "She's here. She's everywhere. In your head. In mine. Every time I look at Ariel, I . . ." His voice breaks and he turns his back on me. "Make sure you lock up tight. Windows, too."

I stare in disbelief as the door closes behind him. *You can't walk away from this. From me. You started it!* Everything peaceful and happy as friends, and then he has to go and stir it all up again. *It's not fair!* I know I sound like a child. Fair has nothing to do with this. Maybe he's loved her all these years. I don't know. So what the hell was that kiss about?

Tears well up, but I'm sick to death of them and I brush them away. I'm so exhausted I can barely keep my eyes open. Things will look clearer in the morning, after a good night's sleep.

I climb the stairs without turning on a light. There's no need. My body knows them by rote. Our old bedroom hasn't changed much since Callie left. I never moved the beds or the dressers. I've grown used to her absence over the years, but tonight her memory is everywhere. Enough light from the street seeps in through open blinds to make the two twin beds visible, and the blanket-wrapped body in Callie's stops me cold in the doorway. Exactly how she always slept, wrapped up like a giant burrito with her feet hanging out. When she was little, sometimes I would unwrap her head and put the blanket over her properly, but an hour later she'd have wriggled her way back to the way she started.

George lies across the foot of the bed. He looks up at me and his tail thumps twice, but he doesn't offer to move.

It's Ariel. Callie's dead. But my heart keeps fluttering. My hands feel like ice. Step by slow step, I cross the room. When I peel back the blanket, I half-expect to see a ghostly, moldering Callie, but it's Ariel's heat-reddened face and blonde hair on the pillow. She mutters something unintelligible and rolls onto her belly. I replace the blanket over her head, and she settles with a long sigh.

Moving across the floor, I crawl into my old bed without bothering to take off my clothes. The mattress sags in the middle. The springs creak when I roll over. The sheets smell dusty. I'm so tired that none of it matters, my limbs molding themselves into the old sleep posture that fits this bed.

But my heart continues to beat so hard I can hear the blood whooshing in my ears, and that internal quaking is going on again, a tremor so deep I can't touch it. Memories swirl around me in dizzying intensity. Callie begging for bedtime stories. Me singing her to sleep when she was sick, worried about her fever. The two of us standing dead center, shouting at each other over points of contention: dresser territory, her clothes scattered all over the floor, the latest theft of my favorite shirt and earrings.

And then, inevitably, there is Dale. Memory shows him sitting on the window ledge, face flushed, pupils dilated, with Callie standing halfway across the room wearing next to nothing. I'd burst in seeking refuge from the most disastrous night of my life. And there they were, the only two people who really mattered to me in the world, completely wrapped up in each other. In that moment, the knowledge of what Dale meant to me came flashing down like a message from God on high.

Rolling over in my childhood bed, burying my face in the pillow, does nothing to make the memories stop. Grabbing the pillow and blanket, I tiptoe out of the room and retreat to the living-room couch downstairs. It's comfortable enough for my weary body, which settles into the familiar hollows with a sigh of satisfaction. But my brain still refuses to cooperate. My eyelids pop open, and a jumble of worries mixes in with the memories. Ricken is probably stealing everything from Callie's house. I should be there to make sure he's gone, to let the attorney and the agent know he's out of the picture and has no authority. I should go through the bank accounts, the properties. How am I going to get my mind wrapped around all that? What about the paparazzi? And is there any way to help Ariel find her father with all of the fakes coming forward to complicate things? Dale is a constant in every one of those threads. And my anger at Callie surfaces over and over again, wrapped up in a web of bitter grief and guilt and failure. I roll from side to side, punch the pillow a time or two, and finally give up on sleep.

I wander around the room, picking up items and putting them down. Mother's old china dog. The pillow I cross-stitched for some school project that was inexplicably kept around, probably because neither of my parents knew what to do with it. Crossing to the double bookcase, I let my fingers trail across the spines of books that have been occupying those shelves since before I was born.

There's nothing in the fridge, but I have been known to store things in the freezer, and I score a half-eaten pint of Ben & Jerry's. Fetching a spoon, I carry the container with me to look out the kitchen window at the little park across the street. The last time I sat on the park bench reading a book and letting the spring sun warm me, Callie was alive, my feelings about Dale neatly contained, my future set.

The ice cream sits cold in my belly, the lingering sweetness on my tongue already turning bitter. Without thinking, I drift across the room to my old piano. It's an ancient upright, already battle-scarred when Dad brought it home. I haven't had it tuned in a couple of years, and guilt over its neglect adds to my already overwhelming emotional cocktail. Sinking down on the bench, I let my hands rest lightly on the keys. They feel faintly gritty; Kelsie has been slacking on the dusting. The A key is chipped, thanks to Callie dropping a paperweight on it.

I'd been furious about that, had chased her down and spanked her, using the advantage of weight and fury to wreak my vengeance. She'd retaliated by tearing up my math homework. But she'd left the piano alone. Even then, we'd both agreed that music was sacred territory.

If I'd been smarter, kinder, more tolerant, maybe things would have turned out differently between us. Anger rises out of the guilt, as it always does. Of all of the things she's taken from me over the years, including Dale, the one that hurts the most is music. When "Closer Home" hit the charts, when I heard her voice on the radio and saw her on TV singing my song, it choked me. I would sit down to sing, and my voice would crack and break and turn into coughing. My fingers sat idle and silent on the keys. No more tunes popping into my head from out of nowhere. No writing songs. No singing. No playing for the sake of letting the music flow out through my fingers. For a time, I took refuge in technical studies, playing scales and broken chords over and over, striving for ever-greater speed and accuracy. I skipped a day. Then another. A month went by. Then a year, and another.

Teaching lessons makes it easy enough to hide the block. I can direct fingers and voices, set assignments, arrange recitals, without ever dipping into the music myself. None of my students know. Dale used to ask, every now and then, if I'd written anything new. But maybe he figured it out, because somewhere along the way, he stopped asking.

Now, in the dark silence of the old house, with Ariel asleep in Callie's bed and all my ghosts alive to haunt me, I set my fingers over the worn piano keys. Weariness steals over me and I just sit there, fingers resting on the keys, moving in and out of the edges of sleep. My head nods and I catch myself, open my eyes. They drift closed again.

"Coward," Callie says, sitting beside me on the bench. She smells of shampoo and floral spritzer. She's wearing my angora sweater. Her sudden appearance doesn't surprise me; I already knew she was here.

"I'm not scared."

"Then why did you stop playing?"

I trace the jagged edge of the broken key, then depress it so slowly the hammer nudges against the string without a sound. "Why did you steal my song?"

"You weren't using it."

"It was mine! You had no right."

She laughs softly and kisses my cheek. "Silly goose. Music is like air. It belongs to everybody."

The laugh, the kiss, are so real my eyes fly open. But the bench beside me is empty. I know ghosts don't exist, that this whole conversation is happening inside my head. So why do I still smell her fragrance and the pressure of cool lips on my cheek? I want to shout at her to get back here and finish this conversation, but if I do that I'll be crazy for sure. Panic beats against my ribs. Maybe I am losing my mind. Maybe I'm imagining this whole thing. Or maybe she's alive and well somewhere, and I'm having some psychotic episode or crazy dream.

Only the familiar keys beneath my hands save me from a full-scale panic attack. They anchor me, ground me. I depress the broken key again, this time a little harder. One clear tone hangs in the air, A440, only a little flat.

I was born with perfect pitch, which is both gift and curse. A certain vibrational frequency produces a certain tone. When it rings true, I feel a sweetness deep at the center of me. The tones can be managed, arranged, organized.

Which is a very different thing, really, from music.

My fingers move into a scale; slow, uncertain. A chord progression, still tentative. Asking something. The vibrations, the tones, are predictable and constant. It's the music makers who are random.

"They're really not predictable at all," Callie's voice says. It's distant now, no longer beside me on the bench. "Don't you see?"

All I can see is that my world is a mess. My fingers stumble on a progression and I close the lid. This time when I lay down on the old couch, sleep is waiting, and I'm mercifully conscious of nothing.

CHAPTER SIXTEEN

Somebody is shaking my shoulder. "Wake up."

"Go away." I roll over, pulling the blanket up over my head, trying to retreat into the warm bliss of nothingness.

"I'm hungry."

"Eat some cereal."

The hand shakes me harder. "There isn't any cereal. There isn't *anything.*"

Not Callie. Ariel. Reality pours in. The paparazzi. Dale. The old house. I burrow deeper into the sofa, wanting more than anything to escape what the day holds in store.

"If you weren't up playing the piano in the middle of the night, maybe you could actually wake up in the morning." Ariel strips the blanket off me, and there's no more hiding from the light. A cold nose pokes into my ear, snuffling, followed by a warm tongue slathering across my cheek.

Ariel giggles. I sit up and pet George's head, mostly to hold him back from more licking. The piano feels like a dream, but if Ariel heard it, then it was real. Not the Callie part, that can't be. But still, the memory of her voice and that butterfly kiss are as physically solid as the sensation of my hands on the keys.

"What are we going to do about breakfast?" Ariel asks. "How do we get anywhere? You don't have a car."

These are all good questions. I do have a car, in fact, but it's parked at the Spokane airport, a two-hour drive from here. My place is a couple of miles away. And I'm not asking any of the neighbors for breakfast. After last night, I can't call Dale.

"Can we order something? George is hungry, too."

"Ha. Welcome to small townsville. McDonald's doesn't deliver." My mouth is desert dry. My head aches. Food is not anywhere on my playlist, but I need coffee.

"What are we going to do?" There's a note of panic in her voice, and for her sake I try to pull myself together.

"We have feet. We'll walk. Give me a minute."

"What if *they* are out there?"

"I'll find you a hat."

"I'm taking a shower." She's already scouted the house, apparently, because the door to the main bathroom slams shut a minute later. I let George out into the fenced backyard, then shuffle through my parents' room and into the half bath.

If anybody needs to worry about being seen, it's me. I look like I've been out on an all-night bender. My eyes are bloodshot. My hair is flattened on one side, wild curls springing up on the other. A red line from the sofa cushion runs the length of my right cheek. The pipes above my head are loud with the running water, and I can hear the shower spray hitting the tub. *Callie better leave me some hot water.* I catch the thought. *Not Callie. Ariel.* I have got to get out of this house before it makes me crazy. Too many memories. A little cold water to my face helps, but not enough.

When I walk out of the bathroom, my mother is lying on the bed. She's on her side with her back to me, a thin hump under the covers.

I blink, and she's gone. The quilt is smooth, the pillows set neatly and precisely on top, exactly where I put them when I made the bed the morning after I drove her to the nursing home. A trick of the light. I smooth the quilt with my hands. Plump the pillows and replace them. Open the blinds to let the full sun shine in.

The sky is the pure true-blue of spring up here in the north country. Cloudless. Sunlight falls across the mountain that marks the edge of the valley on the far side of town, turning the trees to gold. I've never seen this view from exactly this angle before. Mom always kept the blinds closed, the room dark. Now, in the morning light, I see the room with new eyes. Small, cramped. There's barely enough space for the bed and the dresser. Dark paneling on the walls. No pictures. The beige carpet is threadbare, stained on my dad's side from spilled drinks.

I feel like I'm suffocating. The window opens with a crank handle. It's stiff but functional, and I manage to get it open. Cool air flows in, smelling of spring flowers and grass. I rest my hands on the windowsill and breathe. Then, driven by a compulsion I don't stop to think about, I strip the bed. The old quilt feels heavier than it should, weighted with years of depression and despair. Down the stairs, outside, and straight to the trash can.

"Annelise Redding. What on earth are you doing?"

The voice jolts my head up, eyes wide, a child caught with her hands in the cookie-jar. Mrs. Olson stares at me accusingly while her rat-dog terrier sniffs at the trash can and then lifts a leg to water it. Mrs. Olson ruled first grade with an iron fist. Back in the day, I have no doubt she paddled students regularly. Denied that satisfaction by the time I came along, her weapons were a sharp tongue, sarcasm, and bitter homework assignments doled out in retribution for whispers and fidgets.

Since she also lived next door, all of my small indiscretions were reported to my mother, who did nothing but look at me as if I were an extra burden in her already dreary life. Even now, her voice sends my heart galloping, guilt flooding me from head to toe as if I've been caught cheating on a test.

"That's a handmade quilt. Antique. Is something wrong with it?"

"Yes." Let her think it's a spill or a stain, not just accumulated years of depression and an episode of temporary insanity.

Her eyes are as gimlety as ever in her wrinkled face. "You've been busy," she says, implication dripping all over the words. "I saw your magazines."

"They're not exactly mine." I bite back a flood of words out of habit. My body tells me that I'm six and she can hurt me.

"I must admit I am surprised to see you here. I'd think you'd be busy partying, taking up where Callie left off."

"Mrs. Olson, with all due respect—"

"She always was trouble, that one. You were bad enough, but from the minute she pranced into my classroom, I knew."

"What did you know?"

I close the trash can lid. Stand up straight and turn to face her. Her eyes travel over me from head to toe and back again, and she shakes her head, clicking her tongue. "Las Vegas is a place of sin. Look at you."

"What did you know?" I raise my voice a little, take a step toward her. I'm not scared anymore; there's something stronger running through my veins.

"All big eyes and curls, wrapping the boys around her little finger. Where could it go from there? Everybody was so surprised when she turned up pregnant. Me? I told Pastor Montaigne that—"

I take another step toward her, which puts us eye to eye and almost touching. "And what did you do to help her?"

She backs up, dragging the dog away from its ongoing investigation of the trash can. "I don't know what you—"

"When we were kids. You lived right there. Did you notice what was going on with my parents?"

"I—"

"Of course you did. You knew. Everybody knew. Mrs. Redding is depressed. Mr. Redding drinks. Those poor, neglected children, coming to no good. You sat around and gossiped about us with your friends. Picked on us at school because we had no parent to defend us. And now you're going to stand here and talk shit about Callie now that she's dead? Fuck you!"

She gasps, her sharp face flushing scarlet. Her dog starts yipping, loud and shrill. "How dare you use such language to me!"

"You mean fuck? Are you objecting to my particular usage? Do you want me to spell it for you? F-U-C-K you. Now get off my sidewalk and go wag your tongue elsewhere."

I don't wait to see if she follows my command. I turn and stomp back into the house, slamming the front door behind me.

Ariel stands in the entry, eyes wide. "Who was that?"

"A neighbor. You ready to go?"

"I need a hat. And you are not going anywhere like that."

"Why not?"

"Because you look like shit."

"I don't care what they think. Any of them. They can take their shitty photographs and plaster them on telephone poles. I'm through with everybody." I rampage through the house, pulling up all the blinds, opening all the windows. Letting in the air and the light and banishing ghosts. Living room, kitchen, music room. No more evidence of Callie, no lingering fragrance. I open the piano lid I slammed shut last night and run my hand lightly over the keys.

"Feel better?" Ariel asks. She sits down on the bench and starts hammering away at "Chopsticks."

I do, as a matter of fact. Or I did. I press both hands over my ears. "Must you make that racket?"

She grins and bangs harder. "Go take a shower. There's only one towel, which you probably know, and I used it. But hurry up. I'm starving."

***

The coast looks clear when we set out. We will inevitably encounter neighbors, but I'm pretty sure Mrs. Olson won't talk to me for a while. She'll be too busy talking to everybody else. Before we go, Ariel scans the social media feed with the search strings she's inputted. Everybody's busy with the flavor of the day, which isn't us.

Still, I don't want to venture far. There's a gas station at the traffic circle, the closest place where we can buy food. It's not much farther to McDonald's and Zip's, but we would have to walk by Benny's Inn to get there. I'm leery of motel parking lots. We can cut through the park and stick to side streets the way I'm headed.

It feels good to be out and about, stretching out tight muscles, clearing my head. No ghosts out here. It's easy to put the last hours in perspective with the sun shining warm on my face, the sound of lawn mowers, the trees in bloom.

"It was kinda weird sleeping in Mom's old bed," Ariel says, after we've walked a block in silence. "Good weird, though. How come you slept on the couch?"

"The weird was not so good for me."

"I remember visiting," she says. "And that I could stand on the bed and see out the window."

We settle back into silence, my brain setting to work on the problems I need to solve. Car, attorney, paperwork, paparazzi.

"It smelled like her," Ariel says. "Like that perfume she wore."

"Those sheets have been washed a bunch of times since she used them."

Ariel shrugs. "I dreamed about her. That she came in and sat on the bed and kissed me. And when I woke up, I smelled her perfume."

"It was only a dream," I say, but a cold thread runs the length of my spine.

"I wasn't sleeping. You were playing the piano. Scales and stuff."

My left toe catches on a crack in the sidewalk while my right foot keeps on moving. The great divide between immobility and momentum throws me off-balance, and I brace myself for a fall, lurching sideways onto the grass and barely managing to keep on my feet.

"Are you okay?"

"Fine. Just clumsy." Something pulls in my thigh when I resume walking, making me limp a little.

We walk the rest of the way without incident. I'm vigilant for either of the cars from yesterday but see nothing suspicious. Right inside the gas station doors sits a wire rack with the weekly edition of the *Statesman Examiner* staring up at us. Both of us stop as if on cue, staring at the picture of Dale's rental car with a teddy bear blocking the window, the "I ♥ Callie" shirt unmistakable. I don't even read the headline.

"Hurry," I whisper to Ariel, but she needs no such instruction.

Chin tucked, letting her hair hide her face, she whispers back, "I'm not hungry anymore."

But we've come this far and we're getting food. Whatever ancestral spirit possessed me when I was talking to Mrs. Olson is back in command. I hold my head up, bold as you please, and search out bread, milk, eggs, and a small bag of dog food. Ariel follows, after a moment's hesitation, picking out a breakfast burrito from the food warmer and pairing it with a tall energy drink. I look at the drink, then at her. I should insist on orange juice, get a few vitamins into her. Instead, I free up one hand by passing her the milk jug, and fill a twenty-ounce cup with coffee.

The boy behind the cash register hasn't grown into his height and doesn't quite seem to know what to do with a set of very long arms and legs. His face is attractive, though, and he's got beautiful brown eyes, which Ariel appears to notice with some approval. She smiles at him. He smiles back.

And then his face changes. His Adam's apple bobs. A red flush starts at the base of his neck and travels up over his jaw and into his hairline. "You're her. You're Ariel. Oh my God."

I set my groceries down on the counter with a bang, but he still only has eyes for her. "What you're doing—it's so cool. I hope you find him."

"Thanks," she says, the color of her face mirroring his.

"Look, can we buy our stuff?" There's a greasy-haired man behind me, baggy shorts riding low under a beer belly, stained T-shirt, carrying a six-pack in each hand and looking like 9:00 a.m. is way past time for him to get started. Behind him, a sixtyish woman, dressed for the office, taps her toe impatiently, lips pursed.

"Sure," the boy says. "Sorry. I can't believe it's really you." He fumbles the packages across the scanner and into a bag, dropping the egg carton, then checking to make sure they're all okay.

While I run the credit card through the machine, he grabs a copy of the newspaper and sets it on the counter in front of Ariel. "Do you think, maybe, you could sign this?"

"What?"

He flushes even deeper. "Just to, you know, prove you were really here. That I talked to you. Because nobody will believe it." He holds out a pen.

"Ariel, come on. Let's go." I grab the bag of groceries and head for the door, thinking she'll follow. But she takes the pen from the boy's eager hand and scribbles across her picture before scurrying after me.

"What the hell were you thinking?" I ask her, as soon as we're across the parking lot and speed walking down the street.

"He seemed nice."

"Seemed means nothing. Now he has your autograph. You think he's going to cherish that for the rest of his life, in secret?"

"I wasn't thinking, all right? I just . . . he was so nice and polite, and it seemed like a small thing."

"There are no small things when it comes to you. Not fair, not right, but it's the way it is. Besides, what about all of those other people behind us?"

"There were two! An old woman and a drunk guy. You at least don't have to exaggerate." Her voice rises with emotion.

"The old woman took a picture. With her smartphone. You were too busy signing pictures for your fanboy to notice."

Ariel stops in the middle of the sidewalk. Fear strikes me that I've gone too far and said too much, that she'll refuse to come with me and I'll have a runaway on my hands. But she's not even looking at me as she fumbles her phone out of her pocket, her thumbs moving at lightning speed.

"Shit."

"What?"

Mutely, she holds out the phone and I retrace my steps to look. Twitter. The avatar is some spiky comic book character I'm unfamiliar with. The tweet says, "Unbelievable! Ariel Redfern just came into the store & I got her autograph." There's a grainy photo of the newspaper pic with Ariel's signature across it.

I start walking again. "Could be worse. Let's get home."

"You don't understand." She runs to catch up. "He has the location on."

I almost break into a jog, but that would attract attention. It feels like a hundred miles to the house. Every time a car goes by my heart speeds up, then slows a little with relief when it keeps moving. When we turn into our street, both the white compact, still mud splattered, and the brown sedan are parked in front of the house. The two cameras are already aimed in our direction, clicking away.

"I'm sorry," Ariel says.

"Don't be. You were just trying to be nice. I'm sorry for being a bitch."

"What now?"

"If you can't beat 'em, join 'em."

"What's that supposed to mean?"

"Right now, it means that you should act like you did at the funeral. Chin up, eyes straight ahead. They are kitty litter beneath your feet."

"I don't like kitty litter. Gritty. Crunchy."

"Precisely. Ready?"

Shoulder to shoulder, like we're marching into battle with plastic grocery bags as our only weapons, we head for the house. George is barking frantically in the backyard.

The guy from the white compact blocks the sidewalk, his camera right in my face. Click. I stare straight down the lens, unflinching.

"Are you through?"

"You owe me," he says with conviction.

"For what?"

"Yesterday."

I try to step around him. He blocks my path. "Not until you talk."

Behind me, I hear the whir of the other camera, probably aimed at Ariel. He's not in her way, though, and she's almost to the door.

"Please let me go into my house." I try to keep my voice calm. It would be so satisfying to grab the camera and smash it on the sidewalk, but if I did that, I'd be legally in the wrong. Assault charge. Jail time.

"Which possible father is from this little place?" he asks. "Come on, give us a name."

"They're all from here." I push past him, eyes focused on the goal.

Up the steps, onto the porch. I fumble with my keys. The cameras are still clicking behind me.

"How do you feel about the allegations that you're an unfit guardian?" the other camera guy asks. His words freeze me, key in the lock. I turn around and stare at him, at both of them. Before I can open my mouth and ask questions, Ariel drags me into the house.

I lock and bolt the door and then lean against it, breathing hard, weak in the knees. Ariel bulldozes through the house into the living room and turns on the TV. Since even I won't pay for dish on an empty house, all we've got are local channels picked up by the roof antenna. At this hour, there's not much of interest, but ABC has *The View*. No mention of Callie, thank God, and the guest list is not of interest to a teenage girl. Ariel switches off the tube and runs upstairs, returning with her laptop. I don't pay for wireless, either, but apparently the Callahans haven't secured their router and she taps in without difficulty.

A search for my name and Callie's brings up a ton of hits, the most recent all with headlines like, "Is Callie Redfern's Daughter Safe?" and "Custody Battle Looms."

I sink down into a chair, blinking at the grocery sack and the cup of coffee. I'd forgotten I was carrying them. Ariel clicks through links, stopping at a news video. Both of us gaze, mesmerized, at Ricken. His hair is smoothly combed. He wears a subdued pinstripe shirt with a conservative tie. Everything about him says decent, respectable, mistreated.

"Annelise Redding is erratic and unstable. She threw a reporter into a swimming pool, nearly drowning her and ruining her camera. Assault charges are under consideration. She allowed a sixteen-year-old girl to investigate a vehicle in which one of her alleged fathers shot himself in the head. How a woman like this can be entrusted with a grieving child is beyond my comprehension. Ariel needs the structure of school and the support of her friends. I held back from taking action because I thought perhaps being with family would be healing for her. Obviously, I was wrong, and I deeply regret not having expressed my concerns earlier."

Two young, earnest newspeople—one male, one female, and both too beautiful and polished to be believable—discuss the situation. Ariel closes the laptop. I've never seen her look so pale. Her pupils are so big her eyes appear nearly black. "Can he do that? Get me taken away from you?"

"I won't let him." My voice doesn't sound convincing, even to me.

"It's because we fired him," Ariel says. "It's all about the money."

The laptop sits between us, closed and quiet, but I can almost see exclamation marks hovering over it.

"What are we going to do?" Ariel's voice trembles a little.

"Eat," I say, fishing out the greasy paper bag that holds the burrito.

"I'm not hungry."

Me either. The smell of fried food nearly makes me gag.

"Might be your last meal before foster care. They'll feed you corn-flakes with almond milk."

"You're not funny!" But a trickle of laughter escapes her, anyway. The color returns to her face and her voice sounds steady.

I need a lawyer. Fortunately, my old friend Ashley is a member of the bar. We're still close enough that I keep her number stored in my phone. Which is in Vegas. Luckily, my mother was never an adopter of newfangled technologies and always kept a phone book handy. I dig it out of the drawer and dial Ash's number. The receptionist who answers doesn't sound any older than Ariel and probably isn't. Ashley is big on hiring high school kids. Just as capable as adults, she claims, and more motivated by money. Also, it's easier to tell them what to do.

"I need to speak to Ash."

"She said not to bother her."

"This is Annelise Redding. It's important."

"*Ohhhh,*" the voice says. She forgets to put me on hold, just shouts, "Hey Ashley, Annelise is on the phone."

Ash picks up twenty seconds later.

"The news is not good," she says. "I've been watching."

"You and the whole country. I need an attorney."

Silence.

"Ash?"

"I'm not up to this, Lise. Small-town stuff I can do. Your mom's guardianship papers. Wills. Maybe the occasional child custody case. That sort of thing I can handle."

"This is about a will and maybe about child custody. Sounds perfect. Can you get Callie's will sent to you? And all of the financial documents, too, while you're at it? And then we can sue Ricken for defamation of character. Right?"

"Wrong. He's got a point. She's not in school—"

"But—"

"And you did take her to where that guy killed himself. What were you thinking? Forgive me for saying this, but you're acting more like Callie than yourself."

My right hand hurts. I change the receiver over to my left. There are red lines in my palm from where I've squeezed the phone too hard.

"Lise? Are you still there?"

"Yes. I'm counting to ten."

"I'm sorry if I've pissed you off. But somebody has to tell you the truth." She drops her voice, makes it softer. "Look, I'm not judging or blaming. Grief does weird things to people. But that's how it appears from the outside looking in."

"Well, how it looks isn't exactly how it is. You all go on like Ariel is six. Like I'm dragging her around the countryside and forcing her to do all this shit. Did anybody ever consider that she's almost an adult and has a mind of her own?"

"Legally, she's a child. And you are an adult, and her guardian. You're going to need a better story than that. Or make up with that Ricken guy."

"That is not going to happen."

"Then you need somebody besides me."

"So find me somebody. Look, will you at least do this? Call Callie's attorney and let him know that Ricken is, in fact, fired. Legally request that all relevant documents get sent to you. And find me a trustworthy attorney who can help me. Okay?"

I hear her hesitating on the other end of the line. She doesn't want to say yes, but I'm an old friend.

"Ash? Please help me. I don't know much, but I know that Ariel and I need to stay together."

There's a heavy sigh on the other end of the line. "Yeah, okay. Since you're already my client, I will initiate these things for you. But I'm finding you another attorney."

"Thank you."

"And I'm raising my fees."

"Whatever you want."

"Don't tempt me. I'll call you."

The phone clicks off. I'm sweat soaked and shivering so hard my teeth chatter. The idea that anybody might take a custody case seriously hadn't even occurred to me. Ricken seems so pitifully obvious.

Ariel brings me a blanket and wraps it around my shoulders. It's the one from Callie's bed and it does smell like her, for no rational reason. But it doesn't begin to touch the cold.

"You should drink your coffee." She hands it to me and I take a sip. It's bitter and lukewarm, and I hand it back to her with my face all scrunched up.

Ariel rolls her eyes. "It's medicinal. Here. I'll fix it."

Her footsteps run up and then down the stairs and into the kitchen. The microwave purrs for a minute. Then another minute. I can't help smiling a little at the thought of Ariel and her high-tech world confronting my mother's kitchen. The microwave is an enormous thing that is activated by a dial. No touch pad. And it takes forever to heat up anything.

But she comes back with the coffee, in a mug this time. Steam rises off the top. I sniff it, suspiciously. "What did you do to it?"

"Doctored it a little."

I take a sip. It tastes better, all right. A lot better. "Where the hell did you find Baileys?" Mom didn't drink, that I know of. Dad drank hard stuff straight out of the bottle. Besides, I've been through these kitchen cabinets about a hundred times.

Ariel grins. "I was snooping in Mom's dresser this morning. It was in the second drawer, wrapped up in a pair of jeans."

"Seriously? After all this time?" A part of me has to admire Callie's audacity at hiding alcohol right under my nose like that. I take another sip. The coffee goes down smooth and sweet, warming my belly. "You know, if they are trying to make the case that I'm not fit to be your guardian, maybe I shouldn't be drinking at ten in the morning."

Ariel waves her hand dismissively. "It's only one shot. And we won't let anybody in the house until you're stone-cold sober."

"Thank you." It's surreal, having her take care of me instead of the other way around. I pretty much raised Callie. And ever since I was a little kid, I've been taking care of my mother. This small gesture of a blanket and spiked coffee makes me feel warm and nurtured.

"I heard what you said on the phone," Ariel says. "About us needing to stay together. And about me having my own free will and stuff."

"I was kind of pissed."

"It's true, though. And I was thinking that Mom did, too, you know. Like when she hid the booze in her drawer. That wasn't your thing. It was hers. Her sleeping with all those guys and getting pregnant with me—that was her thing, too."

I look at Ariel, as tall as I am, and just as stubborn. The thought of forcing her to do anything seems ludicrous.

"So what now?" she asks, sliding from wise woman back into scared teenage girl in a heartbeat.

"I don't know. It would be great to have somebody from your mom's team to help us out. Definitely not her attorney. And that accountant . . ."

"Genesis? Yeah, she was sleeping with Ricken. But Glynnis would be good."

"Who is Glynnis, again?"

Ariel looks at me like I'm an idiot.

"Humor me, I'm bad at names."

"You weren't paying attention. Glynnis is the agent."

I remember those sharp, intelligent eyes, the no-nonsense face. "Maybe. I don't know how to contact her."

"I do. Mom made sure I had numbers for all of her people. In case."

She flips through her phone and gives me a number. When I dial, I get a receptionist. This one is a lot more polished than the one in Ashley's office and there's no way she's going to just "put me through to Glynnis," no matter who I am.

"Let me," Ariel says, taking the phone. "Hey, Courtney? It's Ariel."

A short burst from the other end that sounds like it ends in a question.

"I'm okay. Sorta. Hanging in. But I really need to talk to Glynn. Can you make that happen?" She nods, looks at me, and mouths, "I'm on hold."

After two minutes and forty-three seconds by the clock, Glynnis comes on. "You've seen the news?" Ariel's voice is hard-edged, older. As if she's talking about stock markets and business, not her personal life.

"Yes, I'm sure sales *are* wonderful. We need some advice and you're the only person on the team who is straight up. How do we play this so I get to stay with my aunt? Ricken goes down, you understand?"

She listens, nods. I fidget, unable to hear the other side of the conversation. Catch myself chewing my fingernails and trap my hands between my thighs. It's all I can do to keep from grabbing the receiver out of Ariel's hand and asking my own questions. The voice on the other end goes on at length. Ariel nods occasionally, says, "Okay," and that's it.

She hangs up and then sits there, looking at me, saying nothing.

"What did she say? Do you need a paper? A pen? You didn't take notes or write anything down at all."

"Three basic things," Ariel says, ticking the items off on her fingers. "One: get a new team—attorney, accountant, PR. Two: do an exclusive.

Three: be photographed going about ordinary-life shit, which includes me doing something about school."

"That's it? That's all she had to say?"

"Pretty much."

"Long conversation for that amount of information."

"I condensed."

We sit and stare at each other.

"We have money," Ariel says. "We can pay for things. Like your car—you could just leave yours at the airport and buy a new one. That's probably what Mom would do. Or get a limo and hire a driver. Do they have those here?"

There is one stretch limo in town. It gets rented out for prom and weddings. I try to picture myself being driven around Colville by a paid driver. I shake my head. "We don't have the money yet. And I don't want a new car. I like my car." But her words do give me an idea.

"You're a dinosaur," Ariel says, as I flip through the alphabet tabs in the phone book. "Or a Luddite. That's a thing, right? Or is it Mennonite?"

"Good thing for us if I am." I punch a number into the landline phone.

"What are you doing?"

"Improving the local economy. Hang on."

The first of my students doesn't answer. The second one does.

"Hey," she says. "You're famous!"

"Yes, well, that's beside the point. You want to make some money, Lexy?"

"Always. I'm broker than broke. What's up?"

"You have choices. Number one: Get somebody to drive you to the airport and bring back my car. I'll pay you both. Forty bucks an hour, plus lunch and obviously gas."

"Okay. What else?"

"I need somebody to run errands—groceries, that sort of thing. Same pay scale. You in?"

"For sure! I can't go to Spokane today, got stuff this afternoon. But I can do errands this morning."

"Can you find somebody to do the Spokane thing? Pick a safe driver."

"Naturally. I'm all over it."

I give her a grocery list. Then I call Safeway and talk to the manager, who's more than willing to set up an account for me. The biggest problem is distracting him from the topic of my face on the magazines in the checkout aisle.

I turn to Ariel. "What's next?"

"School."

It's the middle of May. School's out in a month. We agree that throwing Ariel into a brand-new class for such a short time, especially with all of the media bullshit, would be cruel and unusual punishment. Again, the phone is our friend. A call to the principal at her school in Vegas, an explanation of the situation, and an agreement is easily reached. Ariel is an excellent student. There is no reason why course work can't be e-mailed to her. Textbooks can be shipped. If she'd like to make arrangements to sit for her exams at the local high school, that can easily be arranged. We thank him with the promise of a new scholarship fund in Callie's honor.

We work both phones, her cell and my landline, taking care of business. Ariel is cool and efficient on the phone, and between the two of us, we get things done. Still, we're both more than ready for a break by the time Lexy arrives with groceries and supplies. She and Ariel circle each other a little warily at first, but by the time we've stashed all of the groceries, they've discovered a shared love for some TV show I've never even heard of and are chattering away like magpies.

They exchange numbers when Lexy leaves, with an agreement to meet later online.

"If you want to give me the car keys," Lexy says just before braving the front door, "Dax says he'll go get your car."

"Done. Tell him to be careful, will you?" I'm not in a position to be choosy, but Lexy's brother is known as a risk taker.

She grins. "He's really a good driver. Like he says, speed has nothing to do with it."

I watch her walk down the sidewalk, waving at the cameras like they're old friends, but ignoring all the questions. A bubble of gratitude rises in my chest. There are so many good people in this town. I want to be able to live here, which means finding a way to handle the press.

And so, at last, I do the one task I've been putting off all day.

Melody Smith's business card is still in the pocket of the jeans I bought in Portland. I silently wish for the call to go to voice mail, but she picks up right away.

The first words out of her mouth after I identify myself are, "What on earth did you do to Ricken?"

"Never mind Ricken. Are you ready for your exclusive?"

Ten minutes later, my fate is sealed. Melody will catch the next plane to Spokane. Tomorrow, she'll spend the whole day with us. We'll act normal and responsible and she'll document it. That's the theory, anyway. I have my doubts.

"I don't know how to do this normal thing Glynnis talked about," Ariel says. "That's on you."

"I'm not so good at it myself."

"What do you usually do this time of day?"

"Usually I'm teaching lessons."

"And then?"

"I go see my mother." I feel sick at the thought of a camera in the nursing home, my stomach churning.

"I want to see her," Ariel says.

"She won't remember you. It's not a fun visit."

"I can't remember her hardly at all, and I don't even know what Grandpa looked like. Are there pictures?"

"What kind of pictures?"

"You know—photographs. Of the family. Of Grandma and Grandpa. And you and Mom when you were kids."

I start to tell her no. Nobody was interested in pictures. But then I remember something. I climb the stairs and walk into my parents' bedroom. It looks different with the blinds open. The air smells fresh and clean. Sunshine lies across the bed, lights up the wood on the dresser. Good wood. It glows warm in the light, under inevitable flecks of dust. Tucked into the back of my mom's closet, behind another handmade patchwork quilt, I find what I'm looking for.

Ariel is right beside me and we both sit down in a pool of sun on the carpet, the dusty shoe box in front of us.

"I'm not sure what's in here. Stuff Mom squirreled away. A few pictures, some other stuff. I glanced at it but didn't sort the rest."

"Why not?"

I shrug and don't answer. Ariel brushes away an accumulation of dust and peels open the cardboard flaps. There's a photograph on top.

Mom and Dad stand side by side in front of the house. It's summer. The grass is green, the trees in full bloom. Mom cradles a baby in her arms. She's not looking at the camera; instead, her eyes are fixed on the tiny face at her breast. Just a small smile on her lips, but she glows with happiness and love. Dad stands beside her, shoulders back, chin up, eyes looking directly into the camera lens. No small smile for him, he's laughing outright. One arm is around my mother's shoulders.

I have no memory of ever seeing them that way. They certainly never looked at me or each other like that any time I can remember. I'm not sure where I was when the picture was taken. Staying with friends, probably, while Mom was having Callie. It makes me feel shut out. Forgotten. One moment of pure family joy, and I wasn't a part of it.

"Are there any of Mom?" Ariel asks.

"Besides that one? I don't know. Dig a little."

"This is you," she says, holding out the photo.

"It's Callie. She was born in the summer. I was born in February."

Ariel turns the picture over. "It says here, on the back."

"Let me see." The edges of the photo are soft with wear. The picture itself is a little blurry, taken by an inexpert photographer on a 35 mm, before everybody had smartphones and digital cameras. Printed on the back in my mother's loopy handwriting are a name and a date.

"Annelise. Spring 1979."

My body goes perfectly still. A breeze from the open window stirs through the room, carrying the sweet fragrance of lilacs. In the right-hand corner of the picture, behind Dad's shoulder, there is an unmistakable riot of purple. Callie was born in July, well after lilacs. The baby in the picture might be a couple of months old, but no more.

I'd assumed that my parents could only maintain that level of happiness for a day or two at most, that it must have been connected to a recent birth. But it's not Callie in this picture. It's me. My chest fills with warmth. There's not room enough, and it expands into my throat. Tears well up to make room for it, and for once I let them fall without trying to hold them back.

Ariel glances up at me from under her lashes but doesn't ask questions. Which is good, because I have no words to explain. I lay the picture down beside me, where I can keep looking at it, reminding myself of this new reality. My parents loved me once. They were happy. Maybe whatever happened after that had nothing to do with me and everything to do with forces and circumstances over which I had no control.

A memory floats upward on the warm currents of this new emotion. Just a small one. A soft hand on my forehead, a voice singing me to sleep. I must have been very young. Before Callie, probably. In my mind, I add the face from the picture, hanging over my bed, gazing at me with that kind of love.

By the time I'm able to see through my tears, Ariel has sorted out a small pile of objects. A silk handkerchief, embroidered with tiny perfect stitches: "Jack and Emma, Forever, 1977." Could my mother have done this? I've never seen her with a needle in her hand. There's a little plastic bag of baby teeth. My father's wedding ring. And then the pictures. Only a handful, maybe fifteen at the most. There's me sitting on the couch, smiling a gap-toothed grin at the camera, my baby sister propped against me. Callie and me in the fishing boat with Dad when we're older—both skinny, blonde pigtailed ragamuffins, but grinning ear to ear. Dad wearing a hard hat, either going to or arriving from work, lunch box in hand. He's smiling, but it doesn't reach his eyes. The lines are in his face. His belly is rounding. I remember the hard hat and the not-quite smile.

The last picture Ariel holds for a long time before she passes it on to me.

Callie and I stand side by side, arms around each other's shoulders. She's a little taller than I am. Her hair falls in lazy golden curls; her eyes and her smile are bright and true. My eyes are tired and my smile looks like Dad's in the going-to-work picture. My hair is a darker shade than hers, not quite blonde, not quite brown, but in the sun it gleams like burnished maple. We're huddled in winter coats, black dresses and high-heeled shoes a sharp contrast to the expanse of snow. In front of us, each of us with a hand on her shoulder, a little girl. Wild blonde curls, a mischievous grin.

"I remember Grandma taking that picture," Ariel says. "I mean, I don't really remember her. But I remember it was her that took it. Outside the house. After the funeral."

I remember it, too. Mom in some strange, becalmed place in the grief process, acting like Callie was home for a holiday instead of a funeral. Insisting on pictures, despite the cold and snow. The weird evening meal sampled from the casseroles and potato salads brought in by the neighbors and church ladies, ending with a store-bought, oversweet apple pie. I remember the greasy feel of the piecrust smooth on my palate.

And I remember that night, back in our old room, how it feels like a sleepover. Callie and I talk for a while, cozy and friendly, as if there has never been any bad blood between us. The years of constraint and difficult conversations, like it's been since she ran off when Ariel was a baby, all seem to melt away. Under that influence, I haul out the guitar and we sing some old songs, harmonizing, her soprano and my alto, and I wonder why we never sang together growing up. I get lost in the music until I find myself playing my newest song for her. Callie makes me play it over and over until she can sing it with me.

And then we just sit there looking at each other in the dimly lit room. She's cross-legged on her bed, one hand resting on Ariel's tumbled curls. "You should send that one somewhere. Record it. Do something."

I shrug. "Maybe." The idea sets my teeth on edge. If I put the song out there for the whole world to see, it won't be mine anymore. It will grow and change and wander off until maybe it's a thing I no longer recognize and can't call my own.

"Music was never meant to be hoarded, Lise. It's supposed to be free. For everybody."

I put the guitar aside, leaning it carefully against the wall where it won't fall over. "It's late. We should go to sleep. Mom's going to need us in the morning."

"Just think about it," she says.

That was her last visit. A few days later, she and Ariel drove away, and the next time I saw her, she was lying in the coffin.

"You remember?" Ariel asks now.

"I remember."

"Can I keep it?"

I hand it back to her. "You can keep all of them if you want." Getting up, I leave her there. Too much thinking, too much remembering. Restlessness drives me down the stairs and into a cleaning spree.

Not that the house is dirty; my student has done a better job than Mom ever did. Or me. Cleaning is not my favorite thing.

But now, not daring to brave the reporters outside the door, cleaning gives me something to do with my excess energy. I scrub the floors, vacuum the carpets, polish the furniture with the real polish, not the lemon spray-on stuff. And then I make us a dinner out of the groceries Lexy brought us. Baked potatoes, roasted chicken, steamed broccoli.

What Ariel does during that time, I don't know, but she comes down for dinner with her eyes puffy and her face blotchy.

"That's a lot of food," she says, when the table is all set. "You should invite Dale."

"Too late now. The food would get cold." I hide my face in the process of dishing up my plate.

"There's a microwave."

"Right. That's what we call it, anyway. Just eat, okay? Maybe you can go up to the Elliots' for dinner tomorrow. After we spend the day being normal for the reporter."

She laughs a little bit at that, and we eat in companionable silence. The chicken is chewy and bland, the broccoli overcooked. I focus on my potato, slathering it with butter and sour cream and salt. It's hard to go wrong with a baked potato.

"Don't feed Melody," Ariel says, pushing her plate away with half a piece of chicken uneaten. "She'll call CPS on account of child cruelty."

"Ha. Very funny. The potato is good."

"I don't like potato."

"Then eat bread."

"Can I put honey on it?"

"Do I care?"

"Like I said. Don't feed Melody."

We both burst out laughing. We load up on potatoes and bread, and then we clean the kitchen. Together. There's no dishwasher, so she washes and I dry.

"This is nice," Ariel says, when we get a rhythm going. "Mom never did dishes."

"Tell me about it."

"Even when you were kids?"

"Especially then." She's right: it is nice working together. It's close to the feeling of making music with somebody. It used to be like this when Dale helped clean up the kitchen. But now any thought of Dale makes me feel like a boat adrift on a vast and lonely sea.

All at once my dish towel is wet and clammy; the plate in my hand is slippery, and I nearly drop it. Dale didn't call today, not even to check on Ariel. Tomorrow, Ariel and I have to pal around all day with a camera-toting reporter while pretending to be normal.

We finish cleaning up the kitchen in silence, and my last lingering emotion before sleep comes is one of dread.

CHAPTER SEVENTEEN

"She's here." Ariel stands at the living-room window, self-appointed watch person. She's wearing the same outfit she wore to church the day we went to see Kelvin, freshly laundered and carefully pressed. A touch of makeup, all she ever wears. Her hair is braided, but she's left a few strands loose around her face. She looks softer today, younger, despite the high alert.

I join her at the window, both of us in full view. It's not like the lenses aimed in our direction are sniper rifles. If we're going to be an open book for the media, then they might as well know we're watching them.

The compact from Nevada has been freshly washed and is white again. It's familiar by now, a known entity, and I feel almost friendly toward the driver. He leans against his door, sipping coffee from a paper cup. I catch myself, hoping he found something better than the gas station swill I had yesterday, and then I remind myself he's the enemy and deserves the shittiest coffee imaginable. The brown sedan is missing. There are three unknown cars that might on another day be dismissed as people visiting neighbors, but each one is equipped with a camera.

My own Subaru is back from the airport, parked in the driveway, freshly washed and respectable looking.

Melody Smith climbs out of a midsize rental, red curls like flame in the early morning light. Score one point for her—since I'm paying for the car, she could have had anything she wanted, but she kept it inconspicuous. The camera on the strap around her neck is another story. It looks bigger and shinier than the one I drowned in the pool. I'll be getting the bill for the camera, too, but that's fair. She pauses outside the car to shoot the house and the yard, no doubt with Ariel and me framed in the window. She takes some shots of the scavengers. And then she heads up the sidewalk toward the front door.

White Compact whistles at her back. "Hey, they've got a dog. Maybe guns."

George joins us at the window and starts barking. It's a big, mean bark, but Melody doesn't break stride. Before she has time to ring the doorbell, I've got the door open, hustling her in. George stops barking and starts sniffing her over from the feet up. She laughs and takes his picture. Before she says a word, she snaps a shot of me and Ariel, too.

I know damn well the room behind her is spotless. I saw to that myself. We're ready. The cupboards are stocked. We are neat, clean, pressed, and ready to present the best sides of ourselves to the world. Still, my insides are quaking, and I flinch every time the flash goes off. Social awkwardness swamps me. Do I invite her into the living room? Give her a tour of the house? My palms are damp and I'm breathing too fast.

"Long drive," Ariel says, sounding calm. "Coffee? And let me show you where the bathroom is."

"Coffee would be amazing," Melody says, following her. "That drive from Spokane is kind of terrifying."

"Right?" Ariel says. "Miles and miles of nothing. But at least there's cell service."

This leaves me blank. I've always thought it was a beautiful drive. At night, it's a pain in the ass because no gas stations are open, but the drive through Spokane is much more anxiety provoking for me. All those cars, all those people. Leaving Melody to freshen up or do whatever needs doing in the bathroom, I follow Ariel into the kitchen. She pours out three mugs of coffee. We each doctor our own. About a half a cup of sugar for Ariel, nothing but half-and-half for me.

It's not until Melody comes in and snaps a picture that I realize maybe other people don't pour the cream right out of the carton or get the sugar out of the bag. People like Callie, anyway. The sort of people the paparazzi are used to following. Maybe they have cream pitchers and sugar canisters. My knees have that wobbly thing going again, and I'm grateful that the coffee gives me something to do with my hands.

Melody has no problem fixing her own cup. "Thanks for this," she says, not meaning coffee. "It's an amazing break for me."

"It had to be somebody."

She grins, not taking offense. "Look, I'm sure you're not happy to have me in your house. But for what it's worth, I think you're right to do this. Best way to get the others off your back, at least for a while. Tell the story. Stop the speculation."

"That's just part of it," Ariel says. "Making them go away. We want . . ." Her voice quavers and she takes a drink, her eyes pleading with me over the top of the cup.

"We're also hoping this will help make Ricken's accusations go away. The last thing Ariel needs is to be torn away from her family."

"Which is you." The green eyes are intelligent and laser focused. "I assume you haven't found the father yet, or guardianship questions would be taking a whole different turn."

Ariel chokes on her coffee. I grab the cup to save it from spilling, but it's all reflexes. In the beginning, Ariel finding her father was all to the good. If she found him, and he was a decent guy, he could take over the responsibility of raising her. Now the very thought of her going to live with somebody else feels like an elbow to the gut.

"I'll be staying with Lise," Ariel says. "Looking for my father is on hold until the media thing settles down. Do you want a tour? Or did you want to talk first, or what?"

"I'm camera first, story later," Melody says. "Walk me around and I'll ask questions as we go. Am I right that this is where Callie grew up? I'd love to see her bedroom."

The camera flash lights up every corner of the old house. Hallways and stairway, bedrooms and living room, the broken ivory on the old piano. I follow in its wake, seeing the house with different eyes. Shabby. Run-down. The rooms small and cramped. The curtains old and faded. All of it outdated and scruffy and countrified.

Melody asks questions along the way, and I answer her as best I can. In my parents' room, she takes way more photos than I think are called for. She makes Ariel sit on the bed, stand by the window, hold an old china dog that sits on the dresser.

"Where are they?" she asks.

"Where are who?" The question derails my thoughts, which are on the house, the realtor, the nagging question of why I don't do more to sell the place and move on.

"Your parents."

"He's in the cemetery. She's in a nursing home."

"Excellent." She lets the camera drop to the end of its strap and puts her hands on the small of her back, leaning into a stretch.

"That's not the usual response that comes to mind."

"But perfect for us. We're going to go visit them."

"Wait just a minute. That's not part of the—"

"Have you met your grandma?" Melody cuts me off midthought, swinging around to capture Ariel's reaction with the camera.

"I was six. I don't remember her very well."

"Better and better. We go see Grandma in the home. It will be all very touching. And it presents Lise as a caring, dutiful, and responsible daughter. Then we go put flowers on the grave—"

"My parents are not part of this freak show!" My hands are shaking again. "The house, me, Ariel—that's one thing. We set ourselves up for this. But exposing my mother's dementia to all the world, pretending dutiful visits to my father's grave, that's different! I won't do it."

Melody shrugs. "Your funeral. You're missing a golden opportunity."

"You said you always visit Grandma in the afternoon," Ariel says. Her voice is determined, her eyes challenging. "We're doing normal, remember?"

"There's nothing normal about bringing cameras into a nursing home. What we're going to do is this: We go sit downstairs and Ariel tells the story of why she's looking for her dad. Melody gets to ask some more questions and take some notes. No more pictures. We eat lunch. And that's it. Interview over."

"But—"

"No buts. I'm done."

I turn and march through the door and down the stairs, not waiting to see if they'll follow. The doorbell rings, and I'm mad enough to answer it. If it's paparazzi, all the better, I have some things I want to say.

A stranger stands on the porch, but he doesn't have a camera. Midthirties, navy slacks, pinstripe shirt, tie. His hair is slicked back, his face smoothly shaven. And he's got a name tag that declares he's Erik Crandall, MSW, an employee of the Department of Children and Family Services. He carries a briefcase in one hand.

I stare at him, blankly, all words blown away by that name tag.

He introduces himself politely enough. "We received a call from a concerned citizen that there is a child in your home who is at risk. May I come in?"

"It's not a good time."

He smiles with professional condescension. "It's never a good time, is it? I can come back later with the police if you prefer."

Out in the street, the camera guys are converging on the house like kids on a Christmas tree. I step aside and let him in, locking the door behind him.

"Can you tell me what the allegations are, specifically?" I manage to stay outwardly calm.

"Just some concerns about the child. Is she here? Or is she in school?"

"She's here. Under the circumstances, the principal of her school in Nevada agreed it would be best for her to complete the year with home study."

"May I see her schoolwork?"

"Her textbooks should be arriving today. You do know that her mother just died, right?"

"It's usually best for a child to return to school and her usual routines quite quickly. I'd like to look around the house, if that's okay."

None of this is okay, of course, but I bite my tongue to keep from telling him so. "Where would you like to start?"

"How about the kitchen?"

I lead him down the hallway. At the bottom of the stairs we nearly collide with Ariel, Melody, and George.

"This is Ariel," I say. "And Melody. She's . . . um, visiting."

No need to make introductions the other way. Ariel's quick eyes have already caught the name tag and the purpose of the visit. She throws her arms around my waist and leans her head on my shoulder, turning a high-beam smile on Erik while George goes to work sniffing every square inch of his pants.

"Hi," Ariel says. "I bet Ricken called you."

"Now why would you say that?" Erik pushes George's intrusive nose away from his crotch, brushing at the black fur clinging to his pants.

"We fired him. He got mad and he's worried he'll lose out on the money."

"I can't tell you who called, I'm afraid. Are you happy with your aunt?"

"Of course!"

I should get the girl some acting classes. She's a natural. But I see from Erik's face that her happiness isn't necessarily the point. He opens his mouth to say something, stops, and stifles a sneeze with his sleeve.

"Allergic to dogs," he says, looking down at George, who sits in front of him, panting happily and waiting to be petted.

I'm pretty sure Erik would like me to put the dog outside, but instead I turn and head for the kitchen. Ariel follows, George at her heels. Then Erik, with Melody bringing up the rear. Erik sets the briefcase on the counter and pulls out a pen and clipboard. Then he goes through the cupboards and looks in the fridge, checking off boxes and making notes as he goes. Thanks to Lexy, the fridge is full of milk and eggs, fresh vegetables, chicken, whole-grain bread. The cupboards are also all well stocked. The kitchen is spotless, and evidence of our junk-food binges and high-carb dinner is in the trash can.

He asks Ariel about school and she gives him the same information I did about finishing out the year from home. She volunteers that it's important for her to be with me, her only family. Her smile is bright, her body language relaxed. But there's a set to her chin and an expression in her eyes that reminds me she's Callie's daughter and my father's grandchild. If she explodes while Erik is in the room, God help us all.

"One of the concerns is that both of you are using drugs," Erik says, completely unaware of the storm that's brewing. "Any truth to that?"

Ariel beats me to the retort. "Last I heard, pot was legal in Washington State. Are they taking kids for that now?"

I recognize the sarcasm. Erik misses it. "So you are using marijuana, then?" He pronounces the word precisely, like a medical term, and the wicked part of me wants to play with him, shake him up, scandalize him a little. But the last thing we need is a scandalized CPS guy. So I bite my tongue and dig my fingernails into Ariel's hand as warning.

"Alcohol is legal as well," he goes on, "but often creates an unhealthy environment for a child. Do you drink, Ms. Redding?"

"Rarely."

"And you are aware that any alcohol or marijuana use is illegal for a sixteen-year-old, I'm sure."

"She's not using drugs." Memory of the bottle stashed in Callie's drawer colors my response and makes my voice fall flat. Where did Ariel put it? If he searches the room, he'll never believe it's been there for sixteen years.

"Well, it would be helpful to run a drug screen. Are you both able to do that today?"

"We have plans."

"You can do it tomorrow, of course," he says. "But then there will always be a level of doubt. It should only take a few minutes. Depending on how busy the lab is." He smiles, showing all of his teeth. "Now. We need to talk about paternity and the media and what's been going on the last few weeks. Maybe we should go sit down and get comfortable, yes? And maybe your photographer friend should leave."

"Melody stays."

"It's exactly this sort of thing that makes it appear you are seeking media attention. It can't be good for a vulnerable child to have a photographer actually in the home."

"She's here to make the others go away."

"Or maybe you've been feeding the media information all along. It's not uncommon, I understand, for stars to accidentally leak their location to get press."

Turns out I'm also my father's daughter. Rage, already simmering, flares hot and bright. I want to throw something, break something, slam a fist into his perfect little nose. I dig my fingernails into my palms, focusing on the pain. "If you're suggesting—"

"I'm not suggesting anything. I'm asking."

"Haven't you been watching the news?" Ariel asks. "It was Shadow."

"Oh, come now. And you really didn't know what was going on?"

"Ricken told me they were in Portland," Melody says. "He got the tip from Shadow."

Erik looks at her and shrugs. "I'm not sure of your credibility, given what you stand to gain. Now. This way, yes?" He leads the way back to the living room and sits down in one of the chairs without waiting for the rest of us. Melody takes the chair across from him, pulling out her own notepad and pen. I wonder if we should offer him coffee.

Ariel perches on the edge of the couch and I take the place beside her. Both of us are stiff as boards, spines straight, feet flat on the floor. Our arms and shoulders touch, and I can feel her vibrating with suppressed energy. George sits in front of us, ears perked.

Erik sneezes again, wipes his nose with a tissue hauled out from the depths of his pocket, then glances down at his clipboard and makes a note. "Now Ariel, let's be honest, shall we? I know how hard all this has been for you, but do you really expect me to believe you don't already know who your father is?"

It's like he lit a match and threw it into a barrel of gasoline. There's an instant of supercharged silence. And then the explosion.

"Fuck you!"

She springs to her feet, every muscle in her body rigid, fists clenched.

"Ariel!" I grab for her hand, but she jerks it away from me.

"Do you think this is *fun* for me? Being stalked like some sort of game animal, all of them trying to get the biggest trophy? That's what they think I am. *Meat.* You're just like all of them. I bet you like to hunt. Do you have antlers on your wall? Do you go out every year and shoot yourself a nice big buck?"

"Ms. Redding, Ariel—"

A growl pulses in George's throat.

Ariel advances until she is standing right over Erik. He leans back in his chair, his eyes darting toward the exit, then back to me. Considering his escape route.

"Answer me. *Do you?*"

If she hits him, or George bites him, we're done for. Juvie, court, loss of custody. Without thinking, I'm up, too, grabbing George by the collar. There's no room to get between Ariel and Erik. Yelling won't work. I pitch my voice low, with as much authority I can muster.

"Ariel."

She ignores me, and I say it again.

"Ariel. Go to your room. Now."

Nothing happens. My heartbeat is so loud I'm sure they can all hear it. Melody sits frozen in her chair, mouth hanging open, camera in her lap. George tugs at his collar, still growling. Erik doesn't dare move a muscle. Ariel stands there, panting. And then her mouth starts to work. Her face crumples. And she breaks into huge, wracking sobs that electrify all of us.

I wrap my free arm around her, pulling her in tight. She puts her arms around my waist and clings. "Don't you dare say a word," I tell Erik over her shoulder. "Give us a minute."

George growls again, and I have to jerk hard on his collar to drag him away. Ariel comes with me, compliant, and I get both of them out of the room and up the stairs.

"I'm sorry," Ariel sobs, her words blurred and muffled against my shoulder. "I'm sorry, I'm sorry, I'm sorry."

I sit her down on Callie's bed, stroking her hair. George licks tears from her cheeks and she lets go of me and hugs him, burying her face in his fur.

"You had something to say and you said it. At least you didn't hit him."

"Almost."

"Yeah, well. I almost did, too. And I've never heard George growl at somebody before. All three of us could have wound up in jail."

That earns me a choked laugh. Her sobbing slows and eases.

I cup her face in both hands and turn it up to mine. "We'll fix this, okay? He doesn't really have any ammunition. Nothing but allegations."

She nods, sniffling, then flings her arms around me again and clings. Her whole body is quivering. "I'm scared."

"I know. Me too. We'll get through this."

"I want to stay with you," she says. "Even if we do find my dad. Just so you know."

I tuck her head under my chin and rock her. Her hair is so soft, so warm. Impossible that two weeks ago she wasn't in my world at all. The thought of her not being there going forward is inconceivable. "It will be okay," I say again. "I'm going to talk to him again now."

She nods and sniffles.

"In a minute, when you're calm, you should come back down, too."

Her eyes go wide. "I'm not sure that's a good idea."

"It's a very good idea. And you will apologize to him."

She pulls away from me. "I can't."

"You can. You will. We are going to do everything we have to do. Understand?"

Sniffles. And then a nod. I pat her head and leave her and George to pull themselves together.

Coming down the stairs, I hear voices in the living room. Shit. I've left the reporter and the CPS worker together in the room. This can't be a good thing. They break off when I walk in.

The couch feels empty without Ariel at my side.

"That was quite a display," Erik says. "Maybe some counseling is in order."

I take a breath, plant my feet on the floor. My voice is calm. "Her mother just died. Her boyfriend sold her out. She has a pack of media hounding her everywhere. I can't imagine what sort of emotional state you expect her to be in right now."

"All the more reason why she needs to be in a structured and stable environment. With all due respect, I'm not sure you're providing that for her."

"With all due respect, I think you've let the media color your perceptions." I keep my voice level, but I am not backing down.

"All right," he says, after a long moment. "Suppose you tell me your version of events."

So I do. I tell him everything, from the minute Ariel told me about her crazy plan to where we are now. He listens, takes notes. Melody takes notes of her own. I begin to relax, thinking he understands, that he hears how difficult this has been. For her, for me.

When I'm done, he looks up and says, "There's something I still don't understand."

"What's that?"

"Why did you go with her?"

I stare at him disbelieving. He hasn't understood a thing.

He closes his notebook and slides it neatly and precisely back into his briefcase. "And now you're essentially blaming her for the whole fiasco. A responsible adult would have stopped her. Are we ready to go do that drug screen?"

"That's not fair!" Ariel says. I didn't see her standing at the door, listening. George isn't with her, and I can hear him whining upstairs, most likely behind a closed door.

"So long as you're clean and sober, Ariel, you have nothing to fear."

"I'm not talking about the stupid drug screen! It's not fair to blame Aunt Lise. She was only trying to—minimize the damage."

"I'm not going to argue with you," he says, still patronizing. He edges around her on his way to the door.

I follow him. "What happens next?"

"I talk to some people. We look at your drug screens. And then we'll see. Have a nice day."

The door slams behind him. The three of us stand there looking at each other, three little pigs in a fairy tale that's taken a wrong turn.

"So much for apologies," Ariel says. "What now?"

I sigh. "Now we get the drug screen. And then we go see Grandma. Can we also volunteer at a soup kitchen, maybe feed some orphans or give coats to the homeless?"

Ariel's face droops. She shuffles one foot on the carpet. Callie used to do that, usually when she was guilty.

"About the drug test," she says, in a small voice.

"What about it?"

"There might be a problem."

"Ariel, for the love of all things holy, do not tell me you've been using drugs."

"Don't shout at me." She looks wretched. Mascara is smeared around her puffy eyes, her nose is red.

"I'm sorry. I didn't mean to shout. You'd better spit it out."

"I might, maybe, have smoked some weed with Shadow."

"Might?"

"All right. Yes. I smoked weed. Now I'll test positive and they'll put me in some foster care place."

Ariel stares at her feet. I stare at the wall. Surely, they won't take her away. It's not my fault if she smoked pot. But given Erik's obvious bias, we're going to be screwed if this goes to court.

Melody walks away, but she's back in a minute with a tall glass of water.

"Start drinking, kid. This will help."

Ariel takes the glass without protest.

"Now," Melody says, as the water disappears down Ariel's throat with small glugs, "when was the last time and how often did you do it?"

"I don't know. A week, maybe? It was Pasco. The Timothy time."

"You were with me the whole time," I protest. "You never had the opportunity."

"Outside," she says. "On the balcony. While you were sleeping."

"And before that?" Melody persists.

Ariel shakes her head. "That was the only time. Honest."

"You should be okay," Melody says. "Takes longer to clear for a regular user. A week ought to do it for you."

"It's only been five days! What are we going to do?" Ariel's voice trembles, rising into a little squeak on the last word.

"If it was only the once, you're probably still okay. Drink tons of water. Don't suppose you have any vitamin B floating around?"

We both look at her and she shrugs. "Makes your pee yellow so it doesn't look diluted from all the water."

"How do you know all this?" I ask.

She just smiles. "Let's go visit Grandma while Ariel gets hydrated."

Which is when I suddenly remember who I'm talking to. "Even if Ariel tests negative, you're going to have a fabulous story." I smack myself in the forehead. "I am an idiot."

"Tell you what. You give me Grandma, I don't mention the pot smoking. Deal?" Melody holds out her hand. There's nothing to be done but shake on it and hope she keeps her end of the bargain. I doubt it.

Ariel locks herself in the bathroom for what seems like hours, finally emerging with more makeup on than I've ever seen her wear. I don't blame her; I'd do the same if I thought it would do me any good. When we're ready to leave, I put George in the backyard to watch for overly venturous intruders, but he howls so loudly about being separated from Ariel that I relent and bring him along. To her credit, Melody has no objection to riding in the backseat with a whole lot of excited dog.

She insists on a quick stop at Safeway, so she can run in for water and a bottle of vitamin B. She also brings back a rawhide chew stick and a bunch of flowers. I don't ask what the flowers are for. I know.

Whatever Glynnis meant by normal, I'm pretty sure this isn't it.

CHAPTER EIGHTEEN

There are rules about nursing homes and hospitals. Patient confidentiality means paparazzi can't come barging in, and we leave our little convoy parked in the lot, capturing the front of the building and our backs. Melody is restricted to a small pocket camera. She nearly has a tantrum at the idea of leaving her camera unattended even after I tell her that car theft and break-ins are unusual occurrences in Colville. Besides, George makes for a great theft deterrent. In the end, she downloads all of her photos, just in case, and we leave the camera locked in the car.

Valley View is a good place, as far as nursing homes go. It's clean and airy, with lots of windows and high ceilings, but to me it smells like despair. Two wheelchairs sit facing each other inside the entry. In the first an old man, collapsed in on himself in a twisted wreck of limbs, glares at a woman who can only be called fat. I have no idea how they get her in and out of the chair. She is laughing, toothless gums pink, multiple chins wobbling.

Melody's hand inches toward her pocket. I grab it and shake my head. No pics of the other residents is part of the agreement. We set out down the hallway, Melody beside me where I can watch her, Ariel trailing behind. An aide in cartoon-print scrubs steps out of one of the rooms.

"Hey, Annelise! She's in her room. She missed you." She flashes a bright smile. "Is this your niece?"

"It is."

"Awesome! Dale was great while you were gone, but I know your mom will be glad to have you back. She's quite alert this morning, so it's a perfect time for a visit."

We both know Mom has no idea who she's talking to and that alert means awake, but the staff is like that, always maintaining a cheerful pretense that things are normal. The aide bustles into another room, and we continue our trek, detouring around Mr. Erhler, who is using the handrail to pull himself along in the wheelchair, one slow handhold at a time.

It's a short hallway. Mom's room holds two beds, both empty and neatly made with brightly colored quilts. The TV is on and blaring, Dr. Phil admonishing a teary-eyed woman in black. Mom sits in a chair, pointed more or less toward the TV, but the tilt of her head puts her focus to the left, between the screen and the window where there is nothing but blank wall.

Ignoring Melody, who is already snapping pictures, I bend down and kiss Mom's cheek, cool and papery. She smells of baby powder. Her head turns, slowly, at my touch, and a wavering hand reaches out for mine. Her eyes find my face, the mind behind them wandering in search of a name.

"Callie? You never visit."

"Not Callie. It's Lise." I'm not supposed to argue with her. She gets agitated. The staff says it's better to let her believe I am whoever she happens to think I am. But I can't do it. Not today.

"Aren't you going to tell her?" Ariel says. She's got the look of a deer in the headlights, wide-eyed and skittish, like she's going to make a run for it any minute.

"She wouldn't remember. She's still asking when Dad is coming to see her."

Mom turns her head at our whispered conversation, her hand in mine all fragile bones, vibrating with the tremor she can't control. "Company," she says. "Come in, sit down."

"This is Ariel," I tell her.

"Who?"

"Ariel. Callie's little girl."

"Hi, Grandma." Ariel steps closer.

For just an instant, I think Mom has really seen us. Her eyes focus in on Ariel's face.

"Where's Jack? Let me get him. Jack! We have company."

She rocks forward to stand up, and an alarm goes off, sharp and insistent. It sets my pulse to racing, even though I know what it is and have heard it plenty before.

"Mom, please sit. You'll fall." She's still got a faint-green stain on her cheek from the last time she tried to walk on her own. By some mercy she didn't break any bones, but she probably won't be so lucky the next time.

Once in motion, she's not easy to derail. Her hand detaches from mine, reaching for the chair arm to give herself leverage. She rocks again, manages to lift onto her feet. I stand in front of her, my knees against hers, and push her back down, hands on her shoulders. She's wiry, stronger than she looks. Her face twists with anger. I'm not Callie anymore, not Lise, just an obstacle.

"Get out of my way, you." She takes a swing at me, and I duck my head and take the blow with my shoulder. All the while the alarm continues to bleat.

An aide comes in full steam ahead, a different one, but with the same cheerful smile. "Hey, Emma. What's going on? Why don't you sit down, let me get you a glass of water."

"I need to find Jack," Mom says, her voice quavery and panicked.

"Jack is just fine. I'll find him for you in a minute. Okay? Now, just sit back and drink this. There you go."

The aide turns off the alarm and distracts her with a drink of water, then coaxes her to lean back into the recliner. The touch of a button brings up the footrest. In that position, with an afghan tucked around her legs and over her lap, she's not going anywhere.

She's forgotten all about us, anyway, her gaze drifting back to the edge of the television screen. I keep thinking I'll get used to this, but I never do. Every time my mother looks at me, I hope she'll know it's me, even if it's only for a second. Every time she starts asking about Dad, I remember coming home from the hospital to tell her that he died while she was home sleeping. Time and constant repetition has so far failed to build calluses over the pain, and it's always fresh and new.

Today, though, I carry a talisman. There's a corkboard on the wall by her bed. I pull the picture out of my pocket, the one where she's holding me—me, not Callie—in a way that says I'm the most important thing in her world at that moment. The one where my dad is strong and smiling and alive. I pin it beside the chart that says what day it is, beneath the one that says what's on the menu for dinner.

"I'm sorry," Ariel says, behind me, "but I really need to pee."

***

The only place in Colville to do a drug screen is at the family practice clinic. It's busy. It's public. I run into three people I know in the main waiting area before we even get to the elevator that takes us down to the lab.

Melody with her camera and citified clothes is conspicuous. In the elevator, she says, "You need to call that boyfriend of yours."

"I don't have a boyfriend."

"Whatever. Call Dale. Tell him he needs to go to the cemetery with you."

The elevator doors open, but I don't move. "We're not doing that."

"You want your public to feel compassion. And to see that you're stable. He's a steady guy, right? Well respected."

The doors start to close, and Ariel catches them.

I shake my head. "No. Absolutely not."

"You should definitely think about it," Melody says.

"I thought we were going to do whatever it takes," Ariel chimes in.

I glare at her. "Like apologizing to Erik?"

"But he was an asshole!" She says it with conviction, as if it's a valid excuse.

"Are you getting out?" An elderly couple stands at the doors. Both of them lean heavily on walkers. The man frowns; the woman's face is contracted with pain.

"Sorry." We troop out of the elevator, and Ariel holds the doors while the couple shuffles in.

The waiting room is full. People waiting for the lab and to see the doctor. A young woman rocks a wailing baby while trying to control two rambunctious toddlers. One of them is banging on the closed door marked "Yellow Group." I'm grateful for the squalling baby when I step forward to the window to give our paperwork to the receptionist, but of course he stops crying just in time for the whole lobby to hear our business.

I suck in my breath, but the woman is mindful of patient confidentiality and takes the papers with professional calm, as if we're here to get our cholesterol checked.

Ariel goes first and returns to the waiting room nervous and twitchy.

"It's like we're criminals," she says, and it does feel that way. Before I'm allowed into the bathroom, the lab worker puts tape over the knobs on the sink. My instructions are clear: I must not wash my hands or flush the toilet until I turn over the sample, or it will be disqualified. When I emerge with my little cup of pee in hand, I nearly run smack-dab into Pastor Montaigne. He's decent enough to nod and say hello without asking questions or getting into a "so sorry for your loss" or "it's been a while since I've seen you at church" mode. He pretends he doesn't see the brimming cup in my right hand. Maybe he'll think I'm just here for a bladder infection or something.

Until the headlines surface.

Face burning, I obediently observe the process of sealing the cup and then add my initials next to those of the tech.

There are no stairs that we can see, so we have to wait for the elevator, which we end up sharing with a guy who coughs so hard I expect to see lung tissue bursting out of his mouth. Not a word passes between the three of us. Even when we get to the car.

I'm too weary to argue about the cemetery. The biggest problem is going to be remembering exactly where the grave is. I don't come here. Dad is dead. I don't see how standing around and looking at a stone in the ground will make me feel any closer to him. So while I drive, I'm frantically sorting through my memory of the funeral to get some sort of bearing on where to park and where to walk because it's not going to help my cause if Melody finds out I have no idea whatsoever where to find the grave.

Nobody mentions Dale, and I'm thanking my lucky stars that at least she's forgotten about that little piece of torment. Until I drive up the hill, slowing for the turn, and see a familiar pickup truck parked down one of the lanes. George whines and prances, his tail creating a small windstorm and whacking Melody in the head.

"What's Dale doing here?"

"I called him," Ariel says.

"What? How?"

"Technology. Google."

I lean my forehead on the steering wheel and bang it. I manage to hit the horn and it honks, loud and obscene among the peaceful dead. When I look up, Dale is approaching our car. A little bleat escapes me, a small, ridiculous noise like a sheep in pain.

"Well, you weren't going to," Ariel says. She starts chewing on a fingernail, catches herself, and drops both hands into her lap.

"Come on, everybody out of the car." Melody sounds like a grade-school teacher charged with a bus full of slow kids.

Ariel turns her head to look at the cemetery, then back to look at me. Her jaw has gone soft, and her lip is dangerously close to trembling. She doesn't get out of the car.

"At least there are no horses," I say, finally.

Neither of us moves.

Melody is already busy, camera clicking and whirring in all directions. She's mostly focused on the old part of the graveyard, which is visually interesting. Old tombstones and trees—picturesque and perfect for a photo op. But Dad is buried in the new section, which is just a flat green lawn marked at regular intervals by headstones. Since I still don't know where to locate the particular one that marks his spot, maybe we can just pretend he's buried somewhere in the old and interesting part. It would be as real as the rest of this charade.

Dale presents a whole new layer of difficulty. Melody greets him like a long-lost friend. He answers her greeting politely, but there's no smile.

"Grave's over that way." He gestures toward the boring part of the cemetery on the north side of Seventh Avenue. Melody looks with obvious longing at what would obviously make a better story, then shrugs and heads off in the direction of his pointing finger.

Dale continues on to the car and opens my door, looking down at me. "You coming?"

I want, simultaneously, to fling myself into his arms and ask for comfort like a child, to beat on his chest with my fists, to kiss him. I stay in my seat, hands on the wheel.

"You've been quiet." The bitterness creeps into my voice despite my best attempts to keep it out.

"I needed some time to think." He is so cool, so distant, so controlled. I want him to fight with me, to show some kind of emotion. I feel like I'm suffocating.

"If we're going to do this, let's get it over with," Dale says, after a long pause. He bends a little farther so he can look into the backseat at Ariel. "Come on, kid. Let's go."

She grabs the flowers and gets out of the car. George whines and she pats him and tells him to stay. The three of us start walking in the general direction Melody went: Ariel on one side of me, Dale on the other. A wave of déjà vu hits me. We walked like this to Callie's grave. My feet stop moving. The rest of my body takes a little longer, and I trip over a clump of grass and very nearly fall. Dale and Ariel continue on a few steps before they realize I'm missing and turn back, questioning looks on both their faces. I remember Dale's arm at Callie's funeral, warm and supporting, the strength of his hand, but now he only looks at me and says, "You okay?"

I want to scream that I'm not okay. I wonder what would happen if I were to fling myself on the grass like an unruly toddler and scream and kick and shout obscenities. How would that fit with normal?

"It's been a while," I say, because Melody is just ahead of us with the camera and I've begun to feel like it's really The Camera, all knowing and omnipresent. But he doesn't understand what I'm asking for, can't pluck the thought out of my head, and I finally have to admit the truth. "I don't remember where we put him."

"I do," Dale says, without any hesitation. His brain lays the world out like one of his construction diagrams. He starts walking again, not waiting for me. Ariel moves beside him.

I feel like I'm standing on the edge of a dream, all my losses overlapping like a double-exposure photograph. Dad's funeral superimposed on Callie's, white on green, grief on grief, layer on layer. Ahead of me, Dale and Ariel walk in sunlight. Dale's broad shoulders and Ariel's blonde hair framed by blue sky, their feet moving easily through spring-green grass. My sky is heavy and gray, my feet planted in snow, my arm around my mother's fragile shoulders. Callie is there beside me, just out of reach. I can see her shadow out of the corner of my eye, black on white.

I am the only negative space.

And then, in my heart or my head or somewhere in between, the music starts. Just like the old days, when songs were always writing themselves throughout the day. A single tone plays in my head, and then another, chaining into a thread of melody. Words follow.

If I color you gone . . .

What will my world be then?

The music opens a sensory floodgate that holds me spellbound. Sunlight warms my hair, my slightly upturned face. My feet are cradled in grass, each blade a new life, pushing up out of the earth as if there has never been snow. My chest expands in a breath that reaches to my toes and fills me with the fragrance of earth, of grass, of trees, of sun, and with the distant undertone of lilacs.

I feel at once surreal and more alive than I have ever been. More aware. Even the air through which I move is a presence. The song grows in my empty spaces, fills me, makes me real. All of the memories of music, every pressure of fingers against the piano keys, every touch of guitar strings, every note that ever emerged from my throat into the waiting stillness, these surround me, as real and true as the memories of my dead.

Dale and Ariel and Melody, oblivious to my epiphany, stop at what must be my father's grave, waiting. Melody holds the camera half-raised, looking directly at me, and not yet through the lens. Dale half turns, seeking me out. Ariel's head is bent, gazing down. And then Melody lifts the camera.

With the first click, the reality of the moment sucks me in. My skin feels a little tight, as if I've grown. Words are far away, but I don't need them right now. I take my place beside Ariel, using her as insulation against the problem of Dale. Melody and her camera approve.

The headstone is no more than a flat brass plaque with Dad's name and the date of his birth and death. Both Dale's and Ariel's faces are closed down, their eyes shuttered. None of us look like the expected picture of grief. Melody, if she notices, doesn't seem to care. She continues to direct the action, as though this is a movie and she's the director.

"Lovely. Now, Ariel, lay the flowers on the grave. Perfect. All of you, look up here. There you go."

Ariel doesn't look up on command. Her eyes are turned down, fixed on the bare-bones brass plaque. "I wish Mom was buried here." Her voice quavers.

"I dreamed about her last night," Dale says. "And when I woke up, I could smell that perfume she used to wear."

A shiver runs up my spine. Ariel and I exchange a glance, and I know she's thinking the same thing I am. Callie's been trying to deliver messages to all of us, it seems. I wonder if she stopped by to visit Mom, and if it was possible to get through there.

"Damn," Dale says.

I think he's still on the subject of Callie, but then I see where he's staring and turn my own head. A white compact car turns off Seventh and into the narrow lane leading toward our part of the cemetery. A ragtag procession of other vehicles trails behind it. We are exposed here, with no way to hide.

Nobody needs to say anything; we all head for the cars. Ariel's eyes are full of tears. She stumbles and Dale catches her, keeping an arm around her shoulder.

"Can't you make them go away?" she asks. "I'm so sick of eyes watching all the time. I just want to be left alone."

I don't know what to tell her. Maybe in a few days they'll get bored with us and move on, if we hide out in the house and don't go anywhere. And if nobody else spills any gossip about us or Callie.

"How about I take you to my parents' place for a couple of days?" Dale says. He's talking to her, but his eyes are on me. "Dad will fend off any cameras. My folks get lonely. They'd love to have you."

My heart gives a funny little twist at the thought of being in the old house without Ariel, but one glance at her miserable face settles it for me. "Sounds like a good idea."

"What would I do? Do they even have TV?"

"They have Dish. Or you could help Dad with the car he's rebuilding. Or bake things with Mom. Trust me, they'll keep you busy."

"I like cars," she says. "I don't know how to bake."

"One word: 'cookies.'" He looks at me over the top of her head, his eyes asking something. "You could go too, Lise, if you want to get away."

"I've got work to do." Truth and evasion, all in one. The documents should be rolling in. The will, financial stuff. Time to face the music.

"What about George?" Ariel asks.

"Let's leave George to take care of Lise." Dale's gaze settles on me again. He looks tired. There are dark circles under his eyes. The lines in his face seem deeper. "I really don't like you being there by yourself with all those vultures circling. Are you sure?"

"I'll be fine."

I give Ariel a swift hug. "Call anytime you want to come back, okay? When your books come, I'll get them to you. And I'll bring you your clothes and stuff."

Her arms tighten around my shoulders. She sniffles, nods.

"I still don't like you being alone," Dale says. I wouldn't be alone if he was with me. The words hang on my tongue, but I bite them back. He's cut that avenue off sharply. The least I can do is have some pride.

George is in the front passenger seat of my car, face against the window, whining like his heart is going to break. I open the door for him and he gambols over to Dale, sniffing at his pant legs, then throws himself at Ariel. She wraps her arms around his neck and presses her face against the top of his head. Cameras click and whirr, but she's screened by a whole lot of dog and they all keep a reasonable distance. Maybe they've heard some tales. I doubt any of them have developed a sudden sense of compassion.

Ariel gets into Dale's pickup, George jumping in beside her.

"George, get down here." Dale snaps his fingers and points at the ground. The dog whines but stays right where he is.

I shrug. "I'll be okay. Let him stay with Ariel."

"You sure?" Dale asks. "You could stay at my folks', too."

"I'm sure." I turn and walk back to my car. Dale follows.

"Be careful," he says. "Be smart." He waits until Melody and I are safely in—doors locked, engine running—before he walks away.

"You're a lucky woman, to have a man like that," Melody says.

I hit the gas harder than I need to. Gravel spins under my tires before they find traction and I fishtail a little. Lucky indeed.

Melody's not done. She makes a sizzling noise. "He's hot. Looks great on camera. He's a fabulous addition to the story, trust me."

In my rearview, I watch the pickup turn onto the road behind us. George sits in the middle, Ariel's arm around his neck. Behind them, the other cars string out. We look like a funeral procession, until I turn left and Dale keeps going straight. The cars behind him slow in a moment of indecision. Ariel is the hotter topic at the moment, and they follow Dale, except for my old friend the white compact, which follows me.

"I would have thought he'd have spread the word to his buddies," I say.

Melody cranes her neck to look through the back window. "Are you kidding? It's a cutthroat business. Do you know how much ribbing he'd get if he said he was run off by a dog and a shotgun? Uh-uh. He's not going to tell."

She watches me watching the rearview and says, "You're not worried, are you? About letting her go?"

"Nope. She'll be safe up there. Nobody's getting past Mr. Elliot."
We're quiet the rest of the way back to my parents' house. When
we pull into the driveway, she says, "Thank you for your trust in me.
The story will be good. I promise." She hugs me, like I'm a long-lost
friend. No air kisses, no pretending. I'm surprised to feel a warm little
burst of affection. Stockholm syndrome, I tell myself. She is anything
but my friend and now knows way too much about me. With photo-
graphic evidence to prove it. She'll sell everything to the highest bidder
at her first opportunity. This whole thing could go right, or it could go
horribly wrong.

***

I spend the evening working on the new song. My fingers forget to be
awkward after a while. My voice wakes up. The music takes over, and
I forget about everything until I've got both words and music down.

After, I sit at the keys, hollowed out and cleansed. Even as the
world comes back to me—one responsibility, one problem, one grief at
a time—I feel content. I have made peace with the music.

When I stand up, my whole body feels more like I'm ninety than
thirty-five. The kitchen clock says it's 1:00 a.m. Outside the living room
window, the street is empty.

A whisper of Callie's voice brushes across my mind. *Music is not to
be hoarded.*

"All right," I tell her out loud. "This one's for you."

I get in my car and drive the dark, silent streets back to the house
I'm renting. I have a small recording system set up for some of my
students. It helps if they can hear themselves, particularly my voice
students. Ariel thinks I'm a Luddite; I'm not. I just don't care to be
connected to the world all the time with social media. But I have a new
Mac, and I'm proficient with music software and graphics. Some of

the kids have walked out of my little studio with a professional-quality demo ready to go.

Piano is tricky to record properly, so I use the keyboard. When I think I'm ready, I click to start recording and immediately freeze. My voice sticks in my throat. My hands lock up on the keys. Even in the old days before the music left me, I never recorded myself and got horribly nervous about performing in public. Callie would get up and sing in church given any opportunity. The one time I tried it, I forgot the words to a song I knew upside down and backwards, and my knees shook like a small earthquake.

I stop the recording and wait for the panic wave to ebb. Then I run my fingers over the keys and try the song again. My voice sounds shaky, my pitch is flat. I see my face reflected in the window, pale and strained.

So I turn out the lights and let the darkness fill up the studio. Callie feels closer to me in the dark. I try to imagine what it would feel like to be in her skin, to love singing in front of a crowd. I can't get there, but little by little my self-consciousness eases away. The music is still there, waiting. It's different for me than it was for Callie, but I can see now that this makes sense. There's enough music for both of us. There always was.

In the darkened room, working by the glow of the computer screen, I manage to record one complete take. It's all right, when I listen through. It's a good song, and my performance is clean and competent. I could stop now, take my weary body to bed. That would be the rational thing to do.

But the music, the song, deserves more from me, and I try again and again, until on the final cut I forget about my exhaustion and the little red flashing light that means the mic is on. I even forget the why of this. No Dale. No Callie. It's just me and the music.

And when I listen to this final take, I know it's done.

But there is one more thing on my mind. A wild and crazy compulsion I know I will never do by light of day, after a good sleep and time to think.

Music should be shared, Callie whispers in my ear.

It doesn't take long searching Internet images before I find the ones I want. Callie onstage at the end of her last concert, arms in the air in a gesture of absolute triumph, a smile on her face. Callie singing her heart out, oblivious to the crowds and cameras. And a photo of the shrine in the parking lot outside the motel in Pasco. I put the pictures with the song to make a video, adding a slide at the end that says, simply, "In Memory of My Sister Callie—Thanks for the Music."

The sky outside my window is gray with predawn light by the time I pull up my YouTube account. I sit back in my chair, staring at the screen until my eyes blur. And then I click "Upload" and select the file I've labeled "Color You Gone." For a minute, I watch the progress bar as the video uploads. It's not too late. I could still hit "Cancel."

Instead, I turn off the monitor so I won't know when the deed is done. If the upload fails, then it wasn't meant to be. I know I won't try again. I haven't tagged the video, or done anything to promote it. Maybe nobody will ever find it, and my song will be a secret between me and Callie. Which would be fine with me.

I've done my part. Discovery lies with fate.

CHAPTER NINETEEN

I wake in a sweat, tangled up in my blanket. I don't know where I am.

An obnoxious chiming echoes in my ears.

I bury my head under my pillow, away from the light, but I can't shut out the noise.

Little by little, I wake up enough to realize I'm back on the couch in the old house. It's broad daylight. Somebody is ringing the doorbell. It seems to take forever to free myself from the confining blanket, get my bearings, and career through the hallways like a drunken bat, lurching hard against the wall and bruising my shoulder.

It's Ash. I stand there, door wide open, blinking at her.

"For God's sake, let me in," she says. "Trust me, you don't want them to see you like this."

Over her shoulder, I catch a glimpse of a collection of cars parked in the street and people snapping pictures. One of them is my friend in the white compact. Some of them are teenage kids, using the cameras on their phones.

Ash shoves past me into the house, dragging me in behind her and slamming the door.

She looks at me and shakes her head. "There's drool on your chin. And did you sleep in those clothes?"

I scrub at my face with my hands and try to run my fingers through my hair. Too many tangles.

"Well, you've just given CPS a field day, letting them get those pics," Ash says. "Here. I brought your homework."

She hands me a brown manila envelope, a stack of file folders, and a small FedEx box.

"I obtained a certified copy of the will directly from Callie's attorney. Per your instructions, I avoided Genesis when I contacted the accounting firm. One of the junior accountants was more than happy to oblige. I think he's probably trustworthy, or at least smart enough to know he wants to be on your good side. He did a great job putting together the financial files. He would appreciate you thinking of him when you form your new team. I also talked to Glynnis. She says to tell you Ricken is no longer in the house and the locks have been changed. She'll have somebody send your suitcase. Your cell phone is in the box. Oh, and the contract for Callie's memoir is ready to sign, and she'd like your e-mail address."

I stand there, too overwhelmed to move, my arms full of envelopes and folders. Ash has always been high energy and is super fueled at the moment. Fortunately, she has places to go and things to do. She leaves me with an admonishment to behave myself and never, ever let anybody see me looking like I've been out all night on a bender.

Once I've locked the door behind her, I take refuge in a hot shower, which serves the dual purposes of washing away the grime and loosening knotted muscles. A search through my dresser yields an old pair of faded jeans with holes in the knees, and a clean T-shirt. There are message lights flashing on the phone; I ignore them. Armed with a pot of coffee and a notebook, I start familiarizing myself with my new responsibilities.

The accountant has sent a clear summary, and I stare at my list of bank accounts, business investments, and property holdings in dismay. Why Callie didn't give it all to Ariel is a question that sits on my shoulder day in and day out. I'm now blessed, or cursed, with a fortune in ready cash. There's also the house in Vegas and three other properties, one of them some sort of old castle in France. A handwritten note tells me to expect debit cards from the bank to give me access to the funds in Callie's trusts, which I can use for living expenses for Ariel and me while waiting for the will to clear probate.

I don't need this much money; I don't want it. When I dream about having money, it's about buying my own house, getting a new car, indulging in a grand piano. I'm dazed by this sudden wealth, and I haven't even scratched the surface of what the business interests entail. Capital, royalties, advances, bonuses. Clearly, I'm going to need help to understand any of it.

For today, I jot down my own list of how many accounts there are, what they are for, and available balances. Ten different accounts in Callie's name. The trusts. Ariel has an account for her allowance and expenses, financed by an automatic deduction from Callie's primary checking account. Also in Ariel's name is a savings account that was opened a month after she was born. In the third week of every month since then, without fail, somebody has made a $200 deposit. With interest, it amounts to over $40,000.

As far as I can see, none of this comes from any of Callie's accounts.

My cell phone rings. It came out of the parcel fully charged and ready to use, for which I suspect I need to thank Glynnis. I don't recognize the number. Don't want to answer. But I'm trying to be a responsible adult, so I pick it up. It's Glynnis herself, her voice clear and precise.

"I've been leaving messages on the landline number you gave me."

"I was busy."

"Hmm. Yes. Well, we have business to discuss. First, I need your approval to accept some engagements."

"What sort of engagements?"

"Ellen DeGeneres has asked for both you and Ariel. You should accept that one. Also, *The View* and *Live! with Kelly and Michael.* There are a couple of reality shows I think you should turn down . . ." Her voice goes on, but I'm stalled on the opening sally.

"Ellen?" That's about all I'm able to hold on to from the string she's recited. I clamp my free hand around the solid wood of my chair, squeezing until it hurts, making sure I'm awake.

Glynnis laughs. "Her people said this is a fabulous human-interest story they are sure their viewers will love. Did you hear anything else I said?"

"Not really."

The old familiar kitchen looks unreal, a random collection of meaningless shapes and textures. I feel dizzy and realize I'm holding my breath.

"I suppose you're not accustomed to these sorts of calls," Glynnis says, kindly. "Do you have a pen? I want you to write down names and dates. You can think about them, but get back to me by tomorrow, okay?"

I turn to a new page in my notebook and jot down what she tells me.

"This type of exposure would be very helpful to you, given the Ricken situation. Now, let's talk about your song."

"My song?" The way I keep repeating words back to her, I'm sure she thinks I'm a nitwit.

"While I understand the impulse that made you post the song, I do request that you consult with me in the future. We could have put it out as a single and advertised it as a commemorative song for Callie. It would have made you a small fortune."

"'Color You Gone' isn't about money."

"Everything is about money, dear. And it's a very good song."

Panic flutters around the edges of the room. "How did you know about the song? I didn't tell anybody." How long since I put it up, six hours?

She makes a little clucking noise. "It's all over the Internet. One million hits on your YouTube site just last night, and of course everybody is sharing it. Album sales are already up and it's giving you lots of positive buzz, but I still think it could have been handled better. In the future—"

"You're not my agent."

"Pardon?"

"You're Callie's agent. I don't have an agent yet. I haven't signed anything. So what I do with my music is entirely up to me. Right?"

Silence. "The agency contract is just waiting for your signature. You can scan it and send it back, and we'll get to work immediately."

Music is for everybody.

A vivid sense of freedom rushes through me. The panic recedes, replaced by the glimmer of an idea. "Let's hold off on that a little, okay? I need some time."

"Lise, you need somebody to represent you. Since I'm still representing Callie's interests, it makes sense for us to work together. Unless you want to fire me like the rest of the team?"

"No, no. I want to keep you. I'm just—let's hold off on what we're going to do with my music. Okay?"

She's not happy but is too smart to push. "All right. Let's take it slowly. But I'd like you to get back to me by tomorrow about those engagements. Best not to keep them waiting."

"All right." I want to say no right now, but this is Ariel's life as well as mine. She deserves a say.

"One more thing, Annelise, that I think you should know. That story about Callie being the sole survivor of a car wreck that killed her whole family when she was a baby? That was all Ricken. He fed one tabloid an exclusive scoop, and the story took off like a bat out of hell.

By the time any reputable reporters got around to doing a fact check, it was too late to set the record straight, not that anybody tried very hard. Callie's reaction was something like, 'Lise is never going to forgive me anyway, so I guess it's sort of true.'"

Her call leaves me feeling shell-shocked and buzzing with adrenaline and guilt. I'd like to take a walk, but there are too many people outside wanting to ask questions and take pictures. So I pace around the house a few times and then sit myself down. My plan is to start a list of Callie's business interests and charities, but I can't stop thinking about my song. Glynnis must be mistaken—there's no way it's had that many hits. I figure I'll take a quick peek at the YouTube site on my phone and then get back to work.

But there are already a thousand comments, well over a million views. I google Callie, scrolling through the resulting hits in wonder. Only then am I brave enough to google myself. Melody, true to her word, has already been feeding bits of our story to different magazines, online and off. There's a picture of Mom gazing up into my face as though I am the best and most beloved daughter in the world. Readers will never guess that she thought I was Callie. There's a picture of Dale and Ariel and me at the cemetery. There are also other shots, all taken from a distance, contributed by the vultures, none of them with the same clarity as Melody's. I have to admit the girl has talent.

When the doorbell rings, I jerk like I've been buzzed by a cattle prod. My heart races, my hands go cold. I can't think of anybody good who could be at the door. Maybe it's just another package. Maybe it's Erik, back for another CPS inspection tour. Or maybe one of the paparazzi people has gotten bold.

When I peek out through the small narrow window beside the front door, there's a man standing on the porch. Tall and well built, with close-cropped blond hair and the sort of tan that comes from a lot of time outdoors.

Letting out a sigh of relief, I crack the door and wave him in. The camera-wielding crowd surges forward. It has grown by about ten people since I last looked.

"Gene! Quick, before the vultures get here."

He takes my advice, slipping through the door and brushing at his arms and shoulders as if he's covered in debris. "Quite the party you've got going on."

"Barrel of laughs. All I need is a keg and a truckload of potato chips. What are you doing here?"

Eugene Garrett is from my class at Colville High. Like me and Dale, he's chosen to stay in town. He does pretty well for himself with a carpet and flooring business. Not much by way of a storefront, but that allows him to keep his costs down, and he gets good word of mouth. He's not a close friend, but he is a familiar face, and I'm surprised by how happy I am to see him.

"Come on in and have a seat. Can I get you coffee?"

His eyes don't quite meet mine, and he stays right where he's planted. "I don't suppose you have a beer?" His laugh is nervous and unease winds up my spine.

"Sorry, I didn't stock up on the alcohol. What brings you to the neighborhood?" My gaze falls to the manila envelope he's clutching in his left hand, and the happiness I felt about his visit shifts to dread.

"This isn't really a social call," he says. "I wanted to give you this in person, instead of you getting it from some stranger."

"What is it?" I reach for the envelope.

He holds on to it with both hands. Shifts his weight from his right foot to his left. Sweat shines on his forehead. "I don't want you to take this the wrong way."

Pictures, I'm thinking. Somebody with a telephoto lens skulking around the yard and taking pictures through the window. The only thing I can think of that would make him look so nervous would be either Ariel or me in a state of undress. It's not like anybody's been having any sex. Unless these are pictures of Callie. But how would photos like that fall into his hands?

"How about you show me?" I tug the envelope away from him. What slides out when I open it is not a glossy eight-by-ten. It's a legal document. I can read the words just fine, but they don't make any sense.

I glance up at Gene. He's sweating in earnest now. "It's not like that," he says, in answer to my look.

"Suppose you tell me how it is then, Gene?" The words "paternity suit" dance in the air between us. I blink to make them go away.

Gene takes a deep breath and swipes a sleeve across his forehead. "Well, if it turns out that I am . . ." He swallows hard, shuffles his feet again.

"Her father," I supply.

"Right. If it turns out that I'm . . . if paternity is established . . ."

"Then what? You'll sue for custody?"

He shakes his head and tries a smile. "No, nothing like that. I'm not trying to take her away from you, Lise. I only want to know if she's mine."

"Great. Then we don't need this. She can swab you with her Identi-Match kit and we'll wait for the results." I hold the papers in both hands and start to tear them, my eyes intent on his face.

His hand shoots out and grabs mine. "Now, Lise. It's not so simple as all that."

"You're going to have to explain it better, then. Pretend I'm six. Give me the kindergarten version." My body feels like a block of ice.

"Now don't be that way, Annelise. It's more of a . . . business consideration."

"You want some of Ariel's money."

His face flushes. "It's not like I'm robbing her blind and leaving her in a ditch somewhere. She's got plenty. I figure I deserve a cut."

"Deserve? What have you done to deserve anything?"

"Well, if I'm her father . . ."

"You're not asking to be a father. You want to be the sperm donor of record. Since when does a high school boy get paid for having sex with a pretty girl? Seems like you got damn lucky."

He draws himself up straight and his mouth presses into a hard line. "I didn't come here to fight with you."

"How did you think I was going to react to this?"

"I figured you for a reasonable woman."

"She's a child, Gene. The same age Callie was when you fucked her, by the way. She's not a money machine and she's sure as hell not a media puppet. Her mother just died, and she doesn't know which bastard might turn out to be her father. And you want in on the money?"

"Lise, I—"

"Get out of my house." I open the door and hold it, screening myself behind it and letting the cameras have a clear view of him looking flushed and off-balance. Let them draw whatever conclusions they want.

"What about the testing?" He's red as a beet, but not moving.

"My attorney will be in touch with your attorney. Don't even think about coming here again. And if you go anywhere near Ariel, so help me God . . ." I leave the words hanging there. It's a threat, I suppose. Maybe he'll use that against me. I don't care.

He takes a step toward the door, hesitates.

"Now," I say. "Before I call the cops to remove you."

"You always were the Ice Queen." He tosses the words over his shoulder, a parting volley. "Thought maybe you'd changed, but you're still a bitch."

The vultures close in on him as soon as he hits the sidewalk. I slam the door and stand there, shaking. As soon as I pull myself together enough to press numbers on the phone, I call Ash. Not her office phone, her cell phone. I don't care if she's busy doing something else. I need her now.

"You're in luck," she says, before I have a chance to start talking. "I reached out to a friend from law school. He's a junior partner in a big entertainment firm in LA. They'll take you on. They've got a whole team, so they can handle your financials, your will, any lawsuits. Okay?"

"How are they with paternity suits?"

"Fine, I should think. They handle some other celebrity accounts." She drops a couple of names that make me gasp while she laughs. "You're in the big leagues, baby. I hadn't realized Callie was such a hot commodity. I checked this firm out from all the angles. They've got great credentials. All members are in good standing with the bar. Even their most junior partners were stars at their various schools. So I think you'll be in safe hands. I told Marcus you'd be calling."

I write down the number she gives me, taking care to put it on a separate page marked "Legal."

"Ash?"

"Yeah?"

"I want you to stay on for the CPS thing."

"Lise, we already discussed this. I'm way out of my league."

"You do CPS, right?"

"I do, but—"

"Forget the media. Forget that it's high profile and I have money. Look at it like any other case. You know the judges, the other attorneys. You're from here. I don't want a high-powered out-of-towner for this. You know how people are."

She hesitates. "I don't know."

"If it doesn't work out, I won't hold it against you."

"If it doesn't work out, they could force Ariel into foster care. But that's unlikely."

"What is likely?"

"They'll probably just close the case. They don't really have anything on you. She's sixteen, not a baby. And you haven't actually neglected her or anything. But . . ."

She doesn't want to say what comes next. There's a long silence.

"Spit it out, Ash."

"Well—if she does figure out paternity, the father would have some say in all this. It could get messy."

"It's already messy."

She pauses. "All right. What am I missing?"

I tell her about Gene.

"Could be worse," she says.

At that, my tongue gets tangled on my next words and I choke. Once I can breathe again, I ask, "How could it possibly be worse? He's not even on the list Callie wrote in the diary. Who knows who else is out there?"

"Exactly why it could be worse. Gene's not an axe murderer or a pedophile. And he doesn't want her to live with him. So he gets a little money. Who cares? You might consider saying he's the father and ending this whole mess. It would take care of CPS, too."

"I'm going to pretend you didn't say any of that."

"Annelise." Her voice sounds patient and a wee bit patronizing. "I love you, but you are an innocent. Don't you pay any attention? Gene might be the best you can hope for. Trust me."

"She wants to live with me. I want her to live with me."

"Listen to me. If the real father shows up, he could sue for custody. And he'd probably win. Even with you as trustee, that would give him some control of whatever money she has coming in."

I'm shivering again. Not just outside, but deep inside on a level that no hot beverage is going to reach or warm.

"How do we make it stop?"

"Not sure you can. I can handle CPS, probably, but I want you to use the other firm for the paternity suits. I'll get you a name and a number and set up a consult. Okay?"

It's not okay. Nothing is okay, and I won't say that it is.

Ash's voice gentles. "Honey, listen to me. You need the best legal representation possible. If Ricken really likes the feel of veins between his teeth, he could try to prove you an unfit trustee, maybe even get control of the money himself."

"Oh God. She's been through a lot, Ash. This isn't fair."

"Kids are resilient."

Maybe. But this is asking too much, of her and of me. Fear is a dark, empty space eating away at everything. I press my knuckles against my mouth to stifle a sob.

"Lise?"

Silence. I can't speak. Can barely catch my breath.

"Lise, listen. A good attorney can probably drag a custody suit out for a couple of years until she turns eighteen. Or maybe she can get herself declared emancipated. Or maybe, just maybe, Dad will turn out to be somebody really wonderful. But I think you should consider letting Gene have this one. Give it some time. Call me tomorrow."

Swallowing hard against a lump that feels like a baseball lodged in my throat, I nod and then realize she can't see me. "Right," I manage to croak. "Thanks, Ash. I'll be in touch."

I hang up the phone and sit there. The world around me no longer feels solid. It's like everything I ever believed or thought I knew has been turned upside down. I'm afraid that if I stand up and take a step, the floor won't hold me, that even the laws of physics have been somehow suspended.

And then I remember the worst thing.

I'm going to have to tell Ariel about Gene.

CHAPTER TWENTY

When I get to the Elliots' place, the sun is hanging low over the trees. The whole way there I've been rehearsing how I'm going to tell Ariel about Gene. I'll bring it up in a roundabout way. Ask her again about the guys on the list that we haven't contacted yet, suggest that maybe there are a few more than she's already mentioned. Maybe she's already e-mailed Gene, or he found her Facebook page and messaged her. In every scenario, she's alone, waiting to talk, and I can spill the news and get it over with.

But when I drive into the Elliots' yard, Dale's truck is parked beside his dad's, and his sister Nancy's 4Runner is pulled up alongside it. A rusty old pickup is up on blocks, and Mr. Elliot and Ariel both have their heads and hands under the open hood. Dale leans on the far side, observing.

Dale looks up and smiles when he sees me, and my heart lifts a little, thinking maybe whatever strange mood possessed him is gone. But then the light in his eyes goes out, and his face sets again into reserve. Ariel is wearing a baseball cap, turned backward. A smear of black grease runs across one cheek. The knees of her jeans are dirty.

She straightens up and grins. "We're fixing the truck."

"I see that."

"Hey, Annelise," Mr. Elliot says. "I hope you're staying for dinner. We're cooking the fatted calf. Hand me that wrench, would you, Ariel?"

She passes him the wrench she's got in her right hand, watching intently as he adjusts something in the innards of the engine. I know nothing about cars. Mine runs. I can change a flat if I have to. All the rest is up to the service-and-tire guys.

But Ariel looks happier and more relaxed than I've ever seen her, and completely in her element. Dale still looks tired. I want to smooth the lines of tension along his jaw and forehead, to massage his shoulders. Hell, I just want to touch him, anyhow, anywhere, but his eyes hold me at a distance.

I'm not welcome. That thought shreds what's left of my intact feelings, and I'm about to make my excuses and say that I have plans elsewhere when the door opens and Mrs. Elliot steps out onto the porch.

"Dinner!" she calls. When she sees me, her face lights up. "Annelise! What a delightful surprise. You are staying for dinner, of course. Come in, come in. The rest of you need to go wash up. Hurry now."

Too late for an escape. I cross the yard and am instantly wrapped in a hug. She keeps her arm around my waist and leads me down the hallway and into the kitchen. A wall of aromatic humidity hits me: beef, garlic, a tang of greens. Nancy stands at the stove, stirring something with a wire whisk. Her hair is tied back in a ponytail, escaping strands sticking to her flushed and sweating face. All of the burners are on.

"Oh, thank God," she says. "Can you stir? I need to pee so bad I'm about to spring a leak."

She thrusts the whisk into my hand and trusts me with the gravy. A mistake, in my opinion, since cooking and I are far from friends. But apparently, all I have to do is stir, and I can hopefully manage that.

I hear the back door open, and three sets of footsteps come in. Two heavy, one light and quick. I catch myself separating Dale's tread out from Mr. Elliot's, holding my breath so I can hear whether he's coming this way.

My ears are so tuned to those footsteps that I don't hear Mrs. Elliot coming up behind me and I startle, spattering gravy over the stove top. Without comment, she takes the whisk from my hand, turns off the burner, and gives a final stir.

"Done," she pronounces, placing the whisk in the sink. "Let's get the food out of the oven."

If the kitchen was hot before, opening the oven door heats it up another notch. She hands me a pair of oven mitts, and all footsteps are blocked from my hearing with the clatter of dishes as we pull a roast and a casserole out of the oven. Nancy flits in and out, carrying dishes out to the dining room.

Finally, Mrs. Elliot takes off her apron and hangs it on a hook. She smoothes her own hair, then turns to me and tries to smooth mine. I feel my curls resisting, and she laughs and cups my cheeks in her palms. "I'm so glad you came for dinner, dear," she says. "Dale told me all about the photography people."

This should be a good thing. I wanted him to tell her the truth. But my stomach sinks. Mrs. Elliot pulls my forehead down and plants a kiss on it. "This, too, shall pass," she says. "Let's go eat."

I follow her into the dining room, suddenly self-conscious as all eyes turn in our direction. I manage to take my place beside Nancy without tripping over anything.

"Dale, would you say grace?" Mr. Elliot asks. He sits at the head of the table to my left. Dale and Ariel sit across from me. We all join hands—Mr. Elliot's strong and calloused, Nancy's cool and soft.

"Dear Father, we are grateful for the food provided," Dale's familiar voice begins.

I sneak a peek at him from under my lashes, only to discover that his eyes are open and he's staring at me with an intensity that sends a jolt of electricity straight to the heart. I miss the end of the prayer, head bowed, eyes closed tightly now, heart hammering like a building crew on a framing project.

Nancy elbows me. "Dork," she says, laughing. "Pass the potatoes already."

It's a meal worthy of an occasion. Thanksgiving dinner. Christmas. But it chokes me. I pick at the food on my plate in silence while everybody else laughs and chatters. Ariel is animated like I've never seen her, discussing car repairs and engine parts with enthusiasm. Her face is alive.

I feel like I'm in a time warp. Since I saw her last, I've written a song and sent it out into the world. Gene has come to visit. This makes my world different than her world, or Dale's, or anybody's. I feel terrifyingly alone.

I've drifted again and missed something. Everybody is looking at me, waiting.

"Lise?" Ariel asks, obviously repeating a question. "Can I stay another day? We're going to rebuild the carburetor tomorrow."

"Sure." And with that, I know I'm not telling her about Gene. Not tonight. The kid deserves a day of happiness. As long as she's here, she won't find out by accident. No Internet access at the Elliots'. And nobody's going to be watching *Entertainment Tonight* or Fox News.

I know this is the right decision, but it makes me feel even more alone.

"Awesome," Ariel says. "This roast beef is incredible, Mrs. Elliot."

"Eat up, child. We'll get you fattened up yet. Lise, dear, you've barely touched yours. Did you need more gravy?"

"I'm fine," I say, possibly the biggest lie of my life, and manage to wash down a bite of mashed potatoes with half a glass of water.

"This kid," Mr. Elliot says, waving his fork at Ariel, "is a natural with cars. Make a fine mechanic, if she wasn't a girl."

"Girls can be mechanics, Dad," Nancy says. "It's not like that anymore."

"I'm a weirdo at school for taking all the shop classes," Ariel says.

"Well, you fit right in here." Mrs. Elliot beams at her.

It's true. She looks perfectly at home sitting there between Dale and Mr. Elliot. Part of the family, while I am just a guest. All three of them sit leaning forward slightly, elbows on the table. Ariel's hands are smaller, softer, but engine grease blacks the cuticles of short, squared-off fingernails. My fork clatters onto my plate as I see, finally, the thing I've been missing.

Ariel doesn't look like Callie, or like my family.

She looks like Dale's.

Mr. Elliot's eyes. A softened version of Dale's jaw. Even her expressions are his.

"Lise?" Mrs. Elliot asks. "Are you okay?"

"I'm sorry. I'm not feeling well. Excuse me." My numb lips barely shape the words.

I push back my chair and blunder out of the room, nearly running into the doorframe. The hall seems to stretch, and it takes forever to reach the door and run outside. I feel like I'm underwater and starving for oxygen. When I finally manage to suck in a breath, it makes a whooping sound and gets tangled in my chest. I double over, arms around my belly, forcing labored breaths in and out while blackness grows at the edges of my vision.

And then there is Dale. He doesn't say anything. I hear his footsteps in the gravel, then his boots appear in my line of sight. He doesn't try to touch me or offer any comfort. Just waits.

Little by little, my breathing eases and I'm able to stand up straight and look at him.

"She made me promise," he says, as if this makes all the sense in the world.

"I don't even know you," I say, studying the face that once seemed so familiar. "All these years, and I have no idea who you really are."

He flinches, but doesn't look away. "She said we could never, ever tell you. I swore it, oath of honor. After she died, it seemed wrong to break faith with the dead . . ."

"You've been sending money to Ariel. Every month."

He doesn't confirm or deny this and seems to be having trouble with his own breathing.

"I'm sorry," he says, after a long silence broken only by his erratic breathing and mine. The words sound like they've been wrung out of him after days of torture on a rack.

I should say something, but I can't. It's not that the words won't come, it's that there aren't any. My little world has been blown apart, and the debris is raining down all around me.

Dale is the good guy. The stabilizer. The solid, grounded, strong one who always does the right thing. He's not the guy who has sex with the sixteen-year-old sister of the girl he's supposedly in love with. Who fathers a child he never acknowledges. That's the sort of thing Kelvin does. Or Bryce, or even Gene. But I can't say any of this.

"You knew" is what finally comes out of my mouth. "You knew, and you let Ariel . . ." I choke on the rest of the sentence. This whole crazy paternity thing. The media. The nightmare Ariel has been through since Callie died.

He shakes his head. "I didn't know. Still don't, for sure. Lise, that's the one thing you have to believe."

God, how I want to cling to any shred of decency.

"I told her I wanted to help her. She said Ariel wasn't mine. She said she'd hate me for life if I pushed it. She said she didn't need my help, that Ariel was hers, and to leave her alone. I . . . I asked her to marry me. She laughed."

"But you sent the money."

"I had to do something, didn't I?"

"And now?" I'm shaking again. I hate this weakness of my body, the buzzing in my head. I need to sit down, but I'm not going to show weakness, not in front of him. Not now.

"I started to see the truth when I picked you up at that motel. Ariel seemed so familiar. I thought it was that I was seeing her reflection of Callie at first. Or at least, that's what I told myself. And then yesterday, I looked up once and saw her and Dad side by side, both so intent on rebuilding that engine . . ."

"Are you going to tell her?"

"I needed to talk to you first. I didn't want to break my promise to Callie. But when I realized today, I knew I had to tell you. Was going to come see you tonight. But then you came out here . . ."

"Well, it solves the CPS problem. And it takes care of Gene." I hear my own voice as if it comes from outside of me and from very far away.

"Garrett? What does Gene have to do with anything?"

"He's suing for custody. Needs the money. Not interested in the child. At least you've proven that money isn't your intention."

I dig in my pocket for my keys. There's nothing for me here. Ariel has found more than just a father, she's found a family. They will embrace her with open arms, take her in, give her all of the love and acceptance she could dream of. I'll be Auntie Lise, and she'll come see me on Saturday afternoons. If I even stay in Colville.

The thought of living so close to Dale, of running into him in town, of seeing him with Ariel, is more than I can handle. I choke on a sob. My keys slip through my fingers and fall in the dirt. Before I can bend for them, Dale does. He holds them, not giving them to me.

"Please," he says.

"Give them to me. I have to go." Tears are smarting behind my eyes. I don't want him to see me cry. I need to get home. I need to be alone, to lick my wounds and be still until the world stops spinning and settles on this new reality. Maybe with some time I'll be okay. For the first time in my life, I can't see how.

I start to reach for the keys, but stop. His hand is inches from mine, but I can't bring myself to touch it. A thin scar bisects the base of his thumb at the first joint. The nail of his right index finger is broken. Not long ago, a matter of days, that hand was warmth and comfort to me. It is this that breaks me, the tears coming in a rush I'm not strong enough to hold back.

"Give me my keys." My voice breaks. I turn my face away, not looking at him, tears pouring down all the while.

"Let me drive you. You're not—"

"Give me the goddamn car keys!"

"Lise . . ."

I wait for him to say something, anything, to make this nightmare go away. But after a long silence, he drops the keys into my hand and I flee to my car. A sob escapes me as I climb into the seat and slam the door. My vision is blurred, my hands are shaking, and it takes three attempts to get the key into the ignition. The car starts, reliable as always. I brush at the tears with my sleeve, clearing my vision so I can drive.

The door opens.

"Lise."

I try to pull it shut, but he's blocking it with his body, leaning down to look at me.

"Let me go."

"You have to know I love you," he says.

Disbelief makes me look up. There are tears tracking his cheeks. He looks older, smaller, folded in on himself. There is nothing I can say. I hit the gas, tearing the door away from his grip. When I lose sight of him in my rearview mirror, he's still standing where I left him, watching me drive away.

CHAPTER TWENTY-ONE

Dale is good at fixing things, but this is beyond him. Watching Lise's car disappear down the driveway, he feels helpless and defeated.

Now that the secret is out, he can see how stupid he's been. Any one of the hundred ways he'd thought of to tell her about Callie would have ended the same. Not for the first time, he wishes he could go back in time. Undo his actions that one night. Only now there is Ariel. He can't bring himself to wish her out of existence, can't imagine the world without her in it. Already, she fits comfortably into his heart, as if there was a space ready-made for her there. Now he's afraid he's going to lose her, too.

Behind him, the front door opens and footsteps cross first the porch and then the gravel. He doesn't turn around. It will be his mother, or Nancy, come to see if Lise is okay, and he's hours, days maybe, away from trying to explain. Scrubbing his sleeve across his face to erase the traces of tears, he swallows hard, steadies his breathing.

"Dale? What's wrong with Lise?"

It's not his sister or his mother. It's Ariel. There's fear in her voice.

He wants to comfort her. Put an arm around her shoulder, ruffle her hair, tell her it's nothing to worry about. Lise is having a grief moment and just needs to be alone. For the count of ten, no more, he also considers making a run for it. His truck is right there. The keys are in his pocket. He glances back over his shoulder at the house. It's only a matter of time before the rest of the family comes out. He's not ready for them yet.

"How about we go for a drive?" he says. "And I'll tell you all about it."

Ariel searches his face, and he knows she sees the marks of tears.

"What did you do to her?" she asks, sounding more like the mother of a bullied child than anything.

"Long story. I'll tell you, but I need to drive while I talk."

She accepts this and climbs into the passenger side of his truck. Dale breathes in the familiar, calming smell of sawdust and engine oil, grateful that driving gives him something to do with his hands and eyes.

"Well?" Ariel demands, as he turns around and heads out down the driveway.

"She's upset about a couple of things," he says, buying time. "For one, a guy came to see her today. He wants official paternity testing, says he thinks he's your father."

"But that's a good thing, right? Which one?"

"His name is Gene Garrett."

Ariel frowns. "He's not on the list."

Dale laughs, a dry scratch in his throat. "Apparently, the list was not complete."

"He must be the king of all asswipes for Lise to get all upset like that. He must be worse than Kelvin or any of the other guys. Bryce even."

"Gene's always seemed like a decent guy. He wanted the money, and that turned her upside down a little."

"More than a little."

"She's worried he'll try to take you away from her. Especially with everything else going on."

"Can they do that? I mean, what if he is my father and CPS tries to make me go live with him?"

There's real panic in her voice, and he's going to have to tell her. Driving doesn't seem like a good idea anymore, but there's no place to pull over.

"How would you like to stay here, with my folks? Or maybe even with me?" he asks, keeping his eyes on the road, trying not to hold his breath.

He can feel her staring at him, but if he looks at her, he'll lose his nerve.

"If they won't let me live with Lise, then why would they . . ." Her voice trails off. "Oh," she says.

"Is there a swab left in that DNA kit?" His words hang in the air between them. When she doesn't answer, he dares a glance in her direction. Her head is turned toward the passenger window, and he can't see her face.

"You're him," she says, about a mile down the road. "That explains everything."

It explains nothing to Dale. He'd expected an emotional reaction. Tears, maybe. Anger. Had hoped for excitement. The flatness of her tone, almost a weary inevitability, squeezes his heart in a vise grip.

"I don't understand," he says, finally.

"You're in the journal."

A shock of cold drills through him, wondering when the media exposure will hit, why it's taken so long. Well, he deserves it.

"What did she say?" he asks, carefully. "Since I'm not on the list."

"Can't remember the words," Ariel says. "And your name's not in there. Just something about finally going too far and sleeping with the wrong guy. Figured she meant some super jerk, given all of the wrong guys she hooked up with. But it was you. Because of Lise."

Lise. The vise grip on his heart tightens with physical pain at the mention of her name.

"You were right the first time," he says. "Super jerk. King of all asswipes. That's me."

"Because you had sex with Mom? Or because of Lise?"

"Both. And because I let Callie convince me to keep it secret."

Ariel finally turns to look at him. Slow tears roll down both cheeks. His heart cracks right down the middle. He's never felt so helpless as he does now, not even when he watched Lise drive away.

"I asked her," Ariel says. "Over and over, I asked her who my dad was. She knew all the time it might be you, and she kept you from me."

"I'm so sorry. Oh God, please don't cry." Dale reaches out and puts his hand on her shoulder, half expecting her to pull away.

She doesn't. Her shoulder is thin, but solid. She is anything but fragile. They drive in a silence broken only by an occasional sob from Ariel.

"I can see why Lise went into meltdown when you told her," she says after a while, scrubbing at her face with both hands.

Dale wants so much to be the good guy in the white hat, but he shakes his head. "I didn't tell her. Watching you with my family, she figured it out all by herself. You're a dead ringer for my dad. Not a doubt in my mind where you belong."

"So, do you want me?" she asks, in a small voice.

He squeezes her shoulder. Wants to hug her, but he's driving, and he's not sure if she's ready for that anyway. "More than anything in the world. I should have been there for you. I—"

Ariel sputters, a laugh and a sob meeting halfway in her throat and choking her up. She waves her hand at him that she's fine, and when she can breathe again, she says, "Mom kept you away. I know her better than anybody. And it's not like you knew then, right? I mean, you didn't know for sure?"

"When I saw you at your grandpa's funeral, you looked more like your mom. I didn't see it then . . ."

"Oh my God. You have to talk to Lise. She's going to hate you."

"Too late, she already does."

"Fix it!"

Dale sighs. "I would if I could. Believe me. I tried. She won't talk to me."

"You didn't try hard enough."

"Ariel—"

"You love her, right?"

"You don't understand."

"I understand plenty. How old were you? When you and Mom—well, you know."

"Nineteen. Old enough to know better."

"Yeah, right. Sex. It's all boys think about."

"It's more complicated than that. She was only sixteen—"

"I'm sixteen."

"I'm well aware of that." God. Just the idea of some horny asshole laying a finger on her sets his teeth on edge and his blood to boiling.

Ariel does an eye roll that puts Callie's version to shame. "Don't be stupid. No guy is ever going to get it on with me unless I want him to. God, you and Lise make it seem like Mom was this helpless child or something."

"Helpless" and "child" are not words he would connect with Callie's behavior on that night. In his mind, he's twisted it, somehow, increasing his guilt. Eliminating hers. Now the memory rolls over him again, complete with the state of his emotions.

A knot in his gut untwists. He feels lighter, despite the condition his heart is in.

"You have to talk to Lise," Ariel insists. "Now. Tonight."

Dale shakes his head. "There's no point. She won't forgive this."

"Please," Ariel says. He's stupid enough to look at her, to see all of the pleading in her face, the tears trembling on her lashes. "I finally find you, and now it's going to be horrible because you and Lise won't be speaking to each other. Please fix it, Dale."

"Maybe," he says, turning the truck around to take her back so they can tell his family. "Maybe I will."

He's wary of making any promises right now, but he knows damn well he's going to do pretty much anything Ariel asks.

CHAPTER TWENTY-TWO

I can't go into the old house.

It's not the paparazzi that stops me, although I'm pretty sure most of the cars parked in the street don't belong to the neighbors. What keeps me sitting in my car staring at the old house is Callie.

Never in all of my life have I wanted so deeply to beat on somebody with my fists, to punish living flesh, to feel the crunch of knuckles on bone. But she isn't here to fight, won't ever be. She's gone where I can't reach her with love, or guilt, or rage. For a long time, I sit in my car, looking at the old house. When I find myself wondering where she and Dale created Ariel, I know there's no way in hell I'm going in. If I try to sleep, I'll picture them in her bed, on the couch, even up against my piano.

So I drive back to my place. There are two or three suspicious cars in the street, but I don't care. Don't even bother to try to hide my tear-swollen face. Compared with this last secret, there is nothing out there that can hurt me.

Once inside, I still can't settle. I try everything. A warm shower leaves me shivering. I try to read but can't focus. When I walk into the music room, remembering all the love I felt while writing "Color You

Gone," the rage crescendos into a wave that makes me want to break things. It's not safe to be in my music studio in a mood like this. I walk out, slamming the door behind me so hard the sound echoes through the house.

That feels good and gives me an idea.

In my bedroom, stashed at the bottom of a dusty box shoved back under my bed, is an unopened CD of Callie's *Closer Home* album. She had the nerve to send it to me, right after the damn thing went platinum. I never opened it. Certainly never listened to it. And now it's the perfect item to smash.

I fetch my hammer and set the CD case in the middle of the living room floor. Callie smiles up at me, and I take the hammer to her with all my strength. The plastic crunches beautifully. Another blow, and it cracks and shatters. The damn CD, though, is near indestructible. After beating on it for a few minutes I start to feel better, even if it doesn't break. I also start to feel like a child having a tantrum. *Grow up, Lise. Face the reality. Clean up the mess.*

When I go to throw the pieces in the trash, I find myself holding the insert. For some reason I turn the page to look inside, something I've never done before.

In black felt marker, Callie has written: "For Lise: Thanks for the loan. It's not like you were using it."

I drop the paper like it's burned me. It's a thing she used to say, half an irritation and half a joke between us. I'd complain about a missing sweater, and she'd say, "It's not like you were using it." Mostly, when she'd drop that line and give me a hug, I'd melt, unable to hold on to my anger. Mostly, she was right.

What it means is that she tried to tell me she was sorry. And I didn't forgive her, didn't even hear her. No wonder she went along with telling everybody her family was dead.

My emotions are all over the place now. Grief, rage, laughter, love, and hate, all swirling around and taking turns at running the show.

Maybe I'm the one who needs a counselor. Or a padded cell. An hour later, I'm pacing from one side of the house to the other, still trying to get my turmoil under control.

A knock at the door startles me half out of my skin. I ignore it. There is nobody in the world I want to talk to right now. The knock comes again. And again. Every time it makes me jump, pulls me out of the rhythm of pacing, raises my anxiety level. Finally, I look out the peephole.

On my porch, distorted by the uneven curve of the glass, stands Dale.

"Let me in," he calls.

"Go away."

He knocks again. "Lise, let me in."

I don't answer, just stand there, hands against the door, breathing. "Go home, Dale."

"I can't. Ariel won't let me," he says. "Not until I talk to you."

He's told her, then. Whatever he is going to say, I don't want to hear it. Words can't fix this. I turn my back on the door and return to pacing, my nerves thrumming, my heart in my throat.

I love you.

How dare he say those words to me? They follow me around the house, from one room to another, step after step. He had sex with Callie. Asked her to marry him. All these years, he's held that secret.

I love you.

The words eat away at my resolve, force me to see that the underbelly of my rage is heartbreak and hurt.

I love you.

The words carry me back to the front door. When I peer out this time, he's gone. All is quiet and dark. Nothing moves. I open the door to step out onto the porch and breathe the cold night air, and Dale almost falls in. He's been sitting with his back to the door and barely catches himself with his hands.

"This secret's been burning me up for sixteen years," he says. "The least you can do is listen."

"Get a therapist," I retort, but he's already across the threshold and I can't slam the door on him.

"You're the only one I ever wanted to tell. And the one I couldn't." He holds me in place with a gaze so intense I can't even blink. His eyes and his hands and the whole strong length of him and memory of his lips on mine are overwhelming. I wrench my gaze away and lead the way into the living room, sinking into the chair that's across the room from everything else. At least, I can put some distance between us.

Dale doesn't sit. He paces from one side of the room to the other. He doesn't look at me as he starts talking.

"We need to talk about what I did with Callie."

"Is that what this is about? That one's easy. She was sexy. She was willing. Same reason as Kelvin and Bryce and all the rest of the crowd."

"And that's where you'd be wrong." He comes to a stop at the window and stands looking out, his back to me. His voice is low and intense. "You were the one I wanted. I was so crazy about you I couldn't see straight."

"So you slept with my sister. Makes perfect sense."

He swings around then, turning the full force of his gaze on me. "Let's not forget that you didn't want me. You dropped me like a bad penny the minute somebody else asked you out. I was young and stupid enough to think that was the end of everything. I had no hope you'd come around. And I figured I'd ruined even our friendship by asking you in the first place."

I open my mouth to say something, but he holds up a hand to stop me. "Let me finish, all right? For God's sake, let me spit it all out."

He turns away again, the only sound in the room our breathing. His voice is quieter now. "It was Callie's idea, the prom thing. And then after . . . She wanted to get back at you for bossing her around and making her feel like a little kid."

"So you're going to blame Callie now?" I know it's not fair, even as I say the words. I've been blaming her all night in my own head.

"No. I'm not blaming anybody. Just telling you how it was, as fairly as I can."

I close my eyes against the pain in his face, but then remember him sitting on the windowsill on prom night, see the way he was looking at Callie. The way she claimed him, like property. A conquest. The boy in my memory is young. Conflict is written across his face as she takes his hand and leads him away.

"Anyway," Dale's voice goes on—the man's voice, not the boy's—and I open my eyes again. The disconnect makes me feel like the room is spinning. "I wanted to tell you—"

"Was it prom night?"

He nods.

"Before or after I came home and found you?" I need to know if it happened in my room. In my bed, or Callie's.

"After. I think, maybe, if you hadn't come home when you did, I might have been stronger. Maybe I would have told her no." He tries to smile, but it doesn't get past a quick hitch of the corners of his lips. "At least, that's what I'd like to believe."

"That doesn't make any sense."

"Doesn't it? I was nineteen. Heartbroken and, let's face it, horny. Callie was all over me, and then you come in, your dress ripped half off and soaking wet, like you'd been ravished in the rain. Kelvin had this stupid bet going, and I thought you fell for it, let him . . ."

Time slows again, as I replay his words in my head and try to shape them into something that makes sense. "You thought . . ." It's too absurd. I can't even say the words. "Kelvin got drunk," I tell him. "He attacked me. I beat him with my shoe. Trust me, there was no ravishing."

He wavers a little, as if the ground has moved beneath his feet. "I heard a car."

"Timothy. Knight in shining armor. He's got the scars to prove it."

Dale looks blank and a little lost. I know the feeling. Long-held beliefs that turn out to be so far afield you don't know what to do with them.

"Dear God," he says, finally. "So you escaped from hell and came in to find us . . ."

"I can't believe you didn't hear about the thing with Kelvin and Timothy. Pretty sure there was a lot of gossip."

"The story that Kelvin and his buddies put out was that once wasn't enough and you begged for seconds. Hell, he said you were ready to take on the whole gang, but he fought them off to keep you for himself."

"And you believed that?"

"I figured it was exaggerated plenty. But I guess I thought there was a grain of truth in there somewhere. I mean, surely you knew that's what he was after when he asked you."

His face settles back into the deep lines I've been assuming were all about grief over Callie. "I wanted to tell you. At least once a week I'd call her, tell her we had to fess up. And she'd say that if you ever found out, you'd never forgive either of us. She got me to promise not to tell, right after prom night, and then always held that over my head."

"She was good at guilt."

"And then she got pregnant and I figured, if it was mine, I owed her. Maybe never being with you was the penalty I'd have to pay for my mistake. It was torture sometimes, with you right there in front of my eyes. Sometimes I thought maybe you cared about me, more than friends, but I couldn't ask you out, couldn't tell you how I felt, because I always knew what I'd done."

"God, Dale."

"I settled for friendship. Every time you hooked up with some guy, I'd think this was it, I'd finally lost you. And then feel relief when it was over. When Callie died, God help me, one of my first emotions was relief. I was thinking we could make things work somehow. Maybe I'd finally tell you and you'd forgive me. But when we came back here, she was everywhere, in every room of the old house. And if I could forget about her for a minute, there was Ariel to remind me. I knew you were going to find out; it was just a matter of time. After that dick of a kid stole the diary, I was waiting for it to come out on the news. I would have told you then, but you were out of reach. No phone. I didn't want you to hear it from some reporter or Internet gossip."

"But you still came to get us."

He shrugs that away. "You needed me."

His words resonate. It's not often that I let myself need anybody. Thinking back, I've worked hard to shut him out. To keep the walls between us. But all of my walls are down now. No more secrets. Nothing left to hide behind. The last man I dated, a genuinely nice guy, tried his best to break through. And in the end, when he was leaving and I asked him why, he'd told me, "I need to be needed, Lise. Not all the time. But every now and then."

Sitting here, looking across the room at Dale, all of the versions of him come together. He's the man I know and the boy I remember, not a saint or a hero or a loser. He's both more and less than each of these things. What I feel for him is complicated. Love and rage, friendship and desire, sympathy and judgment, and other more nuanced things for which I have no words.

"Thanks for listening. Maybe it was selfish, but I needed you to know." He smiles, and the tortured look is gone from his eyes.

In return, I need to tell him some of what I feel, but as usual I don't have the words. At my silence, he nods once, as though I've said something profound. "I should let you get some sleep," he says, and heads toward the door.

He doesn't say so, but I know as surely as I've ever known anything that if I let him walk away, I'll have lost him. We'll still talk from time to time. We'll be friendly over Ariel and maybe have dinner together at his parents' place. His words echo back to me from the other night. "I can't do this, Lise. All these years . . ."

And I know, for certain, that he is going to finally let me go.

He stands with one hand on the door, about to walk out of my life.

"I wrote a song." The words surprise me. They come up straight out of my heart, bypassing my brain.

"That's wonderful." His lips curve into a smile. It looks sad, though. I want to see it reach his eyes.

"I want you to hear it."

"Some other time," he says. "It's late."

"It has to be now."

I take his free hand, daring to touch him, lacing my fingers through his. He feels stiff, resistant, and my heart sinks. But then his hand softens, just a little, his fingers closing around mine, and he lets me lead him back into the music room. As we walk, I'm thinking I'll just put the recording on for him, but at the last minute I sit down at the piano and run my fingers over the keys. My heart flutters crazily, and I play a few bars of "Closer Home" while I build up my courage, and then modulate over to the slow ballad tempo of "Color You Gone."

There are four verses. One for my father, one for my mother, and one for Callie. The last is for Dale, for this separation that I've felt coming between us. He's behind me, listening. I can feel him there. And when I begin his verse, I hear the hitch in his breath. My voice cracks once, and I think I'm not going to make it to the end, but I do.

"I want a take-back," I say, when all of the music has ebbed away.

"What?"

I spin around on the bench to look up at him. His eyes are wet. There are tears on his cheeks.

"Callie never took anything I didn't give her. The music. You." My throat closes over the last word, and it comes out with a little tremor. "Can we—"

I don't get to finish the question. He bends down and scoops me off the bench and into his arms.

"Do you love me?" he demands in a hoarse voice.

"Enough to make me write a song about it," I answer. And then, because I'm a little different now, I manage to whisper, "I love you, Dale."

After that, lips and hands do all the talking and words don't seem to matter.

***

It's a small ceremony, mostly family, and all of the attendees are sworn to secrecy. We wanted to have it in the backyard at the house Dale built for us, but just to be sure no media shows up, we've chosen Dale's parents' place instead. Mom Elliot is in seventh heaven, what with the wedding and her ready-made granddaughter and the opportunity to prepare a feast.

Nancy is my bridesmaid. Timothy and Dennis have traveled here for the occasion, and Timothy serves as groomsman. Most of my students are here, and some of the guys from Dale's construction crew. Ariel's friends from school. Ashley and her husband. George, with a red ribbon tied around his neck, works the crowd, looking for handouts. Dale's old dog, Spike, doesn't like other people or George, so we've left him at home. My mother is here, even though she has no idea what is going on, and Callie is never very far away.

The only photographer allowed on the premises is Melody Smith. She's kept all of her promises so far, and we'll keep feeding her exclusives. I get free wedding photos out of the deal, which is not a small thing. Despite all of the money now at my disposal, I can't shake my background and can't ever pass up a bargain.

To be honest, Dale and I aren't crazy about the whole marriage thing. I'm afraid of jinxing our happiness. He feels like we're succumbing to social pressure. Which, to be honest, we are. The whole custody issue goes away if we get married.

Ariel sent in her DNA samples, and the results confirmed that Dale is her father. Due to legalities, we ran a second, official test, which concurred. So he pretty much automatically has the right to custody, barring anything that makes him unfit. And if I'm married to him, then we both hold all assets and things are easy.

Ricken is spending his summer in court, along with his accountant ladylove, and prison looms large in his future. Turns out, they were both skimming so freely off Callie's money that my new accounting team barely had to work at discovery. As for Shadow, he went dark as soon as the tide of public opinion turned against him. He sent an apology once, by text message. Ariel deleted it, unanswered. She doesn't seem to miss him.

Not that everything is perfect, of course. Ariel is seventeen and considers herself an adult. It's been a year since her mother's death, and she still wakes up screaming sometimes from nightmares about that horse. She's used to parenting herself, and there's plenty of shouting between the two of us about rules. Dale stays calm about most things, and she'll usually come around and do whatever he asks of her. When it comes to boys, though, he gets completely irrational and won't listen to reason.

We're a family now, with everything that means.

The music venture was Ariel's idea. Once the honeymoon is over, we'll be opening the doors to the Redfern Music School, a boarding academy for talented kids who wouldn't get a chance any other way. We have to do something with the money, Ariel says, and we're not going to use much of it living in Colville.

Her capable hands have been involved in everything to do with the school, from helping Dale with the construction plans to setting the criteria for scholarships and selecting students. I interviewed and hired three teachers. One for keyboard and guitar, one to teach composition, and one for voice. Looking at the student profiles, I'm thinking we may well need a counselor and a corrections officer, but Ariel insists that the music will win and they'll work out okay. If they don't appreciate the opportunity, she says, then out they go, and there are plenty more where they came from.

We've also put together a small but cutting-edge recording studio. I've written two more songs and Glynnis is pushing me to do an album. I'm not ready for that. I keep telling her maybe one of these days. In the meantime, I want to help other musicians with recording and some distribution. We'll do it free up front, with a clause that if they start making money, a small percentage goes back into funding the project.

I'm not sure what Callie would think about any of this. I regret the lost opportunities to talk to her, to know what thoughts were going through her head after she told me that music was for everybody. But I've made peace with the uncertainty.

After the vows are said and Dale kisses me properly in front of all of the witnesses and claims me as his wife, we plan to make a break for it. I look around for Ariel, to hug her good-bye, but she's nowhere to be seen. A dark cloud falls across my mood, and I start to wonder if she's really okay with this whole wedding thing after all.

Then she reappears from around the corner of the house, four of my longtime students trailing after her, carrying guitars and an electronic drum kit.

Ariel runs over and hugs me, then Dale, then me again. "I had to give you something," she says, laughing, "and this is all I could think of."

Apparently Mr. Elliot was in on the planning, since he's busy helping out with amps and cables and electrical cords. A minute of random music and testing, and then they launch into a blues-rock arrangement of "Closer Home," Lexy's clear voice belting the lyrics out into the summer day.

Dale's fingers close around mine, warm and steady. He shoots me a look of concern, knowing this song is an emotional hand grenade for me. My eyes fill, but the tears are clean now, all of the jealousy long gone. In this moment, standing hand in hand with Dale beneath the blue, blue sky, Ariel at my side and all of the people I love gathered around, I finally understand the meaning of the words I wrote so many years ago.

The wider I wander, the further I roam
The more your love finds me
And brings me back home.
Closer home, closer home
You always bring me closer home.

ACKNOWLEDGMENTS

Living with a writer is not always easy. My heartfelt thanks and much love to my Viking, whose support of my writing is phenomenal. I also owe a great deal to my writer friends. Alex, our morning sprints, motivational planning, and mutual commiseration sessions were lifesavers. Heather and Susan, I can always count on you guys to make me laugh, kick my butt, and be outraged on my behalf when things go wrong. I owe you. Thanks also to Kristina Martin for reading and for your ongoing support. If I start naming names for the rest of the incredible writing community I'm privileged to be a part of, I know I'll forget people. Just know that every encouraging tweet or Facebook comment helped me keep writing, especially on the hard days.

This book would never have come to be without my gifted agent. Thank you, Deidre, for encouraging me to try something new and for believing in me. To the people who read for me at various stages of the manuscript—the Viking, Alexandra Hughes, Susan Spann, and Kristina Martin—your input and support was invaluable.

As always, thank you to everybody who supports and loves books. Because without you, what would be the point?

ABOUT THE AUTHOR

Photo © 2012 Diane Maehl

Kerry Anne King holds a BA in English from York University and a MEd in counseling psychology from Washington State University. She lives with her Viking in a little house surrounded by trees, the perfect place for writing books. Kerry spends her days working as an RN in a clinic, spinning her tales early in the morning and in the evenings after work. In addition to women's fiction, she also writes fantasy and mystery novels as Kerry Schafer.